Praise for
What I Like About You

"Heartwarming, endearing, and sure to leave you swooning, *What I Like About You* shines with authentic characters you will absolutely fall in love with. This story is as sweet as the cupcakes you'll be craving by the end!"
—Rachael Lippincott,
#1 *New York Times* bestselling author of *Five Feet Apart*

"With a charming, modern teen voice and a cast of characters I refuse to believe aren't real people, this debut explores the connections we make online and IRL. A love letter to storytelling, fandom, and all kinds of friendships, I'm still hugging *What I Like About You* tightly to my chest."
—Rachel Lynn Solomon, author of *You'll Miss Me When I'm Gone*

"This book is like a cupcake—delicious and to be devoured in one sitting."
—Laura Silverman, author of *Girl Out of Water* and *You Asked for Perfect*

"We fell in love at first DM with this delightfully readable debut. Equal parts clever contemporary romance and celebration of the joys of reading and connecting with people regardless of distance or medium, *What I Like About You* is what we love about YA."
—Emily Wibberley and Austin Siegemund-Broka,
authors of *If I'm Being Honest*

"*What I Like About You* is real, relatable, and as sweet as a One True Pastry cupcake. Marisa Kanter's voice will resonate with readers. I couldn't put this one down!"
—Gloria Chao, author of *American Panda* and *Our Wayward Fate*

"*What I Like About You* is utterly unputdownable and completely enchanting. Along with fantastic Jewish representation, Kanter's debut is an ode to fandoms, teen readers, and the friendships we make through our communities, on and offline. So fun, so relatable, I was rooting for Halle and Nash the whole time."

—Katherine Locke,
award-winning author of *The Girl with the Red Balloon*
and co-editor of *It's a Whole Spiel*

"Cupcake cute and Belle-brainy. Fans of Miranda Kenneally and Jenny Han will like Kanter's smart (and a little bit awkward) main character whose romance is based on more than the physical . . . but also the physical."

—*School Library Journal*

"With humor and compassion, Kanter's debut is fun to read. . . . Kudos to Kanter for featuring Jewish teens and telling a sweet story that also examines the blurring of online and real lives." —*Booklist*

"A charming, witty story about authenticity in the social media age, told with a wink and a string of heart-eyes emojis." —*BookPage*

"Debut author Kanter realistically paints Halle and Nash's YA-centric universe via Twitter, Instagram, blog posts, and group chats, giving an insider's peek into the fandom. . . . Kanter creates robust characters and a swoon-worthy romance."

—*Publishers Weekly*

What I Like About You

MARISA KANTER

SIMON & SCHUSTER BFYR

New York   London   Toronto   Sydney   New Delhi

SIMON & SCHUSTER BFYR

An imprint of Simon & Schuster Children's Publishing Division

1230 Avenue of the Americas, New York, New York 10020

Text © 2020 by Marisa Kanter

Cover illustration © 2020 by Sinem Erkas

Cover design by Krista Vossen © 2020 by Simon & Schuster, Inc.

SIMON & SCHUSTER BFYR and related marks are trademarks of Simon & Schuster, Inc.

For information about special discounts for bulk purchases, please contact Simon & Schuster Special Sales at 1-866-506-1949 or business@simonandschuster.com.

The Simon & Schuster Speakers Bureau can bring authors to your live event. For more information or to book an event, contact the Simon & Schuster Speakers Bureau at 1-866-248-3049 or visit our website at www.simonspeakers.com.

Also available in a SIMON & SCHUSTER BFYR hardcover edition

Interior design by Hilary Zarycky

Graphic art on page 76 by Tom Daly

The text for this book was set in Adobe Garamond Pro.

Manufactured in the United States of America

First SIMON & SCHUSTER BFYR paperback edition June 2021

2 4 6 8 10 9 7 5 3 1

The Library of Congress has cataloged the hardcover edition as follows:

Names: Kanter, Marisa, author.

Title: What I like about you / Marisa Kanter.

Description: First edition. | New York City : Simon & Schuster Books for Young Readers, [2020] | Audience: Ages 12 Up. | Audience: Grades 7-9.

Summary: When Halle Levitt arrives to spend senior year in her grandfather's small town, she meets Nash, her online best friend who thinks her online persona, Kels, is as confident and popular as he is.

Identifiers: LCCN 2019035672 | ISBN 9781534445772 (hardcover)

ISBN 9781534445789 (pbk) | ISBN 9781534445796 (eBook)

Subjects: CYAC: Online identities—Fiction. | Dating (Social customs)—Fiction.

Grandfathers—Fiction. | High schools—Fiction. | Schools—Fiction.

Classification: LCC PZ7.1.K285 Wh 2020 | DDC [Fic]—dc23

LC record available at https://lccn.loc.gov/2019035672

In loving memory of my grandmothers,
Sheila Shapiro and Beatrice "Peppy" Kanter

Twitter archives—three years ago

Nash Stevens @Nash_Stevens27 3hr
Announcement: I'm launching a weekly web comic series on Outside the Lines! It's called REX, it's about dinosaurs, and I'd love for you to check it out. Posts go up Fridays at 6PM EDT. Issue #1 is now live! https://bit.ly/33OWH4Y

Kels @OneTruePastry 55min
@Nash_Stevens27 hi omg WHAT EVEN. I love this so much?!

Kels @OneTruePastry 50min
I CAN'T BELIEVE THERE IS ONLY ONE ISSUE AND @Nash_Stevens27 ALREADY RUINED ME?! I already know REX will break my heart AND be my newest obsession. Check it out! https://bit.ly/33OWH4Y

Nash Stevens @Nash_Stevens27 6min
@OneTruePastry whoa, thank you!

Direct Messages

Nash Stevens
Hey—thanks again for the shout-out! I just
got 150 new followers in the last ten minutes.
How did you DO that?

magic!

I didn't even know you read my blog.

i read MAUS because of your review
and it changed my life. honestly.

That is the nicest thing anyone on the internet
has ever said to me.

you're welcome! consider me a fan.

You're my first fan, I think. No one IRL really
knows I do this. Or rather, knew. I guess
everyone's going to know now.

yeah, that's the internet.
did you think about using a pseudonym?

Who says this isn't a pseudonym?

okay fair.
wait. not fair. you did, by implying
everyone would know.

🙈 🙈 🙈

so now that you've revealed yourself as an
ARTIST and all, I have to ask . . .
did you design your blog?

i've been trying to customize mine for *months*
but i'm so crap at HTML i want to burn it.
nothing comes out the way it looks in my head.

Oh. I mean yeah I did, But its nbd. I can send
you some of the links that got me started if
you give me the recipe for that red velvet you
posted yesterday.

lol not a chance

ONE

The flowers are dead, I'm surrounded by orange, and a suitcase has been disemboweled in the search for a phone charger. Clothes are everywhere. I mean *everywhere*. Like, you wouldn't know that underneath the scattered piles of my wardrobe is a white carpet kind of everywhere. But I have motive.

The Most Important Email of My Life (so far) could poof into my inbox at any moment before five p.m. EDT and my phone is currently lifeless.

It's waiting for me now, for all I know.

Subject: READ BETWEEN THE LIES Cover reveal: You are NOT worthy.

Subject: We gave it to EW. Who are you?

Subject: If you think THAT'S a lot of Instagram followers . . .

With the toss of one last cardigan, I reveal . . . nothing. The suitcase is empty.

I blink. My charger isn't here. There is literally nowhere else it could *be*.

I know it's not in my purse.

I check my purse for a third time anyway.

It's not even like I can borrow one. Deciding to be an Android in an iPhone family? Literally the worst decision ever right now. I've been offline for three hours and thirty-three minutes and I can think of approximately three hundred thirty-three things that could have happened in that time. My phone died its tragic death in Philadelphia mid–inbox refresh on hour ten of the twelve-hour trek from Charlotte, North Carolina, to my newest temporary home: Middleton, AKA Middle-of-Nowhere, Connecticut.

With no charger in sight, the only connection I have to anything within the realm of normal is impossible to reach. I'm stuck instead with no internet, dead flowers, an entirely unrecognizable Gramps, and orange walls.

I hate orange. After red, my rainbow skips straight to yellow.

But I *chose* this orange. Shortly after we arrived, I stepped into Aunt Liz's childhood 1970s nightmare room and claimed it as mine. I know I'm going to regret this in the morning. But right now? I need this room. It's the only place that still feels like my grandparents' house. Every other room is remodeled and modern, all glass tables and new paint and uncomfortable cream-colored furniture. No more garden. No more pictures. No more books.

Grams would be horrified.

"Halle."

I look up. Ollie is at the door, waving my charger in his hand.

"No clue how it got into my stuff," he says.

Me either. But it doesn't matter. It's *here*.

WHAT I LIKE ABOUT YOU

"You're my *hero*."

I grab my phone off the floor and hold my hands out, expecting Ollie to toss the cord to me. He doesn't. Instead, my fifteen-year-old brother leans back against the doorframe, allowing his light brown hair to fall into his eyes.

"Mom is two seconds away from cry number three. Dad's having an allergic reaction to Scout. And Gramps is ranting about the rise of fascism. He straight-up looked at me and said, 'Do you know what fascism is?' Like, anyone with a pulse right now knows what fascism is. I didn't say that, obviously."

I take a step toward him and place my hand on his arm. *"Ollie."*

He exhales. "This is hard for me, too, okay? I need you out there."

"I spiraled," I say. "I'm sorry."

"Everything looks so different," Ollie says.

"I know."

"Gramps and I have matching *Nikes*."

"I know."

"Maybe this was . . ." Ollie lets the thought trail off, incomplete.

A mistake. That's how Ollie's sentence ends. I know this because I'm wondering it too.

I twirl Grams's *hamsa* necklace between my fingers. "It's only been six months."

Ollie nods. "We'll check your email downstairs? Together?"

"Let's go," I say.

Ollie places my charger in my palm and I smile. Ollie knows all about my blog life. He knows how important this email is. He read the pitch I sent *five times* because he's the best. He reads YA for me and I understand baseball stats for him. It's just what we do.

I follow him down the stairs and through the living room to the kitchen, ignoring the pictureless walls and absent bookshelves. I fixate on the back of Ollie's head and swallow the emotion that's lodged in my throat because Grams would *never* take down the pictures.

All the pictures in my life live in folders on screens. At Grams's and Gramps's, the pictures lived on the walls. Photographs were everywhere—in the living room, on the kitchen walls, lining the staircase, in albums on the coffee table. Familiar faces. Foreign faces. Whenever we visited, we got a new story based on one of the pictures. One story per visit, that was Grams's rule. So we had to think about, and fight for, which picture we wanted.

One day, we'd know all the stories. That's what Grams said.

I wanted to stay in Grams's house.

This isn't Grams's house.

"Found her," Ollie says. "Lured by a phone charger."

Dad sneezes. "Typical."

I open my mouth to retort, but stop short at the sight of him. He's holding Scout, Grams's adorable maltipoo—who is definitely the source of his sudden-onset sneezing—and sitting at a *glass table*.

How does a person decorate cupcakes on a glass table? It's not made for messes.

The kitchen used to be a shrine to baking, with two shelves on the wall next to the stove to display Grams's fancy standing mixer and all her quality cupcake creation equipment. The kitchen table was solid wood, perfect for spreading out all the ingredients for a long afternoon of baking.

Now the table is glass. The shelves are gone.

Gramps is gone. I mean, I know the man sitting next to Dad is Gramps. *I know this.*

But he's also *not*. Like, at all.

He's skinnier. Messier, too. My Gramps was always short-haired and clean-shaven. This Gramps has a full beard and a short ponytail sticking out underneath his baseball hat. He's wearing a graphic T-shirt and cargo shorts. And Ollie's Nikes.

"Hi, Gramps," I say, my voice soft.

Gramps nods. "Hal."

His smile is forced, lips tight and no teeth, and I'm not sure how I'm supposed to react. I should probably hug him, right? A handshake would be weird, right? I mean, this is Gramps. *My Gramps*, who taught me everything I know about Johnny Cash and read picture books to me until I fell asleep on his lap. My Gramps, who always made sure to interject himself into the near-daily conversations I'd have with Grams, calls where we'd go on hour-long rants about *the best books we've ever read,* ever. Until the next best book we've ever read came along. Gramps would attempt to pivot the conversation toward narrative nonfiction and political memoirs. *You ladies and your books*, he'd say, giving up with a hearty laugh. Nothing ever put a bigger smile on my face from hundreds of miles away than his laugh. *React, Halle.* I'm the reason we're here. I'm the one who's been desperate to reconnect with Gramps in this post-Grams world. But now that I'm here, and he's in front of me? Now that I'm about to *move in with him*? I don't know what to say.

That's the problem with words. In my head, words are magic. My thoughts are eloquent and fierce. On the page, words are music. In the clicks of my keyboard, in the scratches of pencil meeting paper. In the beauty of the eraser, of the backspace key. On the page, the words in my head sing and dance with the precision of diction and the intricacies of rhythm.

Out loud? Words are the worst.

"Gramps was just asking us about college," Mom says.

Gramps nods. "Still NYU?"

"Still NYU."

It's always been the plan, to follow in Grams's footsteps.

NYU undergrad. Interning at the Big Five publishers. A publishing job offer after graduation.

"Competitive school these days," Gramps says. "College applications are so different now."

The corners of my mouth drop. "I know."

I know getting into NYU isn't easy. I think about it at least ten times a day. It's why I'm here instead of following Mom and Dad on their next adventure—to focus on nailing AP classes, to continue growing my blog presence, to keep putting myself out there as a viable media opportunity for authors, to prove to the book world and NYU admissions that I'm meant to shout about books for a living and will *thrive* in publishing.

"Well I'm pretty sure since I'm destined to get drafted into the MLB, Halle can get into NYU." Ollie says.

"I mean"—sneeze—"if it's *destined*," says Dad.

Gramps snorts. "MLB? Good luck, kid."

Ollie isn't bothered. He just shakes his head, smirking. "You haven't seen me play, Gramps."

Gramps turns his attention to Mom. "How's preproduction going, Maddie?"

He's the only one who can get away with calling Mad Levitt "Maddie."

"Oh! Really good, actually. Our locations were approved—"

And just like that, before my very eyes, my parents are no longer my parents. They're Madeline and Ari Levitt, Academy Award–nominated directors. Seriously, my parents are the Leonardo DiCaprio of the Best Documentary (Feature) category. Six nominations. Six *and the Academy Award goes to [insert name that's not my parents]*. Zero Oscar dude statues.

Leo had to eat raw bison liver for his.

My parents will spend a year on a kibbutz for theirs.

"—we'll start filming at Kinneret next week and work our way south through four different kibbutzim."

"Wait—" Dad sneezes. "You're saying everything is all set . . . before our arrival?"

"Doubtful," Ollie and I interject.

"Allegedly," Mom corrects herself.

Gramps looks perplexed. "Shouldn't it be?"

Ollie pats Gramps on the shoulder. "Alas, the life of a director is unpredictable, Gramps. You'd hate it."

Gramps nods. "I would."

Mom shakes her head. "You'd think that, Ben. But it's the best kind of unpredictable. It's following—"

I take a few steps backward, toward the free plug above the countertop. Now that Mom is officially in *follow the story wherever it leads you* mode, I can charge my phone. Finally. I can't make dead flowers bloom or make the kitchen look like my memories of it. But I *did* make small talk without bursting into tears. A small victory.

I plug my phone in and tap my fingers absentmindedly on the granite, waiting for it to come back to life. I count the seconds so they pass: *152, 153, 154 . . .*

At last, with a series of vibrations and notifications, Kels—YA book blogger and founder of One True Pastry—is back on the grid.

It's overwhelming, the amount I've missed. Forty-two new emails. Sixty-five Twitter notifications. Hundreds of DMs.

And zero messages from Ariel Goldberg's publicist.

I exhale anxiety because I didn't miss it.

I inhale anxiety because it hasn't happened yet.

Grams introduced me to Ariel Goldberg, one of my favorite YA authors, when I was twelve. So it feels fitting that today is the day I find out if I'm chosen to host the cover reveal of her newest book, *Read Between the Lies*. Fitting, but also ten times more nerve-racking.

What if the rejection email is *no* email at all? What if I'm not even worth responding to? What if Ariel's publicity team read my pitch and *laughed*? Now that Ariel's a best-selling author on her fourth book, now that her books have "critical and commercial success," she doesn't need my cupcakes. Hosting an Ariel Goldberg cover reveal is for sophisticated platforms now. Real magazines with subscribers. Literary reviewers. Adults.

I'm just a kid who bakes cupcakes that match book covers and has an opinion, like everyone else on the internet.

And 20K Twitter followers who care about those opinions, I remind myself.

With my elbows resting on the countertops, I work through the process of clearing my notifications. It's calming. Halle's reality is complete chaos; nothing feels familiar. But Kels's world? Besides waiting for this email, it's so wonderfully the same.

I created Kels when I was fourteen, and Kels created One True Pastry, a blog dedicated to the two greatest things on Earth—YA books and cupcakes. She's pretty much the best thing that's ever happened to me.

Once all my notifications are cleared, I check in on the IRL conversation. Gramps is asking more questions about the documentary. Mom and Dad respond with enthusiasm, all *we haven't been to Israel since birthright* and *this is such a cinematic opportunity* and *the Academy will have to*, and I am definitely okay to dip my toes into my DMs before going back.

I tap the first message I want to respond to.

WHAT.
10:39 AM

w h a t ?
10:40 AM

You've NEVER seen lord of the rings? like ever?
10:40 AM

I am speechless.
10:41 AM

Actually no I'm not. HOW IS THIS POSSIBLE?
10:41 AM

. . . Kels?
11:20 AM

I hope you know that while you dropped a
bomb like this and disappeared, your lord of
the rings initiation marathon is already in the
works. 20 hours. Extended editions. You're
not ready.
12:34 PM

I smile. Nash picking a *Lord of the Rings* fight is easily the best conversation I've had all day. I'm so grateful for the dose of normal.

hey.
12:49 PM

sorry, phone died. (it's true!)
12:50 PM

okay, so hear me out. the hobbit was assigned reading the summer before freshmen year and just? so many descriptions of rocks? idk. i DNF'd it.
12:52 PM

The response is immediate despite my long lapse. Like he's waiting for me.

WOW
12:54 PM

First, you're wrong. Second, you can't let The Hobbit ruin the whole experience!
12:54 PM

but it's PART of the experience.
12:55 PM

YES AND IT'S AMAZING TOO.
12:56 PM

🙂
12:56 PM

"Halle."

Mom's voice makes me jump, and my phone slips out of my hand, clattering on the granite.

"Sorry. I . . ." I look around. The kitchen has been vacated. We're the only two people left. "Wait. Where is everyone?"

Sometimes, being in a Nash phone zone is so intense, everything around me ceases to exist.

"Scout needed to go out." Worry lines wrinkle Mom's forehead. "It's not too late to change your mind, you know. I mean, I don't think we were expecting Gramps to be so . . ."

I flinch. "It's only been six months." Mom's trying to give us an easy out, but there is no way I'm leaving Gramps. More than ever he needs us not to bail. Mom is good at chasing down truths, but she's not so good at witnessing the ones that find her instead.

Her expression softens. "Oh, I know, babe. Of course he's sad, we all are. I mean, well, your dad talks to him almost every day and, well, we just thought he'd be more—together. And the house . . . Look, all I'm saying is I know you wanted to be here, but you can still come with us. We'll hire the best tutors. You'll graduate on time. This time next year, we'll be moving you into NYU. Besides, this trip is going to be life-changing. Think about how much closer we'll be to our culture."

Mom doesn't get it. We've always been A Levitt Family Production, whether we were investigating the ethics of cattle farming in the Midwest, examining the effects of climate change on the beaches of the Outer Banks, or exposing the realities of gentrification in major cities.

I love chasing stories with my parents, but I *can't* go to Israel with them. It isn't even about graduating on time. It's about having a senior year that's *mine*—I have big plans for OTP and building an NYU-worthy resume, a resume that screams *publishing*.

If I say yes, I'll get caught up in A Levitt Family Production— distracted by long days on location, switching out camera lenses to capture the perfect headshot, proofreading interview questions— the familiar, comforting chaos of filmmaking. It's a chaos I haven't felt since my parents moved us to Charlotte for their *raising teenagers sabbatical* three years ago, devastated by Oscar loss number six. Being on location and behind a camera is the closest thing to *home* I've ever had—until Kels.

If I go, OTP will take a back seat to my parents' demanding schedule and fitting school in.

I can't afford to go on hiatus for a year.

My presence will evaporate. NYU will have nothing to look at. Kels will disappear.

"I'm staying. For Gramps."

For *me*.

Mom nods. "I get that. It just might be harder than you think, okay?"

"Every day is already hard."

Mom's arms open and I fall into her embrace. She strokes my hair like I'm a little kid again. It used to be identical, our hair. Long and medium brown. Whatever Mom's chosen hairstyle was for the day, she'd replicate it on me. If Mom braided her hair, she braided mine. Crown braid days were my favorite. Along with matching green eyes and the same small mole above our lip. Everyone on set used to call me Mini-Mad.

Now, I keep my hair shoulder-length and styled in layers.

Mom's is still as long as ever because, quote, *screw ageism*.

I'm going to miss her so much.

Mom lets go first and glances at her smart watch. "We need to get going."

Still chewing my cheek, I nod.

"Come on, the boys are all outside."

I follow my mother's footsteps out the back door. Mom referring to Dad, Gramps, and Ollie as "the boys" gives me flashbacks to sand between my toes and the smell of hydrangeas in bloom. Summers were always for Middleton. If we weren't on location, we were here. But now it's August, and there's a whole year here in front of us.

Dad pulls me into a hug as soon as I reach him. We don't say much, but we don't need to. Dad isn't a man of many words. Mostly, he speaks in cupcakes and cinematography. I can't wait for the pictures I know he's going to send me from Israel.

"Take care of Gramps," he whispers in my ear.

"I'm not going to cry. I'm *not* going to cry," Mom says, then smushes Ollie and me together into one giant group hug and promptly bursts into tears.

There it is. We've been waiting for it. Mom always cries in threes, and she cried twice during the road trip to Middleton. It's like three-act structure is built in her DNA.

On that note, Gramps turns around, Scout in his arms, and

retreats inside. It's the first *Gramps* thing that has happened since we've arrived, him running away from Mom's tears. He kind of always has.

Mom wipes her eyes. "Okay, well." She looks back and forth between Ollie and me. "I love you. We love you."

"We'll love you more if you win an Oscar," Ollie says.

"No pressure," I say.

Mom rolls her eyes, but she's laughing. Ollie always knows what to say like that.

"Okay, one more hug. Then we'll go—I promise!"

After a final round of hugs, Mom and Dad get in the van and they're off to JFK. Then onto a plane. Then halfway around the world.

I don't realize I'm crying until they're already gone.

One True Pastry—three years ago

Debuts You Should Be Reading / Cupcakes You Should Be Eating
FIREFLIES AND YOU by Alanna LaForest

Okay, here we are. #50. The post I've been teasing on Instagram all week.

I can't believe I just typed #50. *Fifty reviews.* Fifty recipes. Do you have any idea how many cupcakes that is? I can't even tell you, because my brother always starts eating them all before I have the chance to count. Thankfully. If you were worried about food waste, rest assured, these cupcakes *never* go to waste.

Today's recipe is lemon cupcakes with lavender frosting, topped off with gold glitter. Inspired by my new favorite book you probably haven't read. Which is absurd! So I thought, *How can I get this book on YA Twitter's radar?* I can write a glowing review (see below!)—but I know way more people are engaged with my #CupcakeCoverReveals on Instagram.

So I turned thirty-six cupcakes into a book cover cake.

Fifty cupcakes recipes later, and I have *finally* taken #CupcakeCoverReveal literally. You're welcome.

These cupcakes taste like spring and are the perfect pick-me-up to get through this endless winter. Which, evidently enough, is how I feel about FIREFLIES AND YOU. If you asked me how many times I've read this book, I'd say two.

I'd be lying. The answer is three. I've read this book three times and I am the definition of book hungover!

So, what's the book about, Kels?

FIREFLIES AND YOU is the YA contemporary book of my dreams—one where the romance elements are squee-worthy as anything, but *nothing* compared to the core of the story—a friendship so complicated, so codependent, you never know whose side you're supposed to be on.

Every year, Annalee waits for the fireflies. Summer is for swimming, working two part-time jobs to save up for college, kissing Jonah Beckett, and fireflies. It's a phenomenon that marks her small town outside of Baton Rouge. No one can explain why the fireflies keep coming back. And when they do, so does Maisy Daniels, Annalee's best friend, and everything is perfect.

Except this summer, Annalee and Maisy are

broken and barely even speaking. Annalee's POV is in chronological order and Maisy's is reverse chronological, both intricately woven together leading up to the night they fell apart. It's *wild*, but *so* worth the ride, figuring out what happened.

With that, I will say no more about plot because spoilers!

But in terms of feels, the thing I loved most about this book was the moments of levity. It sounds heavy, reading a book about a friendship breakup—hoping Annalee and Maisy will figure it out and find their way back to each other. Parts of it *are*. But it's also a lot of laughter, a ton of atmosphere, and the best depiction of summers in the too-hot South I've ever read (speaking as someone who's lived there!).

Anyways, how this book only has 24 ratings on Goodreads is a tragedy—I will be plugging and blasting and screaming about FIREFLIES AND YOU on social media until the end of time!

PLZ READ IT SO ALANNA CAN WRITE MORE AMAZING BOOKS.

With Love (& Cupcakes),

Kels

And, as always, tag me in your cupcake posts!! I LOVE seeing your beautiful bookish creations.

[Showing Comments 1-20 of 1,782]

TWO

You'd think us Levitts would be minimalists.

I mean, we once moved *six times* in *two years* in the name of *Gentrify, U.S.*—a documentary that exposed the realities of gentrification in American cities. From nine to eleven, I lived in Brooklyn, Boston, Chicago, D.C., San Francisco, and Seattle.

By Chicago, I lived out of my suitcases. There was no point in pretending to settle.

With every move and every new doc, my parent promised it was *the one. Gentrify, U.S.* earned Mad and Ari Levitt their fifth Academy Award nomination.

It lost to a doc about chinchillas. Seriously.

I'm just saying. Considering how much of my childhood has been spent packing and unpacking and relocating, stuff should be a burden. I should live a cleansed, clutter-free life.

I don't.

Exhibit A: the tornado of clothes still covering Aunt Liz's floor. Or my floor now, I guess.

I stare at the mess I made. If I move the clothes from the floor to the bed, is that progress? Maybe instead I'll purge everything that doesn't spark joy. Honestly, I probably should've channeled Marie Kondo in Charlotte, *before* I challenged myself to fit my entire closet it one suitcase, just to see if I could.

I decide I can deal with the clothes later. First, my books need to breathe—in alphabetical order, by genre. I empty my suitcase one book at a time, organize, and shelve. Repetitive motion centers me, but I finish too soon. All my books fit on the white lacquered bookshelf next to the bed. It's small—only two shelves. It's kind of a tragedy, all the books I have fitting on only *two* shelves.

I would've had at least five more if my parents hadn't made me donate a bunch to the library before we left. Incomplete fantasy series and old white dude *literature* I read for school now have a new home in the donation bin at the Charlotte Public Library. It's never easy, saying goodbye to books. Especially ones that I have discussed and debated for *years* with my friends. Like, will Nash still be my best friend if he knows I donated the first two books in *The Queen of Stone* series? I'm not about to tell him and find out.

Still, it didn't hurt so bad at the time, when I thought I'd have Grams's collection to fall back on. But I don't. And I'm afraid to ask Gramps what he did with them, because if he trashed them I don't know what I'll do.

I take a step back and assess my work. My bookshelf is small, but it is mighty. It's a collection that consists of my three favorite things: swoony romcoms, twisted thrillers, and anything edited by Miriam Levitt, AKA Grams.

Fireflies and You is face out, of course. Signed, courtesy of being the granddaughter of the editor. It's hands down the most priceless part of my collection.

Everyone on Book Twitter claims it's impossible to pick a favorite book, but *Fireflies and You* is mine—no question. Beyond the beautiful story, it's the book that made OTP. It's the book that told me publicity is my path and showed me that I am in fact good at shouting about books—and making people listen. The one that helped me see I need to work in publishing.

And now it's the book I reread to feel close to Grams.

I squeeze my eyes shut, fighting the pressure that builds behind my eyes. *Fireflies and You* is going to be a movie, so it's been everywhere lately. It comes out in January and it's the first Grams book to ever be adapted and she doesn't even get to see it. She'll never know—

Breathe.

"Hal?"

I twist to face the door, for one brief minute expecting Grams. Then Gramps's head pokes in. I turn back around to wipe my tears, quick. Gramps *cannot* see me like this. I need to be positive. Enthusiastic. I *asked* to be here.

Gramps's expression is neutral behind his too-long beard. If he saw me upset, he doesn't show it. "I'm sorry. The orange. I know you hate it. I meant to paint it. Before. I just—"

I shake my head. "It's okay, Gramps. Orange is a crime to the color wheel, but I'll live."

He nudges the door open enough to step in. "It *is* pretty bad."

I snort, grateful for this acknowledgement. It's small, but it's the first time since arriving that Gramps sounds like *Gramps*. "*So* bad."

"You can repaint. Any color you want."

"I'd like that. Thanks."

Gramps's shoulders relax as he approaches Scout, who's standing at the end of the bed, tail wagging. She blends in so well with the clothes when she's curled up in a ball and sleeping, I honestly forgot she was here. Gramps scratches her ears and my brain is in overdrive, trying to figure out what to say next, what words to form when Gramps seems sort of okay, to broach the topic that's the hardest.

"Her books?" I blurt out.

Gramps flinches. "Boxed up in the garage."

I nod. "Can I—?"

Gramps is gone before the question fully forms.

Of course, I said the wrong thing. I *always* say the wrong thing. It's just—I needed to know. The absence of Grams's bookshelves and the hundreds—no, *thousands*—of stories that lined them? It's a tragedy.

I close my eyes and clutch Grams's *hamsa* charm.

I open my eyes, exhale a shaky breath, and power on my laptop.

The screen comes to life, full brightness, and my pulse

steadies as I type in my password. I can at least focus on the blog and checking to see if I got this cover reveal email, things that aren't totally out of my hands. Except my inbox isn't refreshing, and I notice my laptop is refusing to connect to Wi-Fi. Weird. It worked fine last summer, when we stayed in Middleton for three weeks. It should automatically connect, but of the six routers that appear, none are familiar.

I close my laptop and venture to ask Gramps. Also because I can only be surrounded by orange for so long. It's too loud. Impossible to focus. Ollie's already shut into Dad's room, J. Cole blasting from his new speakers as I head down the stairs.

I park myself on the living room couch and open my laptop again. There's so much to do, but connecting to Wi-Fi is priority number one. Tomorrow's posts need to be edited; tweets need to be scheduled. Once all One True Pastry–related duties have been conquered, tonight is for organizing, sweatpants, Netflix with Ollie and hopefully Gramps, and catching up with my friends.

"Hey, Gramps?"

"Huh?" he yells from the adjacent kitchen.

"Did you get a new internet router?" I ask.

"Nope!"

I place my laptop down on the coffee table and peek my head into the kitchen. Gramps is sitting at the table, reading the newspaper and eating popcorn. Like a newspaper is popcorn-worthy entertainment.

"Then where's the old one?" I try to keep the panic out of my voice.

Gramps shrugs. "My desktop is hardwired. So I didn't need it anymore, you know?"

I soften. *"Gramps."*

He doesn't look up from the newspaper and my heart shatters. Even Wi-Fi is triggering and everything about being here is suddenly *too much.* Why did I think this was a good idea? How can I possibly live in the house that has been stripped of every memory, of everything I love? Except Gramps. But even Gramps isn't *Gramps.*

"I know you kids need it for school," Gramps says. "It's getting reinstalled next week."

"I have some things I have to take care of, like, right now," I say.

Translation: I need to get out of here *now.* I can't be offline for a *week.* And I can't run One True Pastry from my phone.

"Then go to the library." Gramps says, not even looking up.

And wow, his indifference? It *hurts.*

But I want to go. I *need* to go.

"Okay. Well, I'll be back before dinner. . . ." I run upstairs for my backpack. Then remember that I left my laptop in the living room, so I double back and shove it inside the sleeve, then tuck the sleeve inside the backpack. Zip backpack. Retie shoelaces. Yell up to Ollie that I'll be with the books, which he'll get if he even hears me. *Get out of here.*

I dash out the door, craving my Kels life like a drug.

Twenty minutes later, there's still no Ariel Goldberg email, but I'm reconnected and feeling about a million percent better. I'm supposed to be writing a guest post for *Teen Vogue*. Instead, I'm assuring my friends that I am, in fact, not dead.

Amy Chen
i mean in all fairness what were we supposed
to think?
3:34 PM

you went off the grid for SIX HOURS.
3:34 PM

Elle Carter
IN THE SUMMER. DURING NORMAL
BUSINESS HOURS.
3:35 PM

Samira Lee
Really, Kels. You'd be just as worried if any of
us vanished mid-convo with no explanation!!
3:36 PM

OMG
3:36 PM

the only thing that died was my phone
3:37 PM

Elle Carter
The first rule of internet friendship? Inform

your comrades when your phone is on the
brink of death
3:38 PM

Amy Chen
lol also we know you've been messaging Nash
3:39 PM

Amy Chen
he confirmed your semi-on the grid status two
hours ago!
3:40 PM

Samira Lee
We see where your loyalty is!!
😊
3:41 PM

🙈🙈🙈
3:42 PM

Amy Chen
lol you don't even deny it anymore
3:43 PM

i'm sorry it's been a day okay!!
3:44 PM

Amy Chen
whatever. i get it. you have to admit it to
yourself before you can admit it to your
besties. i'll be here to say I TOLD U SO when
you do.
3:45 PM

. . . what am I admitting?
3:45 PM

Elle Carter
Girl, you know.
3:45 PM

. . .
3:46 PM

My friends, along with the rest of the internet, *love* to act like something is going on between Nash and me. For the record, it's not. Nash is the first person who left a comment on my blog, which led to me discovering REX, which resulted in our first DMs. He's the first real friend I ever had. My *best* friend.

Amy, Elle, and Samira's jokes cut closer to home though because they're friends with Nash too. Book Twitter is already a bubble. Teen Book Twitter? It's such a niche subsection of the Twitterverse—pretty much everyone knows everyone. Or at least, knows *of* everyone.

Samira Lee
an extremely natural segue
Brooklyn wants to know how moving went,
Kels?
3:50 PM

Samira sends us a string of portrait-mode photos of Brooklyn, her perfect queen of a cat. I save them to my camera roll, because Brooklyn photos make the best memes. On Twitter, she's a star.

ok. i'm used to it, you know?
3:45 PM

it's not really a big deal anymore
3:46 PM

My friends think I'm an army brat. It explains why I move around so much. If I told them the real reason, it would get complicated. And the best thing about being Kels is how uncomplicated she is. She bakes cupcakes inspired by book covers, reviews YA books, and always knows exactly what to say. She never thought-spirals or blurts out the wrong thing at the wrong time. She makes a religion out of the backspace key. She doesn't have Halle's Academy Award–nominated parents or a publishing royalty grandmother to live up to.

And she has actual friends. Even though we've never met, they aren't just pixels to me. Amy, Elle, and Samira are the people

I talk to every day—whether about the latest drama on Book Twitter, the disappointment in an ARC I was so excited for, or asking their opinions on which photo to use for the next cupcake Instagram post. Even though they don't know my real name, they know me better than anyone. Well, except Nash.

Amy Chen
not a big deal! i cried for a week when i
moved into my dorm.
3:47 PM

Amy Chen
i'm still crying because i'm going to be paying
off student loans until i'm 40. 😭
3:47 PM

Elle Carter
Wait! Didn't you settle on UT Austin to SAVE
money?
3:47 PM

Amy Chen
yup!! college is a scam!! if more sponsorships
came through i'd honestly consider
booktubing full time
3:48 PM

omg so then I could say I'm friends
with a NEW YORK TIMES BESTSELLING
author /and/ a CAREER YOUTUBER???
3:49 PM

Elle Carter
omg stop it I'm blushing!
3:49 PM

Amy Chen
pray to the gods of monetization for me please!!
3:49 PM

Samira Lee
🙏 🙏 🙏
3:49 PM

Elle Carter
🙏 🙏 🙏
3:49 PM

🙏 🙏 🙏
3:49 PM

Samira Lee
Also. Hold up. Elle. You let Kels read
IT'LL NEVER BE YOU????
3:50 PM

SHE DID AND IT'S AMAZING
3:51 PM

Elle Carter
You think anything pitched as "hate-to-love"
is amazing, Kels
3:52 PM

BECAUSE IT IS
3:52 PM

Samira Lee
BECAUSE IT IS
3:52 PM

Elle Carter
Well. Thank you. It actually might not be
trash? Lilah thinks we can go on sub next
month. 💀

I send a string of screaming emojis, then thank Samira for the super-casual segue in our private chat. Amy and Elle frequently spiral into a *Kels + Nash = Endless Hearts* rabbit hole. It's pretty cringe-y, but at least Samira is always on my side.

Samira Lee
Totally natural segues are my specialty. See.
3:54 PM

My phone blows up again with twelve new pictures of Brooklyn. Back in the group chat, the subject shifts.

Samira Lee
Wait. Kels. Have you heard from AG's people?
4:01 PM

not yet!
4:02 PM

i'm stressed!!
4:03 PM

Elle Carter
Don't stress! It's PUBLISHING. So like.
Expecting a response today most definitely
means you won't get one until next week.
4:03 PM

Elle is probably right, but I can't focus on blog content now anyway, so I let my eyes wander to the shelves around me. I have a prime window seat in the YA section, which I finally found after climbing up a winding staircase and through a narrow corridor. I've been here a handful of times, only on the off chance that Grams didn't have a book I was looking for, but the YA section is somehow smaller than I remember. Then again, it's a small library. My eye lands on the first two books in a new epic fantasy series that Amy recommended to me, so I get up to grab them. Then I pause at the NEW AND NOTEWORTHY endcap, stalling. I know I should check these out and go home, but I'm not ready to go back to that house and face Gramps.

I sit down instead and refresh my email while the group chain fires away in the background. Still nothing.

Well, if I'm not leaving, maybe I can at least be *somewhat* productive, with the promise of two new books to read as a reward. I minimize the group chat and reopen the article for *Teen Vogue*. It's not due until next week, but I'm hoping to get a draft prepared before school starts. It's a feature on Jewish YA—listing all my favorite books with Jewish protagonists, written by Jewish authors.

Ariel Goldberg is of course at the top of the list. Her twisty psychological thrillers star Jewish teens and her debut was the first time I felt *seen* in genre fiction. I want this article to help others feel that way too.

I put on headphones, play my #amwriting playlist on Spotify—a perfect combination of soft rock and acoustic covers—and find my rhythm in blurbing each book I've selected for the listicle.

"Hey. Mind if I sit here?" I barely notice the voice, but I do register the tall shadow standing above me.

"Go for it," I say, not breaking eye contact with my screen. I can't lose my flow now.

It's my first *Teen Vogue* piece, but I'm planning to pitch a monthly column to an editor I'm a Twitter mutual with. All posts would include a link to One True Pastry, which would be *huge*. I'm currently being hyped as their teen contributor, so I feel like there's a decent shot. I'm aware that my *teen* factor has an expiration date, but for now? I totally embrace it. Let me be a *teen voice* on any and all major media platforms! I'll never say no. I built One True Pastry on being for teens, by a teen.

Because engaging with adults who think YA is for them? It's exhausting.

Twenty minutes later, I click "save draft." It's not exactly what I needed to do today, but after twelve hours in the car and narrowly avoiding a panic attack, it's something.

My laptop dings with a new email notification—and my chest tightens for the millionth time today.

I glance at the clock.

It's four thirty-two. Almost the end of the workday. Unlikely. But possible.

I exhale and click the "Inbox (1)" tab.

Subject: READ BETWEEN THE LIES Cover Reveal

Oh God.

It's a rejection.

I feel it in my bones.

My cursor hovers over the email. It might seem small, waiting for a cover reveal, but it's *everything*. Ariel Goldberg hasn't released a new book in *three years*. In publishing, where so many popular authors are on a book-a-year schedule, this feels like a *lifetime*. Hosting a highly anticipated cover reveal like this one? One that should probably go to a major media outlet? It's exactly what One True Pastry needs to keep the momentum, to rise above the everyone-has-one kind of blogs out there, to be noticed by industry professionals and impress NYU admissions.

Now that the email is here in front of me though, and I have the power to click . . . I almost don't want to know. I thought no email was worse than a rejection. I take it back. Why did I ever think I wanted something in writing telling me I'm not good enough?

I wait a full minute, then click on the email before I change my mind.

Hi Kels!
I'm Alyssa Peterson, Ariel Goldberg's publicist. I'm so excited to confirm that Ariel would LOVE for One True Pastry to host the *exclusive* cover reveal for *Read Between the Lies.*

I reread *confirm* and *love* twelve times before I am convinced that's really what it says.

I got the Ariel Goldberg cover reveal. *Me*, Kels from One True Pastry.

Oh my God.

I slam my computer shut.

The sound reverberates through the silence.

Sorry, I mouth to the person sharing my table, trying to contain the stupid smile that must be spreading across my face. I make eye contact with him and for the second time in literally thirty seconds, I don't believe what I'm seeing. I blink once.

I'm hallucinating. It's the only logical explanation.

"Good news?" he asks—but really, he's trying not to laugh.

"You could say that," I say.

How am I speaking? How am I *breathing*?

He isn't a hallucination.

I know him.

Well, *I*, Halle, don't know him.

Kels knows him.

In fact, he's kind of Kels's best friend.

July, the summer before Middleton

BookCon @thebookcon 1hr
Calling all bloggers! Do you want to be a voice at one of publishing's biggest events? For the first time, we're opening applications for a blogger-only panel, aptly called Bloggers IRL! Applications are due September 1.
Apply here: https://bit.ly/2IX3iAs

Nash Stevens @Nash_Stevens27 1hr
👀 👀 👀
@thebookcon @OneTruePastry

Direct messages

Nash Stevens
Heeeeey! Did you see that BookCon is having a blogger panel at next year's conference?
2:27 PM

Dumb question. I tagged you. You saw it.
2:27 PM

So. Proposal. I think we should apply for it.
2:28 PM

hahaha okay sure
2:29 PM

Kels. I'm serious.
2:30 PM

you are? come on. CALLING ALL BLOGGERS
is code for famous, influential bloggers. the
people who write think pieces for national
publications, but actually know nothing about
YA or the blogging community.
2:32 PM

Wow. Harsh.
2:32 PM

You need to give yourself more credit
sometimes, you know? Don't you have like . . .
100K Instagram followers?
2:33 PM

110.2K
2:34 PM

SEE. I think you're probably exactly what
BookCon is looking for.
2:35 PM

only my cupcakes are viral. my actual blog stats
are still pretty mid-level. i don't know.
2:37 PM

Well, I think we should give it a shot. What do
we have to lose?
3:00 PM

our dignity when the BookCon
committee laughs at us
3:01 PM

. . . You are so dramatic.
3:02 PM

okay. i thought about it. let's give it a shot, why
not. on the miniscule chance this works, we're
definitely getting into NYU with this on our
application.
4:34 PM

That's a valid point.
4:35 PM

We'd also meet. Like. In person.
4:35 PM

really? that thought did not cross my mind,
not once
4:36 PM

Ha?
4:37 PM

don't you ever worry it'll be weird? meeting?
4:37 PM

Sometimes I guess, but I think we should let
the BookCon gods decide. Because like . . .
if we both manage to somehow get onto this
thing?
4:38 PM

I'm pretty sure that means we're supposed to
meet.
4:39 PM

THREE

If words weren't the absolute worst, I'd say, *Nash, It's me.*

I don't know how to explain it so it makes sense. *Nash. It's me, Kels. We were just talking about how I've never seen* Lord of the Rings *and oh, by the way, I got the cover reveal! I'm Kels— except I'm not Kels, I'm Halle. But . . . you can call me Kels. Though everyone else will probably call me Halle, so that could get weird. But yeah! Wow! Hi!*

It would be a catastrophe. I would be a catastrophe.

He's so *boyish* in person. Without the thick black hipster glasses he wears in his Twitter picture, he looks younger. His dark hair is longer, too, falling into his eyes. His *eyes.* I knew they were brown, but they also have specks of gold—I had no idea. I don't think I've ever thought of him as a height, but he's tall and all limbs. I mean, Kels knows he runs track. But now I *see* it, you know? I see how all the pieces fit together and become Nash IRL.

"I'm Nash."

His voice is a melody I never imagined I'd hear. And I almost don't understand why he's introducing himself, but of course he has no clue who I am. Why would he? My current picture is an artsy photograph of the back of my head, my hair long and blowing in the wind. My face is always obscured in posts. It helps to mold my persona, a version of me that is cooler and more mysterious than I am in real life.

I'm Kels. That's what I should say.

"Halle" is what comes out.

It's the truth, but it feels like a lie.

"Cool." He smiles, and my God, it's so much better than the smiley-face emoji. "Are you just visiting?"

I shake my head no because words are stuck in my throat.

"Wait—"

Oh, thank God. I don't have to tell him. He knows.

"—you're Professor Levitt's granddaughter, right?"

Professor Levitt? Nash knows *Gramps*? *My* Gramps. What?

"It's not weird that I know that, I swear. I'm in his art history class. First class was supposed to be tonight, but he postponed it. Said his grandchildren were moving in. We don't get too many new people in Middleton, so I kind of put two and two together."

I exhale, not sure whether to feel relieved or disappointed.

Wait. Nash is in high school, I thought. We're working on college applications—not *in college classes*. Next year it's supposed to be us, meeting as freshmen at NYU, spending time in every bookstore downtown between classes and exploring the rest of the city on the weekends. If Nash takes classes with Gramps at UConn, if Nash is *in college*—well, that calls into question pretty much everything I know about him. Oh God, what if Nash is a catfishing liar?

"So . . . you commute?" I ask.

He looks at me funny and I can already feel my neck flush pink.

"To UConn," I clarify.

"*Oh*. No, I'm not—MHS doesn't have any art history classes, so your grandfather offered to let me into his. But yeah, high school. I am in it."

Breathe. Nash is just perfectly nerdy and not a creep.

"Me too," I say, which is when it hits me.

MHS. Middleton High School. As in *my* new high school.

"Cool. Where'd you move from?"

"New York. Upstate," I lie without flinching, the words flying out of my mouth before I can even think them through. I have never been to upstate New York in my life. I don't know why I say this. As far as Nash knows, Kels is moving from an army base in Georgia to North Carolina. Kels is comfortably in the South— hundreds of miles away from Nash.

"Well, welcome to Middleton," he says. He looks down at his watch and frowns. "I have an ungodly stack of books to check out before the library closes, but I'll see you around?"

He stands up as I nod, swoops his messenger bag over his shoulder, and is gone with a wave.

Oh my God. I knew Nash was from Connecticut but—I never thought to ask *where*.

I didn't think it mattered, because it's not like I planned on telling him that I—well, Kels—moved to Connecticut. Never did I ever think he'd be *here*, with me, in Middle-of-Freaking-Nowhere, Connecticut. Because who really lives here? No one I've ever talked to has even *heard* of this place.

If Nash knew Kels was in Connecticut, he'd want to meet. I wasn't—I'm *not*—ready for that. We were supposed to meet in Washington Square Park, ready for orientation.

It was supposed to happen then, when I would be the closest version of Kels, for real, living the life Nash and Kels always talked about.

I glance at my phone-clock. Ollie texted me that dinner was almost ready fifteen minutes ago. I pack up my laptop and wipe the sweat beads off my forehead. Breathe in and out slowly to try to force my heart rate to recover.

Nash is here. In Middleton.

We're going to school together. We're going to *graduate together*.

He has no clue who I am.

And . . . I have no clue what to do.

If I could never tell Nash who I really am online, where I'm the most confident, chill version of me, how can I ever form the words in person?

Ollie heated up ramen noodles for dinner and nothing is okay.

I got the Ariel Goldberg cover reveal, but Nash is *here*.

Ollie is twirling noodles with a fork and watching Netflix on his phone. My bowl is set up at the seat adjacent to his and my chest tightens because Ollie made dinner. He set the table, even filled a pitcher with water, but there are only two place settings.

"It's probably cold," Ollie says, pausing his show. "If you want to, reheat it on the stove."

I sit next to Ollie. "Where's Gramps?"

Ollie shrugs. "Asleep, I think. I don't know. He hasn't come out of his room since you left."

I pick up my fork and twirl noodles. "It's not even six."

"Yeah. I'm really confused."

"Me too," I say. "Thanks for dinner."

Ollie snorts. "Ramen isn't dinner. But honestly, it was the best option. Gramps only has cereal and snack foods, basically. We need to go grocery shopping."

I eat the cold ramen. Ollie returns his attention to his show. If Grams were here, we'd be eating matzo ball soup. It'd be a whole production, Ollie and me helping to roll the matzo meal into walnut-size balls after the stock has been simmering on the stove all afternoon. I wasn't expecting a Grams-quality dinner tonight—but I did expect the three of us to at least eat dinner. Together.

He's not okay, Grams, I think, looking down at the necklace resting against my heart. In my head, I talk to Grams a lot. Like whenever I read a really great book, or see a movie I know would make her laugh, or have a Major Life Event.

Does meeting Nash in person qualify as a Major Life Event?

Grams would call it destiny.

We were making frosting together when One True Pastry was born, three summers ago.

"Did you always know you wanted to be an editor?" I had asked, adding two drops of purple food coloring to buttercream frosting. We were going to surprise Gramps with lemon lavender today, even though red velvet is his real favorite.

Grams nodded. "Always. I love stories. Figuring out what makes them tick, how the pieces fit together. Seeing people like you fall in love with them." She winked at me as she stirred her own bowl of yellow frosting, her eyebrows pinched in concentration. Lavender lemon meant we had to use two piping bags to swirl the colors together.

"Do you think I could maybe be an editor?"

My cheeks flushed immediately. I loved talking about books with her, but I'd never vocalized my publishing dreams out loud before to anyone. It seemed absurd to even try when Grams was already, like, the Judy Blume of children's editors.

Grams looked at me. "I think you'd be an amazing editor, Hal. But the way you talk about books, you're already a publicist."

I dropped my spatula, contemplating. "Publicist?"

I had never even thought about it, but I liked the way the word sounded on my lips. Talking about books was the only time I felt like my words fit together.

"You should start a blog. See if it's a good fit," she said, wiping her hair out of her warm eyes, looking at me like she could see right through me.

I laughed. I loved reading book blogs—I got so many great recs from my favorite YA bloggers. But writing one? I was fourteen. Who would even listen? But . . . maybe that didn't matter.

Maybe if Grams thought it was a good idea, my dream wasn't completely crazy.

"I could call it One True Pastry." I laughed at my own silliness as a splatter of purple buttercream landed on the counter instead of in the bag. "Like One True Pairing. OTP."

I thought of all my favorite forums filled with passionate debates re: OTPs and every combination of characters who were just meant to end up together.

Grams stopped mixing and faced me. There was a speck of frosting smudged on her nose and I'll never forget the smile that burst onto her face.

"Hal, that's perfect. There's your hook. Cupcakes and books. What's better than that?"

I've been Kels from One True Pastry ever since.

Creating a profile meant crafting an identity. It wasn't that I *couldn't* be Halle Levitt—I didn't want to be. If I used my real name online, I wouldn't be Halle. I'd be industry giant Miriam Levitt's granddaughter. I'd get opportunities *because* I'm Miriam Levitt's granddaughter. Or worse, people would compare me to her and tell me there's no way I measured up. If people were going to follow me, I wanted it to be for the content.

I wanted to know if I was really good, or if Grams was just saying that.

Still, Grams presence has seeped into every part of my blog. I write my reviews the way I'd tell her about a book. And when I had to choose the name of my persona, well, that came from her too.

I wanted your parents to name you Kelsey, Grams said.

So I became Kels Roth, a combination of Grams's favorite name and her maiden name.

With some experimentation and Grams's guidance, One True Pastry grew. Kels was good. And I love that one of Grams's books proved it.

Fireflies and You was the first time I re-created a full book cover with cupcakes, and it's what put Kels on the map. Originally, the premise of One True Pastry was *cupcake inspiration* and I paired cupcake recipes with reviews. Then I started posting #CupcakeCovers on Instagram. The posts were simple—a close-up shot of a single cupcake on a plate. The details were in the design, the swirl of frosting colors and topping choices that were always directly influenced by the color scheme of a cover.

Then *Fireflies and You* happened and the book just changed something in me. It felt like I had to do more. Like I could. I didn't talk to Grams about it at all first, like I usually would when I had a brand-new idea. I just did it and now the photo I posted two years ago has 110K likes on Instagram—a number that continues to increase.

Yeah, I check.

The buzz for the book got real. But honestly, so did the buzz for my blog. Thanks to the cupcakes, people started to read my reviews. Thanks to cupcakes, publishing began to *notice me*. Now publicists send me advance reader copies, with an enthusiastic exclamation point note attached hoping to connect. Beyond that, I found a whole community of people who love YA books as much as I do. I have friends.

I have Nash.

So really, this entire situation is all your fault, Grams.

"Halle!"

My eyes snap up and meet Ollie's. He's looking at me funny. "Huh?"

"I said your name three times," Ollie says. "Are you okay? You're, like, not here."

I shake my head. "Sorry, I just—"

Nothing I say will make sense, so I twirl too many cold noodles with my fork. Raise the fork to my mouth, and take a bite. Half the noodles land on my lap, soy sauce splattering all over my white shorts.

Awesome.

I stand up. Brush off Ollie's concern. "I need to change. Yeah."

Upstairs, I clean myself up in the bathroom and change into sweatpants. Sitting on the toilet lid, I scroll through Nash's social media when my phone buzzes with a new message.

Nash Stevens
OK. I've waited for you to text me first long
enough. Did you hear from Ariel's fancy
publicist? Did you get the cover reveal? I'm
kind of dying here.
6:44 PM

I read the text in Nash's voice for the first time. His actual vocal cords vibrating *voice*. It's honestly wild.

maybe I did

6:47 PM

OKAY SO
6:47 PM

SO MAYBE I GOT IT
6:47 PM

NO WAY
6:48 PM

I mean, I totally knew you would.
6:48 PM

LOL nice save ☺
6:49 PM

You cold emailed Ariel Goldberg's publicist!
And weren't ignored! You're a total badass.
6:50 PM

This is who Nash is expecting to meet. The girl who cold emails publicists. A *badass*.

what can I say? it's a gift.
6:50 PM

You'll totally get the panel now, at least!

6:51 PM

like bookcon is going to be interested in
aesthetically pleasing cupcake photos.
6:53 PM

I migrate from the bathroom to the bedroom as I try to message Nash and pretend everything is normal, that I don't know the exact color of his eyes or the sound of his voice. I settle on the most generic of generic messages.

what's up with you?
6:57 PM

Not much. Some new kids moved into town. A
sister and brother. The girl's our age, I think. I
met her at the library.
6:59 PM

She's me. Two words have never been more impossible to type.

oh?
7:00 PM

Yeah! Seems cool. Kind of quiet, but we were

in a library. I'm mostly basing my assessment
off meeting her in the YA section.
7:00 PM

You know, where the cool kids hang.
7:01 PM

exactly what I was thinking.
7:01 PM

It was nice, meeting someone new under the
age of 55. Most people come here for the
senior life.
7:02 PM

they do NOT
7:02 PM

Swear to God.
7:03 PM

But anyways, meeting her got me thinking.
Like, it'll be cool when we meet.
7:03 PM

My pulse quickens. How would he feel if he knew we already

had?

i'm a terribly awkward human

7:03 PM

I mean . . . mood?

7:04 PM

fair enough.

7:04 PM

but new girl is probably most definitely cooler

than me.

7:05 PM

Eh, probably.

7:08 PM

He doesn't say anything else, but I can feel his disappointment in the non-immediate response.

A knock on the door makes me jump.

"It's me," Ollie says and he comes into the room, Scout on his heels. She jumps on the bed and makes herself comfortable between my crisscrossed legs. Ollie takes a seat on the end, fists curled at his sides.

"You should apologize to Gramps," he says.

"What?" I ask.

Ollie's eyes are fire. "You couldn't *not* be Kels for one day? We hadn't even been here for an hour and—"

"Nash is here." I blurt out. I know Ollie is pissed at me but I need someone else to know.

Ollie blinks. "What?"

I wrap my arms around my knees, letting my toes sink into Aunt Liz's mattress. "I, um, kind of met him at the library—and I'm *shook*, Ollie. Seconds after I learn that I'll be hosting Ariel Goldberg's cover reveal, I look up and Nash is just *there*, like, trying not to laugh at my reaction."

"Wait, pause on Nash—you got the cover reveal?"

We bump fists and I smile because in the middle of this mess, I can't forget something good happened today. Something amazing, actually. Ollie holds out his hand. I pull up The Email and he reads it and can't stop smiling and wow, it feels so good when he's proud of me. He repeats "This is so great!" probably half a dozen times before relinquishing my phone.

Ollie flops down on his back so he's staring at the ceiling. Scout lies on his stomach and it's too adorable.

But then he says, "Okay, back to Nash. What did he say?"

"Oh. I mean, I didn't tell him."

He turns his head toward me. "Wait. Didn't tell him about the cover reveal?"

I stare at my knees. My eyes are burning a hole in my right kneecap and I'm silent one beat too long.

"*Halle.*"

"*Ollie.*"

"He's your best friend."

"*You're* my best friend."

"Nope." He sits up so fast, Scout is startled. She jumps off the bed with a quiet yelp and retreats out my ajar door. I wish I could follow her right out and away from this conversation.

I look at Ollie, who has the sternest expression I have ever seen on a fifteen-year-old. When Ollie is disappointed in me, I forget that *I'm* the older sibling.

"So, what? You're just going to spend all year pretending you don't know everything about him?"

"I—I don't know, okay? I haven't exactly thought that far ahead."

"I repeat: *He's your best friend.*"

"*Online*—and maybe it should stay that way. IRL me will ruin everything."

He crosses his arms. "That is literally the stupidest thing I have ever heard."

Ollie doesn't understand, because Ollie is braver than I will ever be. Ollie's gut reaction would've been to tell Nash—and he would've been *excited* to do it. It would never even cross his mind to keep himself a secret from his best friend, not for one second.

"You'll tell him, though? Once you know him better?"

"Yes," I say, and it's the second time today I lie instantly.

"You have to promise. If you become friends, you'll tell him the truth."

"I promise." I pinky swear for added believability.

"Also promise you'll apologize to Gramps."

I nod. That, at least, is a promise I can keep.

Ollie exhales, because I've never broken a pinky swear.

As soon as Ollie exits the room, I stuff my face in my pillow. Attempt to suffocate the fact that I, Halle Levitt, am at a total loss.

I can't jeopardize Kels's friendship with Nash. *I won't.* I don't know how to *friendship* IRL. Behind a screen, it's easy to talk to Nash about the possibility of meeting. It's easy to imagine an offline friendship, us studying for midterms together at the library and going to book events in the evenings. It's easy to imagine because it's theoretical. We both have to get into NYU first. It's not real until that happens, and there are so many ways it could not. BookCon feels like an even bigger long shot. One of us getting it would be insanely lucky. Both of us? Impossible. There's every possibility none of it will ever be real.

I'm not ready for real. How can I be certain the truth that is me won't be a total letdown? I imagine the flash of disappointment that crosses his face when I tell him who I am. His disappointment—it would *ruin* me. I can't deal with that.

So for now, I won't.

September 3

6:41 AM

Mom
WE'RE CONNECTED

Dad
👏 👏 👏

omg hi

Ollie
what up

how are you? how is Israel? how is everything?

Dad
👍 👍 👍

Mom
We scouted this morning . . . locations for
b-roll, other kibbutzim to interview . . . it's
going to be great

Dad
😎 🤑 🙌

awesome!

Ollie
I've already told all my friends that you're
going to win an Oscar

Mom
Oliver

Dad
😵 😵 😵

Ollie
Just raising the stakes

Mom
If you're going to brag about your fab parents,
at least tell them something true!

Mom
How are you doing, Hal?

like socially? school starts today! so I'm not
sure to whom ollie is referring to with regards
to "friends"

Mom

I miss your regular uses of whom

Dad

😭😂😭

Ollie

I don't

FOUR

If school and I had a relationship status, it'd be it's complicated.

Ollie and I sit in plush chairs in the guidance office, bent over the official MHS map. I oscillate between fidgeting with the hem of my black shirtdress and wiping off my cherry lipstick. I don't know why I listened to Elle this morning when she helped pick my first-day-of-school outfit and insisted red lipstick was a good idea. Amy and Samira agreed, and so did Kels. In my room, alone, the line between Halle and Kels feels more blurred. Lipstick makes me feel like the badass Kels is online. Out in the world? It's a calculated risk, and this is definitely not the time for it.

I should know better, honestly. It's my fifth first day in a new school system, and as a veteran newbie, I have developed a comprehensive list of rules for the first day at a new school. It's published on the blog, for those interested in reading the whole list; 1.2K retweets. Rule number one: Don't draw attention to yourself.

I rummage through the front pocket of my backpack for a

muted neutral lip gloss, swipe it over my lips, and instantly feel more like me, just Halle.

Ollie is fixated on the map. He runs a hand through his hair and sighs. "This map is the *worst*, Hal. Useless."

It's a relief, being in the same school. We may have no clue where we're going, but at least we have no clue where we're going together.

"Homeroom starts in ten. Do you have any questions?"

Ms. Connors, our guidance counselor, reappears and hands us our schedules. Ollie opens his mouth to speak, but I cut him off. "We're good."

She nods and escorts us out of her office. "Sophomores are in the science wing, down to the left. Seniors are in the English wing upstairs."

"Thanks," Ollie says.

Ms. Connors flashes a plastic smile that screams *good luck* before closing the guidance office door behind us.

We're officially on our own.

I reassess the map. Ollie is right. It *is* the worst. It's nothing short of illegible—the colors don't contrast, the symbols aren't obvious, and the typeface is tiny. The printing is so bad that the inky route is just meaningless lines connecting meaningless places.

"I'm making a new map tonight," Ollie says. "It will be in Ms. Connors's box in the morning."

I snort. "Not again."

"I want to contribute to *the community*, Halle. My motives are pure."

We're headed in opposite directions. So we bump fists, promise to reunite at lunch, and go our separate ways. Ollie will probably have his own crew by then.

For a small school, it still feels like people are everywhere. I go upstairs and down two hallways, my pulse speeding with each wrong turn. I pause against a row of lockers, giving the trash map one more pass, as though I can will some useful information to appear out of nothing. Alas, this is not the Marauders Map.

"Hey, Upstate. Need help?"

It takes me a second to look up.

Of course. My stomach can't decide if it wants to twist or flutter.

"This map is horrible," I say, finally.

"The worst," Nash agrees. "We're probably in the same homeroom, though; let me see . . ." He plucks my schedule out of my hand. Heat radiates from my ears. I feel it when I tuck back a lock of hair. "Yup. H113."

Levitt to *Stevens* in one homeroom? That can't be right. MHS is small, but it's not *that* small.

"Alphabetical?"

"Mhm. K for Kim and L for Levitt. Looks like you're stuck with me. . . ." He looks down, scanning my class list. "Also looks like we're taking all the same APs. Cool."

Wait. That's not right. He's supposed to be Nash Stevens.

I blink. "Kim?"

My face is on fire the moment the words spill from my lips.

"I'm so sorry. That's not what I—"

Nash laughs. "It's okay. Seriously, it's not every day you meet a quarter-Asian Jewish person in semi-coastal Connecticut. My friend Sawyer calls me a unicorn. I like the term *enigma*, personally."

Nash thinks everything is an enigma. That's literally his Twitter bio. *An enigma, tbh.*

"I'm the worst."

I don't tell him the truth. I know Nash is a quarter Korean. Of course I know that. It sounds like I'm shocked his last name is Kim. But really, I'm shocked that it's not Stevens. And that maybe I, Kels, don't know him as well as I thought I did. So now he's going to think I sputtered *Kim* like I've never seen a multiracial human in my life.

Where is backspace when you need it?

My stomach muscles constrict. Day one at Middle-of-Nowhere High, and I, Halle, have already made a complete ass of myself. To Nash. Before homeroom, nonetheless. The day hasn't even started yet!

"Most people are surprised." Nash shrugs. "Because I'm definitely white passing. Long story short, my grandpa is Korean. My dad is half. And now, here I am. Boom, math."

We stop in front of H113. I've never been more relieved to get to class.

Middle back. That's my first day of homeroom seat. Front is too eager. Back corner is too angsty. Middle back is just right, a place where I can sink into my chair in humiliation, open a blank notebook, and start brainstorming titles for a fall roundup post.

Nash will be distracted enough by all the talking heads around me that he won't even notice I've slipped away.

"Nash! Hey!"

I turn to the voice, but all I see is raven-black hair. Tight spiral curls cascade down her back. She waves to Nash and points to the two empty desks behind her. Middle right. Nash motions for me to follow with a head nod, and I do because all the middle back seats are taken and I can't ghost after that. At least middle right is an okay alternative, and we only have homeroom on the first day of school. It's not like I'll be stuck next to Nash all year.

I follow him and everyone's eyes follow me.

Okay, do I have lipstick on my teeth? A quick tongue swipe confirms no. Nash told me that Middleton doesn't get new people often; I guess he wasn't kidding.

I try to avoid eye contact with all the staring and focus instead on Nash's seat saver. She's cute, with a petite frame and soft features. Her makeup is on point—bronze eye shadow makes her brown eyes pop and her deep red lipstick looks perfect. A neutral eye matched with a bold lip is Kels's favorite combination.

Nash slides into the seat behind her, so I sit next to him. I pull my water bottle out of my backpack and take a long sip. Stall for a few seconds so I don't have to speak. Introductions mixed with small talk are especially cruel.

"How was the shore?" Nash asks.

"Painful," the girl says.

She slips down the sleeve of her sunflower shirt dress, revealing a red, blistering shoulder.

"Gross. What happened to SPF 100?"

She sighs. "SPF 1000 wouldn't be enough."

Nash laughs and the girl turns to me. "Wait. You're Halle. Hi! I'm Molly."

"Hi," I say.

I almost said *I know.*

Because now I do. She's Molly Jacobson. Nash's IRL best friend. Wow. Meeting Nash is enough to process. Being introduced to the people in his IRL world? People who are now a part of *my* world? It's too much. Online, talking to Nash as Kels, it's easy to forget that he has *people*, real people, outside of Book Twitter and blogging.

He's my best friend. I'm his best *internet* friend.

I hate that distinction.

Nash and Molly swap schedules and discuss The Situation. AP overlaps, study blocks. Important details, like who's where when. They're calculating how many minutes they can possibly spend with their core crew until the final bell rings at two-fifteen.

Meanwhile, I'm counting down the minutes until I can go home and update my blog and message *my* Nash, not the actual human sitting a foot away from me.

"I have the second lunch block," Nash says.

"Me too!" Molly says.

"Third period study?"

"Fifth."

"Damn."

Molly glances at her cell. "Sawyer is second lunch too—and, hey, so is Autumn!"

"Sweet, Le Crew lunch is complete."

I pretend I'm studying my *Welcome to Middle-of-Nowhere High School!* pamphlet. Then pretend there's someone on the other side of my phone, not just the overwhelming amount of OTP emails I already have at eight in the morning.

"Halle," Molly says, "what lunch block are you?"

I look up. "Second," Nash and I say.

Molly swats Nash's arm.

He shrugs. "What? We have, like, the same schedule."

"Dude, it still sounded creepy."

"Whatever."

Molly looks at me. "Nash's creepiness aside, you can totally sit with us. We can introduce you to everyone."

I should say no. Given our near-identical course load, it looks like Operation: Avoid Nash is already a no go. He's going to be a part of my Middleton life whether I like it or not. But if this morning's disaster showed me anything, it's that I should keep things strictly academic between us. I shouldn't socialize with him. I shouldn't get to know Le Crew. I shouldn't get to know *him*, IRL.

Still, lunch is always, without a doubt, difficult on day one. I see myself standing in the cafeteria, frozen, with no choice but to crash Ollie's sophomore table. So despite my self-imposed No-Nash Policy, I nod, and Molly smiles.

I'm grateful I have some sort of *place*, any sort of *situation* that does not involve a massive panic attack. Now Ollie and I can pretend not to know each other at lunch, like normal siblings do.

And it's just lunch. It doesn't mean we have to be friends. It'll be great.

It's not great.

I'm the seventh seat at a six-person table, which is uncomfortable in an infinite number of ways.

In dropping my fork on the floor and awkwardly trying to decide if I should squeeze out and maneuver my way back to the cutlery station or say *Screw it, I didn't want my salad anyway*.

In being wedged between Molly and Nash.

In brushing shoulders with Nash multiple times—and feeling like all my secrets are going to spill out of my soul every time I do.

In checking and rechecking that I've silenced my cell, just in case Nash sends a DM to Kels.

In everyone talking all at once, but being unable to access any of the conversation.

". . . having Weisner for English *blows* . . ."

". . . dude, yeah, I have McAlister and she's amazing. Her book list is exclusively women and people of color . . ."

". . . I didn't think it was possible to screw up cheese pizza, yet here we are . . ."

". . . Sawyer, if you make a *that's sexist against men* comment I'm breaking up with you . . ."

". . . right? It's so bad . . ."

". . . If you have that little faith in me, maybe I should break up with you . . ."

". . . I actually think it's pretty good . . ."

My eyes flicker in circles, my eardrums bounce from conversation to conversation, attempting to piece together the web of relationships. Nash. Molly. Sawyer. Autumn. Taylor. Beth.

Nash + Molly = BFFs

Molly + Sawyer = 😍😍😍

Sawyer + Nash = Bros

Autumn = Molly's other BFF

Taylor + Beth = Autumn's theater friends. Not Le Crew, but clearly lunch regulars—unlike me.

Overwhelmed by my total inability to naturally insert myself into the conversation, I look down at my phone. It's the only place I never feel out of place. The home screen displays a string of texts from Amy.

Amy Chen

Happy LAST first day of high school, Kels + Elle!!

12:05 PM

Amy Chen

And happy FIRST first day of high school Samira, our freshman child!!

12:06 PM

I lock the screen. I can't even respond to the string of texts from my friends, because Nash is here. Next to me. He *knows* my friends. They're his friends too.

"So what is your thing, Hal-lee Levitt?" Sawyer asks.

My eyes snap up to meet Sawyer's. "Huh?"

Could I *be* any more eloquent?

Sawyer Davidson is Molly's other half. We met this morning in AP psych, when I took the seat Nash had gestured to behind him. *I'm not the new kid anymore*, Sawyer had said. I laughed and I don't remember what I said because between the wavy blonde hair and ocean-gray eyes, I was too busy thinking *Damn, Molly. Good job.*

"You know? Your jam."

"Like how sometimes Sawyer speaks in syllables," Molly says.

"And says 'jam,'" Autumn adds.

Sawyer rolls his eyes.

"Um," I stutter. Six people, twelve eyes. All on me. "I like books?"

Great. Where's the instant lie impulse when I *actually* need it? I should've made up some sort of fake hobby. Or said *literally anything other than "I like books."*

Because of course Nash says, "Me too."

"Nash likes comic books," Taylor says.

"Graphic novels," Nash clarifies, since I, Halle, am not supposed to know that.

Heat creeps up my neck when Nash looks at me. "It's an underappreciated genre, honestly. I, um, kind of blog about it. I'm trying to make graphic novels mainstream, one review at a time."

"Nash, don't be modest," Autumn says, dipping a potato

chip in ketchup and popping it in her mouth. She swallows, then looks at me. "He writes and draws too. They're good—I've already called dibs on the option."

I would've known Autumn Williams was a director even if Nash hadn't already told Kels that she's destined to be the next Ava DuVernay. Her mostly black, trying-without-trying aesthetic screams *film school*. Her braided black hair is tied back into a ponytail and she carries around a little black notebook, where she jots down what she calls *moments to remember*, all through lunch. From what Nash has told me, USC is her dream, but for now she has A_Williams Films, a Vimeo account where she posts short films that are the epitome of black girl magic.

"They're okay," Nash says.

"Shut up, they're so good," Molly says.

It's the second time today I almost say *I know*.

"He posts them online," Autumn says.

"*Autumn*," Nash says, his cheeks flush pink.

"www.outsidethelines.com/rex," Sawyer chimes in.

Nash is full-blown red, but it's adorable the way they're hyping him up, like retweets in real time.

REX, Nash's weekly web comic, is about two dinosaur brothers—Terry and Rex—exploring the modern world. At the end of the first series, they are separated and it is devastating. The second installment is from the POV of the younger dinosaur, Rex, searching desperately for his brother. It's action-packed and adorable and heartbreaking all at once.

Online, Nash shouts about REX to his thousands of Outside

the Lines subscribers. He's always posting links, constantly liking tweets, and retweeting reviews.

IRL, he's shy about it. It's really cute.

I cannot think Nash is cute. Amy and Elle would go insane if they knew that thought even crossed my mind.

Nobody understands not wanting to talk about something more than I do, so I attempt to steer the conversation away from REX. Half for Nash's sake, half for my own. But when I do I say, "*Maus* kind of changed my life."

"Seriously?" Nash says. "Me too!"

His smile is grateful—not at all suspicious—but that doesn't stop my heart palpitations and sweaty palms. Luckily, the bell rings and I take the opportunity to pretend I've left something in my locker and bolt.

I don't know what I was thinking. I am the *worst* in group settings. I never know what to say, or the right questions to ask, or how to apply a face that reads *approachable, I promise.* It's somehow always surprising if and when I'm directly addressed. It absolutely would've been better to sit with a different group, where even if it was uncomfortable, at least there were no stakes. No *I like books* and mentioning things I know he likes. I'm not supposed to know what he likes!

The whole point of not telling him is to protect our friendship because I won't live up to Kels—and every awkward thing that's happened today just proves me right.

FIVE

Friday is a cupcake day.

A reward for making it through my first week at MHS in one piece. There's flour in my hair, the electric mixer is plugged in, and I feel unstoppable.

I feel like I can design a cupcake cover cake worthy of Ariel Goldberg's cover reveal.

Earlier today, Alyssa Peterson emailed me. Subject line: *Confidential*. When I saw it at lunch, I promptly excused myself to go to the restroom, doing everything in my power to not *gasp* and run. I opened the email in the bathroom stall and stared at the cover for five minutes, stunned that someone from the real New York publishing universe trusted me with this information that thousands of fans will want. Not because I'm Miriam's granddaughter—because I'm *Kels*.

It's a piece of notebook paper, the cover. The page is filled with words, but they're all redacted—except for the title words, *Read Between the Lies*—each on a different line. It has a three-dimensional effect, so the paper looks like it was crumpled up. Splatters of red, like blood, make up the only color on the page.

As soon as I saw it, I knew how I am going to introduce it to the world.

It's going to be my first ever *cinematic* cupcake cover reveal.

My friends are already *obsessed* with this idea.

Elle Carter
A VIDEO??? Kels, that's going to be
AMAZING
4:31 PM

> i hope so!! i'm picturing it, like, time-lapsed
> 4:32 PM

> so each cupcake will be laid out one at a time,
> row by row . . . and then boom! full cover
> 4:33 PM

> maybe I'll even do some ~ fancy ~ animation.
> Swap out the cupcake cover for the actual cover
> at the end? i don't know, i'm still experimenting
> . . .
> 4:33 PM

Samira Lee
👀 👀 👀
4:34 PM

Amy Chen

I'm just impressed you can animate anything,
tbh
4:34 PM

> well, hopefully my brother will
> help with that part
> 4:35 PM

Elle Carter

So. Are we now done pretending you don't
care about the bookcon panel?
4:35 PM

Samira Lee

Yeah. This is too next level to "not care."
4:35 PM

> it's less about not caring, more like how can
> i even think i have a shot against every other
> amazing blogger?
> 4:36 PM

Elle Carter

Because you make cupcakes LOOK LIKE
BOOK COVERS?!
4:36 PM

Samira Lee
And write KILLER reviews?
4:36 PM

Amy Chen
and you don't let adults get away with any
of their garbage YA takes!!
4:37 PM

Elle Carter
. . . have we inflamed your ego enough?
4:38 PM

too much!!
4:39 PM

Okay, yeah, if my post goes viral, I can admit to myself how cool being on a panel at BookCon would be—and also how *amazing* it would look to NYU. If it goes viral, BookCon will start to feel less like *not in a million years* and more *probably not, but maybe*.

The only problem with totally falling for the idea of Book-Con? Nash.

If I get in, Kels won't be anonymous anymore. I'd submit a photo for the announcement—and even if I managed to avoid *that*, I'd be all over Twitter during the actual convention.

I'd have to tell Nash.

Right now? That feels impossible.

But I can't talk to my friends about this, obviously, given that they have no idea I'm actually a girl named Halle living in Connecticut sitting with Nash at lunch every day.

So I place my phone down on the countertop a safe distance away from the chaos of ingredients on the table, and focus on them instead. Batch one is in the fridge cooling and Gramps's kitchen smells like red velvet batter. Batch two—dark chocolate for Ollie—is in the oven. For my cover reveals, the batter flavor doesn't matter as much as the look, so for tonight's dry run I can make everyone's favorites.

I'm making cream cheese frosting from scratch with Grams's standing mixer when my phone buzzes. I glance over my shoulder and see the Instagram notification. Right on time, it's a new post from Mad Levitt's account.

I have notifications turned on for all of Mad and Ari's social media accounts. It keeps me in the loop and helps me feel like they're not so far away. It's jarring, not being on location with my parents, not sitting in on their top-secret meetings, not being in the *same time zone* as them.

Mom plans on sending a weekly email and we have an ongoing text chain in WhatsApp, but the electricity of being there doesn't translate in emojis. Instagram is better. The candid shots of my parents scouting locations and exploring Israel are as close as I can get. Today's post is an obnoxiously cute selfie of my parents, floating in the Dead Sea. While the legal team is crossing Ts and dotting Is, Mom and Dad have been playing tourists in their temporary home.

I double tap to like it.

The emails and texts remind me that I do, in fact, still have parents. But Instagram is where I *miss* them. With everything going on in the past week, I've barely had brain space to think about it, but now I wonder if maybe this was the wrong decision. If I was with them, Nash would've continued to exist only in my phone and I wouldn't be in this mess.

It's fine.

I'm fine.

I separate the frosting into three bowls and add the appropriate food coloring—black, white, and red. Mix it until it's the perfect shade of blood red or pitch black. Even though they won't *look* like traditional red velvet cupcakes, they'll still taste like them. When my timer beeps, I pull out the cooled cupcakes in the fridge and swap in the fresh-out-of-the-oven chocolate ones.

Then I fill a piping bag and begin frosting.

Maybe if I make some of them not bloody cupcakes, Gramps can even bring them to Shabbat services.

I know he's disappointed Ollie and I are not going. We *can't*, though. We're Jewish but we don't know Hebrew or the melodies of the prayers or the order of the service. Mom and Dad never took us to temple. I've already had enough *firsts* for this week— I'm not ready for another situation where my anxiety will most definitely be on display.

I can't Shabbat, but I *can* bake epic cupcakes. That'll make Gramps happy. It always does.

I snap a picture of the first completed cupcake and send it to

Ollie, even though he's just upstairs—it's easier than yelling over Kendrick Lamar.

Then, while I wait for him to rush down and give me an opinion, I remember I owe Nash flailing commentary on the new REX panels he emailed me this morning. It's beautiful and devastating and starting to feel like Rex will never find Terry.

> hey! sorry my notes are late, i'm just busy over here sobbing forever!!! seriously.
> HOW DARE YOU?
> 4:31 PM

> how does. REX. keep. getting. better???
> 4:31 PM

> *flails*
> 4:31 PM

Please stop crying 🐧
4:32 PM

> 😭 😭 😭
> 4:32 PM

Thank you—I think? I hope NYU thinks so
🙏
4:33 PM

THEY ABSOLUTELY WILL
4:34 PM

My parents will let me go if I get in? Right?
4:35 PM

i hope so.
4:36 PM

Every time I try to talk about it, I totally freeze.
4:37 PM

mood. they're THAT against NYU? why? let me
guess, your mom has a vendetta because they
didn't accept her a million years ago
4:38 PM

LOL no. It's a lot of things. It's expensive. It's
in the middle of a, quote, "big dangerous
city." It's the fact that Wesleyan has an
amazing art program, and it's right here.
4:39 PM

so you have to convince them. WHY NYU?
4:40 PM

Because if I don't get out of this town now, I
don't think I ever will, tbh.
4:41 PM

It feels so good talking to Nash from my phone, as Kels,
like before. At school, the best strategy when it comes to dealing
with Nash is total, complete avoidance. I always arrive to our
shared classes right before the bell. I claim the lunch seat wedged
between Sawyer and Autumn. Any and all school-related talk is
strictly about assignments and due dates.

It's the only way to avoid a repeat of that awkward first day.

Because already I can see that Nash is just as smart and funny
and filled with book puns for every situation as he is on my screen.
If I get to know him, I know I'll think he's even more wonderful,
and I'll wish I were brave enough to tell him the truth and take
his reaction, whatever it is. Which I won't be.

When we have conversations like this one though—where
Kels can talk to Nash as if nothing has changed, where Nash
confides in Kels—the IRL awkwardness is worth it to risk not
losing this.

Enough about that. Are things going
okay at the new school?
4:42 PM

i'm trying to make friends, i swear, mom!
4:43 PM

That's not what I meant.
4:43 PM

. . . ok that's kind of what I meant.
4:43 PM

is there even a point? It's senior year. i'm at yet ANOTHER new school. maybe it's better to save the whole IRL friends thing until college
4:45 PM

That sounds lonely.
4:46 PM

who needs real people when i have the internet?
4:47 PM

You mean when you have me ☺
4:45 PM

"What is all of this—?"

My eyes snap up from my phone, meeting Gramps's voice, and wow, his pained expression wipes the Nash smile right off my face.

Okay, so I kind of made a mess . . . and am in the process of frosting two dozen cupcakes.

But Gramps is looking at me like—I don't even know. Like I've done something *wrong*.

I place my phone facedown on the table. "Peak stress baking?"

"Is this—it's all Miriam's stuff? How?"

His voice cracks when he says Grams's name and my eyes instantly start watering. The mixer, the bowls, the pans and spatulas—they were all Grams's. But she always let me use them, and all of it was just sitting in a box in the garage, clearly labeled KITCHEN STUFF.

"I just needed to bake, Gramps. I didn't think—"

"No, you *didn't* think."

I swallow my words. I don't know what to say next. Whatever I do say will be wrong.

"You can't just start taking things that aren't yours, Hal. You didn't even ask. You can't just bust in here like nothing has changed when *everything*—"

He pauses. Blinks once. Twice.

"Just clean it up, okay?"

He turns his back to me and walks upstairs without another word.

I lean forward and press my hands against the counter. All the emotion I've kept in since we got here bursts out now that Gramps looked at me like I'm the *worst* granddaughter in the world and just *left*. Tears stream down my face. I *am* the worst. The real reason it was all in the garage is so obvious now. Gramps literally stripped the house of everything Grams in a matter of months and I *hate* it.

My movements through the kitchen turn static. I'll work on the cover reveal another day. I frost the cupcakes standardly and put the ingredients away. I scrub the bowls until my fingers prune and there are no more signs of sugary batter or memories of Grams. Scrub until I can convince myself that it doesn't even look like I used them, not really, and I can forget the broken heart plastered on Gramps's face.

I can't.

I dry the bowls and pack everything back into KITCHEN STUFF. Tears dry on my cheeks as I lift the box and carry it into the garage, back to its spot on the shelf that I now realize is all Grams's stuff. Cupcakes gave me tunnel vision—because it only now hits me that everything that was Grams, everything that *is* Grams, has been reduced to boxes in a garage.

CLOTHES (1/4)

SHOES (1/2)

BOOKS (1/10)

PHOTOS

Someday, we'll all just be boxes in someone's garage.

The KITCHEN STUFF box nearly crashes to the floor, my hands shake so violently. I can't breathe, my chest is in knots, and I'm so hot and I'm gasping for air, gasping for anything to make this stop.

It doesn't stop.

I am going to die, I think.

I'll only be three, maybe four, boxes when I die, I think.

"Hal?"

In an instant, Ollie grabs my hand and pulls me away from the boxes, toward the steps of the garage.

"Breathe," he says.

I squeeze my eyes shut. Listen to Ollie.

Breathe.

Ollie holds my hand tightly and lets me breathe my way through this. And I do get through it. Slowly my muscles relax, my breath steadies, and I'm not going to die—at least not today.

The first time I had a panic attack, Ollie was nine. Our uncle had died suddenly—I didn't know him well, but the idea that he was just gone? The idea that someday *I'd* just be gone? It was too much. I cried so hard I couldn't speak, or breathe. I thought, *This is what dying is, isn't it? It's not being able to breathe*—which only exacerbated the situation.

Ollie found me on my bed, sobbing my brains out and hyperventilating. He didn't say anything. He just climbed into my bed and held my hand until it passed.

He's held my hand through every panic attack since.

The tightness in my chest eases and I let go of Ollie's hand. "Sorry," I say. "I thought I was—"

I don't finish my sentence because whatever I thought I was, I clearly wasn't.

"You good? Maybe you should talk to Gramps about—"

I shake my head. "Gramps hates me."

Ollie shrugs. "He's just triggered, you know? He'll get over it."

I cover my face with my hands. "I just wanted to bake. He just wants to forget her."

"Maybe he's not ready to remember yet. Maybe we're making it worse. I don't know. Dude can barely take care of *himself*—it's pretty brutal to watch."

I squeeze my eyes shut. "I'm sorry, Ol."

Ollie waves me off and nudges my shoulder. "Did you bake double dark chocolate?"

I open my eyes and nod.

"Excuse me while I go eat one. Or five."

He holds his hand out to me and pulls me up to standing. I swear, he's even taller than he was just a week ago. He says something that makes me laugh—I can't remember what though, because when we reenter the kitchen a second later, Gramps is there, eating a red velvet cupcake over the kitchen sink. Scout sits patiently at his feet, waiting for any possible crumbs to fall.

Seriously? Moments ago, Gramps's grief *crushed* me into a panic attack and now he's just—eating my cupcakes? He can't *see* Grams's baking equipment, but the cupcakes they produce are apparently fair game. I can't.

"What?" Gramps asks, voice flat. "You made my favorite."

At least that hasn't changed.

"I made them for Shabbat, Gramps," I say quietly.

"Oh." His eyebrows lift with surprise. "Well, I'll bring them, I guess."

I make a decision before I can unmake it.

"I'll bring them myself, I think."

I don't know Hebrew and I'll most definitely fumble through the service, but Gramps asked me to go—and now I'm sure he needs me more than I thought.

"Really?" Gramps is expressionless. "Why?"

"I want to," I say, and the funny thing is, I mean it.

We've only been in Middleton for a week—and we haven't seen Gramps outside the house, not once. If I can ignore the anxious thoughts that always accompany a new social situation, I can see Gramps interacting with the outside world—beyond this sad house. Maybe I'll catch a glimpse of who my Gramps used to be.

I need that.

"Me too," Ollie says, and I know he feels the same.

If cupcakes can't fix us, maybe Shabbat can.

September 6

5:05 PM

> i know it's late but you need to know i have no
> clue what to wear to shabbat services
> AND I BLAME YOU

Mom
Omg your first shabbat??

Dad

Ollie
Gramps gave me a kippah but it keeps
falling off

Mom
Bobby pins!!

> come into my room, I have some Ol

Dad
 ?

fine! gramps is fine! everything is fine!
except I HAVE NO CLOTHES FOR THIS

Mom
Your purple dress. The one with the flowy
sleeves? It's perfect! Wear that.

oh that's a good idea. thanks!!

Mom
Let us know how it goes!!

Dad

SIX

Temple Beth Shalom is happy. So much happier than I expected.

Every wooden pew is filled with life, with chanting and praying, and I don't know if I believe in God, but I do believe in *this*. In people. Together. I believe in the unity of voices and Hebrew, an ancient language I don't understand, but I swear tonight it makes perfect sense.

Because though Gramps is quiet beside me, he follows along in the prayer book with his index finger, silently mouthing every word. He may not be as loud and boisterous as some of the other members of the congregation, but he knows this service by heart and his shoulders relax with each new prayer. He flips to the next page before Rabbi Goldman announces the page number and utters *amen* after each recitation.

I spend half of the service watching Gramps love the service.

And another quarter of it trying to ignore Nash and Molly two rows in front of us.

Grams's necklace twirls between my fingers, calming me. A *hamsa* with *chai* engraved in the middle. *Chai* is Hebrew for life, and a *hamsa* is the shape of a hand. Usually, the evil eye sits in the middle of a *hamsa*, but I like Grams's version better. A hand protecting life. It's comforting, centering. Right now, it keeps my anxiety at bay.

After the sermon is completed and the final prayers are recited, everyone heads downstairs for the *oneg*. Gramps says the *oneg* is kind of like the after-party. There's challah and pastries and wine and socializing.

I'd really love to skip the socializing part. Ollie and I don't know how to socialize here, how we're supposed to *be* here. Ollie downs the grape juice before the prayer and Gramps gives him major side-eye.

"I know nothing," Ollie whispers.

"Clearly," I whisper back.

In all fairness, neither do I. I tug at the hem of my purple dress, wondering why Mom suggested I wear something so short. Okay, it's not *short*. It falls just above my kneecaps—but everyone else is in longer skirts. My knees feel so exposed. I completed the look with matching lavender lipstick that I am now itching once again to wipe away.

I didn't know. Why didn't Gramps tell me? I have no frame of reference for this kind of thing. Mom's limited cooking skills feature an exclusively Jewish menu: kugel, cholent, brisket, and lots of challah. We have a plug-in menorah that travels around the country with us. Dad makes us watch the old *Ten Commandments* film on the first night of Passover. And growing up, Ollie and I had two special days off per year for holidays we didn't really celebrate. But while Mom practiced her religion through food and traditions, and Dad in movies and menorahs, we never celebrated the rites.

I've never been in a Conservative synagogue before now.

Once the food prayers are over—there really is a prayer for *everything* here—Gramps introduces us to some of his friends. We shake hands and smile at a string of names we'll never remember. This at least we are good at after years with film crews.

Ollie and I sit with Gramps at one of the many eight-person tables scattered throughout the space. I spot Nash and Molly across the room, sitting at a table with their own cups of grape juice and slices of challah, laughing, so at ease with each other.

My fingers twitch for my phone, for the hundreds of messages that have most likely accumulated in my group chat with Amy, Elle, and Samira. Our chats are always most active once the weekend begins because school is now, in fact, a thing.

Molly makes eye contact with me and smiles. I look away, embarrassed she caught me watching them. When I glance back in the general direction of their table, Nash is gone and Molly is in motion, walking toward Ollie and me.

"Halle!" Molly leans in for a hug like we've known each other forever, not just a week. I'm still sitting. Should I stand? I can't decide, so I wrap one arm awkwardly around her, turning it into a weird sort of half hug. "We've been waiting for you to come over and say hi!"

I step out of the awkward hug and blink. Molly and Nash were so deep in their conversation, there didn't seem to be a moment to interrupt. Also—I don't believe Molly. There's no way they were thinking of me before I awkwardly made eye contact.

"Hi, Molly," Gramps says, fondness in his voice.

"Hey, Professor Levitt," Molly says. For a second, I expect Molly to hug *Gramps*—but she just smiles at him. "How are you?"

Gramps nods. "I'm glad you've met Halle."

"Oh yeah! We have a lot of classes together. Didn't she tell you?"

I did not. In all fairness, though, it's not like Gramps asked.

"I'm Ollie," Ollie says with a small wave, pulling focus.

Once again, Ollie is my hero.

"Hey! Nice to finally meet. You have classes with Talia Davidson, right?"

Davidson. Sawyer's sister?

Ollie nods. "We're the only sophomores in pre-calc."

Molly sits in the empty seat next to me. "Right! Mr. Benson is tough, but he grades on a curve. I still have my notes, if you need them."

Ollie looks surprised. "That'd be great."

"Of course!"

Gramps coughs. "You kids good here? Don't want the boys to feel like I'm ditching them for a cooler crowd."

By *the boys*, Gramps means a group of men seventy and over, all in patterned button-down shirts, *kippahs* on top of their gray and/or bald heads, who seem to be saving a space for him in their circle. It's kind of adorable and exactly why I'm glad I came tonight.

"We're good," Molly answers for us.

Gramps excuses himself and Molly turns her attention back to me, tucking a flyaway curl behind her ear. "It's so cool you're here. I mean, I assumed you were Jewish because your grandpa is, like, in the brotherhood. But also, you can't *assume* anything, right?"

I nod. "Right."

"You should definitely join USY. I'm on the executive board of the local chapter. We're doing a beach cleanup in two weeks with a few other Jewish communities across the state—you should totally come!"

Ollie and I look at each other. What's USY? Other Jewish communities? We've never had *a* Jewish community.

It's always just been another thing that has sort of isolated me. In Charlotte, I was the only Jewish kid in my entire class. The only one whose mom and dad forced us to skip school on the high holidays. But here, school is closed for Rosh Hashanah and Yom Kippur. I didn't even know some schools did that, that some areas are overwhelmingly Jewish and actually care about their Jewish population.

"Maybe," I say, ripping my challah into smaller pieces.

"Awesome," Molly says, like *maybe* means *yes*. "I'm trying to get my sister Sarah to come home for it. She's a sophomore at Boston University. It's right before the high holidays, so I figured she'd be coming home anyways. But she doesn't want to celebrate them this year. It's honestly *bizarre*."

Molly takes a sip of grape juice.

"You have an older sister?" I ask.

Molly swallows. "Two. But Rebecca is doing her PhD at Oxford, so, like, *that's* obviously not happening. It'll be the first high holidays without my sisters."

"It's our first away from our parents," I say. "If that makes you feel better."

Molly smiles at me and tips her cup so it clinks mine. "Solidarity."

I smile back. I like Molly. It's easy being around someone who does all the talking.

"Hey." Nash is suddenly standing above us with a plate of cupcakes. *My* cupcakes. "I come with cupcakes. Which is pretty nice of me, considering I was totally abandoned."

The calm I felt moments ago, clinking cups with Molly? It's gone.

Molly rolls her eyes at the word *abandoned* and pats the empty seat next to her for Nash to sit.

Is it time to leave yet?

"We were just talking about USY," Molly says. "Isn't it so cool that Halle and Ollie are practicing too?"

Ollie shrugs. "Oh. We're not. Practicing, I mean."

"You're here," Molly says, confused.

"For the first time," I clarify.

"Sorry." Molly places her empty cup on the table. "I guess I did assume, after all."

"We've moved a lot," Ollie says. "Our parents raised us with, like, the culture. But there wasn't really time to do the synagogue part."

I kick Ollie's foot under the table because what if the phrase *moved a lot* triggers a light bulb in Nash's brain and everything is ruined.

He just flashes me a *what the hell?* look.

"Did you like it?" Molly asks, not noticing our exchange.

"Yeah," I say. "I really did."

"It's boring," Ollie confesses.

"It gets better once you learn the prayers," Nash says. "I get it, though. My mom raised us—*me*—very Jewish. But when I'm with my Korean relatives, I'm so lost."

"But *will* I learn the prayers?" Ollie says. "I didn't even know how to hold the book—the *siddur*—before tonight."

Nash nods. "You will. Give it a few Fridays."

"Also! Still going to plug USY. There are a lot of Reform and secular Jewish kids involved," Molly says. "I can text you more info."

She recites her number to me and I plug the digits into my phone. She doesn't pull hers out, so I'm guessing Molly keeps Shabbat—which means no phones after sundown on the Sabbath. Nash pulls out his phone and . . . does not ask for my number. Thank God. I mean, Nash and Kels only communicate via DMs and G-Chat. So Nash *could* have my cell number, theoretically. If I wanted him to. Which I don't.

Once I've saved the number, Molly excuses herself for the bathroom. Ollie gets up to grab more challah, ignoring the look I'm shooting him to keep him in his seat.

It's just Nash and me. Pretty much a nightmare scenario.

"Molly's the community outreach chair. She can be kind of intense about it, but it's okay to say no to the USY stuff. I do it all the time."

"She thinks I know what USY is," I say. "I have *no* clue."

Nash raises his eyebrows. "United Synagogue Youth. It's just a youth group for Jewish teens, basically—"

"Yeah, I got that part, obviously. I just didn't know what the acronym stood for."

Nash blinks, clearly taken aback by my abruptness. Ugh. Nash is talking to me, unprompted, when I've very actively been *not talking to him* all week. I don't want to encourage it—but I don't have to be full-on *rude* either. Not here. Not on Shabbat. It's the first time we've talked, just the two of us, since the first day of school.

"Thanks," I say.

I can reset Operation Avoidance on Monday.

"You could've just asked Molly," he says.

"And cut her off in the middle of her spiel? It seemed easier to nod," I say.

Nash laughs. "Mood."

I laugh too, and for the smallest moment, it feels like we're behind our screens. Nash says *mood* all the time. But we're not behind screens—we're here. Together. IRL. And Nash just *laughed* at something I, Halle, said.

I thought I liked making him lol. But *this*? His laugh is so much more than lol. The way his eyes crinkle in the corners and he covers his mouth with his hand if he's laughing too hard. His one dimple.

This is a million times better. And that's definitely going to be a problem.

Nash peels off the liner of his double dark chocolate cupcake—*my* cupcake—and I wait for his reaction, my stomach in knots. I don't know if I want him to like it or not. It feels like a neon sign over my head. Ollie returns to the table just in time to witness the bizarre reality that is Nash eating one my cupcakes.

"Oh my God, *this is so good*," he says, his mouth still full of cupcake.

I exhale because I am not a hack—my cupcakes *are* good. Online, no one gets to taste them.

Molly returns to the table with a red velvet of her own. "Are we talking about the cupcakes? We totally are, right? My God, who made these?"

Ollie is always the first to brag, so I nudge his toe gently before he can, reminding him of our secret—*my* secret. Instead of the confession, we both shrug and affirm the amazingness.

The four of us talk and laugh and drink an entire bottle of grape juice. Temple Beth Shalom is a happy place and I feel okay, safe, which is weird because I'm only Halle tonight, a complete stranger to Nash. Okay, maybe a familiar acquaintance at this point.

At the end of the night, Molly offers another hug, but this one comes with an invitation.

"You should come bowling with us tomorrow!" Molly says.

If I say statements as questions, Molly does the opposite. She makes statements out of things that should be questions.

"It's a Saturday night tradition," she continues.

"Mostly because it's when Molly is free again." Nash teases.

"Hashtag Conservadox Problems."

"You should come," Nash says, smiling.

His invitation is so *earnest*—and it's exactly why I can't. I have to say no. Tonight was a one-off—spending just five minutes alone with him is already messing with my head. I can't get too close.

"Rain check?" I ask. "We kind of already have dinner plans with Gramps tomorrow."

Ollie's eyebrows scream, *No, we don't!*

My pinched lips scream, *Shut up, Ollie!*

"Oh! Fair enough. Next week, then," Molly says. "Shabbat Shalom! See you Monday!"

"Night," Nash says, following her out. I can't read the expression on his face.

My Kels heart wants me to change my mind.

My Halle head says avoid that boy like the plague.

Nash is Kels's, not mine, and it needs to stay that way.

September 21

Elle Carter
. . . have y'all seen this?
7:35 PM

LINK: ALANNA LAFOREST CRITICIZES
REVIEWERS WHO CALL FIREFLIES AND YOU
PERFECT FOR TEENS AHEAD OF WINTER
FILM RELEASE

"While FIREFLIES AND YOU centers on
the teen experience, I don't think it's fair to
assume I wrote this book for teenagers. I want
my work to resonate with everyone, whether
they're 13 or 93."
7:38 PM

HOLY SHIT, KELS. ONE TRUE PASTRY IS
MENTIONED
7:40 PM

. . . excuse me WHAT
7:42 PM

Elle Carter

"That's quite a statement for LaForest to make, especially when you consider teen fandom launched FIREFLIES AND YOU out from obscurity—starting with the account One True Pastry, when Kels Roth, a viral teen influencer in the YA community, posted a rave review."
7:45 PM

i . . . need to lie down.
7:46 PM

Elle Carter

"When this is mentioned to LaForest, she said, 'And I appreciate my teen following, I truly do. I just don't think they're my only audience, and I don't understand why we put books in a box.'"
7:48 PM

Amy Chen

IT'S CALLED POSITIONING YOUR BOOK IN THE MARKETPLACE
7:49 PM

Wow I am so mad!! This is such a bad take.
Because writing for teens is somehow LESS
THAN.
7:50 PM

Samira Lee
Okay, let's all agree that this is a trash take
but also KELS YOU WERE CITED IN AN EW
REPORT. Holy crap!!!
7:52 PM

Amy Chen
How does FAME feel?
7:53 PM

. . . kind of nauseating, not going to lie.
7:54 PM

SEVEN

Sawyer is behind the counter at Maple Street Sweets, and I instantly second-guess what I am about to do. I watch him through the window, packing orders and chatting with customers, a pastel-blue apron tied around his waist.

I chew on my lower lip, wiping sweaty palms against my jeans. Maple Street Sweets was supposed to be a solution, not a problem. A place where I can *bake*, since Gramps's kitchen is off-limits.

But clearly, I need a Plan B. Maple Street Sweets isn't safe if Sawyer works here.

"Seriously, Hal?" Ollie says, exasperated.

"I'm good. Just give me a sec," I say.

I don't know why I didn't connect Maple Street Sweets to Sawyer. I know that Sawyer's parents own the best bakery in Middleton. I know that Maple Street Sweets is, without a doubt, the best bakery in Middleton.

The first time Grams and I stumbled into this bakery was the summer after I turned twelve, in need of an immediate sugar fix. It was brand-new then. It's part of the Main Street Shoppes—"a giant tourist trap" according to Gramps, who hates the spike in population during the summer months. Middleton is close to the beach without being a beach, making it the perfect affordable alternative for a family vacation, but Maple Street Sweets is a year-round draw.

It's quiet in the bakery for a Sunday morning—typically, a line wraps around the L-shaped counter and ends out the front door. The first time I visited the bakery, I fell in love with the three pink walls, the cake-patterned wallpaper on the fourth, and the way the white countertops gleamed in contrast with the dark wood of the tables and chairs. But mostly, I fell in love with the rainbow of cupcakes behind the cases and the cinnamon-sugar scent that refuses to fade.

Last week, after the Cupcake Incident, I noticed there was a HELP WANTED sign plastered on the front door, so I picked up an application and decided this job, this place where I can bake freely without breaking Gramps's heart, is *mine*.

But Sawyer's presence is a sign that screams *no*. He's Nash's friend. I should not be getting any closer to the people in Nash's life and creating more opportunities for slipups. Also, working in a bakery is too on-brand for Kels. Totally suspicious.

Still—maybe the rewards outweigh the risk. I can bake in a *real professional kitchen*. And I'll have money that's *mine*. I have a savings account, filled with money from birthdays and holidays, but I've never had a job, apart from helping out on Mom and Dad's sets.

It'll round out my NYU application. Colleges *love* teens with a good work ethic who seem to balance it all.

The scale in my mind tips and my decision is made.

"Okay, let's do this."

I pull down the hem of my T-shirt and smooth down my hair. Fix Grams's necklace so it's not sitting on the clasp. Before I change my mind, I reach for the door, ready to swing it open and march inside.

"Wait," Ollie says.

"What?"

He drums his fingers against his thigh.

"Sawyer *does* have an effect on people."

Ollie blushes. "Shut up. He's captain of the baseball team."

"Is he?"

"Do you live under a rock?"

"It's not baseball season!"

"I just need to get on his radar, you know? Please don't embarrass me," Ollie says.

I roll my eyes, but brother-sister banter centers me. When we approach Sawyer, the nervous butterflies are gone, and I just want to get this whole interaction over with.

"Oh hey, Hal-lee, how can I help you?"

Ollie interjects. "Hi. I'm Ollie. Halle's brother. Yeah. Um."

He holds out his hand to shake and Sawyer takes it and oh my God where is my brother? Swear to God, Ollie's ears are bright pink and I am loving every moment of this. He'll snap into character, I'm sure, but his fumbling shows that he *does* have the awkward Levitt genes inside him, deep down.

"I'm just dropping off an application," I say.

"Sweet! I can take it from you, no problem."

I hand him the papers. Instead of doing whatever it is you're supposed to do with new applications, Sawyer starts reading through mine. Right in front of me. Which I'm pretty sure is a violation of something. I think. Yeah.

"Availability looks good—is there any time that will change? Any sports? Theater?" Sawyer asks. "It's cool if there is. My parents just prefer a heads-up on any seasonal extracurriculars."

"Um," I say. "Nope, no sports. Or theater." Group activities give me hives.

"I play baseball," Ollie says, even though nobody asked.

"Dude, yes!" Sawyer moves in for a fist bump and Ollie relaxes. "We need some fresh blood on the team. What position?"

"Center field."

"Are you free this afternoon?" Sawyer asks. "I'm out at one— let's hit the batting cages."

"Sure." Ollie my brother is back. Cool. Calm. Casual. As if this moment isn't everything his little baseball heart had hoped for and more.

He's totally, without a doubt, dying inside.

They exchange cell phone numbers and coordinate plans and, wow, Ollie is good. I don't even have Sawyer's number yet, and I've sat with him at lunch every day. At school, he's *Molly and Sawyer*, so to be honest, having Molly's number in my phone is like having Sawyer's, too. But still.

"So when can you start?" Sawyer asks me.

"Whenever."

"You're hired."

I laugh, because that's so not how this works. Sawyer cannot just hire me; I need to botch an interview first, at the very least.

"Yeah, okay," I say, skeptical.

He makes a face at me, like I've wounded his ego or something. "I mean it. It's my parents' bakery, you know? So if you want the job, it's yours."

"You can do that?" I ask.

"Technically, no. Practically, yeah. Be right back."

Sawyer folds my application in half and disappears into the kitchen. I don't even have time to process what is happening before he returns with a stapled packet in his hand.

"Start the paperwork," he says. "At school tomorrow, get a work permit from the office. It needs to be signed by a parent or guardian. Fill everything out, and boom. You are employed."

"Okay," I say. "Thanks."

"Cool. I'll have Dad, *ahem*, Mr. Davidson, give the final okay when he comes in later today. Let me . . ." His voice trails off and his attention shifts to another sheet of paper. "Can you start Wednesday?"

That seems so fast and I am not prepared for any of this. But I have a ton of reviews to bake for and this is my only shot, so I swallow that answer and say, "Sounds good."

"Cool," Sawyer says again. "Welcome aboard!"

"Thank you," I say. "Seriously."

"Of course!" He looks at Ollie. "See you later?"

"Yup." Ollie's pupils practically have heart-eye emojis in them.

"I'll see you around," I say, trying to be casual.

Sawyer nods. "See ya, Hal-lee."

I exit Maple Street Sweets high on cinnamon sugar and *having a job*. So on the car ride back to Gramps's, Ollie and I blast music and freak out.

"I have a job!" I say.

Ollie pumps his fist in the air. "I'm going to make varsity!"

Then his face falls. "Wait. Why did you let me agree to go hit with him?"

I turn down the music. "What?"

"He's so cool *and* he's captain," Ollie says. "What if I botch this? I'm out of practice."

"He has a girlfriend, you know," I say.

He flips me off. "That's not what I'm worried about."

"Ol, you got this. I promise. Baseball is like breathing for you. And as for the social part, he's nice. You're nice. He's funny. You're funny. If there are any awkward moments, well, just start speaking baseball. But it won't even get awkward. Because you've got this."

Ollie breathes. I crank the music again.

"It's just baseball," Ollie shouts over the music, which confirms it is *so* not just baseball.

"Keep telling yourself that," I say. "Admit it. You have a crush on Sawyer."

"*Crush* is a strong word."

"Lust?"

We burst out laughing because it's true and because Ollie will never admit it, especially since I've referred to Sawyer as *cute* once or twice. We can't have the same taste in anything, let alone guys. He didn't talk to me for a week after I discovered he followed my *Les Misérables* Spotify playlist.

Ollie turns the music back down. "Gramps doesn't need to know," he says. "Most days, *I* don't even know, and he'll want to label it and I'm not ready for that."

"Okay," I say.

"I mean—I want to figure it out before I tell him. If I do."

I nod. "Totally."

"And, Hal? Thank you for saving my ass back there. I don't know what happened."

"I do," I say, wiggling my eyebrows.

Ollie rolls his eyes but cannot for the life of him wipe the stupid smile off his face.

Neither can I, honestly. I am giddy the entire drive home because I have a job I can be excited about.

A job where I can almost be Kels, for real.

If I could work at Maple Street Sweets every day, I think I would.

Okay, so it's only been a week, but I'm *so* in love.

It's Saturday afternoon and I'm behind the counter, taking orders and making recommendations along with Sawyer. Our cupcake of the day—vanilla bean with rosemary lilac frosting—sells out by noon. It is a line-out-the-door kind of day and at this rate it'll be six p.m. before I blink.

Diana Davidson is behind the register and Max, her husband, is in the kitchen checking inventory.

Sawyer's parents are the coolest. On what I thought would be my first day, I actually just met with Diana for an informal interview over coffee and cupcakes. I started to freak out, but it didn't take long for my stomach to untangle and my hands to uncurl from fists because Diana gets it—gets *me*. With the help of the magical red velvet cupcake I consumed, I breezed through our chat. I showed her a few images of my One True Pastry cupcakes—shots that were never posted, of course—and that sealed the deal.

I am guaranteed at least twelve hours a week, I get a key to the shop so I can open on weekends, and best of all, I'm allowed to use the kitchen after hours, so long as it looks *pristine* when I leave.

The first time I saw the kitchen, I almost passed out it's so beautiful. All the equipment is state of the art with its convection oven and cooling racks and *multiple* industrial cake mixers. Seriously, it's next level.

There's thankfully not much time for chatting with Sawyer during rush hour, so we spend most of the afternoon on autopilot. There are a lot of people in the small space, but in moments when I start to feel overwhelmed, I inhale the scent of fresh-baked cupcakes and pretend I'm in the kitchen, and everything is okay.

At last, it slows down around five p.m.

"Kitchen duty," Diana calls and Sawyer groans.

Diana's Mom Smirk is on fire today. "Halle can help too, after her break. Show her how we clean the mixers."

"Fine," Sawyer says, pushing the EMPLOYEES ONLY door to the kitchen open.

I head to the back room for my fifteen and the chance to finally check my phone.

The break room is super basic, with a row of lockers for employees and two circular tables with four plastic pink chairs at each. I spin my combination lock, swing the door open, and reach into my GO AWAY I'M READING tote bag for my phone.

There are *so* many notifications. It's mostly everyone still fuming about the revelation that Alanna LaForest, author of the book of my heart . . . hates teenagers. It's horrifying. If Grams were here, she'd be in total damage control mode. Grams was always a staunch believer in publishing books that speak to teenagers, in finding authors who did that better than anyone. It feels almost like an attack against her just as much as us teens.

I don't know how to *process* this information. So I leave the group chat messages unread and reply to Nash's instead, time-stamped an hour ago.

Nash Stevens
Question.
4:01 PM

I only have fifteen—well, twelve—minutes until kitchen duty, but I'm too curious to not immediately respond.

answer
5:04 PM

**When do you throw in the towel? Re: like,
trying to be friends with someone.**
5:04 PM

My face gets hot reading Nash's words. He means *me*, Halle. I know he does. This keeps happening. Every time we text lately, she—*I*—somehow comes up. It's weird. I don't know how to answer his question honestly, so I revert to Kels's defense mechanism. Snark.

when you start speaking in clichés
5:06 PM

. . . Wow. I'm being serious right now.
5:06 PM

by someone you mean halle?
5:07 PM

Talking about myself with Nash? It's the worst part of this whole situation.

Yeah.
5:07 PM

you don't have to be friends with everyone
5:08 PM

You don't get it. I've never been iced like
this before. But then I'll make a stupid joke
at lunch and she'll laugh. I don't understand
anything.
5:10 PM

I *do* laugh at his stupid jokes.

pity laughs, prob.
5:10 PM

. . . Can you at least TRY to be serious?
5:11 PM

OK FINE
5:11 PM

maybe you're coming on too strong?
5:12 PM

He's not.

She got a job at Sawyer's bakery. Sawyer
says she's cool at work. But when I try to talk
Shakespeare with her in AP lit, she's total ice.
And she's supposed to like books! But she's
clearly able to talk to my friends. Why not me?
5:13 PM

Because if we become friends, Nash, I'll have to tell you the truth. Everything will change, and I'm still too attached to this version of us.

. . . i can't answer that
5:14 PM

question
5:14 PM

Answer.
5:14 PM

why do you care so much?
5:15 PM

The typing text bubble appears, and I can see Nash on the other side of the screen, typing and deleting and typing and deleting. The bubbles disappear and I'm *dying* to know what Nash is trying to say—but before he can send anything my fifteen is up and kitchen duty awaits me.

I toss my phone back into my tote and make my way toward

the kitchen, toward the cupcakes, but my head is still with the three bubbles, locked up tight.

The worst part about baking cupcakes is without a doubt cleaning up the mess.

Sawyer fiddles with the hot and cold handles on the faucet until he achieves the perfect dish-washing temperature. The sink is large enough that we can work together to finish ASAP.

"So how was your first Saturday rush?" Sawyer asks.

"Pretty good," I say.

"You're like a different person here," he says. "It's cool."

I almost ask what he means by that, but I don't need to. At Maple Street Sweets, I'm not worried about giving myself away. I'm comfortable around cupcakes. Also, it's just easier for me to talk to the members of Le Crew one at a time. In groups, my brain goes into overdrive and it feels like I never know how to naturally contribute to a conversation. One-on-one is better. My anxious brain shuts off and I can even joke around. It's new. Almost like I'm writing a killer line for OTP. My words flow instead of sputter.

I make a face, then deflect. "Must be the sugar. You love cup-cakes too."

"I do," he says. "I'd be here more, if I could."

"You can't?"

"Baseball," Sawyer says.

"Right," I say.

"It's my ticket out of Middleton," Sawyer says. "My parents

are so serious about *my future*, you know? I tell them I'd be happy to stay, to someday take over the bakery. I don't know what I want to study, I don't even know if I *want* to go to college. I do know I want to keep the bakery in the family. They won't hear it, though."

I nod. Conversations with Sawyer don't usually get this *real*, and for the first time all shift, I'm not sure what the right thing is to say.

A moment later, the kitchen door swings open.

"Oh. Hey, Upstate," Nash says, plucking an unfrosted vanilla cupcake off the cooling rack and jumping up to sit on one of the countertops.

My heart twists in my chest every time he calls me by my lie.

"Hi," I say, wondering what gives Nash the privilege to sit on the countertops we just wiped down.

"Employees only, dude," Sawyer fake deadpans.

"Diana said you were wrapping up," Nash says, undeterred.

Sawyer grins and grabs a rag and a bottle of disinfectant spray from the cabinet. "We are. If you can finish up in here, Hal-lee, I'll take care of the tables."

I nod. "Got it."

I reach for a clean dishrag and continue doing the dishes, hoping Nash will follow Sawyer from the kitchen to the seats out front. Nope. He hasn't moved from the countertop, where fresh crumbs are accumulating. I try not to look at them. Or Nash. How is he always just *there*, wherever I am?

"What's up?" I ask.

"Bored," Nash says, his mouth full of cupcake. He swallows and looks at me. "Like the job? The Davidsons treating you okay?"

"It's good," I say, drying cupcake plates.

The stack of dirty plates is almost as endless as the silence that follows, so I reach for another rag and toss it to Nash.

I wish I could screenshot the look on his face right now. He raises his eyebrows, like, *seriously*? I step to my left to make room for both of us at the sink. If Nash Kim has the audacity to come into my nearly perfect kitchen and crumb it all up—he can at least make himself useful. If his idea of a fun Saturday afternoon is loitering in a bakery kitchen and stealing cupcakes and stressing me out, he's going to help me finish early.

He takes the spot by my side at the sink.

"I'll wash. You can dry," I say. "You do know how to dry a plate, yeah?"

Kels's snark comes out of Halle's mouth so effortlessly it's shocking—and that's when I *know* he's already messing with my head. Nash just rolls his eyes. "Of course."

In between passing plates and humming along to the Ed Sheeran song on the radio, I learn that Nash has a scar on his right palm. It begins at the midpoint between his thumb and pointer finger and runs down the center of the palm, following the curve of the lifeline crease. Every time I pass a plate to him, I steal a glimpse of that scar, fixated on a flaw I never knew, and never *could've* known, as Kels.

"What happened?" I ask.

Nash's eyebrows scrunch together. "Huh?"

My eyes point to the scar. "Your hand."

"Oh." Nash coughs. "Bike fail when I was seven. I hit a rock and flew right over the handlebars. Thought I was ready for the training-wheels-free life. Clearly, I was not. Stitches in the palm suck, by the way. Do not recommend."

I pass another plate to Nash. "That is tragically generic."

Nash laughs. "Oh, for sure. But it was still traumatizing! For my mom, at least. I don't remember much of it." He holds out his palm so I can see the full extent of the damage. "I don't remember my hand ever *not* looking like this."

If I were Kels, I'd trace his scar with my thumb.

But if I were Kels, I'd never know there's a scar to trace.

What else don't I know about Nash?

It's just a scar, I remind myself. *Anyone can fall off their bike. You* know *Nash.*

He curls his fingers into a fist and returns to drying dishes and we revert to a more comfortable quiet.

"Do you bake?" he asks.

I blink and my heart skips a beat. "What?"

Nash stacks the dry plates. "I am clearly the master of segues."

"And bicycles."

He clutches his hand to his heart. "Ouch. Too soon, Upstate."

I ignore his theatrics. "Sometimes," I say. "But I like eating cupcakes more than baking them, I think."

Nash nods. "Dude, same! My friend and I argue about this, like, *all* the time. She bakes cupcakes that are *art*, cupcakes that could win

Food Network competitions. I know it's her brand, but sometimes I wonder why she—why *people*—put so much effort into a product that is temporary, you know? At the end of the day, cupcakes are meant to be eaten. But if you love them, you have to see these."

His phone displays One True Pastry's Instagram page and I am dead.

Nash scrolls through my most recent #CupcakeCoverReveals and shows me his favorites—zooming in to point out the details of my artwork. I chew on the inside of my cheek because Nash is so proud of One True Pastry, so proud of Kels.

I've never heard anyone I'm not related to speak out loud about the work I do.

Nash doesn't just speak, he *brags*. Like, *This girl is my friend, how lucky am I?* Just like how Molly and Autumn talk about REX. It's surreal but also wonderful. It makes everything about our online friendship feel valid.

It also makes me feel like the biggest liar.

"They're okay," I say, focusing on scouring one of the mixing bowls.

Nash talking to Kels about Halle is one thing. I *can't* listen to Nash talk about Kels. It's too much.

"I was just trying to—"

I cut him off. "Nash. Stop. I have work to do, okay?"

This mixing bowl is going to *sparkle* by the time I'm done with it.

"You're right."

"You don't," I say. "I mean, it's not like you're getting paid to be here. I can finish up."

I expect him to leave. Anyone else would. Not Nash. "We're almost done. May as well finish what I started." He tucks his phone in his back pocket and returns to his dish-drying duties.

We finish in a silence that is as far away from comfortable as you can get.

September 28

Kels @OneTruePastry 2hr
NEWS! I am so excited to announced that One True Pastry will be hosting the EXCLUSIVE cover reveal for READ BETWEEN THE LIES by @ArielGoldberg! Tuesday 10/1 @ 2 PM EST. Watch this space—I'm almost positive I outdid myself with this one 🤲
[45 comments] [104 ↻] [552 ♥]

Ariel Goldberg @ArielGoldberg 55min
AHH I'm so excited that @OneTruePastry is hosting the cover reveal for READ BETWEEN THE LIES. I'm so obsessed with this cover & her cupcakes. I can't wait to see what Kels comes up with!
[245 comments] [557 ↻] [2.2K ♥]

Nash Stevens @NashStevens_27 52min
@ArielGoldberg it's going to be EPIC @OneTruePastry is killing it

EIGHT

On the last Saturday of September, I am neglecting homework for *Read Between the Lies*.

Ollie and I filmed the cover reveal on Thursday night at Maple Street Sweets, after hours. Since Gramps's house is a no-cupcake zone, the process of baking and executing a cinematic cupcake cover was complicated. We draped a white tablecloth over one of the tables. Ollie stood on a chair and pointed the camera down, careful to make sure the table was the entire shot.

I wore a long-sleeve black shirt and swapped my chipped blue nail polish for black. It took a few takes to get the lighting and cupcake placement right. Once we did, we got a few extra takes for good measure.

Now I'm editing the footage in Premiere and it feels so right, so natural, after spending so much time with my parents in post, that I can't believe I never thought to do this before.

It looks exactly how I pictured it in my head and I can't stop smiling. I baked chocolate cupcakes, since most of the cupcakes are black frosted to mimic the redacted lines on the cover. The splatters of red blood pop. The timing between placing the next cupcake is even, allowing me to manipulate the footage to make it as fast or slow as I want.

It's too perfect.

My followers are going to freak out.

While the final cut renders, I continue reading my very own, very *not* edible version of *Read Between the Lies.* I may or may not have screamed when I opened the mailbox and the ARC was waiting for me inside. It's a book worth dropping everything for—which is exactly what I plan to do, once the video is all set. I'm already one hundred pages in and completely enthralled. I'm *so* picky when it comes to thrillers, mostly because I have a weird sixth sense and can *always* predict who the killer is fifty pages in. But with Ariel Goldberg, I'm still guessing.

It's such a nice break from the Alanna LaForest Twitter drama. Since the EW article, my Twitter following has grown exponentially, which is awesome timing with the cover reveal coming. But also not, as the level of trolling has increased along with it.

Elsie Porter @ElsiesShelf 2hr
How can @OneTruePastry straight up disappear at a time like this? Alanna NEEDS our support! Like, literally she just said she wants her book to be read by a wide audience? And now she's being boycotted? Pile-on culture is TOXIC.

Jamie K. @jamiereadsya 2hr

lololol that's a real interesting interpretation. alanna's statement implies that it's not enough for her book to be read and loved by teens??? which is pretty hurtful?? as a teen?

Abby In Wonderland @abbyinwonderland 2hr

So much for seeing FIREFLIES & YOU. Also . . . so much for @OneTruePastry being a teen advocate?!

For the first time in the history of One True Pastry, I don't know what to say.

I don't want to isolate my followers who are hurt by Alanna's words.

But every time I think about signing a *Fireflies and You* film boycott, I think of Grams.

I know Alanna wrote it, but it's Grams's too. She was *so* excited for the movie. Even when her health was deteriorating and she was hospitalized more than she was home, she believed she'd be around long enough to attend the red carpet premiere. And—I *can't* boycott it. I just can't.

At this point, my big hope is that Alanna comes to her senses and apologizes and this whole thing blows over. At least the cover reveal video is dropping in a few weeks—which will, hopefully, be enough get the Alanna drama out of my mentions.

"Hal?"

I look up from the book as the door swings open and Gramps comes in, Ollie trailing behind. He pulls out Aunt Liz's desk chair and takes a seat. Ollie sits at the end of the bed and Scout jumps onto my lap. I don't know how or when Aunt Liz's room became the family meeting spot—sometime between the cupcake incident and Gramps and me being on speaking terms again—but at least I don't have to move.

"The Jacobsons invited us over for dinner tonight," Gramps says.

I put *Read Between the Lies* facedown on the bed so I don't lose my page. *Okay, Gramps. You have my attention.*

"Why?" I ask.

"It's Rosh." Ollie says this like *duh*, even though he knows as well as I do that we've never celebrated *Rosh*, at least in the proper way—never mind called it that.

"Well, almost," Gramps says. "It technically starts tomorrow night. But every year, the Jacobsons host a big dinner party the night before. A New Year's Eve *Eve* party, I suppose, for everyone to celebrate, together."

"Why the day before?" Ollie asks, his nose wrinkled in confusion.

"Because," Gramps explains, "tomorrow night, the Jacobsons will be at services. They keep the high holy days like Shabbat—no electricity, no technology."

Ollie and I nod, sort of understanding. Wow, we have so much to learn. Then I swallow because it's Molly's party, which means Nash is going to be there.

"I have homework," I say.

He eyes my blood-spattered book. "Clearly, nothing urgent."

"We're on vacation, basically," Ollie says.

He's right. Rosh Hashanah is a two-day holiday and because of how it falls this year, we have Monday and Tuesday off.

"We're leaving at seven-fifteen. *L'shanah tovah.*"

Scout follows Gramps out the door. Ollie makes a face at me before he leaves too.

Goodbye relaxing evening reading *Read Between the Lies.*

It's not the dinner part I'm worried about, it's the party. Food. Talking. Ollie will ditch me for his friends. I'll be stuck attempting small talk with Le Crew but actually trying to find a place to disappear. Maybe I can hang by Gramps. Can that be an option? Yes.

Ollie will be social and I'll hang with the old people and everything will be fine.

Small group dynamics make me uncomfortable, but crowded spaces are my kryptonite.

Everything about hanging out in Molly's decked-out basement is too much, and I regret following Ollie down here instead of sticking to my original plan. There are too many voices, too many faces, too many bodies in one space. It's so hot in here I instantly regret wearing a long-sleeve blouse. The music is so loud, I can't think. Everything, everyone is staring at me. Except Nash. Nash is helping set up karaoke and it's so weird because the thing I want to do most right now is text him. And for a moment, I hate that I'm a secret. I want to yell at him, *Why can't you see that it's me and I need you?*

As expected, Ollie has ditched me for Sawyer's sister Talia, his friend Trevor, and normal social interaction. He's concentrating on an intense game of air hockey with Talia. A bunch of nameless faces surround my brother, rooting and cheering and clapping him on the back whenever he scores.

How does he *do* this?

I'm sitting at the bar with Sawyer, far enough away from the music that we can speak without screaming over each other. Sawyer is the easiest to talk to of everyone in Le Crew because we can go into cupcake mode. I pour myself a glass of water and fill a paper plate with veggies. Individually dip each stick into the ranch dressing because that takes time. One, two, three, celery sticks. Four, five, six, baby carrots.

"You know, we thought you wouldn't show," Sawyer says.

I swallow celery and my face starts to burn. "Oh. Sorry to disappoint."

He looks confused. "That's not what I meant."

"Hey, Halle." Autumn appears on my other side with a plate of apple wedges and honey. She's traded her black skinny jeans and graphic tee for a black and purple striped skater dress matched with bedazzled combat boots.

"Hi," I manage.

"Nice win, Sawyer," Autumn says, mid-chew. "Molly and Sawyer made a bet on whether or not you'd show."

"Seriously?" I ask.

"Yup," Sawyer says. "And I just won twenty bucks *and* a *Kung Fu Panda* marathon."

"Molly hates *Kung Fu Panda*," Autumn says.

"Oh," I say, because what do you say when every anxious

thought you've had around Le Crew is validated? Also, I have zero *Kung Fu Panda* opinions.

Across the room, Molly turns on the giant flat-screen TV. She's in a blue floral-print dress, her hair curled in soft waves and bangs swept to the side. She puts the controller down and smiles, waving over to Autumn and Sawyer.

"Hey, Halle!"

And me, I guess. I'm somehow included in the group Molly is waving to?

We move through the crowds, toward the actual *media* side of the media room. Molly uncoils microphones, while Sawyer plugs his phone into the speakers and queues up a playlist. Molly tosses a mic to Nash, who is now sitting at the end of the navy-blue sectional, feet up. I swallow. Every time I look at Nash, even for a second, it feels like too long, so I take a seat on the ottoman in front of the couch with my back to him. Great plan. Yes.

Until he taps my shoulder.

I twist slowly to face him. Music is blasting in my ears and it's loud, so loud. Nash leans forward in his seat so I can hear him, his forearms resting on his knees. He's so close and I'm grateful for the music because without it, Nash would hear my hammering heart. I'm sure of it.

"Hey," he says over the music. "I need food before the singing commences and all the good drinks are upstairs. Do you want anything?"

I consider saying *no thanks*, but a drink would be great and I'm afraid if I go upstairs, I'll never come back down.

"Ginger ale, please?" I ask.

Nash stands and his eyebrows raise, surprised. He smiles, almost to himself, as though this is *progress*. He'll definitely message Kels about this. "One ginger ale, coming right up."

Nash leaves and I move into his corner spot on the now-empty couch, claiming my space, and I can finally scroll through my phone in relative peace. There is even more Alanna LaForest drama in my Twitter feed and I've definitely missed something in the last half hour. I click one of the dozens of articles that have taken over my timeline.

Eva Louise @EvaReports 23min
FIREFLIES & YOU author @AlannaLaForest slams creative team behind the film adaption. Says it's "not just a teen movie." Full story here: https://bit.ly/2KZOzpw
[550 comments] [1.1k ⮁] [4k ♥]
|
Elle Carter @ellewriteswords 17min
but you'll profit off teens like @OneTruePastry's free labor lol ok @AlannaLaForest
[979 comments] [10k ⮁] [25k ♥]

I click the link and put my hand over my mouth to stifle the groan that escapes. Seriously, Alanna? You are *not* making this easy. There are too many messages in my group chat with my friends to scroll through, and if I start responding I won't be able to step away, so I'll catch up later. First the EW article, now this? Now you're going to target your own movie? Do I not have to sign a boycott, since she seems to be boycotting it herself? And would that now make it somehow okay to see the movie? I'm not sure.

All I know is my mentions are worse than ever.

Breathe.

"I didn't peg you as a *Fireflies and You* fan, Upstate."

I drop my phone facedown on my lap, flipping the switch from vibrate to silent. Nash hands me my ginger ale and laughs, taking a seat next to me. There isn't even a cushion of space between us.

I need to be way more careful with my phone in public. Thank God it was another EW article and not the OTP Twitter feed.

"*Fan* is a strong word right now," I say, taking a sip of my soda.

"I know," he says. "It's hard to admit fandom when the creator turns out to be trash. Miriam would be so pissed."

I blink. "You knew my grandmother?"

It's shocking, hearing her name come out of Nash's mouth so casually. Kels's Nash is—*was*—on a first-name basis with Grams? I swallow the lump in my throat and fight the pressure that builds behind my eyes. How is it possible that she never told me this? Did the last name throw her off too or did she know the whole time? I'll never get to ask her.

Nash nods. "Yeah. She saw me reading during an *oneg* one time. I think I was, like, nine. The next week, she gave me an advance copy of the sequel. It was the best day ever."

Grams knew Nash. "What book?" I ask.

"*Ridley Myers Had a Bad Day.*"

I nod. "Grams loved working on those. Good choice."

I'm so desperate to have a normal conversation about Grams, to *talk* about her, I ignore the fact that talking about books with Nash is not a good idea. Still, I'm grateful when we're cut off by Molly announcing that karaoke is finally set up. Le Crew surrounds us with plates of food and laughter and Autumn says *scooch* and plops down between Nash and me. I'm grateful there's a person separating us and the subject is changing, but then my phone lights up against my thigh.

Nash Stevens
Omg the Alanna drama? Shit is going DOWN.
8:17 PM

I peek out of the corner of my eye to confirm he's not paying attention before I answer.

yeah. it's SO bad
8:18 PM

i don't know what to do
8:18 PM

You don't have to do anything?
8:19 PM

everyone is waiting for me to say something. Like I'm just supposed to not love F&Y anymore. alanna is SO wrong and her takes are so bad that I want to stick up for my people, but i still think i want to see the movie. does that make me terrible?

8:20 PM

I don't think you owe anyone an explanation. Plus, the people who are making the movie probably aren't big fans of Alanna right now either. . . .

8:22 PM

It's not their fault or yours that she's isolating her audience in the name of some backwards idea of Literary Merit, or whatever.

8:23 PM

I frown at my phone, confused because this is so different from Nash's reaction IRL. To Halle, Alanna is trash and it's hard to admit fandom. To Kels, he says it's okay to still love the book. Is it me, Halle, who gets the truth? Is he just telling Kels what he thinks she wants to hear?

do you think so?

8:24 PM

huh, i actually kind of feel better about it all.

thanks.

8:25 PM

I'll see the movie with you.

8:26 PM

Well, not, like, WITH you. Obviously. But we
could go opening night and debrief after?

8:27 PM

let's do it

8:28 PM

We sit like this on Molly's couch, together as Nash and
Halle, but talking as Nash and Kels. And I can't help but think
it's funny, the way you can be literally *so close* to someone, but
somehow closer with words and social media accounts and pixels
in between.

Nash to Kels, at the party

Also quick Halle update: There has been
Progress! We had a conversation that didn't
end in awkward silence!
8:45 PM

And honestly, it's all thanks to the F&Y mess?
8:46 PM

[typing]
8:47 PM

[bubbles disappear]
8:48 PM

NINE

Karaoke is terrible.

By *terrible*, I mean *amazing*. One dude, Adam, stages a dramatic reading of "Achy Breaky Heart." Two girls named Louisa and Rebecca belt an off-key rendition of "Don't Stop Believin'." Turns out, being surrounded by so many strangers isn't as anxiety-provoking once everyone starts singing off-key.

I'm hanging by the air hockey table with Autumn and Nash, away from the main karaoke action. Molly appears in the space between us, her previously perfect curls loosened to soft waves in the humidity of the crowded basement.

"It's so great you're here," she says to me.

"She knows about the bet," Autumn says.

"Autumn." Molly's eyebrows pinch with concern when she turns to face me. "I really thought you wouldn't come. But that doesn't mean I'm not glad you're here."

"It's fine," I say, looking down.

"No, but seriously," Molly says. "You know we want you around, right? Sometimes I think you don't know that."

When it comes to my anxious brain, it's less about knowing and more about *believing*.

"I'm not Le Crew," I say.

"You're not," Autumn says. "You could be, though."

It's surprising, the words coming from Autumn. There have never been any one-on-one opportunities to get to know her—I don't work with her and she's not Jewish, so I pretty much only see her at school. She has no reason to assure me I could be a part of their friend group.

So for the first time, I consider believing it.

Before I can answer, I see Autumn has a contemplative look on her face and pulls out her memo pad. Out of the corner of my eye, I watch her write down our exchange in dialogue.

"Seriously?" Molly asks, looking at Autumn.

"What? This is as organic as it gets," Autumn says before taking a long sip of her soda and turning to me. "I need to write a scene. I'm not a writer—I'm a DP. I'm applying to film school, but most creative portfolios need a writing sample in addition to a short film. In other words, I'm screwed."

"DP?" Sawyer asks, appearing behind Molly and wrapping his arms around her.

"Director of photography," Autumn and I say at the same time.

Autumn's head snaps up, her eyes meeting mine. "Wait, you're into film too?"

That's when I get my first real smile from Autumn Williams.

I shake my head. Swallow. "My parents. They're a directing team—"

Autumn cuts me off. "Levitt—oh my *God*. Madeline and Ari Levitt? They're your *parents*?"

"Yeah, that's them," I say, kind of shocked she knows them by name.

"Oh my God! I mean, I thought maybe, for, like, half a second. I almost asked, but that's like asking if you're related to Joseph Gordon-Levitt."

"To be clear—you're not, are you?" Molly asks.

I laugh. "I wish."

Molly sighs. "Damn."

"I loved *Gentrify, U.S.*, like, *so* much," Autumn continues, ignoring Molly's disappointment re: JGL. "Your parents got screwed."

"They'll appreciate that," I say. "Do you want to go into doc?"

"Maybe," Autumn says. "I just know I need to be behind a camera, telling underrepresented stories. Whether that's through narrative or documentary, I'm not sure yet."

"That's what college is for," I say.

Autumn smiles at me. "Exactly—which is why my writing sample needs to be perfect. But my dialogue is trash, Halle. *Trash*."

"It's true," Nash says.

Autumn flips Nash off. "And I don't have Sophie to rewrite it for me anymore. She was brilliant." She sighs. "So I've been writing down lines I think would make good dialogue. For inspiration."

"Let's remember that *you* broke up with *her*," Nash says.

Autumn swivels in the bar stool to look at Nash. "Shut up." Then she turns forward to face me. "Soph is a freshman at the Savannah College of Art and Design. We were never going to work long term."

"I can help. If you want."

Autumn lights up. "Really? That would be *amaze*. Did your parents let you on location?"

I nod. "I kind of grew up on location."

Autumn hangs on my every word as I fill her in on what life is like as Mad and Ari Levitt's daughter. I can feel Nash listening, but thankfully this part of my life is safe, solely Halle's, so I try to focus on Autumn's enthusiasm. Most teens don't care about doc, so it's super cool meeting someone who does. I almost forget what an important part of my identity it is until I start talking about it, and I kind of fall in love with it all over again.

My chest pangs and I make a mental note to send a *l'shanah tovah* text to my parents tomorrow. I've been so wrapped up in the Nash-Gramps-Alanna drama, I've barely read Mom's updates.

"What about you?" Autumn asks.

I blink. "Me?"

"College?"

"Oh." I pause. "NYU is my top choice."

"Dude, same," Nash says. "NYU is everything, but I'll probably end up at Wesleyan or UConn or some other in-state school."

"Why?" I ask, even though Kels was just talking to Nash about his overbearing parents.

Nash starts mouthing words to me but I can't hear them over the opening notes of "Islands in the Stream," coming from the karaoke machine. The chords leave me breathless. My necklace feels like a weight on my chest and *I can't breathe.*

I haven't listened to this song since Grams died.

"Sorry," I say, standing up in the middle of Nash's sentence.

Ollie. I scan the room for his eyes, but he's not here anymore.

I can't even imagine listening to two strangers sing it, so I bolt.

I'm halfway up the stairs before I realize that Nash is following me.

"Are you okay?" Nash asks. *"Halle."*

"I need air."

"Okay."

Nash laces his fingers through mine. The fingers that type the words and hit send on the thousands of messages he's sent to me, Kels. It's the first time he's ever touched me, Halle, and it must be the panic overtaking me because I don't think to flinch. Not even for a moment.

I follow Nash up the stairs and out the back door and thank God hands can't talk because if they could, my sweaty palm would be screaming the truth.

Nash sits with me on the swings until I catch my breath.

I bend my knees and let the wind sway me back and forth. Breathe with the wind until my pulse steadies to a normal pace. Nash doesn't say anything. He just swings in sync with me. He looks ridiculous, this tall body on a tiny swing. Every time he tries to straighten his knees and propel his body forward, his feet scuff against the mulch and the chips fly forward. Adjusting his strategy, Nash leans back in the swing to give his legs more space.

Spoiler alert: They're still too long.

In the attempt, he almost falls backward out of the swing. He catches himself at the last second, but for a moment he looks *scared*. Like he's going to fall a full fourteen inches to his death.

I cannot stop laughing. I'm used to laughing at Nash via banter, but this kind of laughter? It's totally new. He sits up and plants his feet on the ground, the swing still beneath him. I focus my eyes forward and keep swinging. This is the part where Nash asks *what happened* or *are you okay* or any other variation of an attempt to acknowledge that I heard a Dolly Parton and Kenny Rogers duet and lost my shit.

"We don't have to talk about it," Nash says.

This surprises me. It also kind of makes me *want* to talk about it.

"It's a stupid song," I say. "Every Thanksgiving, Grams and Gramps would blast 'Islands in the Stream' and bust out in this epic drunk duet."

Nash laughs. "Really?"

"Gramps only sings when tipsy," I say. "And they were *awful*, but watching them, it was like, *this is what love is*, you know? And I miss her. Most days, I'm okay. But then Dolly Parton slaps me in the face and it feels like I'm just being told all over again."

"I know what you mean," Nash says softly. "Memories tend to mess with us like that, don't they?"

I nod, wiping my cheeks. "But also I didn't know losing her would mean losing both of them. Missing her is hard enough. I wasn't prepared to miss him, too. That's the worst part. Gramps isn't *Gramps* anymore."

Nash's forehead wrinkles. "That's really hard. It sucks so bad, losing the people who are supposed to still be here."

He breaks eye contact, his voice fading with the wind. The way Nash says this, the emotion in his voice, it's so genuine and I don't think we're talking about my grandparents anymore. I have no clue what he means. These aren't the conversations he and Kels have.

I know Nash worries his parents won't let him go to NYU. He knows Kels has a complicated relationship with the word *home*. But it occurs to me, here on this swing—we don't let ourselves get *sad* around each other. We thrive on sarcasm, banter, and angst.

After Grams died, talking to Nash was an escape because he didn't know.

Maybe Kels is Nash's escape too.

Who has Nash lost? How can I even ask?

His phone buzzes and he pulls it out to check the message.

"I'm okay," I say. "They must be—"

He shoves his phone into his pocket. "I'm good here."

Me too. It's honestly a revelation, how comfortable I am in this moment.

"You know," he says, "this is the first conversation we've had where you don't have The Look on your face."

"What look?"

He scuffs the toe of his Chucks against the mulch. "I don't know. You always look at me like you'd rather eat broccoli or something than engage in a conversation."

I roll my eyes. "If you want me to stroke your ego, that's not—"

Nash shakes his head. "That's not it."

"So, what is it?" I ask, surprised by how much I want to know.

"Why is your broccoli face only for me?"

I shake my head. "Stop saying that. For the record, I like broccoli. Olives, though—"

"Not the point."

"Nash."

"Halle."

"You're not broccoli."

Nash opens his mouth to say something, but his phone buzzes again.

"Sorry," he says, his eyes fixed on the screen. "It's Molly. Your brother is looking for you. And Molly, apparently, is looking for me."

I stand up and smooth down my skirt, then glance at my watch. It's later than I thought. "I guess we should probably—"

"Probably," Nash says. "You okay?"

I nod, following Nash back toward the warmth of the house. Away from the magical three-slide playground, away from the shadows and saying too many things and not enough at the same time. Away from telling Nash he's not broccoli.

Inside, Gramps is sitting at the head of the Jacobsons' table with

Ollie by his side. A half-eaten piece of apple pie is in front of Gramps and he's laughing with another Old Man Friend, but something is up. He's slumped in the chair, his hands hanging over the arms. When he leans forward and scoops a piece of apple pie sloppily into his mouth, drops of vanilla ice cream drip onto his lap.

"Halle!" Gramps slurs, mouth half-full with pie. "I was saving you some pie. But now I'm eating it. Because I got hungry. Sorry."

"Oh," I say. "That's okay, Gramps."

I don't know what to do, Ollie mouths to me.

I've never seen Gramps like this before. Okay, so most of the adults in the room are well past sober—but this is *Gramps*. And this isn't *"Islands in the Stream"* on Thanksgiving tipsy.

He waves for me to lean closer. Then closer still. I bend down to Gramps-in-a-chair level and rest my hands on my knees. It's like he wants to whisper something in my ear and oh my God Molly and Nash are watching. This is so embarrassing.

"You might need to drive home tonight," he whisper-shouts.

Home sounds great. Home sounds like it should happen *right now.*

"Okay. Should we—"

"There might be more apple pie left. But probably not. It's really good."

I stand up, face burning as Gramps laughs too loud. Nash makes eye contact with me and he's the only one in this kitchen, besides Ollie and me, who looks genuinely concerned. Ollie chugs a glass of water. It's not funny when the drunk old guy is *your* drunk old guy. And now Gramps is giggling like crazy about

God knows what, octaves higher than normal grandpa laughter.

Add giggling to the list of things grandpas shouldn't do.

I squat back down to Gramps's level and fake a yawn.

"Can we go?" I ask. "I'm super tired."

Gramps rolls his eyes.

"Me too," Ollie says.

"Halle. Oliver," he says mid-chew. "It's only"—he glances down at his watch—"ten o'clock."

"Gramps," I say. Firm, this time. "Let's go."

A statement, not a question.

"Let me finish my damn pie."

The harshness in his voice takes me aback. The playfulness that accompanied him moments ago vanishes. He's never raised his voice to me, not even when he was upset about the cupcakes. And it's just—that's it. I'm so tired. It's too much. Too much social interaction, too much constant tension, too much *everything*. I know that he's hurting, but I'm done.

I hold my hand out to Gramps. "Keys."

Surprised by my tone, he reluctantly hands them over.

"I'll be in the car," I tell Ollie.

Then I bolt, weaving through the nameless strangers. I need to get away from everything about tonight ASAP. Away from the side eye, "Islands in the Stream," the broccoli. All of it.

"Halle! Halle, wait!"

I don't wait. I twist the handle and push the door open. Walk down the steps and across the lawn to where Gramps's Corolla is parked halfway up the sidewalk.

Nash catches up to me as I'm fumbling with the car keys, trying to get the door open. You need to manually open the doors with, like, a *key*, and my hands are shaking. It can't just be easy. *Shit.*

"Halle." Nash's voice is quiet. "Can I help?"

I can't deal with Nash right now. I thought splitting myself made sense. I thought nothing would change. Now everything is changing. I have to file Nash stories in two sections of my brain: stories for Halle and stories for Kels.

Things got way too blurred tonight. It needs to stop.

He needs to be Kels's. Only Kels's.

I turn around, the jagged edges of the keys digging into my palm.

"Take the hint. Leave. Me. Alone."

Nash blinks. Takes a step back. "Wow. Okay. I get it. Message delivered, loud and clear."

I can't deal with the hurt on his face for one second longer, so I turn my attention back to unlocking this freaking door, while Nash's footsteps become farther and farther away.

I pull the handle, throw the door open, and lock myself in, then pull out my phone to . . . what? Message Nash? He's fifty feet from me, silhouetted in the front window of Molly's house. He's never felt farther away.

I look away, back at my screen without seeing it.

Tap. Tap tap.

When I look up, Gramps is looking at me through the passenger-side window, his nose squished against the glass, his breath fogging it up. As soon as I unlock the doors, Ollie slides into the back and Gramps flops into the passenger seat. His bloodshot eyes look into mine and he smells like grapes and whiskey.

"What?" Gramps snaps. "You wanted to go. Drive."

"Fine."

I shift the car into drive and my foot tentatively releases from the brake to tap the gas. My heart beats a million miles beyond the speed limit but it's okay because we're on the road and I'm driving and we will get back in one piece. I focus on the road, on getting us back to Gramps's.

Gramps shifts in his seat. Adjusts the back multiple times, unable to find a comfortable position. Then he flips through the radio stations, shunning all things country before cutting the music entirely and stewing in the silence.

"It's the first one," Gramps slurs. "That damn song."

My breath catches in my throat because *of course*. When Nash led me up the stairs and through the soundproof basement door, the music followed me.

"I miss her," I say. It's the first opportunity he's given me to say it, to talk about her.

"Me too," Ollie adds.

"You don't even *know*," Gramps says. He leans back in the seat and closes his eyes once more, his index and middle fingers rubbing his temples.

I grip the steering wheel so hard my knuckles turn white. He acts like he's the only one who's allowed to be hurting. It's been almost a month and I'm still completely walking on eggshells around him. He can eat the cupcakes but can't bear the baking. He can laugh and joke at temple but ignores us completely in the house. We can talk about Grams, but only if he starts the conversation. I'm so sick of grieving on his terms.

"I want the books," I say, the words falling from my lips before I can take them back.

"What?" Gramps's asks.

"Grams's books. I'm going to get them this weekend. I want them," I say.

Gramps shakes his head. "They're not yours."

"Because you're definitely putting them to use," I snap.

"Halle," Ollie says. "Stop it."

"If you won't remember her, someone should."

My hands shake violently and tears blur my vision. We're on a residential street that connects Molly's neighborhood to ours. I pull over and put the car in park.

Gramps exhales. "Just take us home, Hal."

I shake my head. "Grams would hate what you did to the house."

"I know." Gramps's voice is hollow.

"*I* hate the house," I say.

"Damn it, Halle, *I know.*"

Gramps's voice reverberates off the windows before silence settles in the car; the only noise I can hear is the angry beat of my broken heart. I don't think I've rendered Ollie silent before. *Ever.* I'm never loud enough. My words are never sharp enough.

For the first time since I arrived in Middleton, I don't try to filter what I'm feeling.

"Then why did you do it?"

"You can't even *imagine*." Gramps's voice cracks. "It's like half of me died."

I exhale. Twist the key in the ignition and shift the car into drive.

"Me too. But *you're not dead, Gramps*. You're not."

We shift into silence and eventually I start to drive again. I'm struggling for the right words to say, the right way to tell Gramps, *I am hurting too and I am here.*

Instead, I hold my breath the rest of the ride home, thinking for a girl who loves words, I'm pretty much the worst at articulating the first draft.

September 29

Nash Stevens
LOL remember when I said "Progress!" re:
Halle? I take it back.
8:30 AM

You were right.
8:31 AM

As of today, I am officially done trying to be
Halle's friend.
8:32 AM

i'm sorry
8:33 AM

You're not going to say "I told you so"?
8:33 AM

there are, in fact, some cases in which i don't
like gloating about being right. this happens to
be one of them
8:34 AM

i DID, however, screenshot
"You were right" for future reference
8:34 AM

I set myself up for that 🧍
8:35 AM

seriously though—are you ok?
8:36 AM

Yeah.
8:36 AM

I always feel better when I'm talking to you.
8:36 AM

[typing]

TEN

Halle's life has been particularly Not Great in the three weeks following the Rosh Hashanah disaster, but at least Kels is thriving.

It's only been four days, and the *Read Between the Lies* cover reveal has already surpassed *Fireflies and You* in terms of most-liked OTP Instagram post. As of this morning, it has more than 200K likes. Ariel boosted the video on her personal Twitter account, which got the attention of other YA authors and publishers. My inbox is *nuts* right now—totally overflowing with cover reveal requests. Next level officially unlocked.

Read Between the Lies has been the perfect distraction from all things *Fireflies and You*. I know it's temporary relief. Alanna will say something else to make everyone upset soon enough. But for now? I'm living for all the OTP love currently happening in the feed. Every time I check Twitter, I have more followers.

Creating content that people are content with? That makes people excited to *read*? It's the best feeling in the universe. It's a feeling I'm going to write about in my NYU admissions essay. Once they see OTP, how much love goes into it and how much traction it receives? I know it'll make up for the lack of traditional extracurriculars on my application. Who has time for student council or debate team when you're actively pursuing your dreams?

Plus, it's super validating, being able to bask in my success with my friends, given that Ollie is the only person I can talk to about this IRL.

Amy Chen
KELS! Bustle shared your post!
10:32 PM

Samira Lee
You're going to be the go-to person for major reveals now—this is HUGE
10:34 PM

Elle Carter
. . . and lucky. Enjoy the break from Alanna angst while it lasts ☺
10:34 PM

Samira Lee
IGNORE ELLE. YOU'RE THRIVING
10:34 PM

I cling to my online world and how great it feels to be Kels right now because IRL, time passes not in days of the week, but in Jewish holidays. I never knew how many important moments were crammed within the three weeks following Rosh Hashanah. Yom Kippur, Sukkot, and Simchat Torah come one after another. Temple makes my stomach twist in unfamiliar knots because though I love it, ever since Rosh I'm feeling more and more like I don't fit in with these people.

Molly and Nash are at every service. Nash pretends I don't exist. It's like, now he looks at me and he doesn't even see me. I eat lunch in the library now, where I'm free to message him and my friends and work on OTP stuff. But now when I message Nash, I'm wondering what he's talking about with Le Crew. It was too hard to keep sitting with them—too impossible to ignore Nash ignoring me. It *hurt*. And it's the worst because it has no right to hurt—I asked for this. I *wanted* him to leave me alone.

It worked. Everything is great between Nash and Kels. Better than ever, theoretically. Except for the ways it isn't. Nash is real now. He has a voice and a laugh and I can't stop thinking about us on the swings and how good it felt, being able to talk about Grams with him.

How there are conversations I can have with Nash that Kels never could.

At least now it's the first Saturday I'm free since the whirl-wind of holidays, so I try to refocus on catching up with my mentions and chat with my friends.

Halle's problems can wait until Monday.

There's a knock on my door and I look up from my screen, expecting to see Ollie.

I blink.

It's *Gramps*.

"Oh," he coughs. "You're still in your pajamas."

Gramps is dressed before eleven on a Saturday. He's wearing a green sweater over a white collared shirt and jeans. I'm so shocked by the clothes, it takes me a moment to meet his eyes, to register his face and see that the beard is gone. It's just *gone* and Gramps looks put together for the first time in over a month—but he acts like it's weird that *I'm* still in my pajamas?

"It's Saturday," I say slowly, trying to mask the emotion in my voice.

"We're going to Ludlow's. Get dressed. I'll be in the car."

Gramps is gone before I have a chance to catch my breath, to form words, to ask what the hell is going on. It's the first time Gramps has looked at me, I mean, *really looked at me*, since I snapped in the car. I'd say we've been avoiding each other, but that's pretty impossible. Whenever we're in the same space though, just the two of us without Ollie, the tension is so thick, and neither of us breaks it.

Gramps is trying to break it—with a trip to a home improvement store?

I'm dressed and out the door in minutes.

We pick through paint swatches at Ludlow & Sons as though our relationship depends on it.

Gramps selects two shades. "One of these? Are we getting closer?"

We've been standing here for an hour. It's not that I'm incapable of making a decision. It's more like I'm processing that I'm here. I'd pretty much accepted my orange room fate until now. And I'm still skeptical of the normalcy of this outing, that we're finally getting the paint he promised on day one.

"They look exactly the same."

Gramps analyzes the swatches. "You're right. Hm." He places the swatches back in the shelf and takes a step back, assessing. I'm ready to close my eyes and select at random at this point.

"Aha!" Gramps reaches for a swatch in the top row, for a shade that has been out of my line of vision. "This one. It's like the frosting."

Gramps's voice catches on *frosting* and I look up at him, allowing myself to wear my emotion on my face. Gramps swallows and holds out the swatch. I'm so scared I'll say the wrong thing and send Gramps spiraling back into his grief. I take the swatch from his hand and study it. *Lily lavender.* I close my eyes, imagining lavender walls and dark mahogany bookshelves. For the first time, I see a space that is *mine.*

I nod. "It's perfect."

"Hal," he says, his voice hoarse from participating in weeks of services. "I—"

I shake my head. "It's okay to not be okay."

It comes out in one breath, forced from my throat before I can overanalyze.

Gramps is here. For the first time since I arrived. He's hurting—but he's *trying.* It's all I've wanted, for us to be in this, together. *My*

Gramps is still in there, somewhere, and it's such a relief to see him. This might be temporary. Next Saturday he might revert back to his pajama weekend ways. For now, it feels like he heard me.

I'm sorry, says the weight of the can in my hands, a whole gallon of lily lavender. I have paint and Gramps and I are on speaking terms—and it's because of *me*. Because of my words.

I'm always so hung up on saying the *right* thing, on stringing the perfect sentence together. Maybe it's okay for my words to come out messy and wrong sometimes, as long as they're true.

A few hours later, Kels and Nash are texting, and for the first time, I wish we were talking.

Nash Stevens
Well, now it just feels like you're using me for my design skills.
1:21 PM

oh, absolutely
1:22 PM

you're just figuring this out?
1:22 PM

come on, learning to use editing software is a skill, not, like, a whole freaking ART
1:23 PM

Okay maybe not the art part. But I'm just
saying, if you can shoot and edit a video in
high-def, you can learn HTML
1:24 PM

but why learn HTML when I have you 😊
1:24 PM

HA. But seriously. You're getting the BookCon
panel. You know that right?
1:25 PM

maybe? i hope so? a girl can dream . . .
1:25 PM

So you want it now?
1:25 PM

i've always wanted it. i think i just believe it's a
little more possible now??
1:28 PM

It's always been possible for you.
1:28 PM

i appreciate the optimism on my behalf
1:31 PM

My face flushes. I can't talk to Nash now without picturing him here, in front of me, speaking words. I used to spend so much time wondering who Nash is *offline*, if the real him could possibly live up to the profile. I can't do that anymore, because Nash isn't an internet persona. I don't get to imagine who he is—he's exactly who I thought he was, maybe even more.

I *like* who he is.

So even though these DMs are like every other conversation we've ever had, they feel off. I want to tell him about the paint, about Gramps and things getting an incremental step better.

Nash wouldn't have tried so hard if he didn't at least like Halle-me enough to want to be friends, right?

I stare at my phone, rereading our most recent messages until my vision blurs. We could have this—the banter, the real conversations, all of it—IRL. For the first time, I let myself imagine it and it's not so scary anymore.

I owe Nash the truth.

But first, I owe him an apology.

I can't tell him the truth when he's mad at me. If I open up to him and he doesn't take it well, all it takes is one tweet to shatter the persona I've crafted. I'm not ready to be Halle online and open myself up like that. The trolling about Alanna has been bad enough—if they make the connection that I'm Miriam Levitt's granddaughter, I'll be even more in focus. And it'll influence the BookCon decision.

Kels needs to get the BookCon panel first.

It'll prove to NYU that I'm enough without Grams' editorial legacy.

But the original plan to keep my worlds separate? It's not working.

The truth is, if the BookCon gods want me, Nash *is* going to find out. If we can exist as Nash and Halle once I stop pushing him away, maybe he'll be excited if I tell him I'm Kels.

Before I can overthink it, I text Nash.

> Hi
> 11:13 AM

Embarrassment slays me as soon as I hit send. He's not going to respond. *I* wouldn't respond to me either. This is a terrible idea. How have phones not invented the ability to unsend a text yet?

When my phone buzzes, I almost drop it.

Nash Kim
Wrong number?
11:16 AM

Right. Molly plugged Nash's number into my phone after I declined bowling invite number three with a casual *Text him if you change your mind*, since she can't get texts on Shabbat. She said it almost like she believed I *would*. It's the first time I've ever put Nash Kim's number to use. Of course, he doesn't have mine.

> Oh! Sorry—it's Halle.
> 11:17 AM

Not funny, Sawyer.
11:17 AM

I'm positive I don't want to know what *that* means.

No! It's really me! The girl who assured you that you're not a vegetable and then was a total jerk.
11:18 AM

Yeah, you kind of were.
11:19 AM

The jerkiest jerk. That was me.
11:19 PM

. . . And you're texting me now because?
11:20 AM

Ugh. I deserve that.
11:21 PM

I'm just confused.
11:21 PM

Are you free today?
11:21 AM

. . .
11:25 AM

Seriously?
11:25 AM

I type and delete and type and delete. The amount of tension conveyed in a . . . *Seriously?* is nauseating. Every interaction between Nash and Kels is on the same page, whether light or serious.

It's never like this.

Can we hang out? And by "hang out" I mean
can you help me paint my room?
11:28 AM

I thought I'm supposed to be leaving you
alone.
11:29 AM

Maybe you should ask Molly?
11:31 AM

a) It's Shabbat.
11:33 AM

b) I want to hang out with you.
11:33 PM

Fifteen minutes pass without a new notification.

Thirty.

Forty-five.

I am in a staring contest with my phone. My cheeks flush with embarrassment even though I am one hundred percent alone in this ugly AF more-orange-by-the-minute bedroom. I feel like an idiot for texting Nash out of the blue like this.

The rejection stings more than I expect, even though I deserve it.

My phone battery is running on empty, so I plug it in and place it screen-down on the night table. I will not obsess over it. Instead, I drown out the endless loop of anxiety with a new Lola Daniels book, because romance novels are perfect escapism. I get lost in the world of hockey boys and skater girls—until a knock on my door snaps me out of it.

"Hal?" The door swings open and it's Ollie, dressed head to toe in his Middleton Market uniform. Khakis, forest green polyester shirt, and a matching green visor. At fifteen, he's legally only allowed to bag groceries, but he likes having money of his own as much as I do.

I'm not sure what Ollie needs from me before his shift, but he looks pretty freaked out. His mouth is a straight line and his eyes are all bugged out like I've never seen.

"Ol?"

He shuts the door behind him and presses his back against it. When he speaks, his voice is low.

"Gramps asked me to come get you. Nash is in our living room?" Ollie's voice goes up at the end like it's a question.

The hockey boys and skater girls fall to the floor.

"What? Why?"

"You tell me, Hal, since you're allegedly the one who invited him."

I grab for my phone, grab for any explanation—but the only notifications that light up my screen are for Kels.

"I *did* invite him. He never answered, though."

Ollie raises his eyebrows. "Why?"

I shake my head. "I just wanted to, I guess."

"Are you going to tell him?" Ollie whispers.

I shake my head fiercely. "Not yet."

Ollie sighs. "This is a terrible idea and I do not condone it one bit. Nope."

"What if he blasts me online?" I ask. "He's pretty pissed at me right now."

He crosses his arms over his chest. "Seriously?"

"I don't know, *Oliver*. It's a risk I can't take—not before BookCon announces their panelists and my NYU application is in. Not until I'm sure."

He flips me off for using his full name, like I knew he would.

"Oh, so that's still the plan? Wait until you graduate and hope he doesn't find out?"

I bite my lip and shrug. "It won't be *that* long."

He rolls his eyes and I can't remember the last time his frustration has been so palpable. "But you like him, yeah?"

I feel my cheeks flush.

Online, Nash is my best friend. In person, though? When

he's nearly falling off swings, or blushing when his friends gush about REX, or joking in terrible book puns? It's kind of impossible to ignore how cute Nash is.

I've been trying *so* hard to ignore how cute Nash is.

"He's my best friend. Of course I like him."

Ollie shakes his head. "That's not what I meant." He checks his phone. "I really need to go. I'll tell him you'll be down in five—enough time for you to change?"

I look down at my Snoopy PJs. Even when we're tense, Ollie is always looking out for me.

"This sucks—I hate lying, Hal. If he's going to be around more, you legit have to tell him."

"What if I can't?"

Ollie puts his hand on the knob and twists. "You've read this book before. It's going to blow up, and it's going to be your own stupid fault."

He doesn't get it, I think as the door slams behind him.

I change quickly into a *cute but not trying* look of leggings and a long T-shirt. Brush my hair. Hide my books in the closet because my collection *screams* Kels. Pick up my phone and read a message from Nash to Kels. The last one he sent says I guess you're busy, talk to you later and it makes me laugh and hate everything all at once because, if only he knew.

Operation: Rebrand this Orange Hellhole has commenced.

Problem: I, Halle Levitt, have forgotten how to speak in the presence of Nash Kim.

"So first, I think we need to tape the walls," Nash says.

"Okay."

I pick up one of the rolls of blue paint tape and toss it to Nash.

It bounces off the floor a few feet away. Fail.

Nash's eyes are on the tape. "So you invited me over to throw things at me. Got it."

"I didn't—"

He turns his back to me and starts taping before I can finish my sentence. I can't stand the awkwardness, so I pull up Spotify. We spend half of *Hamilton*'s first act taping the room—because *Hamilton* is universal.

Once the room is sufficiently taped, we dip our roller brushes into lavender and start painting.

Time to permanently delete orange from my life.

Except, the orange isn't completely disappearing under the lavender.

"Are we doing something wrong?" I ask. "I think we're doing something wrong."

"Seriously?" Nash asks, annoyed.

"Is that your new favorite word or something?"

If Nash is going to be passive-aggressive to me, I can give it back. I don't know why he's here if he's not even going to give me a chance to apologize. We step back from the wall and assess the work we've done so far. Something is *definitely* wrong.

This isn't the lily lavender I was promised on the swatch.

"Primer," Nash says after a beat. "Duh. We didn't prime first."

"That's important?" I ask.

"When the new color is lighter . . ." Nash walks over to the corner of my room where the second, unopened paint can is. He picks it up and brings it over and it's actually not paint at all. It's primer. "Of course, it's been right here the whole time."

"I thought they were both paint," I admit.

Nash scrunches his eyebrows. "You thought you needed two cans of paint for one room?"

"I haven't exactly done this before," I say.

"Clearly," Nash says, opening the can of primer.

I want to note that Nash didn't exactly point this out before we started either, but instead I stand beside Nash and try to roll primer in sync with him—though his reach extends much higher than mine ever will. I jump to try to make up the difference. If I look ridiculous, he doesn't laugh. My thoughts swirl trying to figure out how to bring up Rosh Hashanah, how to say I'm sorry. I'm not prepared to interact with this version of Nash.

"I get that you're still mad at me," I say. "I get it and I deserve it. But I don't get why you're here."

"I'm not sure either, tbh," Nash says, and even though we're tense, a part of me *dies* because he says text-speak out loud too. "I mean, to be honest."

"Got it," I say.

His exhale almost sounds like a laugh. "Sorry—bad habit from the blog. My friends give me so much shit for it."

"AF is my weakness," I admit.

"Well, don't say it in front of Molly. You'll never live it down."

"Noted."

I prime walls with Nash and for a moment we are okay.

I don't know what to say next, so I start rapping along with "Satisfied" and Nash smiles his real, one-dimpled smile. I don't know if he's laughing at me or with me, but honestly, I don't care.

The song ends and I'm out of breath.

I step backward, so ready to launch into Lafayette's part in "The Story of Tonight—Reprise". . . that my right foot lands in the container of primer.

I look down at my primed foot. "Well."

Nash chews on his lower lip. "This is going well."

"We could do this professionally."

Nash laughs. "Totally. Kim and Levitt Painting. Don't worry, we'll realize what primer is for eventually—"

"—and definitely step in it."

"We also rap, and not just the furniture!"

Tears are streaming down my face and I don't even know why because this is easily Nash's worst pun yet. "We'll charge extra for the rapping."

Nash considers this. "I'll add 'rapping not included' to the fine print."

"Perfect. I see no flaws in this business plan. But I . . . need help," I sputter through my laughter. I am ankle deep in the thick white primer, which might as well be Super Glue.

"You're a mess, Upstate," Nash says.

And suddenly, Nash is, like, *right here*—his face is inches away from mine as he stands up and holds out his hands to help unstick me. He's so close I see the gold flecks in his eyes. Those eyes are the reason that avoiding Nash indefinitely will never work.

"I'm sorry," I say.

He shrugs. "You confuse me, Upstate."

"I confuse me too."

"I never know what you're thinking. For all I know, I'll get the cold shoulder at school tomorrow."

I chew the inside of my cheek and shake my head *no*.

"It's either cold shoulder or this. It can't be both."

"I like this," I admit.

It's as close to saying *I like you* as I'll ever get. If I were the right combination of brave and stupid, I'd tell him the truth.

Instead, I swipe my paint roller across his right cheek.

Nash gapes at me. Did I go too far?

He picks up a brush and flicks it so paint splatters all over my shirt. It's so on. I dip my hands in the fresh lavender and press them against Nash's chest, leaving handprints on his shirt.

The wildest part of all of this is that I am the one who is stuck in a container of primer. Nash can run away whenever he wants. But he doesn't move. It's like a challenge almost: What will Halle do next? How far will she go?

This isn't a text message. I can't change the subject. And for the first time I don't *want* to.

Nash paints my nose lavender, grinning.

Then the door swings open and Nash jumps back two steps.

"Am I interrupting something?"

Gramps's voice jolts me out of the moment. He's smirking in the doorframe, Scout tucked under his arm.

"I can't be trusted with paint," I say.

Nash is trying to be serious in front of Gramps but he can't stop laughing.

"I had too much faith." Gramps laughs—he *laughs*, and wow, I've missed that sound so much. "Paper towels?"

"Please," we sputter through giggles.

It's *fun*, letting myself just be around Nash.

I want to know him, but I also want him to know *me*, Halle. I want to build a friendship with Nash, IRL, so when I'm ready to tell him the truth, he'll understand the full picture. Kels comes with expectations, with almost three years of history. Kels, who always knows what to say, who gets cited in major publications and thrown in the middle of YA scandals, who manages to run One True Pastry like it's a full-time job.

I know he likes her, but she's the branded version of me— she's not *me*.

Could Nash like *this* version of me?

I actually want to find out.

November 1

From: mad@madandariproductions.com
To: halle.levitt@gmail.com

can't wait to hear your voice!!

Hi Halle!

Just wanted to remind you that Dad and I are calling tomorrow at 10 AM eastern. Did you get my emails? I know you're busy, but you can't even humor your parents and shoot us a few messages in the group chat? I know you see those!

Gramps says you seem overwhelmed by college apps. Are you working on your personal statement? I know this whole process is stressful—I wish we could be there to help you navigate it! We might be far away, but we're still here for you, Hal. Don't forget that!

Talk soon!
Love,
Mom

Halle's Inbox

Mad Levit
Ollie has assured us you're still alive
Oct 27

Ari Levitt
camels
Oct 21

Mad Levitt
update #4: a genealogist and a minor tech disaster
Oct 17

Mad Levitt
where are my children? i need details!!!
Oct 12

Ari Levitt
more baby goats
Oct 5

Ari Levitt
baby goats
Oct 5

Mad Levitt
look what you're missing out on!!
Oct 1

ELEVEN

Y ou can't put so much pressure on yourself, Halle," Mom
says.

Her voice cracks when she says my name and it
makes me feel like trash re: the collection of unopened emails
accumulating in my inbox. I've been so overwhelmed with my
double life, I honestly haven't even checked my Halle email in the
two weeks since I became friends with Nash.

Ollie reminds me we have parents who miss us, but I've been
positive they're too busy for that.

Now that I'm on the phone with them? Well, I'm wrong.

"How're the interviews going?" I ask.

"Great!" Mom says. "But I'm not letting you change the subject."

"It's time for a pep talk!" Dad says.

"I was leaning toward *reality check*," Mom says.

I drum my fingers on the kitchen table, waiting for whatever
is coming next. Currently, the table is a command center of application checklists, essay drafts, and SAT prep books. The math

section is the *worst*. I've only improved thirty points from when I took the test the first time in Charlotte, last spring.

I need fifty more points to hit NYU's median score, but right now that feels impossible.

Dad jumps right in. "Here are the reasons why NYU will love you. You're smart! You're tech-savvy! You've been building a brand since you were fourteen! Publishers reach out to *you* for publicity opportunities. We'll have a talk another time about how it's maybe time to try to start monetizing this thing, because I have feelings about free labor—but regardless! Instead of thinking about all the things you *aren't* doing, maybe take a step back and be proud of everything you've accomplished."

"Dad," I say, emotion thick in my voice.

My parents know about One True Pastry—I just had no idea they paid attention to it.

"Wow," Mom says. "That was unfairly good. How do I follow that?"

"You're the only one who thinks a reality check is necessary," Dad says.

I smile. I miss Mom and Dad banter.

"It is," Mom says. "Halle. Listen to me. One college does not determine the course of your life. If you don't get into NYU, you will be okay. There are other options! You could take a gap year. Just remember, you *have* options—and you're lucky that you do."

"I know," I say.

It's true. I *do* know.

But knowing isn't going to minimize NYU stress. It's just not.

Mom sighs into the phone. "Ugh—I'm *so* sorry to cut this short, but Tavi needs us for more last-minute interviews."

"Last minute?" I ask.

"It's our last day at Kinneret," Dad says. "Tomorrow we're heading to Naama."

"It's all in the emails." Mom's delivery is blasé, but I hear the disappointment.

"I'll read them," I promise. "I'll answer them, too."

"Thanks, babe. We love you!"

"Travel safe. I love you too," I say.

We disconnect and, wow, do I wish my parents weren't an ocean away. I wish I could have an Ari Pep Talk and Mad Reality Check every time I need it.

I wish it were enough to make me put away the practice tests.

My eyes focus on the last one I took, blurring around the 600 math score. I am a 600. That's me. How can I *not* put pressure on myself when NYU might throw my application in the rejection pile before they even read about One True Pastry? They receive a ridiculous number of applications—so many that their acceptance rate *decreases* every year. Before I'm a person, I'm a number.

"Hal?" Gramps's voice is behind me. He took Ollie out for breakfast this morning to give me some space to study. I didn't even hear them come back.

I can't look at him. "I—"

Gramps closes my laptop and tucks it under his arm. Places his other hand on my shoulder to steady me. "I think we need a day off from this."

Gramps heads upstairs with my laptop and locks it in his room and I don't even protest. If Dad were here, he would've pulled the same thing. It's a relief, honestly. Gramps has been so refreshingly *Gramps* lately. Not always. He still has days where he'd rather be alone. But his concern right now? It's *everything*. When he returns, he goes straight to the freezer, pulling out a brand-new tub of mint chocolate chip ice cream. Then he pulls a bowl out of the cabinet and a metal spoon from the silverware drawer.

"Gramps, it's not even noon," I say.

His eyebrows raise. "It's never too early for ice cream."

"I don't think that's an actual thing."

Gramps pauses scooping. Looks at me. "Are you rejecting ice cream?"

I shake my head. "No. I'll stop talking."

"Good." Gramps pushes all my college stuff into a messy pile and takes a seat next to me at the table, placing my bowl of ice cream in front of me. "Do you have any plans today?"

I take a spoonful of ice cream. "I'm helping Autumn with her portfolio piece for film school. But that's not until later."

I didn't expect to miss Le Crew while Nash and I weren't speaking. I was so nervous returning to their lunch table after weeks of library lunches, but they acted like I'd never left. Which I'm pretty sure means they missed me too. I don't know. I'm not exactly used to navigating these friendship feels. But I *am* glad to be back.

Yesterday, I sent Autumn notes on her script, as promised,

and wow, she *is* bad at dialogue. But her concept is amazing—and the idea of being on a film set tonight is more exciting than I'll ever admit out loud. My college future feels so out of my control, it'll be nice to focus on someone else's.

"Next up, *To All the Boys*?" Gramps asks.

I nod.

Gramps loves romcoms and he never even knew it. He resisted *To All the Boys I've Loved Before* hype even though Grams could not have been a bigger fan, but now he'll finally see the perfection that is Lara Jean and Peter K. We've been making our way through my favorite romcoms, one each weekend. Now that he's actually giving them a shot, he's obsessed.

It's kind of adorable.

We transition to the living room, ice cream bowls in hand. I set up Netflix while Gramps takes his preferred couch corner, Scout claiming her spot in the middle.

"Ready?" I ask, opening Netflix.

"I don't know. The first movie ended so perfectly."

I settle into my spot on the couch and scoop a giant spoonful of ice cream. For the next few hours, there is no college anxiety, no One True Pastry, no wondering if Nash is texting Halle or Kels—or worse, both, now that we're friends. I shut everything out and focus on Lara Jean and her love letter problems.

But honestly, it's watching Gramps that's the best distraction.

After LJ and Peter K's happily ever after, Autumn is filming her masterpiece at Maple Street Sweets, and it's all hands on deck.

Actors have been recruited from the MHS drama club—two juniors, Lil Rivera and Monique Jackson, are Autumn's stars.

Molly handles all aspects of design—set, costumes, hair, and makeup. Sawyer bakes two dozen cupcakes to have on standby. Nash sets up grip and electric. And I have the distinct honor of being Autumn's AD—assistant director—as well as the resident reviser of scripts. I don't even realize how much I miss being behind a camera until I'm holding one in my hand again. The equipment may be amateur and, okay, we're shooting a five-minute narrative, not a ninety-minute documentary, but it's fun using this part of my brain again.

Autumn's film is called *Look Down, Swipe Right.* "OBJEC-TIVE: Queer WOC on a date because WE EXIST" is written in Autumn's handwriting at the top of the storyboard attached to my clipboard.

If it comes out the way it looks in my head, she's getting into USC. It is current—the use of dating apps and cell phones as both an initiating and distracting device. It is sweet (cupcakes!) and it is light (seriously, why is every portfolio piece on YouTube so dark?). Yet there's a depth to it—not a coming-out story, but a first-date story.

I'm trying to set the white balance on the camera when Nash jumps into the frame and strikes the most ridiculous pose.

"Hey," he says.

"Not camera shy. Noted."

Every time I pivot to reposition the camera to focus on the white backdrop, Nash follows the lens. His lips are tinted frosting blue and I'm shaking my head like, *If you're going to eat the props, at least be more stealth about it? Maybe?*

I let the camera hang heavily around my neck and put my hand on my hip, half annoyed. "I'm trying to white balance."

"What's that?" Nash asks.

"It's so the camera understands the lighting of the room, basically. There's a setting for incandescent light already, but my parents taught me to never trust the presets. So I always do it manually."

Nash is perplexed. "You need to tell a camera that white is white?"

"Yeah. Look." I hold the camera up, pointing it toward Autumn and Molly, putting the finishing touches on the date-night table set. "See how everything is kind of tinted yellow? It means the last time Autumn used it, she was probably shooting outside in natural light. Our eyes compensate for this light change automatically, but the camera needs help. So . . ." I point the camera back toward the white backdrop and scroll through the menu to the white balance setting. Accept the changes, and pivot back to get Molly and Autumn in the shot. "We white balance."

Nash looks ridiculously impressed, like I'm speaking in quantum theory or something. "That looks so much better. Why don't I know this?"

I shrug. "It only matters to professionals. Our phones do it for us."

Nash jumps back in front of the camera. "How do I look? Now that I'm properly white balanced?"

"Your blue lips really pop now," I say.

"I'm going to pretend you said the camera loves me," Nash says.

It does.

"The cupcakes are for the film, you know."

"Autumn said they're for talent. As Hetero Boy Number Six, I'd argue I qualify as *talent*."

I turn the camera off and pop the cover on the lens. "Nash is also a diva. Noted."

This is what we're like now. Behind a screen, we actively stress about NYU and gossip about the latest publishing drama. In real life, I'm still anxious and awkward, but also surprisingly good at bantering with Nash.

In both worlds, Nash is my friend.

It's kind of a perfect situation as long as I don't think about it too hard.

Nash looks like he's about to retort, but he's cut off by the sharp pitch of Autumn's whistle. She's standing on a chair, looking authoritative AF, and announces that we're ready to go, filming is about to commence, quiet on the set.

"Thanks for the camera lesson, Upstate," Nash whispers before moving to his assigned post.

The buzz of chatter settles into quiet as everyone disperses to their designated spots. Nash's is by the counter with the rest of the Hetero Boys. Mine is by Autumn's side. I hand her the camera and give her the rundown of the settings I've selected, all based on her instructions. She double-checks anyway. I'm not offended; it's what any good director would do. It's her film, after all.

She looks at me. "Am I ready?"

I nod. "You're ready."

Autumn smiles at me. "Let's do this."

The next few hours are a blur of cinematography and cupcakes. First, we shoot a montage of boys for the opening scene in which the camera is Lil's eyes. With each new boy, each new date, the shot doesn't change—only the face at the center. Tall boys and short boys and black boys and Asian boys and multiracial boys (Nash) and blonde boys (Sawyer). In editing, I imagine these shots will be cut like a flip book.

Cut into this montage will be shots of Lil's phone under the table. First, we're not sure what Lil is doing, but as the dates continue it becomes clear that she is swiping through girls on a dating app. She swipes right and matches with Monique, and after suffering through a string of boring hetero dates, we move into the final scene we're shooting now, Lil and Monique's first date.

"Think about how much of our life we spend looking down," Autumn says.

She's standing on the second to highest step of a ladder, her Nikon D800 pointed downward to capture an aerial shot of two heads looking at their phones—cupcakes uneaten and coffee cups full. Autumn captures cinematic angles of Lil and Monique holding their phones under the table. Lil and Monique laugh off the awkwardness as they realize okay, yeah—they're both still swiping through Bumble. More laughter as they decide to place their phones on the table—facedown—and finally, *talk*.

It's beautiful, I think.

The magic is going to be in how Autumn captures the moment. Whenever I have an idea for a different camera angle or a creative shot, I suggest it. Sometimes it works, sometimes it doesn't—but it's so fun to be a voice behind the camera again.

But this is different from working on my parents' docs. Those were so professional, so detailed as to be predictable after a while. Not in content but in process. Working on Autumn's film with Le Crew is all about discovering the unknown. I learn Molly is an *incredible* designer—she handmade the dresses Lil and Monique are wearing. Sawyer has an unexpected eye for light design, and by the end of the shoot he's adjusting the placement of a light for each scene without me even needing to ask. Nash is stupidly charismatic on camera even with just two lines, and I'm grateful Autumn is the one with the camera in her hand, controlling the shots.

Three hours later, Autumn says, "That's a wrap!"

In my head, the final shot of *Look Down, Swipe Right* zooms out on Lil and Monique through the bakery window and everything slowly fades to black.

Less than twenty-four hours later, Le Crew is back at Maple Street Sweets after hours—this time, though, we're off camera, eating takeout pizza and studying for the SATs. Except no one besides me is actually, you know, *studying*. The exam is being administered next weekend and all seniors are taking an in-class practice test tomorrow. I pretty much need to accept my 600 math section fate, but I'm stubborn. So more practice tests it is.

". . . I mean, it's easy money and I'm building a portfolio so, like, win-win," Nash says.

I'm scoring practice test number three, but my focus shifts from the College Board to Nash and Molly's conversation. It's everything Kels already knows—Nash is turning his art skills into a business. Still, it's cool hearing Nash talk about Outside the Lines out loud.

"At this rate, I'll have enough in no time," he says.

Molly sighs loudly and it's extra.

"For your applications?" I ask.

He shakes his head. "Have you heard of BookCon?"

I almost choke on pizza crust.

"BookCon?" I ask.

"It's, like, this giant epic conference for YA fandom. Every major publisher is there, there are tons of author signings, and you're allowed to fill suitcases with books. It's basically the Holy Land."

"He's not going for fandom," Molly says.

"He's going for a *girl*," Sawyer adds.

Nash throws popcorn at them. "Shut up." He looks at me and hesitates, like he can't believe he's about to tell me whatever he's going to tell me. "You know my cupcake bookstagrammer friend? We met online—"

"Kels," Autumn interrupts. "Her name is Kels."

"It's not weird, I swear," Nash says. "We like each other's blogs, and we've been best friends for years, but we haven't met yet. Well, we applied for this blogger panel. It's a long shot for me, but not for Kels. She's pretty popular. I'm, um, kind of hoping we meet there. Either way."

I process Nash's words. *Either way.*

It's not like I forgot about BookCon. It's just—clearly, I haven't been thinking about it as much as Nash has.

"It's not weird, I swear," Nash repeats.

"It's a little weird," Molly says. "I mean, no one even knows who Kels really is."

Nash looks at Molly like this is a constant point of tension in their friendship; like he's so tired of having this conversation. "I do, though. In the ways that matter, at least."

Autumn grades our practice exams.

Molly rolls her eyes.

Sawyer gags.

"I don't think it's weird," I say quietly.

"Thanks," Nash says. His ears are tinted pink with embarrassment, but his smile is sincere. The subject changes, *thank God*, and I'm just sitting here in silence, still pretending to work on another stupid practice test while I try to process what this means.

". . . You should! *Please*, Halle."

My attention snaps up from my test to Molly, who is making puppy dog eyes at me.

I have no clue why, but I pity Sawyer because it's an extremely hard face to resist.

"Okay?" I answer.

"Oh my God, seriously?" Molly pumps her fists and yells, "Victory!"

"Um." *What did I agree to?*

Autumn smirks. "You just got her out of the *Kung Fu Panda* marathon she's been putting off since Rosh Hashanah."

Nash shakes his head. "Now *I* have to watch five hours of *Kung Fu Panda*."

Molly is doing a victory dance around the bakery.

"Molly bet that she'd get you to come bowling with us before Nash could," Sawyer says.

"Oh," I say, a bit blindsided. I really wish they'd stop making bets about me.

"It's cool," Nash says. "I'm just glad you're coming."

Molly, high on her victory, sets a timer and insists that we settle in for an *actual* practice round. Pencils scratch against paper and calculators crunch answers around me but I can't even comprehend question one. Occasionally, my eyes shift to Nash, watching him answer questions with scrunched eyebrows through my peripheral vision.

I should cross my fingers behind my back and hope I don't get the panel.

But I can't. I want BookCon to want me so bad.

Even if it's a complication, I can't pretend I'd pass up this opportunity. I won't.

It's been weeks and people are *still* engaging with my *Read Between the Lies* content. *Fireflies and You* hype has dwindled since Alanna's been quiet, and the next YA publishing scandal has since unfolded and the discourse has moved on, for now. One True Pastry is more perfect than it's ever been.

Which makes me believe Kels has a shot at BookCon. For real.

The BookCon gods are emailing me in December, either way.

I need to tell Nash the truth, before this theoretical problem becomes a real one.

November 15

Elle Carter
HI. AN EDITOR TOOK MY MANUSCRIPT TO
SECOND READS
5:28 PM

Amy Chen
elle. oh my GOD
5:29 PM

Elle Carter
I mean, it probably won't amount to anything.
But it COULD.
5:31 PM

Samira Lee
Positive thinking only, please!
5:32 PM

Amy Chen
can we video chat ASAP? please?
TONIGHT???
5:35 PM

Samira Lee
YES
5:36 PM

Elle Carter
YES
5:36 PM

Samira Lee
Kels? Join us this time?!
5:37 PM

Amy Chen
WE MISS YOU
5:40 PM

November 16

OMG just seeing this now—congratulations,
elle!! that's SO ridiculously amazing
8:36 AM

Elle Carter
Thanks, Kels.
8:39 AM

Elle Carter

Glad you're still here with us! We were about to send out a search party.

8:40 PM

TWELVE

Fact: Bowling nights are stupidly competitive.

It's kind of hilarious.

Like, I haven't taken bowling this seriously since I was twelve and determined to beat Sinclair Daniels, the product of the douchiest producer Mom and Dad ever had the—ahem—*privilege* of working with. Us doc kids usually made our very limited social life at the bowling alley, because every town in this country has a bowling alley within a ten-mile radius. If my parents had a late night or a long weekend of interviews and filming, one of the assistants would corral all the kids into the minivan and take us to the nearest one.

Sinclair Daniels was the only brat to ever give me a run for my money.

Because, plot twist: I, Halle Levitt, am a bowling prodigy.

Okay, fine, *prodigy* is a strong word for what is probably the most useless talent on the planet. But I'm good. I can't draw or run a mile without running out of breath, but I can consistently bowl over 200 like it's my job.

It impressed Le Crew the night of my first bowling appearance. Now, they're just annoyed.

Because that's the thing about bowling. It's the type of game that everyone thinks they can win, with no actual skill.

When Nash and I arrive at the bowling alley, Autumn and Molly already have their shoes on. Sawyer is sitting on the floor, his feet in the butterfly position. He leans forward, his head barely touching his toes. Of course, Sawyer is stretching before the bowling begins.

"It's a sport," Sawyer had said the first time I witnessed his elaborate routine. "Gotta get limber."

Do you, though?

"Hey!" Molly says, greeting us with a hug.

I've learned to lean in to Molly's embrace instead of flinch away. Autumn waves from her seat on the bench in front of our lane. She's hunched over the table, writing phrases on notecards and putting them in Sawyer's upside-down Red Sox hat.

"Is it lyrics night already?" Nash asks.

Molly shakes her head.

"Shakespeare?" Autumn asks.

"Sports metaphors?"

See, Le Crew doesn't just bowl. That would be too easy, after years of doing it weekly. No, to raise the stakes, there is a challenge string. During this string, there is a very particular set of rules that must be followed. If someone breaks said rules, the first person to shout penalty gets to throw a gutter ball on the rule-breaker's behalf.

Like I said, stupidly competitive. But also, stupidly fun.

Last week, Molly filled our score screen in with the most ridiculous names, and we could only call each other by those names all night—I lost that round so bad. We've also practiced our Spanish skills, and I don't know if Señor Carpenito would be proud of us or horrified.

I don't think I've ever laughed as hard as I do bowling on crisp November Saturdays with Le Crew—and sometimes I wonder what challenge strings I've missed out on and why it took me so long to say yes.

Molly holds the Red Sox hat out to me.

"Pick one."

I do.

Lefty, it reads.

"First round, you're bowling lefty," Molly says.

"Just me?" I ask.

"Just you," Molly confirms.

Since when do the challenges not apply to everyone?

Molly bats her eyelashes at me, all innocent.

"Come on, it'll be fun! You can stink like the rest of us."

"Speak for yourself!" Sawyer says, now standing up and bent over in a forward fold.

"Find your breath, Sawyer," Autumn says.

Sawyer flips her off.

She's so competitive, Nash mouths to me.

I smile at him, but this weird feeling settles in the pit of my stomach. I shake out my hands and go over to pick up my ball, but I still can't quite calm the bubbles building up in my throat. It's all fun when everybody has stupid rules against them to hinder their game. And okay, I get it, they're targeting me since I'm *good*. But if my winning streak is so detrimental to their good time, why am I even here?

Maybe I'm getting worked up over nothing. I'm not going to overthink it.

Holding the ball in my left hand makes everything feel off-balance. I know this isn't going to go well, so I attempt to position myself to minimize the damage. Step back, three steps, except now my right foot is in front and it's all wrong. I release without really meaning to, but the ball doesn't curve off into the gutter like I expect it to. Five pins fall. That was . . . not terrible?

Molly's face melts out of its confident smirk.

My second ball still feels awkward but knocks down four more pins.

Maybe I *am* a bowling prodigy.

"Damn, Levitt. You could've mentioned you're ambidextrous," Sawyer says, hand up for the high five. Then he leans in. "Please excuse my girlfriend," he says, voice low.

I sit at the score screen seat and Nash slides next to me with a basket full of fries. I take one and dip it in ketchup. It's a good fry—it has the perfect ratio of crunch and salt. It'd just be better dipped in honey mustard, but that's a Kels-Nash argument.

"Nice work. Molly's going to pop a blood vessel before the night's over."

"Is she okay?" I ask.

"SAT scores," Nash mouths.

After we took the in-class practice SAT, Molly asked everyone their best scores from previous exams. At lunch. It was awkward for me, but everyone else is used to Molly's grade nosiness, so they spilled their numbers without hesitation.

But October scores were emailed this morning. Molly took the SAT last month too—she's extra like that. If she liked her number, she'd have been the first to share it.

"Did she tell you?" I ask.

Nash nods. "It's not even *bad*. It's just not Molly."

"Damn."

Nash's box lights up on the score screen and he is off to bowl. "Uptown Funk" blasts through the Rock n' Bowl speakers and Nash dances over to the balls like he's Bruno Mars.

It's adorable. He's adorable.

Nash, a lefty, bowls the frame with his right hand. The first ball flies into another lane and knocks down four pins, to the absolute delight of a giggling toddler. The second ball is much less aggressive in execution and rolls down its proper aisle, but barely clips two pins off the left side.

"What are you doing?" Molly asks.

"Only Halle can bowl lefty, right?" Nash asks.

Molly rolls her eyes. "You *are* a lefty."

"That was not specified."

"I probably would've yelled *penalty*," Sawyer admits.

"You can't . . . I didn't. That's not the rule!"

Molly has the look on her face that I get when everything

is Suddenly Too Much and it doesn't matter that she's been cold and competitive to me all night. I grab her hand, look to Autumn to grab the other, and we drag her across the alley and into the bathroom. Inside, I see Molly's eyes are wet. Her perfect eyeliner is smudged at the edges.

"Breathe," I say.

Molly exhales.

"I'm not going to college," she says.

"Don't be ridiculous," Autumn says.

"Well, I'm not going to Cornell," Molly says.

"Screw your parents' Ivy League expectations," Autumn says, rubbing Molly's back.

I hold Molly's hand like Ollie would hold mine.

"Their faces," Molly says. "The first thing Mom did when Shabbat ended was check my score, and when she saw it I couldn't run away fast enough."

"Molly," I say, "you're the actual definition of well-rounded. If Cornell doesn't want you because of a number, NYU is definitely not going to want me for mine."

Molly wipes her eyes. "You're stressed about scores too?"

I nod. "I've been *killing* myself to improve my math score. It's not happening."

"Also, look at it this way. If you don't get into Cornell, it's because of something arbitrary. If I don't get into USC, it's because I straight-up suck at my dream career!" Autumn says, biting her lip.

Molly shakes her head at Autumn. "But that's completely subjective!"

"Exactly," Autumn says.

Molly pulls a paper towel from the dispenser and wipes her nose. "So what you're saying is we're all stressed about things we cannot control?"

"No. I'm saying we *can* control not being stressed about this!" Autumn says.

"I don't think it's that easy," Molly says.

"Me either," I say.

"Well, I say if Cornell or NYU doesn't want you because of a number, screw them," Autumn says.

"Screw them," I repeat.

Molly squeezes my hand.

"Screw them," she whispers.

I win again, but I throw two genuine gutter balls with my left hand.

"You did it for Molly," Nash says as he drives me home.

Yeah, Nash drives me now. That's a thing. It's kind of the only option, if I want to socialize with Le Crew on the weekends. I don't have a car and Gramps has rejoined his brotherhood friends for Saturday night card games. I'm so happy he's going out and socializing that I don't even care that I had to stop treating the Corolla like it's mine.

"Did not. Bowling lefty is *hard*," I say.

"If you say so. But thank you," Nash says. He turns the radio down so the soft rock guitar hums in the background. "I love Moll, but sometimes it's hard to empathize."

"I'm stressed too," I say. "I get it."

"But at the end of the day, Molly is going to get into Cornell. If not, well, at least she knows she can still go wherever she wants. Molly is getting out of here, and . . ." Nash's knuckles are white against the steering wheel.

"You're not," I say, finishing his sentence.

Nash nods. I suck in a breath and think about what words should come next. At first, I was nervous accepting rides from Nash—I almost said no. But I've been starting to like hanging out with Le Crew too much to continue to turn down bowling. The rides are usually a mash-up of stupid jokes and car karaoke, though. Not this.

"Why?" I ask.

Nash shrugs.

"Money. Paranoia. Fear. Hypochondria. All of the above. It changes daily. I swear, if my parents had it their way, I'd never leave the house. I get it, sometimes. But I'll be lucky if I can convince my parents to let me live on campus at UConn. Molly is sobbing over Cornell and Autumn is lusting over USC and Sawyer has multiple offers from recruiters—and it's hard not to hate them sometimes."

"That sucks," I say.

"A lot," Nash says.

Rain ricochets off the windshield, beating down heavier than the quiet drizzle that has accompanied the first part of our drive home. I focus my eyes forward, watching the windshield wipers crank up in speed, trying to imagine what the hell will come out of Nash's mouth next.

Online, Kels and Nash are going to New York. We've always acted like it was never even a question. But it's so much more complicated than getting in or not. Especially if his parents are seriously not letting him leave Connecticut.

"Yesterday, my mom asked me what I thought about getting my degree online. She tried to argue the economics of it, but she's so transparent. I nodded along and told her I'd consider it, but seriously? Just because Nick left home and died doesn't mean I'm going to."

Nick? Nash's words don't compute. Am I forgetting something? This seems like a major thing to forget. My brain runs through every story Nash has ever told Kels or Halle—until it hits me like a punch in the stomach.

Neither of us knows who Nick is.

And now Nash is driving too fast and it's downpouring.

"Nash," I say.

He's never told Kels about anyone named Nick. He told me he's an only child. Or maybe I assumed. I don't know. I *do* know I'm the last person in the entire world who should be in this car with Nash right now. Where is Molly or Autumn or Sawyer or *literally anybody else*?

"Nash, slow down."

We hit a giant puddle and the car hydroplanes. Headlights blind my vision, so I cover my face with my hands and scream. Nash regains control of the car and I'm suddenly having an out-of-body experience, because I'm literally screaming at him to pull over, to pull over *right now*. He pulls into the parking lot of the

Middleton Public Library, the first place we met, *of course.*

Nash presses the heels of his hands to his eyes. "I'm so sorry."

He's crying. Then I'm crying.

We're a hot mess.

And I can't help but think if we had just hydroplaned into a tree and this was the end, Nash would never know I'm, well, me.

"Nash," I start.

"I don't know why I said that," Nash says.

"Nick?" I ask, thinking back to Rosh Hashanah and our moment on the swings. Nash saying, *It sucks so bad, losing the people who are supposed to still be here.*

My insides clench before Nash even speaks, and for the first time, I really hate that I haven't told him I'm me. I've been collecting Nash stories that are *mine*, Halle's. Things about him Kels never could know—the scar on his hand, his goofiness in front of a camera, his smirk whenever I say something that surprises him, his Bruno Mars dancing.

I don't know if I'm ready for this story.

"My brother," Nash says. "He was so excited that my parents were letting him go to soccer camp, right? He was twelve, finally old enough to attend a whole week of sleepovers and soccer with his friends. He couldn't stop bragging about it. I was eight—too young to go. Also, I hate soccer."

It takes every fiber of restraint in my body not to say, *I know.*

"He had a collision with another kid during a scrimmage. Bonked heads. Everyone thought he was fine. He *was* fine. Kids hit their heads all the time. Except it turns out Nick had a tiny bomb in his brain and that set it off. He never came home."

I close my eyes. *Breathe*.

"I'm so sorry," I say.

Nash shrugs. "It's just bad luck. But Mom and Dad—they blame themselves every day. There are zero symptoms of a sitting brain aneurism, but it doesn't matter. They think they should've known. They shouldn't have let him go. It's bullshit, but they believe it and now I'm the only kid they've got left."

"That's not fair," I say.

"The worst part, though? I barely remember him. Like, at all."

"You were little," I say.

Nash shrugs again. He leans back against the seat and closes his eyes. The rain isn't letting up. If anything, it's getting worse. "It's what my comic's about. REX? It helps me to process things, I guess. Figure out what memories are mine or stories I've been told. I don't know."

I can't stop the tears that continue to stream down my cheeks. When Nash says it straight like that, it's so obvious that REX is personal. I—I thought it was just art. Fiction. I'm an idiot. Art is never *just* art.

"It doesn't get easier," Nash says. "People will say it does. They're wrong."

I wipe my cheeks. "I know."

I think if I'm going to tell Nash the truth, I'd better do it now. This is probably as close to the point of no return as it's going to get. Maybe past it. He told me, Halle, about Nick. If I can't tell him about *a blog*, if I can't trust him after that, I don't deserve him.

I reach for his hand resting over the gearshift and cover it with mine. He doesn't flinch away and I can do this *I can tell him*. But then he looks at me with his bloodshot eyes and tearstained cheeks and it hits me all at once—I *can't*. He just trusted me with something major, how can I tell him he didn't know who he was telling it to?

It'd be selfish to overtake Nash's emotional moment with my own drama.

Except, now I'm not sure *what* to say.

What would Kels say if the screen were between us? Why didn't Nash tell her?

"I'm sorry," Nash says. "That was so stupid—driving that fast."

"It's okay," I say. "We're okay."

"I'm applying anyways," he says. "To NYU. I need to know if I can get in."

"You will," I say.

It's late, way past curfew, but we stay put until the rain quiets into a soft pitter-patter.

Nash turns the car back on. "Thank you. I don't talk about Nick enough. But it felt okay, talking about him with you."

"Grief is weird," I say. "I get it."

"I know," Nash says.

Nash drives us home slow and silent.

November 21

Kels @OneTruePastry 3hr
Welcome to #ReadWithKels! This month, we're rereading
FIREFLIES & YOU by @AlannaLaForest because FILM
ANTICIPATION!!!

Kels @OneTruePastry 3hr
If you're reading along, introduce yourself! Name, favorite
genre & link your blog if you have one! #ReadWithKels

Kels @OneTruePastry 3hr
"Summertime is for Mama's blueberry pies and fireflies" GIVE
ME A MORE ICONIC FIRST LINE, I DARE YOU.
#ReadWithKels

Kels @OneTruePastry 3hr
JONAH. Grateful every day that I now can picture him as
Elijah Rhodes. A++ casting, imo #ReadWithKels

Kels @OneTruePastry 3hr
Where is the Daisy to my Annalee? #friendshipgoals
#ReadWithKels

Kels @OneTruePastry 3hr
"Sometimes, I wonder what's beyond the bayou. Sometimes, I believe that one day I'll find out." #ReadWithKels

Kels @OneTruePastry 2hr
Thanks for another excellent #ReadWithKels!! We'll be back next week for ch. 3-4. Same place, same time, same book <3

#ReadWithKels
[See 100+ new Tweets]

Olivia Brooke @livlaughlove333 2min
Rereading along with @OneTruePastry! CAN'T WAIT FOR FIREFLIES AND YOU. #ReadWithKels

Deja Louis @dejavuwho 5min
Are you even a true F&Y fan if you're planning on seeing the movie?! #ReadWithKels

Jamie K. @jamiereadsya 11min
WHY ARE WE STILL HYPING THIS? #ReadWithKels

Abby In Wonderland @abbyinwonderland 17min
I'm just staring at my screen like 🙃
#ReadWithKels

THIRTEEN

Turns out, functional Gramps is kind of a hard-ass.

November blends into December, and I am still grounded.

"You're always on that phone, and you couldn't answer one of my three calls?" Gramps had said to me when I got home.

"It's called silent mode?" I tried to joke.

Gramps does not appreciate sass unless he's the one giving it.

I was sentenced to two antisocial weeks, too shocked he was so upset to argue further. If this had happened when we first arrived, I don't even think he would've noticed I was missing. I got too used to the freedom, to not expecting anyone to account for me.

There are still five days left until I'm free. Gramps didn't confiscate my phone or laptop, though, thank God. Halle and Kels's simultaneous absence would have been a ridiculous coincidence.

In some ways, the sentence has recalibrated me. Without the ability to spend my free time with Le Crew, I'm able to focus on the thing that matters most: One True Pastry.

I send my first-ever pitch rejection.

I also block my first troll.

My following ironically has plateaued, thanks to the *Fireflies and You* trailer drop. The film is back in the YA Twitter spotlight—and most of my movie tie-in content has gone live. Posts I scheduled *months ago*—an interview with the cast before production started, Twitter chats encouraging my followers to reread the book, a throwback post boosting my original, spoiler-free reviews. It has been extremely divisive with my followers.

I wish I could tell Twitter I'm not pro-Alanna—I'm pro-Grams.

But I can't.

And OTP isn't the only thing I've been neglecting.

I've never been so disconnected from Amy, Elle, and Samira. Now that I spend most of my weekends with Le Crew, it feels like I'm always catching up on their conversations. Elle's novel is on submission, Samira's submitting her art portfolio for a competitive summer program, and Amy is drowning in midterms. I know this. I do still *read* the messages when I can.

It just feels impossible to respond after five or seven or twelve subject changes.

Not to mention I don't even know how to talk to them right now. They're Nash's friends too. What if I slip up and say something about Nash? I want to tell them so badly, but they'll freak out. Ollie is on my case enough. Besides, they don't know who I am either.

My friendship with Nash isn't the only one at stake. Pretty much all of them are.

I need to find a better balance between Halle's life and Kels's.

It's the Sunday after an uneventful Thanksgiving and I'm spending my morning working on my personal statement. The cursor blinks in an empty word document and I stare at the screen, totally stuck. How can passion be infused onto the page? This essay has to compensate for my below-average SAT score—but it can't be a gushing blog post. This needs to be professional, but still show who I am.

All in six hundred fifty words or less.

I twirl Grams's necklace between my fingers, unsure how to essay.

I text Nash.

question.
12:00 PM

Nash Kim
Oh! Hey. What's up?
12:01 PM

I almost drop my phone when his answer comes through as Nash Kim. *Crap.* I can't talk to Nash about my college essay! Obviously, it's about One True Pastry. This is supposed to be a Kels-Nash conversation. I contemplate what to do, staring at the screen for so long the brightness fades.

Actually.

Maybe Nash *can* still help me.

What was your college essay about?
12:02 PM

It was about Nick. I wrote about why I started
REX and the elusiveness of memory.
12:03 PM

Wow. That sounds really smart.
And kind of sad.
12:04 PM

I hope so. Isn't that a college admissions
reader's dream?
12:05 PM

Valid.
12:06 PM

That's helpful. Thank you!!
12:06 PM

I'm glad I texted the wrong Nash. It feels like we've been online talking about NYU since the beginning of our friendship. Him writing about REX. Me writing about OTP.

But of course, Nash's essay is about more than a web comic. Mine is about more than a blog.

Grams. Everything I know about publishing is because of

Grams. She's the reason I know I need to work in publishing; how I know I *need* to scream about books for a living. How many eight-year-olds sit on their grandmother's lap at Thanksgiving and ask, *Grams, how are books made?*

Grams, do you know Junie B. Jones?

Grams, can I be an editor, just like you?

She told stories to me about the life of a book, a tale of Bella Book's journey from inception to production to distribution, á la the *Schoolhouse Rock* "I'm Just a Bill" song. Yes, of course she knows Junie B. Jones. And if I want to be an editor, great—but there are so many aspects to publishing that I can explore, like publicity or marketing.

Tears splash against my keyboard.

Breathe.

I can't write an essay about One True Pastry and not write about Grams. But I'm not sure if I'm ready to.

The words might not flow out of me today—but they will.

Decision made, I close my laptop to take a much-deserved break from my emotions. I stand to stretch my legs and reach for my phone on the nightstand, just as Gramps knocks. His knuckles rap against the door four times, evenly, so I know it's him before the door swings open.

"Hal?"

I plaster a smile on my face and tell Gramps to come in.

"How's it going?" he asks.

I'm instantly suspicious. Gramps has never, not once, asked me, *How's it going?*

"Okay. I'm just working on blog stuff, you know. The usual."

Gramps knows about One True Pastry because he did, in fact, threaten to take my laptop away and I freaked out. *Take away my miniscule social life*, I said. *Take away my driving privileges*, I said. *You can even take away my phone if you really want to. But I need my laptop.* I typed in onetruepastry.com and showed him what it is, who I am. The website, the Twitter account, Kels.

I told him none of it would even exist without Grams.

This is why you're always online? he asked.

I nodded.

It's amazing, Hal. Seriously.

I retained my laptop privileges. Thank you, OTP.

"You're on parole, kiddo," Gramps says. "Honestly, this doesn't even feel like a punishment anymore. You, Halle Levitt, are free."

I'm frozen, unsure what to do or if I even *want* to be free. It's like now that I've gone back behind the screen, I'm not ready to burst the bubble again.

"*Free* as in, get out," Gramps clarifies.

I reach for the oatmeal cardigan draped over my desk chair. "Are you *that* sick of me?"

"Yes," Gramps deadpans. "No, I just have a house project I need to work on today. I kicked Ollie out too—he took Scout to the dog park with Talia."

"Project?" I ask.

"Don't worry about it," Gramps says.

"Thanks?"

Gramps nods. "You have thirty minutes to vacate the premises."

He disappears down the hallway and I'm not sure what he's working on, but I'm just glad he seems *excited* about something. Grams had to leave the house during Gramps's project days too, so this feels like more movement in the right direction.

I'm free. What to do with this freedom? I *should* go to the library and continue working on my essay. Instead, I send a message to my group text with Le Crew.

I'M FREE
12:32 PM

Molly Jacobson
OMG FINALLY
12:33 PM

Autumn Williams
🎉 🎉 🎉 🎉
12:35 PM

Molly Jacobson
🛍️??
12:37 PM

So I spend my first hours of freedom dress shopping at the Middleton Mall.

Winter formal is two weeks away, and I don't know how many times I have to tell Molly I'm not going before it sinks in. She's had her dress for weeks, of course, but Autumn still needs one. I agree to tag along because I need to get out anyway, and for the first time in almost two weeks, I *can*.

"In and out," Autumn says. "I need to pick up Marcy and Max at four."

"Dogs have no concept of time, Autumn."

"Marcy knows when I'm late."

Autumn is the most popular dog walker in Middleton, with a client list that continues to grow. There is a winter chill in the wind—signaling that Autumn's peak season is about to begin. At thirteen, she started the business when no place else would hire her because, well, child labor laws. She managed to charm most of the neighbors into paying her to walk their dogs with USC fliers and her perfect smile.

If Autumn is on a mission to be in and out, Molly's mission is to take her sweet time. She scours H&M's sales racks and pulls no less than half a dozen dresses for Autumn to try on in a variety of colors and styles. Autumn rolls her eyes but takes the stack of dresses into the nearest fitting room.

"You're not wearing black," Molly says to Autumn's only pick, a trademark black A-line cut with lace sleeves.

"Why not?" Autumn asks.

"You always wear black!" Molly says.

"Is senior year really the time to go off-brand?" Autumn counters.

Molly holds out a fitted jade dress. "Just try this one."

Autumn takes the dress. "That is going to be way too tight."

"Just try it—and toss that one over for Halle to try on."

"How come Halle gets to wear black?" Autumn asks.

"Halle isn't going," I say.

"Because Halle isn't allergic to color—and oh my God, stop," Molly says.

Autumn sighs and shuts the dressing room door behind her. Moments later, the black dress flies over the top of the door. Molly catches it and hands it to me with a pointed look that says, *Don't even argue.* If trying on a stupid dress will placate Molly, fine. I'll do it. It's not like she can force me to go to the dance. Friday was the last day to buy tickets.

In the fitting room, I shimmy out of my jeans and T-shirt. Fitting room mirrors are the devil incarnate, so I avoid looking at myself too much. I thought I did a better job covering up the stress zit on my chin, but even a brief glance shows, lol no.

I slip the dress over my head and—I don't hate it. The A-line skirt flatters my hips and the lace sleeves are totally my style. Give me a pair of red pumps and some lipstick to match, and I'd look pretty fierce.

I'd look like Kels.

"What do you think?" Molly asks.

I open the door.

"Oh my God! You look *so* good!"

"Wait, but that's my dress," Autumn says, opening her door. But then she looks at me. "Ugh, no it's not. You do look good in that."

Immediately, she turns to Molly. "And this, as predicted, is too tight."

"Okay, agreed. Try the purple one next. That's Halle's dress, I do declare."

You can have it, I mouth to Autumn.

"Hey!" Molly says. "No!"

The rest of the dressing room session goes pretty much like this: Molly dictating Autumn's fashion choices and my life choices. Autumn settles on a dark purple knee-length dress. The skirt has a sheer black overlay with floral appliques. It's a fair compromise and Autumn looks gorgeous in it.

Molly is still holding my lace-sleeves dress in her arms and trying to convince me that it's destiny, that it was made for me to wear to the Middleton winter formal. We finally move on to shoes, but she keeps it up.

"Give me one good reason why you're not going," Molly says.

"Well, it'll probably induce a panic attack, for one thing," I say. "I don't do crowds."

"That's a good reason, Moll," Autumn says.

"Oh," Molly says. "I don't want that, obviously."

She pauses to consider but I know she's not done. I turn in to the size-eight section of the sale rack, putting distance between us.

"But . . . okay. I totally wasn't supposed to tell you this, and I'll deny it if you say I did, but now that we found the perfect dress and if you leave this H&M without it—well, you just need to know this. Nash wants to take you."

"What?" Autumn asks.

"What?" I repeat, stunned.

"He told you that?" Autumn asks.

"He did," Molly says. "Which is, like, such a breakthrough because, well—honestly, because you're not Kels."

My face is turning red.

I can feel it.

Do not betray me now, face.

I stay hidden in the next aisle of shoes.

"I swear he thinks he's in love with her. Nash has never been on a date, and I know it's because of her."

Molly is so dramatic, I almost start laughing. I cover my mouth with my hand to stop myself from bursting into a fit of hysteria. It's as ridiculous as the time my phone blew up with ship names. Amy decided ours is *Kash*, which is so bad I let her have it. *Love?* That is such a loaded word. Nash really hopes to meet Kels at BookCon, sure. But Nash can't be *in love* with Kels? Can he?

I believe one thousand percent you can be friends with someone you've never met.

But *in love*?

"Anyways," Molly says, "he wants to take you and I think you should say yes. Please say yes."

We meet face-to-face at the end of the size nines.

I cannot say yes.

"I don't have a ticket," I say.

"Please. I'm student council treasurer for a reason."

I want to say yes.

"I don't dance," I say.

"You don't have to!" Molly says.

She's getting close and she knows it.

The idea of going to a dance with Nash, who wants to go to a dance with me, Halle, is breaking me. There are a million—a *billion*—reasons why I should say no. But the idea of going on a date with him? Once the possibility is out there it's impossible not to think about.

I want to more than I even realized. Because the whole internet says Nash is into Kels, but that can't be true if he wants to go with me. He wants *me*. In this moment, thinking about being at a dance with Nash, Kels has never felt further away.

Maybe this is what we need. Maybe if we do this, he'll figure it out without me having to say anything.

"Fine," I say, before I can change my mind. "Okay, I'll go."

Molly sucks in a breath. "Really?"

I nod.

She throws her arms around me.

Molly has an impossible way of always getting her way.

Ollie raises his eyebrows when I show him the dress.

"You're going?"

"Molly coerced me."

He sits up on his bed, closing his laptop and sliding his headphones down so they're around his neck.

"But how? I, your own flesh and blood, have yet to achieve such a feat."

"Nash wants to take me."

Ollie narrows his eyes at me. "Halle."

I sit on the end of Ollie's bed, legs crisscrossed. "I know. How do I do this?"

"You don't?" Ollie says.

"Thanks," I say. "Really supportive."

"Sorry, I just—what the hell, Hal? Is this a *date*? Are you, like, *trying* to mess with him now?"

I stand. I'm already insecure enough about this whole ordeal. I don't need shit from Ollie.

"Okay, bye."

I leave Ollie to his *Star Trek* marathon and he slams the door behind me. I fully plan to collapse onto my mattress belly first, wondering what the hell I got myself into. Does Nash want to take me as, like, a *date*? Or as friends? The way Molly said it, well, it *sounded* like a date. But now I'm wondering if she meant as friends.

Either way, it's complicated.

I kind of hate how much I want it to be a date.

Across the hall, my bedroom door is shut tight, which is weird because I never leave it closed, mostly because I love coming home to find Scout curled up in a ball on my bed. There's a piece of paper taped to the door.

SURPRISE! is scrawled in black Sharpie.

I instantly tense because I don't do surprises. But its Gramps's handwriting, so I twist the doorknob, and push.

Disbelief smacks me in the face.

Grams's bookcases line my lavender walls—and they're filled

with her books. Placed side by side, they take up an entire wall, just as I imagined they would in the floor-plan sketch of my dream room. Five matching mahogany bookcases with six shelves each.

I can barely breathe, but I step closer and see they're organized in reverse alphabetical order like Grams would have them, because A should know what it feels like to be last sometimes. I take a tour of the shelves, my fingers brushing along the spines. Her library is truly a force—featuring classic and contemporary YA fiction, heart-pounding mysteries, and the most epic collection of foreign editions of *Pride and Prejudice*, the book that made Grams fall in love with words. I haven't read all these books, not even close.

Now, they're mine.

I sink to the ground and cover my mouth with my hand to keep my sob inside because *this* was Gramps's project. It must've taken him all day, and it must've been so hard—but he built her shelves for me.

"Whoa."

I look up and Ollie is there. Even though I know he's pissed at me, he holds out his hand and I take it, letting him pull me up to my feet.

"This was the super-secret Halle project?"

"You knew?" I ask.

Ollie shrugs. "Sort of. Not really; he wouldn't say. But I didn't think he'd be able to do *this*."

I know what he means. Every day, I worry that Okay Gramps will revert back to Super Sad Gramps. But maybe I haven't been giving him enough credit.

Downstairs, Gramps is watching *Jeopardy!* on the couch, Scout curled up in his lap.

I sit down next to him. If I look at him, I'll sob and make it awkward.

So I say, "Thank you."

Gramps just squeezes my hand, then asks me if I know the question to a *Hamilton* answer before someone buzzes in and says, "Who is Lin-Manuel Miranda?"

We spend the rest of the night shouting the questions to Alex Trebek's answers.

Nash to Kels, at the dance

Nash Stevens
So. I don't think Halle's gonna show.
7:15 PM

This is why I don't go to school-sponsored
programs . . .
7:15 PM

The music blows.
7:16 PM

This blows.
7:16 PM

Sometimes I think it'd be cool if, like, we went
to the same school.
7:16 PM

We'd totally make fun of this together.
7:17 PM

Maybe I'd even dance with you.
7:17 PM

FOURTEEN

With my red pumps and matching lipstick, I look fierce.

Except all the lipstick in the world isn't going to make me *feel* fierce.

The Middleton High School gym has been transformed into a winter wonderland. We enter under a blue balloon arch to a cacophony of white noise humming beneath the boom of the deejay's speakers. Everyone is in the middle of the gym floor, dancing to a new Beyoncé track that is absolute fire. Teachers and parent chaperones line the perimeter of the gym, and it must be awkward for them to watch their students and children dancing like one giant mob.

Even off the dance floor there are too many people. Too many voices and bodies.

Nash and I are meeting here. He offered to pick me up, but Gramps wanted to drive Ollie and me together and, well, how could I say no to that? Turns out, Gramps is so soft when it comes to his dressed-up grandchildren attending school-sponsored events. He spent *way* too long taking *way* too many pictures. Seriously, it took five minutes just for him to realize his camera was in selfie mode.

Except now I'm twenty minutes late and I can't find anyone.

I need something to do, so I make a move for the snacks table while the line is still relatively short. I bypass the chips, veggies, and cookies, and go straight for the beverages.

"Hal-lee! Hey, we've been looking for you."

Of course, Sawyer is at the snack table. This should've been my first move, really.

"Hey! Where is everyone?" I ask as I grab a bottle of water.

The song changes to a loud rock ballad.

"What?" Sawyer yells.

I lean forward and yell into Sawyer's ear.

"Molly and Autumn haven't left the dance floor! Nash is over at the table!"

Sawyer points to Nash. He's hunched forward with his elbows on the table, typing into his phone. Mine is on silent, but I can't help but wonder if those texts are for Kels or for me.

"Cool! I'm just gonna—catch you later!"

My fingers itch for my cell phone as I approach Nash, but I figure I'm already anxious enough. It's probably better that I don't know whatever he's saying to Kels or me. Away from the speakers, the music isn't deafening anymore, and though I might have partial hearing loss, I can at least now speak at a normal level.

"Hey," I say.

A flustered Nash immediately stands up and stuffs his phone in his pocket.

"Oh, hey. I was just going to—"

"No need to stand on my account."

He's dressed in a light blue button-down shirt and black dress pants, no tie. His hair is styled with the lightest touch of gel. He's seriously leveled up from his typical sweatshirt-and-jeans combos.

He looks really cute.

"You look nice," he says.

I don't know if that's a compliment or not. *Nice* is a terrible word. A non-word really.

"You too," I say.

"Thanks."

I sit down and take a sip from my bottle of water. *Nice?* Nash is being so weird. I'm not sure why. Ever since the night of the storm, Nash and I talk pretty much every day. But now we're at a stupid high school dance and we can't even say hello without fumbling.

"Are you going to dance?" he asks.

"Oh. I don't."

Nash raises his eyebrows. "Really? Me either."

It's almost as though Nash doesn't want to be here just as much as me.

"Halle!"

Molly and Autumn appear from the crowd of dancers, faces shiny with sweat. Yet somehow, their makeup hasn't moved. I need to learn what this magic is. Autumn looks amazing in her compromise dress, and Molly glows in gold.

"Come dance!" Molly says.

She grabs my hand and pulls me up so I'm standing.

"No, I don't—"

"Tell me if you're feeling anxious and we'll disengage. Promise," Molly says.

She takes me by one hand and Nash by the other. Nash just looks at me and I hope he can read my face, because it says, *I am getting the hell out of here as soon as Molly lets go of my hand.*

Molly pulls us toward the dancing, but we barely graze the perimeter of the sea of bodies. Everyone is jumping around to the music, hands in the air, singing along to the lyrics. Molly bops her head to the music and raises our hands in an attempt to make us dance with her. Nash moves his shoulders in the most awkward fashion. My feet stay planted firmly on the ground. I shift my weight as I count the beats of the music, making sure my heart isn't beating faster.

Sawyer joins our awkward non-dance circle.

"Wow, you two are the life of the party," Sawyer says to Nash and me.

I fold my arms over my chest. Nash flips Sawyer off.

But Sawyer just pulls Molly away from us and twirls her like a ballroom pro. Or at the very least, like he's seen a few episodes of *Dancing with the Stars.* Molly laughs so loud amid the twirls. She lands in a dip just as the song's final notes sing through the speakers.

They are kind of couple goals right now, and Sawyer is our savior for taking her attention away from us. High-energy pop transitions to a slow song, one of Ed Sheeran's many ballads, and

Nash and I make eye contact. He gestures toward the tables and I agree, grateful. We make our grand escape, with a pit stop at the drinks table.

"Boring," Molly shouts, her arms draped around Sawyer's neck.

Nash sighs. "She is too much sometimes."

I sip on a Sprite. "She thinks she wants to see me dance," I say. "I promise that's something nobody needs to see."

Nash laughs. "Hey, do you want to get out of here?"

"What?" I ask.

"Well, I don't want to be here. You seem to be having second thoughts. Why are we here?"

"Second thoughts?" I say, feeling my face get hot. "This wasn't my idea."

"What?"

"Molly said . . ." My voice trails off because suddenly, it clicks. "Oh my God."

It clicks for Nash too. "She told me—"

"—that I wanted to go with you?" I ask, eyebrows raised.

We have been totally, completely, duped by Molly Jacobson. This is all an elaborate setup orchestrated by Molly to—what, exactly? Help Nash realize whatever feelings he thinks he has for Kels can't be real?

Kels. Thinking about her sends my thoughts spiraling and oh my God, the gym is too hot. My dress is too tight; the lace sleeves scratch against my skin. My hair is too curly; my lips are too red. Everything is too much. Too Kels.

Nash never wanted to go to the dance with me, Halle.

"Ugh. *Molly*." Nash runs his hands through his hair. "Not that this is terrible or anything, I just don't do dances."

"Me either. Okay, yeah, let's go," I say.

I text Ollie that Nash and I are heading out and to text me if he needs a ride home.

Ollie
I'll be fine. TELL HIM.
7:45 PM

I slip my phone into my purse and Nash and I exit out the back door before Molly notices we're gone. We run to his Prius like this is a prison break, like we're moments away from getting caught and dragged back into the hell that is a school-sponsored party.

In the car, I ask Nash where we're going.

"It's a surprise," he says.

We drive to the tunes of our car karaoke choices and I have no idea where we're going, but it's okay if it means I'm no longer suffocating in a high school gymnasium.

An hour later, I'm sipping the best chai latte I've ever tasted.

Nash brings me to the Main Street Café, his favorite coffee shop in downtown Westport. It's a fusion between coffee shop, bar, and live music. The bar stretches along the entirety of the back wall, displaying a variety of sandwich and pastry options.

Dark wood tables fill the space, each with their own display of succulents as the centerpiece. Nash and I sit at one of these tables, with a perfect view of the corner stage. It's open mic night, and on the stage currently is a woman with dyed red hair, singing what I am convinced is the entirety of Alanis Morissette's *Jagged Little Pill* album.

I keep my hands wrapped around my mug, the heat warming my cold fingers.

"This is so good," I say.

Nash sips on his flat white.

"Yeah, this place is great. I came here a lot during my 'musician' phase."

"Oh? Tell me more," I say. Kels knows nothing about a musician phase. Nothing.

Nash laughs. "Not much to tell. I'm a self-taught mediocre guitar player, and Kat, the manager, was nice enough to let me play at open mic, so I'd take the bus in on weekends when my parents thought I was getting lessons. I sing decent enough to offset my terrible guitar technique."

I nod to the stage. "So you brought me here to show off your skills. I see."

"No way. It was a dumb hobby," Nash says, laughing.

"In fourth grade, I started a knitting club. Mind you—I only knew how to knit scarves out of fuzzy yarn. But I was committed. *That's* a dumb hobby," I say.

"It's practical?"

"Twenty-five fuzzy scarves are not practical, they're a problem.

By the end of *Gentrify, U.S.*, I had every doc kid knitting their own scarves."

"You were quite the trendsetter."

"Us doc kids had to stick together." I nod.

"That must've been so cool," Nash says. "Being on the road like that. Going place to place. I'm jealous."

I shrug. "It's cool. But it's lonely, too, you know?"

Nash nods. "Yeah, my friend—Kels—it's the same for her. She's an army brat, but she says that too."

My brain screams, *You are a lying liar*.

I ignore it.

"Okay, I'm sure you get this a lot, and I don't want to be *that* person. But I'm totally going to be that person. Have you met any, like, celebrities?" Nash asks, leaning forward in his seat.

"Not to brag, but I went to the Academy Awards last year," I say with a hair flip.

"No way," Nash says.

I nod. "Way."

"That's so cool," he says.

"It's great at first. But you can't skip through the boring parts when you're sitting in the audience."

"Ouch."

"It'll be cool when my parents finally win. But also kind of scary. They've been working toward their Academy Award for, like, literally my entire life. If they win—*when* they win—what happens next? Will it be enough?"

Of course, it's a question without an answer.

Nash takes a long sip of his coffee and Alanis Morissette transitions into a pitchy Jason Mraz.

"I'm jealous of *you*, you know." I say this so softly I'm not sure Nash hears me at first.

He looks up at me from the brim of the flat white.

"Why?"

"You have people," I say.

"So do you," Nash says.

"I don't have anyone's embarrassing diaper pictures or falling off bikes or classroom inside jokes. I don't have history, not with anyone."

Nash shrugs.

"You're lucky," I say.

"Yeah," Nash says. "History is relative, though, right? Like someday you'll look back fondly on your first and only winter formal, in which you lasted approximately thirty minutes before ditching for a chai latte. This'll be history."

If my life were a novel, I'd totally kiss him right now.

Instead, I lean back in my chair and listen to the music. Nash's phone vibrates again on the table, once, twice, three times in a row. Molly, Molly, Molly. He scans through the messages, blushes, rolls his eyes, and then stuffs his phone into his pocket. In that order.

I don't know what to say next, so I check my own silenced phone. There are a million Molly texts too, ranging from the calm where are you? to the panicked where are you?!?!? to omg please don't hate me please don't hate me please—

I lock my phone and toss it in my purse.

We're quiet through the next few sets, enjoying the mash-up of singer-songwriter and bluegrass music. It occurs to me in this moment that I've never had a friend like Nash, not in my entire life. Nash the person, not Nash the pixels. Nash doesn't make me feel like I need to have something to say all the time. This friendship isn't based on words.

I can just sit back and listen to the music.

We sit until the lights dim and the music has faded into tomorrow. I need to make a playlist of acoustic covers from tonight and carry it in my pocket. Songs that will remind me of winding up in a coffee shop in lace sleeves and red lipstick, of Nash and Halle in real life, of the most perfect chai latte in the entire world.

I wake up in the passenger seat of the Prius, Nash shaking my shoulders.

"Halle," Nash says.

I jump. "What the—?"

"You fell asleep as I was giving my grand moonlight tour of Westport. Can't say I'm not a little bit offended, but you're forgiven," Nash says.

I yawn. "Time?"

"Like, quarter to seven."

"In the *morning*?"

I rub my eyes—mascara flaking off from the night before—and blink some moisture back into my sticky contacts. I wipe the drool from the corner of my mouth—oh my God. I try to orient myself. It is tomorrow morning, and I am in Nash's car. Why am I still in Nash's car? It's still dark outside and we're parked in a spot overlooking the ocean. Ice-gray waves crash against the shore, and not going to lie, my breath catches in my throat when I see that we're at a beach.

I can't remember the last time I've seen the ocean.

I'm kind of in this half-awake ocean trance, until I catch my reflection in the rearview mirror and see the residue from my once-perfect red lips smudged around my mouth. Instinct—and embarrassment—makes me swipe the back of my hand over my mouth, which admittedly does little to fix the situation.

Nash pops open the center console and hands me a napkin.

I take it, wordless. What do I even say, seriously? Sputter one of my many questions? *Why didn't we go home last night? Why are we at the beach, in December, at dawn? Why do you still look so perfect and I'm, like, a zombie with a half-melted face?*

"My parents think I'm at Molly's," Nash says. "But I really didn't want to go to Molly's."

It's tomorrow. I didn't come home last night.

I reach for my phone. "Oh my God, Gramps." I'm going to be grounded until graduation. At least.

"I texted Ollie. You're at Molly's too."

Ollie is going to give me *so* much shit.

"Where are we?" I ask.

"The beach," Nash says.

I roll my eyes. "Thanks."

Nash laughs. "We're still in Westport. Sherwood Island, technically."

"Okay. But why—?"

"Give it, like"—he glances at the dashboard clock—"thirteen more minutes."

"That is specific," I say.

"Well, sunrises are kind of like that, you know," Nash says.

That escalated quickly. With the word *sunrise*, my heart does this weird thing in my chest, like it's constricting with all its might so it doesn't explode. I try to decode Nash, his expression, his body language. He can hear my heart, I'm sure of it.

"I haven't been here in a while, actually," Nash says, looking toward the ocean. "We used to come here when I was little. Every summer solstice, I'd fall asleep in my bed and wake up at the beach. Nick would try to drag me out of bed. That's the part I remember the most. But it was also peanut butter banana sandwiches my mom packed in a Goofy cooler and watching the sunrise, the four of us. Together."

Every time Nash opens up to me, I'm a confusing mix of elation and guilt.

"I love that," I say.

"Yeah," Nash says. "It's one of the few memories of us that I know is mine, so I try to get down here whenever I can. To remember. Molly and I sometimes still make the solstice trip. My mom tried, for a while, but I think it hurts her being here just as much as it helps me. I don't know if that makes sense."

"It does," I say.

"Thanks for being here," Nash says.

"I mean, it's not like I had much of a choice," I say.

Literally, I don't know why I speak most of the time.

Nash just laughs. "Shut up."

Before long, the sky is illuminated in iridescent shades of orange and it's the most beautiful thing I have ever seen. Like, there are no words. I don't even think to take a photo with my phone because Instagram is not going to do this sky justice.

How do we spend every day sleeping through this sky?

Nash shifts so he's facing me better, one shoulder pressing against the back of the seat. His smile is so big and I am a puddle. He looks at me like . . . like I don't even know, and I lose my words. Something has shifted, though, I can tell. He looks at me from behind his glasses, like he's trying to form the right words to say next. I adjust in my seat, mimicking his sideways position, ignoring the lace sleeve scratching against my skin, but his eyes don't move from mine.

He's going to kiss me.

Nash is going to kiss me.

I *want* him to kiss me.

"I'm sorry about Molly," he says.

I blink, confused. "I mean, I think it worked out okay."

"Yeah, but what she did wasn't cool. I forget sometimes how controlling she can be." Nash pauses. "I just—"

Something has shifted, again. And not in the *Hey, let's kiss each other's faces under a romantic sunrise* kind of direction. Nash chews on his lower lip and runs a hand through his hair, smile gone.

What did I say? He's the one who brought up Molly, not me.

"It's Kels."

My heart plummets.

"I'm sorry," Nash says. "It's just—I feel. I don't know how to say this in a way that makes sense."

I lean back in the seat and stare straight ahead, straight through the windshield. I can't look at him. I can't. I need to know what he's going to say next. What he's trying to say.

"I'm sorry. I didn't mean to, like, lead you on or anything," Nash says.

"We're watching the sunrise."

"Right," Nash says. "I can't believe—look, I like you. I really do. That's why I'm so pissed at Moll right now. Because it's not you, it's just . . . there's someone else."

"Kels," I say.

Me, I don't say.

"I just—I can't explain it, okay?" Nash says. "I am *so* sorry."

"Stop apologizing," I say. It comes off sharper than I intend it to.

"I think I might love her. Maybe," Nash says.

"You don't even know her," I say.

If you did, Nash, you'd know she's me.

Nash shrugs. "I don't expect you to get it. No one does."

I want to scream that I'm the only one who *would* get it. The whole stupid truth, but it's too late. The magic of the sunrise has faded into the typical morning sky. Reality punches me in the stomach. He doesn't like *me*, Halle. Not like Kels. I was right this whole time.

"Can you just take me home?" I ask.

"Halle—"

"Don't."

We drive back toward Middleton through the morning haze, the sunrise in the rearview.

Nash's fingers fumble through the radio stations, unable to settle on a song.

I close my eyes because I can feel it coming, the panic that starts in my stomach and rises up through me. I hear Ollie's voice in my head telling me to *breathe*, imagine the pressure of his hand. *You will not cry in front of Nash right now. You will* not *cry in front of Nash.* He thinks I'm embarrassed or hurt or whatever because he rejected me. But really, I feel so *stupid.* Stupid for thinking I could split myself like this. Stupid for romanticizing sunrises. Stupid for thinking anyone would like me as much as they like Kels.

Stupid for thinking that I, Halle, could just be Nash's friend.

Kels's Inbox

Tori DiVitto
LILAH ROSE LIVED HERE: a twisted psychological thrill . . .
Dec 12

McBride, Alissa
Sadie Thompson Interview Confirmation
Dec 12

BookSparks
12 Winter Romances for Perfect Fireside Reading
Dec 12

Maria Trapp
THE DISTANCE BETWEEN US cupcake cover reveal pitch
Dec 12

Nash Stevens
REXXXXXXXXX
Dec 12

Becca Holloway
Re: BookCon Bloggers IRL Panel Application!
Dec 12

[1-50 of 1,044]

FIFTEEN

I hear Michael Scott's voice the moment I enter Gramps's house.

Ollie only watches *The Office* when he needs to shut off his brain. He has every episode memorized, I swear.

I find him stretched out on the couch, eating a bowl of Rice Krispies in neon orange sweats and his Darth Vader T-shirt. He has something to tell me.

"You look terrible," he says.

"You too," I say on my way upstairs to change.

I put on leggings and my THE BOOK WAS BETTER T-shirt. Wash all the makeup and residual mascara away. Brush out my knotted curls and twist my hair into messy bun. Remove my contacts and put on my plastic frames. I feel infinitely better.

I still look pretty rough when I catch my reflection in the mirror, but at least I'm comfortable. I'm not planning on leaving the house today. Being friends with my boss's son has its perks—Sawyer got us the day off. Bless him.

Scout pokes her head out from Gramps's cracked door.

"Morning, girl," I whisper. "Come on."

She follows me downstairs.

Ollie hasn't moved, and he's not laughing at any of the jokes.

"Okay. What's up?" I sit on Gramps's leather recliner chair, legs crossed, and reach for the remote to pause the TV. Scout jumps onto my lap and curls herself into a tiny ball of floof. "Something is definitely up."

Ollie sits up. "You're not the only one who had a date last night."

"What?"

Ollie goes to every school-sponsored social event ever created, but he never goes with anyone. He prefers to fly solo—it's more fun with friends, he usually says.

Ollie shrugs. "Everyone paired off, and Talia asked me if I'd go with her. As friends."

"Whoa," I say. "I just thought—"

Ollie cuts me off. "Yeah. I know. You kind of *just think* a lot lately."

I flinch. *"Ollie."*

He scrolls through his phone. "So, is Nash a good kisser?"

It's *so* Ollie to make a passive-aggressive quip and then segue, leaving me feeling like trash. Ollie needs to know that I want to hear all about his friend date with Talia. But I'm also *dying* to talk about Nash, to let all my confusing feelings spill out of me all over the living room floor.

So I take the bait.

"I wouldn't know," I say.

Ollie looks up at me. "Wait. Is he mad?"

"No kissing ensued—and I didn't tell him."

"But . . . you were out all night. What happened?"

"There's someone else," I say. "Kels."

Ollie *ugggggghhhhs* into his pillow—the only appropriate response, honestly. I tell him what happened, every detail. The music, the chai, the stories. Falling asleep in the car and waking up to the sunrise. The moment I wanted to tell him—and all the reasons why I didn't.

"I . . . don't understand. A *sunrise*?"

"*Ollie.*"

"He's *so* into you!"

I shake my head no. "He's into Kels."

"Exactly. *You* are Kels—or did you forget that?" Ollie says. "I'm sorry, but you officially make zero sense."

"I'm not Kels."

"Whatever, Hal. You're literally both sides of this love triangle. *You win.* But you're determined to sabotage yourself."

He un-pauses Netflix and now I want to scream into a pillow. Ollie doesn't get it because a) he's a hopeless romantic; and b) he's totally jaded. He's barely even on social media—his universe revolves around baseball stats and his multiple, simultaneous crushes. He doesn't understand the nuances of building a brand. He doesn't understand I'm Kels *online*, for One True Pastry—to build a reputation in the industry separate from Grams. But *I'm not Kels.*

Not really. She's a version of me, a narrative, not truth.

Nash loves *a narrative.*

I pick up the remote and re-pause in the middle of a Dwight monologue.

"So," I say.

"So," Ollie says.

"Don't pretend there's not more to the Talia story and you're not dying to tell me. I'm sorry I've been distracted. Spill."

Ollie crosses his arms and we have a stare-off.

The tension is killing him, I know it. Even if he's annoyed with me, he wants to spill.

Ollie breaks. "Fine. Okay, don't freak out."

"I won't."

"Talia kissed me," Ollie says.

My brain is all exclamation points at this information.

"I kind of kissed her back," he adds.

"Oliver! What!"

"And . . . I liked it? I think. I don't know, we were dancing and then out of nowhere her mouth was on my mouth. And then her tongue was in my mouth. And I didn't hate it. At all."

"Wait, your first lady kiss was PDA?" I ask.

Ollie snorts. "A truly hetero moment."

"You don't have to, like, know what this means," I say.

"If you give me one more 'sexuality is fluid' spiel—"

"It is!"

"I *know*. It's still confusing, though."

"Fair," I say.

"Talia is super cool, I just never thought of her like—like *that*. But now that it happened, I can't stop thinking about it," Ollie says.

"Theory: You're attracted to Davidsons. Exclusively."

Ollie laughs. "Shut up."

"At least one of the Levitt siblings got some action last night."

Ollie launches a pillow at my face and everything else in my life is a mess, but we are okay again. We watch a couple of episodes of *The Office* together, quoting the lines of our favorite characters in real time. Ollie is a Dwight stan. I'm Pam forever. It feels good, just hanging out with Ollie. It feels like I need to do this more.

After one too many *that's what she said* jokes, I head upstairs to OTP and midterms. Ever since the *Fireflies and You* drama resurfaced, I've turned off my social media and email notifications. It's easier to conquer the trolls when I'm in the right headspace rather than letting them sneak up on me whenever. It's always the worst in the twelve hours following a new post. I'm trying to stay neutral for Grams—but it's *hard*.

First, I check my email, scanning the fifty-four unread messages for anything important, not really expecting to find anything. Until I see it. *Re: BookCon Bloggers IRL Panel Application!*

I stare at the subject line, unsure I'm reading it correctly. It's from *two days ago*. The BookCon gods popped into my inbox and . . . I didn't even know it? How is this possible? I should've been *obsessing* over this email, like I did when I was waiting for the *Read Between the Lies* cover reveal. Now it's just here and my brain is not prepared. My heart hammers against my chest, anxiety coursing through my veins.

Oh my God.

I click.

From: rebecca.holloway@bookcon.com
To: kels@onetruepastry.com

Re: BookCon Bloggers IRL Panel Application!

Dear Kels,

Congratulations! We are so excited to formally invite you to be on the Bloggers IRL panel to represent your blog, One True Pastry.

This panel brings together the most popular young adult book bloggers for a Q&A moderated by *Bustle's* Stella McQueen. Blogger panels have been in demand for years, and we're so excited to offer you a spot on our very first one!

A much more detailed email regarding the panel and BookCon itself will be emailed to all confirmed panelists this spring! To confirm your spot, please follow this link and RVSP via the Google form by no later than January 15th.

All the best,
Rebecca Holloway
BookCon Panel Coordinator

Congratulations.

BookCon.

RSVP.

I stare at the email for five minutes, overwhelmed by the validation. One True Pastry is good. *I'm* good. As far as the BookCon gods know, I'm just a teen who loves pairing cupcakes with books—and they still decided One True Pastry is worthy of being featured on a panel, that Kels is worthy of being a *Blogger IRL*.

BookCon wants *me*. I can put this on my NYU application.

Grams would be so proud.

I can't believe I went *two whole days* without checking my OTP email. Was I that distracted by the concept of going to a school dance with Nash? Definitely.

Oh my God, *Nash*. Where is he? How did he not immediately burst into my DMs when the email came in? That's not like him. This isn't like *us*. We've been talking for weeks about the inevitable BookCon decision coming soon. So where is he? Has he been just as distracted as I have? By what? *Me*?

No. He made it pretty clear last night where he stood. There's someone else. Kels.

My phone buzzes on my desk with a DM and my stomach twists.

Nash Stevens

Huh. So cone of silence, but I heard via Samira
that Annaliese de la Cruz got a spot on the
Bloggers IRL panel.
12:31 PM

I guess notifications went out to panelists
a few days ago?! I didn't get anything. I'm
assuming you didn't either.
12:32 PM

I'm still planning on going, I think. So if you still
wanted to meet up, I like wouldn't hate that.
12:33 PM

I stare at the messages from Nash, totally at a loss.

Nash has no clue I got the panel. But he's going to find out.

Which means he's going to find out everything.

I type and delete and type and delete.

Turn down the panel. He never has to know. Can you even handle speaking on a panel?

The reality of being on a panel, of *speaking* on a panel, hits me all at once. What if Stella McQueen asks me a question and I totally freeze up? Or what if I say the wrong thing and embarrass myself and ruin everything—for Kels, for OTP, for Halle?

Turn it down. It's smart. It's safe. Protect yourself.

Except . . . I can't. I might be an anxious mess, but I'm a *proud* anxious mess. I worked on my application for weeks. I genuinely love books and the YA community. I was *chosen*. I am enough. If there's anywhere I can be Kels, for real, it's BookCon.

Also? If I turn down BookCon for Nash and don't get into NYU, I'll never forgive myself.

My phone buzzes with another string of messages.

Elle Carter
Hey, Kels. Not sure where you've been lately, but we heard that BookCon panel emails have gone out. Here for you if you need it 🖤
12:45 PM

Samira Lee
I'm honestly shocked. I mean, Annaliese is ridiculous, but you're totally at her level.
12:46 PM

Amy Chen
do we know who else got it?
12:46 PM

Samira Lee
Nah. Everyone else is being pretty hush. Annaliese and I just go way back from our fanfic days.
12:47 PM

Elle Carter

I'm sure we'll know soon enough.

12:49 PM

I stand up from my desk chair and fall backward onto my bed. I can't tell my friends I got the panel without Nash finding out. Which means this is real. BookCon is happening.

Nash is going to find out I'm me. It's stupid to delay the inevitable, right?

What will he think? How will he feel?

He thinks he loves Kels.

I *definitely* like him.

He doesn't *hate* me.

I tap back into my messages with Nash. All questions of love aside, I'm just *so* tired of lying to him. But it's not like I can tell him the truth via a DM.

My phone buzzes. Three new messages.

I lock the screen and place it facedown on my night table, leaving all messages unanswered. I don't want to lie anymore. Every single time Kels texts Nash, it's a lie. I won't tell him about the panel from behind a screen, where I'm going to have to match his enthusiasm about meeting and pretend like we haven't already. I can't do that.

Until Kels can be honest with Nash, it's probably better she doesn't say anything at all.

Nash to Kels, a week in December

Sat, Dec 14, 1:14 PM

Rumor has it Celeste Pham also got a panel spot. So I guess maybe we shouldn't feel so bad that we're not BookCon adequate. ☺

Also, I have more REX. Whenever you're ready for it.
2:31 PM

I'm going to assume you are intensely studying for midterms. Which is probably what I should be doing tbh . . .
8:34 PM

Sun, Dec 15, 11:31 AM

link: If Alanna LaForest is against F&Y, So Am I.

lol so now it's actually pro-alanna to NOT see the movie? This is becoming more and more absurd . . .

I'll be working on my portfolio (read:
questioning everything) all day. Have you
finished your application yet?

Mon, Dec 16, 3:37 PM

. . . Is everything okay? I don't think we've
gone a whole weekend without talking in
literal YEARS? i don't even think i'm being
hyperbolic here.

Tues, Dec 17, 6:37 PM

Okay. I'd be legit concerned, but I know
you're fighting with trolls on twitter right now.
What's going on?

Thurs, Dec 19, 4:45 PM

So. Alanna tweeted and we're not talking
about it and that's just fundamentally
wrong.

Sat, Dec 21, 10:31 AM

I'm going back through our most recent
messages and I'm just really confused? Are
you mad at me?

Is it about Halle?

I HATE that I'm even asking that. But the last
time we really talked was before the dance . . .

Sun, Dec 22, 4:54 PM

Kels . . . ?

SIXTEEN

December is a blur of midterms and awkward Nash. We're not exactly *avoiding* each other. It's more like we try too hard to pretend everything is fine. He'll sit next to me at lunch to prove a point, but every time his arm accidentally brushes against mine, I am electrocuted. It's a miracle I'm still alive, honestly.

In Kels land, I RSVP to the BookCon panel, pray that time slows down between now and the March announcement, and take a midterms hiatus. Am I avoiding Nash online? Absolutely. Am I still reading every message he sends me? Totally. Do I *want* to answer them? Of course.

I *can't.*

Every time I think I'm ready to type words, I freeze. It's the *worst.* I've never been so *Halle* online before. But the ability to maintain my persona for Nash has shattered, thanks to what is otherwise the best thing that has ever happened to me. Now that him finding out is inevitable, it's impossible to be Kels.

So I'm not.

Kels is on hiatus. Halle has been taking midterms and polishing college applications.

There's no time to tell Nash, even if I knew how to formulate the words. It makes matters worse that I can't talk to my friends about this, that I can't freak out about this mess I made. Samira's reaction would be in cat memes. Elle would say, *This is a shocking development,* in a way that makes me know she's rolling her eyes behind the screen. Amy would be no-chill flailing. But at this point, I've also managed to be absent from their conversations for so long that I don't even know how to begin to insert myself back in.

So I don't. For days. For *weeks*.

I'm on hiatus.

Before I know it, we're lighting candles on the first night of Chanukah.

Real candles. Gramps doesn't have an electric menorah like we're used to. It's late this year—the first night is just two days before Christmas Eve. Gramps's menorah is the table centerpiece. Ollie does the honors, taking the lit *shamash* and lighting the first candle while Gramps mumbles the prayers under his breath. I just stand there and watch it burn, the one singular candle and the elevated *shamash* in the middle. The best part of Chanukah is the last night—it's only when all nine candles are burning in unison that I can fully appreciate the story of the Maccabees and miracles.

"Check the applesauce?" Gramps asks, and I come out of my trance.

We've done the secular version of Chanukah my entire life. Exchanging gifts and eating boxed latkes from Trader Joe's. Chanukah has never been a process or the kind of all-day prep that is associated with Thanksgiving. It has never been latkes from scratch and applesauce that simmers on the stovetop until the entire house smells like it.

In case it's not obvious, Gramps *loves* Chanukah.

I set the silverware and fill glasses with water and we all settle around the burning menorah for our Chanukah dinner. Ollie, Gramps, and me—we're a pretty great trio now, I think. Sure, it was a rocky start, but I can't believe we've only been living with Gramps for four months, and how much has *changed* in those four months.

Ollie sits next to me, dramatically thwacking a tub of sour cream on the table. I spoon a generous amount of applesauce onto my latkes and give Ollie major side eye. I don't know why latke toppings are so controversial. I just know that applesauce is the right choice, the *only* choice.

Ollie licks the sour cream spoon and I make gagging noises. We are the epitome of maturity.

I send Mom and Dad a Happy Chanukah message, along with a photo of my dinner plate and #TeamApplesauce. Ollie is the only #TeamSourCream mutant in the family.

Moments later, my phone buzzes with a text from Mom.

Mom
The superior topping!
6:14 PM

Ollie
#TeamSourCream4Life
6:16 PM

Dad
🍎 🍎 🍎
6:17 PM

Ollie looks up from his latkes. "Why are they even still awake?"

"Probably reviewing footage," I say.

It's almost one-thirty in Israel, but the better a project is going, the later my parents work into the night. At this point, Dad's probably trying to wrap up and go to bed. But Mom's glued to the raw footage. Every time Dad goes to press pause, Mom blocks the keyboard with her arms and says, *Just five more minutes.*

It's the filmmaker equivalent of *Just one more chapter.*

Gramps joins us at the table, reaching for the applesauce because he's on the right team. "It'd be nice to not have the phones at the table tonight."

"The parents say Happy Chanukah," Ollie says.

"Happy Chanukah. Go to sleep," Gramps says. "Tell them that's from me—and then put your phone away! It's present time."

Gramps is very serious about the Chanukah table being a No Phone Zone while we exchange gifts. Instead of one present every night, we decided just one gift each on the first night would be enough.

My present is for both Gramps and Ollie, but it's kind of the best.

I hand Ollie the envelope. His eyes bulge out of their sockets when he opens the card and *boom*, I am the best older sister on this planet. Success.

"How?" he asks, mouth open in awe.

"I'm the best," I say.

"Obviously! Oh my God . . ." Ollie's face scrunches. "There are only two tickets."

"It's a bro date," I say.

"It's too much," Gramps says, eyes wide, but he's smiling and that's how I *know* I've nailed it.

"Clear your schedule for April sixth, Gramps. We're going to the Red Sox home opener!" Ollie throws his arms around me. For a split second, I forget that lately he's annoyed at me ninety percent of the time. I forget that I haven't even told him about the panel yet. With this gift, I am the best, coolest sister again—if only for one night. I'm a pretty awesome granddaughter, too, if I do say so myself.

The small fortune was worth it just for the look on their faces.

Gramps gives Ollie his old baseball glove, but his gift for me is hand-wrapped—*not* in a bag—and suspiciously book-shaped. It's . . . kind of disappointing. I mean, I know I *am* books. It is my brand. I guess I thought maybe Gramps would branch out into other realms of my interests. I contain multitudes. I rip the menorah wrapping paper, wondering which book on my TBR will be inside.

I'm not expecting a book I've already read.

Pride and Prejudice—a collector's edition from Bath, home of the Jane Austen Center. All proper and British, like Grams promised. When she came back from the London Bookfair with Cadbury chocolate and a Harry and Meghan royal wedding mug, I just thought she forgot.

"*Oh,*" I say. I have the biggest lump in my throat. "Gramps—"

"It's from *us*," Gramps says. His voice cracks on us. "From our trip, before—well, you know. It was supposed to be your birthday present. I found it when I put up your shelves. You should open it."

There's a handwritten note on the first page. *Gram's hand-writing.*

> Happy birthday, Hal! Your collection
> is now complete. We love you. —Grams
> & Gramps

It's so *normal*, so *Grams*. Like she had no idea this would be the last gift she'd ever give me. But just seeing her writing again is the real gift. I throw my arms around Gramps before I have the chance to overthink it.

I hold the book close to my heart and it hits me all at once—

this Middle-of-Nowhere house is home. I can't even imagine saying goodbye.

"Thank you," I whisper into his scratchy grandpa sweater. "It's the best."

"Pretty sure these"—Ollie holds up the Red Sox tickets—"are better."

We laugh and I'm grateful he's always here to lighten the mood, even if he doesn't need to. Gramps has been doing better. *I've* been doing better. We can miss her without spiraling into sadness. It's *Chanukah*. We eat tons of latkes and tell stories and are comfortable sitting at the kitchen table for hours. Comfortable in our *togetherness*.

Before I know it, Ollie eats the last latke, his potato-to-sour-cream ratio a new level of disgusting, and the Chanukah festivities come to an end. Gramps turns the TV on, but the only choices are Christmas specials, so he turns it off and we start to clean up.

"Play that Chance guy," Gramps says to Ollie and I *die*.

Near the end of dish duties, long after Gramps has retired to his room for the night and in the middle of yet another Chance the Rapper chorus, the doorbell rings. At first, I think it's in the music, but then Scout jumps off her spot on the couch and runs to the door, so I know I'm not imagining it. The bell rings again. And again. And again.

"Answer the door, Hal," Ollie says, elbows currently deep in dirty dishwater. "Please make it stop."

My phone vibrates in my pocket.

Nash Kim

Open the door, Upstate

9:01 PM

I stare at the text, processing.

Nash is here? But we're still stewing in our awkward. I can't answer the door. I don't know how to be around him. I don't know how to *think* around him. Especially now that he's been texting Kels not just check-ins but actual worries about me, asking if I'm mad at him—for going to the dance with me? Almost as if I'm—Kels—is jealous? And I hate that. I *hate* that he thinks I'm mad at him about myself. I hate that this has all spiraled so far.

Mostly, I hate that he *wants* me—Kels—to be jealous.

The doorbell keeps ringing.

"Hal!" Gramps yells from upstairs. "Nash's car is in the driveway."

"Ollie's getting it!" I yell up to Gramps.

"No, I'm not," Ollie says, drying his hands with a paper towel.

"Can you tell him I'm not home?" I ask.

Ollie shakes his head. "It's *Chanukah*, Hal. Absolutely not."

I inhale a nervous breath. "Okay. I'll get it. Can you, like, stay out of sight?"

"Ouch." He clutches his hand to his heart.

"If you're going to eavesdrop, at least be stealth about it."

"You got it," Ollie says.

I exit the kitchen and walk through the living room to the front door. I reread the text five times before I'm brave enough to open it.

"Hi," Nash says, holding out a small gift bag. "Happy Chanukah."

"Hey," I say.

I don't know what else to say, so I take the bag and hold the door open for Nash to come inside. Less because I want him to, and more because it's too cold *outside* to join him. Nash follows me into the living room, and we sit in on the couch. Neither one of us knows what to say.

"Are you going to open it?" he asks.

"Oh. Right."

I remove the tissue paper to uncover a wrapped box sitting at the bottom of the bag.

"You are not that guy," I say.

"Oh, I am totally that guy."

Inside the box is, oh wow—an embroidery hoop. I live for this crafty stuff. Grams tried to teach me embroidery when I was younger, but she just ended up finishing all of my hoops for me. In the center of this hoop—it's a Nash original drawing. There's no mistaking it. It's a girl with long hair, her face hidden by the book she is reading. The muslin fabric is tie-dyed purple around the Book Girl, only she is not colored in.

It's beautiful.

"I saw that you had a few when we were painting your room. I drew it—and sent the sketch to one of my blog friends who has an Etsy. I know things have been weird since, well—"

"I love it," I say. "Thank you."

Nash relaxes. "Really? Cool."

"Really," I say.

It's such a small detail in my life, such a Grams detail. I can't believe he noticed. I can't believe he drew something for me. It's another complication, another check in the *Nash is wonderful* box and an X in the *Halle is trash* one.

I have no clue what this means.

"Can we talk?" Nash asks. "I'm really sorry—"

I cut Nash off. "I don't want to be awkward anymore."

Kels is on hiatus, while I am processing the reality that IRL, Nash and me are temporary. That's the truth, isn't it? I'm frozen in type because there is no way to spin this story where Nash won't see me as a huge liar. If I can't talk to him as Kels and things are going to blow up anyway, I think I'd rather enjoy these next few months being not awkward with Nash, as *Halle*, before we go down in flames.

"Me either," Nash says, relieved.

"Let's stop being awkward," I say.

"Yes. Okay. Good plan," Nash says.

We shake on it. To not being awkward anymore. I mean, awkward is an inherent part of the Halle genome. I will never be Not Awkward—only incremental amounts of Less Awkward. And before I went off in Book Land, romanticizing sunrises and creating A Thing out of nothing, I was at my Least Awkward around Nash.

Even if it's temporary, I want to get back to that.

Since we're now officially Not Awkward, I pop open a bag of Smartfood and we catch up. Scout is curled up in ball on the couch cushion between us.

"Have you sent in your applications yet?" he asks, passing me the bag of popcorn.

Scout has no chill around snack food. As soon as the bag crinkles she's up and sniffing, trying to convince us to share. Nash passes the bag to me and scoops up Scout, so she's sitting in his lap. He's scratching her ears and for a moment, I swear she forgets about the popcorn.

Scout on Nash's lap might be the cutest thing I've ever seen.

I shake my head no. "Still tweaking my supplemental essays. Did you?"

Nash nods. "Yesterday."

"How're you feeling?"

"Honestly? I'm not sure what to do with myself. You?"

I scoop a handful of popcorn and nod. "My application is ready to go. I *know* it is. But every time I go to press send, I think I should reread my essay one more time, or make sure I filled out all the forms correctly."

"How many schools are you applying to?"

I shrug. As much as I don't like the idea of applying to other schools, I know I need options. Since the first time Grams took me to New York, I've only pictured myself there, so I don't have a proper backup plan.

"I'll panic apply to twelve other schools, I'm sure. At least," I say.

Scout jumps off Nash's lap and runs toward the kitchen, toward the actual possible chance of treats. We've been stone cold with our Smartfood, and she's totally over us.

"I only applied to four. Should I be panic applying?" he asks.

I shake my head. "Nope. Not a recommended strategy."

"I feel like I need to be doing *something*." Nash drums his fingers against his thigh. "It's, like, as soon as I knew I wanted to study studio art at NYU, everything snapped into focus, right? I studied harder, started freelance designing websites, and took REX more seriously. It's always been this *thing* to work toward. Now I've applied and all I can do . . . is wait? It feels *wrong*."

"I mean, you could convince your parents to let you go."

Nash gives me *a look*. "I'll tell them if I get in," Nash says. "I don't need to deal with their Emotions and the pile-on of guilt if it's a nonissue."

"That's fair," I say. I want to throw my arms around him in a supportive hug. Instead, I throw popcorn at him. Because that's *not awkward*.

It's usually Kels talking about NYU in hypothetical future speak. Talking with Nash about NYU as Halle? It feels more real. The possibility of us getting in. But also? The possibility of us *not*. Maybe it won't happen for me. Maybe I'll be screwed over by standardized test scores. Maybe Nash won't be allowed to go. But there *is* a scenario where we're both there. Just now there's no scenario where we are both there and actually friends.

But we're not there yet. We're in Gramps's house, throwing popcorn at each other because we're trying to be *not awkward*. It's not easy like it was, but it's so much better than the way things have been these past few weeks.

We talk until he has to be home for curfew, then I walk him to the door.

"Thanks for the hoop," I say. "It's seriously great."

The tips of his ears flash pink. "I'm really glad you like it."

We stand in the doorway and stare at each other.

"So yeah," I say.

"So yeah," he says.

I put my hand on the doorknob and twist it open. Cold, crisp air whips into the entranceway, the kind of cold that comes just before a storm. I'm coatless so I shiver, but I step onto the porch and close the door behind us.

"See you next year?" Nash asks.

"I suppose so," I say.

"Happy Chanukah, Halle," he says, walking backward down Gramps's walkway, through the light snow that accumulated the night before. He unlocks his car and opens the driver's door. "We're good, right?"

I nod. "Welcome to the friend zone."

Nash's blush is so fierce, I have to laugh.

Kels's DMs, winter break
Amy, Elle, and Samira

Mon, Dec 30, 7:00 PM

Elle Carter
I don't expect you to answer this, but what
the hell is going on? I know you've been busy
and I'm trying not to take it personal, but you
also cut NASH out and now I'm even more
confused.
1:37 PM

Amy Chen
we've come to the conclusion that you're only
our friend when nothing is going on with you
IRL. and kels? that's not friendship. it's just
not.
1:39 PM

Samira Lee
I'm mostly confused.
1:41 PM

Elle Carter

We've been talking and decided we're starting
a separate Group chat. So it's gonna be quiet
here now. Sorry, but you can't just see our
conversations and not participate in them
1:43 PM

Samira Lee

Yeah, that's weird.
1:45 PM

Amy Chen

bye
1:48 PM

Nash
Tues, Dec 31, 11:01 AM

So. 3 weeks. Have I been officially ghosted?
Elle says you've been weird for MONTHS.
But . . . we haven't been weird. I don't think. I
honestly don't know anything right now. What
the hell?

Thurs, Jan 2, 2:13 PM

I hope everything's okay. I really wish you
would've just talked to me if it wasn't. It
sounds so stupid now—but I thought we had
something real. I guess we don't.

Bye, Kels.

SEVENTEEN

ireflies and You fandom is the definition of *extra*.

It's ten-thirty p.m., and the line for the midnight premiere nearly wraps around the building. It's mostly tweens and teens, all dressed in F&Y swag from the official Alanna LaForest Shoppe. Some even have brought the book with them and are rereading it in line. It's a sea of book covers—both the original and movie tie-in editions—everyone counting down the moments until their favorite book comes to life.

All the tension on Book Twitter? In this moment, it doesn't exist.

"I hate you," Autumn says.

Okay. So much for no tension. Her voice is muffled because she has a thick purple scarf wrapped around her face. It's January in Connecticut, meaning waiting for anything outside should be illegal. We're all huddled together like a cluster of penguins, trying to steal each other's body heat.

"I keep my double pinky swears," Molly says. "Autumn and I

were obsessed with *Fireflies and You* when it first came out."

"*Obsessed* is a strong word," Autumn says.

"Obsessed," Molly reiterates. "It's kind of the reason we're best friends."

"I'd prefer not to give Alanna LaForest credit for our friendship, k thanks." Autumn shivers. "She doesn't even want us here. Every opportunity she has, she says that her books aren't for us—that this movie shouldn't be for us."

"Can't you just, like, separate the art from the artist?" Molly asks. "And remember the good times? This means something to me."

"Me too," I whisper.

Autumn looks at me and her expression softens, then she turns back to Molly. "Halle gets a Grief Pass. You don't. Alanna acts like her teen fans are less than. Look around. Look who's here and who she's profiting from. Doesn't that piss you off?"

"Yet here we are," Sawyer says, as the line inches forward.

"It sucks," Nash says.

"Tell that to your girlfriend," Autumn says.

Nash takes a step backward as if the wind has been knocked out of him.

I bury my face in my scarf.

"*Autumn*," Molly says, her voice low.

Autumn crosses her arms over her chest. "What? Kels has a platform to call out Alanna, but instead chooses to post Twitter chats and *fifteen feelings about fireflies and you, in memes*, or whatever. I don't know if she's afraid to speak out because Alanna's fandom is ruthless—or if she's still very much a part of the ruthless fandom and doesn't want to alienate the critics. Either way, she's playing both sides like we're too stupid to notice."

Oh my God—Autumn reads OTP?

Nash opens his mouth to speak, but I cut him off. "Maybe Kels doesn't know what to say."

I don't.

"That's not an excuse," Autumn says. "Kels's silence? It's *so* loud. She's a total coward, Nash! Like, she can't *not* have an opinion."

"Autumn." Molly's voice lowers. "I think we can all agree that Alanna is gross. But she's not even affiliated with the movie so—"

"So what?" Autumn cuts Molly off. "You know what? I'm not giving my money to this movie, to her, especially not when there's a new Barry Jenkins film that deserves support playing across town." She picks her backpack filled with contraband snacks off the ground, tosses it over her shoulder, and marches toward the parking lot.

Molly chases Autumn and Sawyer follows Molly and somehow, only Nash and I are left in line.

"I get why you want to see this movie," Nash says. "I do too."

Do I want to see this movie? For the first time, I let myself think about this—what I think, without all the contributing factors and interests. Even without Grams.

Do I want to see it?

Not really. It hits me all once. Alanna has had every opportunity to apologize to the teens she has hurt. She has not. Alanna brushed off my cupcakes in an interview like it didn't matter. I didn't let it hurt until Autumn called out a truth that's so painfully obvious, even Grams would agree. This is just wrong. This whole time I let myself be caught in the middle, believing I didn't have a choice. But I can love *Fireflies and You* as Halle and criticize Alanna as Kels. That's supposed to be the whole point of Kels! Clearly, Halle has influenced One True Pastry just as much Kels has complicated my real life.

We're not the same—but maybe we're not as distinct as I've always believed.

So it's clear to me now that Kels would never see this movie.

And as for me, I can love the book that Grams helped create, but that also doesn't mean *I* have to see the movie either.

"Autumn is right," I say. "If Alanna doesn't think her teen audience is valid, why are we throwing the little money we, as teens, actually have at her?"

"I guess I don't think about it like that," Nash says. "I think I loved the book, the creative team behind the movie is awesome, and I want to support them—not Alanna."

"I know," I say, digesting this.

Our phones simultaneously light up with a text from Molly.

Molly Jacobson
There's an 11:30 showing of the Barry Jenkins movie at the Omni. I can't see F&Y when A's like this. You coming?
10:57 PM

Tonight is supposed to be sharing popcorn and staying out too late with Le Crew. Part of me wants to stay, to be with Nash, to pretend like it's a date. But it's not. And I know now I can't give my money to this film, not when Autumn slayed me with the truth like that. I'll deal with the Kels consequences in the morning.

I look at him. "I'm going to go."

His eyebrows rise, surprised. "Really? Okay."

I shoot Molly a text before I change my mind. "Yeah. Let me know if Grams would've approved, okay?"

I walk away from Nash before he responds, heading toward the front of the theater, my arms wrapped around myself because it's so cold. Molly says they'll wait for me at the curb and, wow, I am having a Feeling—because I've never had people like this, people who will wait up for me.

"Halle. Wait!"

I turn around at the sound of Nash's voice. He's here, not in his spot in line. And it was a decent spot, too, only maybe a third of the way back. He's here, his hood fallen in his haste to catch me, revealing a green-and-white knitted Celtics hat. Under the streetlights, his nose is bright red, and I see his breath every time he exhales.

"I'm coming too," Nash says.

Now it's my eyebrows that rise. "Really?" I think back to his offer to see this with Kels. The Kels who isn't speaking to him. The *Bye, Kels*.

"Let's go," he says.

"Are you sure?"

Nash stuffs his hands in his jacket pockets and nods. "Yeah. I want to see a movie with my friends. I want to see a movie with *you*."

I want to see a movie with you.

We wave to Molly to go ahead and I follow Nash to his car, processing what this means, thankful my face is already red from the bitter cold.

Damn you and your beautiful movies, Barry Jenkins.

Seriously, the way he's able to capture the smallest moments is breathtaking.

How I'm even paying attention when Nash's arm keeps brushing against mine is a testament to his cinematic skills, honestly. It keeps happening—every time Nash whispers an observation in my ear or offers me more popcorn or a sip of his cherry slushee. During a tense moment between the main character and his father, Nash's arm is against mine for ten whole seconds.

Yeah, I counted.

Ten-second arm touching is not an accident. It's definitely a lot more than *not awkward*.

To my right, Molly and Sawyer are holding hands. Autumn is on the end crying into her popcorn and thank goodness I'm not the only one wiping away tears.

By the time the credits role, we're up to thirty-two arm-brushing incidents.

We exit the theater, Autumn, Nash, and I trailing behind Molly and Sawyer. They're always holding hands, and I hate how much I want that. Despite all the friend zone conversation, I would reach out and hold Nash's hand right now if I could. I hate that in an alternate universe, I could.

Nash bumps against me on the way to his car and my God, why can't he stop touching me? I'm going to pop a blood vessel before this night ends. My heart rate spikes and my palms start to sweat and it's a rush of blood to the head every time Nash's skin brushes against mine.

I know he's not going to take my hand, even if he's feeling what I'm feeling, because of Kels. Even if he's mad at her, mad at the silence, those feelings don't just go away.

I know I should want it to stop. But I also know that I don't.

We say goodbye to the rest of Le Crew and the drive home is filled with car karaoke, film banter, and thought spirals. Every time Nash looks at me and cracks a joke, I think about brushing my arm against his one more time, or running my fingers through his messy hair, or holding the hand that's resting against the gearshift. The thirty-minute drive back to Middleton passes too fast.

Nash can't maneuver up my snowy driveway in his tiny Prius, so he shifts the car into park at the sidewalk. Middleton was slammed with a blizzard over New Year's—and I never want the snow to melt. Snow means puffer coats and knitted mittens, learning the shape of my breath, and vats of hot chocolate.

I open the passenger door even though that's the last thing I want to do.

"Thanks for the ride."

Nash opens his door too. "I can walk you up, um, if you want."

I nod, even though Nash has never, not once, walked me up. "Okay."

We walk along the snow-covered grass, avoiding the icy driveway.

"Sorry, but I still can't believe you cried." He laughs.

"And my tears are funny to you because—?"

"It wasn't a sad movie?"

I swat his arm with my hand, because if Nash can do flirty touching, so can I.

"Can't I just cry because something is beautiful?"

Nash smiles. "You can. But I will laugh at you. Always."

The way Nash says *always*, well, my heart actually skips. Because I have tried so hard to justify my secret, to write Nash off as just a boy, as transient, to avoid doing the hard thing— and then he uses words like *always* and reminds me that whatever this is doesn't have to be temporary if I can just figure out the right words to explain everything. Even if we're only ever just friends.

But the way Nash looks at me, I don't think he wants to be just friends. I have no clue what's changed. What about Kels? I know it should matter, but I think of what Ollie said. *I'm Kels.* I can explain that to him in a way that makes sense. Everything will change, but for the first time, I'm not afraid.

So I stand on my tiptoes, close my eyes, and kiss him.

Because I can. Because I want to. Because I'm going to tell him everything.

It's a quick kiss. I press my cold lips against his and . . . Nash just, like, becomes a statue. I mean, I am getting nothing from him and oh my God what did I do?

I step back.

Nash blinks.

Embarrassment slays me.

"Can we talk?" I blurt out.

The cold air whips through the space between us. If I were Kels, I'd delete that last sentence before I hit send. Come up with something witty. Actually, it doesn't even need to be eloquent or profound or witty. Not a cliché will do.

"I really, really don't want to just talk to you, Halle."

His lips smash against mine before I even have a chance to process the words. Lips that are ice cold, but the kiss is fire and I melt into him. Nash's hands are on my hips and mine are in his perfect hair and oh my God, I am kissing Nash.

Nash is kissing me. Halle.

When the kiss breaks, it's like coming up for air, except I don't want air anymore.

"Wow," Nash says.

"Wow," I say.

I know I should say something, but now I really, really don't want to talk either. And then Nash kisses me again and my mind goes blank. I forget who I am, where I am, and how to be a rational human. All sense of dignity flies out the window because I taste the want in Nash's kiss. I get lost in that want, in his hands on the small of my back and my hands on his face, pulling him closer to me, if that's even possible.

It's possible.

Until he pulls away.

"Is this okay?" he asks.

"Kels," I say.

I mean to form a full sentence. To blurt it out, lay it all on the table while my head is still foggy from Nash's kiss, in this moment when we are so close.

I am Kels.

Nash's mouth parts in a perfect *O* and his arms drop. "We should—"

I step back. "Yeah, we should."

It's almost two-thirty, according my cell phone. If we go inside, Scout will a hundred and ten percent wake the entire house up. *Don't wake me up* was literally what Gramps said when I asked if I could go to the movies tonight, when I told him it'd mean I'd be out past curfew. But we can't leave it like this, so we walk back down the driveway to Nash's car. I don't realize I'm shivering until he cranks the heat. We sit side by side in the front seats, looking straight ahead. There's an awkwardness to this moment, like the weight of what just happened slaps us in the face, but there's somehow still a charge in the air between us, too.

Nash chews on his bottom lip.

I play with my hair.

"So," Nash says at the same time I say, "Kels, I—"

"I'm so into you," Nash blurts, followed immediately by his deep blush. "Kels doesn't matter. It's just imaginary internet bull-shit I've held on to since I was, like, fourteen. I spent so much time waiting for her to give me a hint, but it's never going to happen. Seriously. Kels isn't real. This—you, are. Real, I mean. This is real."

Kels isn't real.

"I can't believe I just said that out loud," Nash says.

Words, Halle. Form words.

Nash waits for me to say something, but I can't. Nash chose me, but Kels isn't real. And I get it, but she also *is*. She's half of me, half of us in a way—but now she's reduced to just a series of zeroes and ones sending messages to a boy who loves graphic novels. For Nash, this supposed "hiatus" isn't temporary. Kels and Nash? That's over.

Truth is a bomb; it'll desecrate this moment.

I don't know how to form the words, so I lean forward and kiss Nash.

Because it's easy. Because I'm Halle, and I'm so into him, too.

Because Kels isn't real.

From: Alyssa Peterson <apeterson@sparkbooks.com>
To: Kels Roth <kels@onetruepastry.com>

unique cupcake inquiry!

Hi Kels,

Thank you so much again for the FANTASTIC cover reveal for *Read Between the Lies*. Ariel just about died when she saw your #CupcakeCoverReveal—and this might sound crazy, but we were wondering if you do catering?

Okay, hear me out. Ariel is launching *Read Between the Lies* at Central Square Books in Boston on April 6th—we would LOVE to have OTP cupcakes at the event! Obviously, we don't know where you're based or how realistic this is. However, if there's any way this can happen, we believe that it will bring amazing publicity to both *Read Between the Lies* and OTP. And of course, there will be compensation.

Let me know if this is something you'd be interested in!

Best,
Alyssa Peterson
Senior Publicist—Spark Books
apeterson@sparkbooks.com | 212-555-5059

EIGHTEEN

I wake up to the smell of bacon and eggs.

Gramps is at the stove, frying the turkey bacon. Ollie is chopping veggies to the beat of Fleetwood Mac's "Go Your Own Way." Scout runs around in circles, sniffing our scraps. I pause in the hallway to watch the well-oiled machine that is Gramps and Ollie making breakfast together and wow, my heart is so happy.

"Morning, Hal," Gramps says. "How was the movie?"

I hope my lips don't look as raw as they feel.

"Fun," I say. "Super fun. Yeah, so fun!"

"Sounds . . . fun," Ollie repeats.

We lock eyes and I hope mine scream, *We need to talk!!*

He gets the message and his look replies, *My room after omelets!!*

Gramps smiles. "I'm glad. Breakfast?"

I plop into my chair at the kitchen table. "Please."

Gramps slides a plate in front of me and I basically inhale the fluffy egg, cheesey turkey bacon goodness. Not as good as regular bacon, but Gramps keeps the *no pork* part of kosher, which means we can't have the real deal. Usually, I have a jab or two in me to complain about it, but this morning I'm too famished/anxious to care.

Ollie's eyebrows ask, *What's going on?*

My pursed lips scream, *News! News, I have!*

I don't know how I'm so calm because my insides are exploding with all the gooey shit that comes with kissing someone for the first time. It's the aftereffects of the kiss that remind me it happened, it was real, I didn't dream it or read it or make it up. I kissed Nash and he kissed me back and I am already thinking about kissing him again.

I'm dying slowly through the longest breakfast ever, I swear. When we're finished eating, we help Gramps clean up, thank him for the awesome breakfast, and then bolt upstairs to Ollie's room.

"Tell me everything!" Ollie whisper-screams.

I don't speak until the door clicks shut behind me. The moment it does, I spill the details of the entire night, from the flirty beginning, to the awkward middle bit, to the perfect ending. I love telling Ollie stories because he is the best listener—he animates at all the right moments.

"Finally!" Ollie says.

"I know."

"I told you so."

"You did."

Ollie plugs his laptop into the TV monitor on his desk and

opens *Toy Story* because it's the only appropriate thing to do when something major happens. *Toy Story* is one of our many things—we got in heated toddler fights about Woody vs. Buzz.

But now, we share them whenever Something Big happens. Like the morning Mad and Ari got their first nomination. Or the day last year when Ollie kissed Mark Lieberman under the bleachers after hitting the game-winning home run. Or the first time One True Pastry got a shout-out from an author on Twitter.

And now, hours after Nash said, *I'm so into you.*

It's definitely a *Toy Story* occasion.

Ollie looks up from his screen. "Wait. What did he say when you told him? I mean, you're glowing, so it must've not been terrible, right? He understood? Everything is great?"

I chew my lower lip. "Oh. I mean—"

As soon as it clicks, all enthusiasm drains from his face.

"*Halle.*"

"I know."

He speaks slowly. Emphatic. Like I'm a toddler. "You're going to BookCon. Kels got the panel. So I really think it's time—"

"I almost did, okay?"

I figure even though I failed, telling Ollie how close I was to spilling my soul will get him off my back.

"What happened?"

"I don't know, I tried to bring up Kels—but he shut it down and called his feelings for her, um, me, *imaginary internet bullshit.* I don't know, he was all *Kels isn't real,* and I just . . . Maybe he's right. Maybe she never was."

"Kels *isn't* real. Not if you don't own it."

I *ugh* into a pillow. I want to ride the high of last night before reality sets in. Like, why can't Ollie be happy for me for two seconds before the patronizing begins?

"Until you tell him," Ollie says, "stop talking about Nash to me. You can't have it both ways. Now you're legit just playing him."

"Fine," I say, standing up and storming out of his room. "Done."

We don't watch *Toy Story*.

Instead, I'm dealing with the *Fireflies and You* fandom.

I can't be on hiatus indefinitely—especially not if people think my silence is complicit. It's not even *people's* opinions who matter—it's *Autumn's*. Autumn thinks my silence is support. Yesterday, I proved to her in actions that it's not.

Today, I want to prove it to her in words.

So I spend my morning putting together a blog post that is very much Not About *Fireflies and You* and shoot a tweet off into the ether before I can overthink it.

Kels @OneTruePastry 2s
it's heartbreaking when an author you loved disappoints you.
did I see fireflies & you? yes! will i be talking about it? no!
instead, here's a list of incredible authors who shout about
how much they LOVE writing YA.

Kels @OneTruePastry 1s
my F&Y feelings are vast and complicated, but that's no excuse to keep giving the author a platform. silence is absolutely not my brand & i'm sorry to anyone who has been hurt by mine.

It's not enough, but it's a start, so I mute Twitter notifications on the tweet, close my laptop, and turn my attention to the messages that have accumulated on my phone while I've been in OTP land. I blink at the sheer number of notifications, for *Halle*. I'm used to Kels's messages blowing up—for *me* to have so many notifications is a relatively new concept.

Autumn Williams
Um? Why is Nash only communicating in nonsensical emojis??
11:39am

Molly Jacobson
Wtf did I miss?!?!
11:42am

Autumn Williams
HALLE
11:51am

Autumn and Molly must be dying.

Then, I see:

Nash Kim

Hey 😊

12:17pm

Such a dork.

Then again, I am alone in my room and blushing so hard from a text that just says "Hey."

So who's the dork, really?

I tap out of my texts and into my OTP email, which I've been trying to be a lot better about since almost missing the BookCon email. If I answer their texts right now I'll go straight down a squee rabbit hole.

I browse through until I see one subject line that reads: *unique cupcake inquiry!*

It's from Ariel Goldberg's publicist.

I read the email and the speed of my heart triples and oh my God, *what even*? It was one thing to host a cover reveal for her. Now Ariel Goldberg wants One True Pastry cupcakes, *my* cupcakes, at her book launch? *And* it's in Boston.

I screenshot the email to send to Nash and Amy, Elle, and Samira.

Then I don't send it. No one wants to geek out with Kels right now. Nash and Kels aren't speaking. Amy, Elle, and Samira called me out *literally* last week for ghosting Nash. I can't tell Molly or Autumn because they don't know I'm Kels either. I can't even run into Ollie's room and scream with him. Everything is *off*, everything is tense—and for the first time, my phone is in my hand, and Halle's not alone.

Kels is.

I reread the email instead. Can I do this? It wouldn't be me in a front of a crowd, but it puts my work out there. I read the date again, hardly believing my luck. The offer, the date, the timeline—the stars have aligned and I, Kels, have an early opportunity to test the waters and make a splash in the real world before my BookCon debut.

My followers are going to *love* this. This is my chance to take OTP's brand to the next level. OTP fans eating OTP cupcakes. How cool is that? It's not for three whole months, plenty of time to daydream up which flavors to make, what the perfect cake/frosting combos would be for Ariel Goldberg's launch party.

My phone buzzes—it's Nash, again. For Halle.

How have I not answered his texts yet?

Nash Kim
Wake upppp
1:45 PM

I'm awake!
1:48 PM

Hi 😊
1:48 PM

Oh hey! Finally!
1:39 PM

Are you busy before Shabbat?
1:40 PM

Nope!
1:41 PM

Nope *exclamation point*? I seriously have no chill.

Cool.
1:42 PM

?
1:45 PM

It's a surprise. Pick you up in an hour?
1:51 PM

Okay!
1:51 PM

Is this going to be our first date? Do I get to go on *dates* with Nash now?

Instead of spiraling, I shift my focus back to One True Pastry. Edit some new cupcake cover reveals in Photoshop. Avoid Twitter and draft an email to send to Alyssa Monday morning, during business hours. It's probably a world record for longest amount of time to type up an email one hundred words or less. I read and reread it until I am positive there are no errors, positive I don't sound too unprofessional or use too many exclamation points.

I love exclamation points, okay?

I'll probably rewrite it again in the morning, but I save it as a draft for now.

Then, I reread Alyssa's email and Nash's texts and swoon—though over cupcakes or him, I'm not quite sure.

Halle and Nash, January 3

OMG can't stop won't stop reading THE
SAPPHIRE PRINCE. Thanks for introducing me
to my new favorite series!!!
12:31 AM

And for introducing me to A Novel Idea. How
does Middleton not have its own independent
bookstore?
12:33 AM

It's a tragedy I've been mourning for YEARS
12:35 AM

Oh! You're still awake.
12:37 AM

Reading too?
12:39 AM

Working on REX
12:40 AM

Well, trying to anyways. It's kind of hard to
focus on anything right now.
12:40 AM

Yeah, I know what you mean.
12:41 AM

How far are you into TSP?
12:42 AM

Truth? I haven't even started yet. I just wanted
an excuse to text you 🙈
12:44 AM

LOL
12:45 AM

BRB FOREVER WHY AM I SO AWKWARD
12:47 AM

Halle?
12:48 AM

Nash?
12:50 AM

I had so much fun today.
12:51 AM

Me too
12:52 AM

NINETEEN

It's been six weeks since the first kiss.

Five weeks and six days since our first independent bookstore date.

And thirty-four days since Nash Kim became my boyfriend.

It's such a weird word to type and think and say out loud. *Boyfriend.* Because nothing about my Halle life has changed. We still eat lunch in the same seats at the same table. I still sit two rows behind him at Friday night services. I still crush everyone at bowling on Saturdays, and Nash still drives.

We just kiss now. A lot.

Also, Nash and I have a dinner date with his parents every Tuesday while Gramps is teaching.

Tonight, we're having beef bulgogi lettuce wraps—David cooks the best Korean food from scratch. The four of us sit around the table, passing food and making small talk. Well, Nash's parents talk—about how much Middleton has changed over the years, about Nash. I listen. Chew my food slowly and sip on water and try to make my anxiety *chill*. Nash's parents are nice. Really nice. It's just, what even are appropriate topics of conversation to have with your boyfriend's parents? I have no idea.

I mean, I have known Andrea and Dave for *years*, really, but only as the composites that Nash constantly complains about. In my caricature of Nash's parents, they have clouds over their heads. But Andrea has a kind smile and loves to embarrass Nash. And David cracks basic dad jokes and loves to embarrass himself. Still, it's easier just to nod along and answer any direct questions than introduce my own topic.

"Halle," Andrea says, passing me a plate of lettuce wraps for seconds. The way she pauses after she says my name, I know it's time to brace for a Casual College Talk. It happens *every* week. "Did Nash tell you we're going to tour Wesleyan this weekend?"

I take two pieces of lettuce and nod. "He told me."

Nash didn't *tell me* so much as *lament to me*. I try to make eye contact with him, but he's turned his attention to his food like it's a plating challenge on *Top Chef*—so focused on achieving the perfect beef-to-veggie ratio. I understand. Admissions decisions loom near. The closer it gets, the more Andrea and David want to talk about it.

"It's such a beautiful campus," Andrea says.

"We know," Nash says.

Wesleyan is twenty minutes away.

Painfully close, Nash wallowed. *Like, live at home close.*

"Clearly, Nash *can't wait*," David says. "His enthusiasm? It's too much!"

Andrea shakes her head. "Sure, we drive by Wesleyan all the time, but it's not a *tour*. You need to see the classrooms! Talk to current students about campus life! *Try* to imagine yourself there! At least be engaged in this process."

"It almost feels like *we're* the ones applying to college," David says.

Andrea turns her attention toward me. "Did you go on any college tours, Halle?"

I shake my head. "Not officially, but when I was twelve, my grandmother took me around NYU. And I kind of just knew."

Andrea crumples a napkin in her hand. "When you were twelve?"

"Yeah. I remember just having this *feeling* when I was there. I can't explain it. My family has always moved around, so I have a weird relationship with the idea of *home*. But walking around NYU with my grandmother? That day felt like home. Or at least the possibility of it."

Nash shoots me a look, like he's grateful the conversation has pivoted away from him.

David points his fork at Nash. "Maybe you'll have a *feeling* this weekend, Nash."

Nash shakes his head and stands, bringing our empty plates to the sink. "The only *feeling* I have right now concerns finding out what happens to Eleven in the next episode of *Stranger Things*. I'm so stressed. Seriously."

I drum my fingers against my thigh and count thirty-four seconds of silence.

"Very funny," Andrea says, finishing her glass of wine.

David begins clearing the table too. "Well, I guess you'd better go do that. If you're *so stressed.*"

"I truly am."

Nash grabs my hand and leads me away from the kitchen, away from Andrea and David and their not-so Casual College Talks.

"You can't keep doing that."

We're in Nash's basement, hanging out like we do after the dinners that have become more and more *awkward* with each passing week. Usually, the best part about Tuesday nights at Nash's is after dinner, because we always get at least two full hours of *alone.* His basement is a media room—the perfect spot to, um, binge watch a Netflix series.

"I'm not doing anything," Nash says.

He turns on the TV and sits next to me on the floor, our backs pressed against the cool leather chair. There isn't a couch, just four matching chairs that recline, almost like movie theater seats. We opt for the carpeted rug, padding it with blankets and a deflated beanbag because the chairs are definitely made for one-person occupancy—trust me, we tried.

"Do you even know what episode of *Stranger Things* we're on?" I ask. "Because I definitely don't."

Remote in hand, he clicks into the series page. "No clue."

"Nash." I reach for his hand. Cover it with mine. "Your parents seem worried. I really think you should—"

I stop short. What? *I really think you should tell your parents about NYU?* Because I totally am an authority when it comes to honesty.

"I know," Nash says. "If I get in."

"Okay, but—"

"Halle." Nash rotates his hand in mine so our fingers intertwine. "Please. Can't we just watch *Stranger Things*?"

Then Nash leans in and kisses me and I know I shouldn't let him off the hook this easily, but it's literally *impossible* to focus when his mouth is on mine, so I do. Of course I do. Because this TV time is the only time we're alone for, like, an entire week. I didn't realize until I wanted to spend all my free time kissing Nash's face that we are never, in fact, alone.

Nash breaks the kiss and stands up and I don't know why because we *literally* just got down here.

"Pause. I want to show you something," he says. "I'll be right back."

I sit up and wrap my arms around my knees. "This'd better be good."

Nash runs up the stairs two at time. I run my fingers through my hair to detangle its unruly waves. Count the beats of my heart until it steadies. Then I use the moment alone to check the stats on the latest OTP post. Kels's hiatus is over, but besides keeping up with One True Pastry's post schedule, I'm quiet online. My NYU app is in, my numbers are maintaining, thanks to Kels's response to the Alanna drama being overwhelmingly well received. It's never been better to be Halle, so it seems like as long as I'm actively posting engaging content, no one really cares if I reply to every tweet.

Every day I'm with Nash, Kels feels less and less real.

I almost forget I still have a very real problem. *Almost.*

The basement door swings open and I swipe out of all Kels content. Nash reappears at my side with his laptop and a sketchpad.

"Hey," Nash says.

"Hi."

He opens his laptop and swallows before turning the screen toward me.

I freeze and breathe because I need to react in a normal way, in a *Halle* way.

It's REX—the very first panel he posted two years ago. I'm so invested in the current series, I've never gone back to the beginning. It's *good*. Of course it's good. But it's also cool to see the improvement from the more amateur early work to his current stuff that, well, looks professional.

It has 454K views.

"I've never shown you . . ." Nash's ears turn pink and he lets out a nervous laugh. "Um, yeah. This is kinda why I'm online so much. It gets better, I swear."

"I know," I say before I can stop myself.

Nash blinks. "You do?"

This is not an appropriate Halle reaction.

"I mean . . ." I stall, trying to grasp a logical explanation out of thin air. "I already read it. I found it the first day of school, after everyone was gushing about it at lunch."

"Oh," Nash says, closing the laptop and setting it on the floor beside him. "I forgot about that."

I exhale.

"You never told me you read it! It's because you hate it, right? Do you hate it? Sometimes I think dinosaurs are, I don't know, juvenile, and no one is going to take me seriously and—"

"*Nash.*" I grab his hand and intertwine his fingers with mine. "It's *so* good."

He looks at me. "Really?"

I nod. "I never said anything because it reads *so* personal, you know? Like, especially once I knew about Nick. I guess I just figured you'd show me when you wanted to."

"I want to."

"I do have one question."

"Oh?"

"Stevens?" I ask.

I've been wondering since the day I learned that Nash Stevens is actually Nash Kim—and I'm not about to waste an opportunity to ask.

"*Oh.*" Nash laughs. "Steven is my middle name. I don't love it—not using Kim—but it's the only way my parents would let me create a public profile to blog. Keywords from my digital youth include *privacy* and *underage* and *safety*."

With everything I know about Andrea and David, that checks out. "Makes sense."

"I'm changing it as soon as I turn eighteen, though," Nash says.

"Even though everyone knows you as Nash Stevens?"

Nash nods. "Yeah. That's not my name. It's not like I haven't thought about sticking with Stevens. A pen name is kind of a safety net, you know? But if I publish REX someday, it'll be as Nash Kim. That's who I want to be to the world."

My pen name kind of feels like the opposite of a safety net right now, but I know exactly what he means. "It's cool."

Nash releases his hand from mine and reaches across me for his sketchbook. "This is cooler, I promise."

He flips through the pages and opens to panels I've never seen before, upcoming REX pages. An establishing sketch of a skyline—*oh,* so Rex is going to look for Terry in New York City next. Rex tries to interact with pedestrians, but they're all either indifferent or unhelpful or scared of the timid dinosaur.

I run my fingers over the pages because it's amazing seeing the beginning stages of art. Each line is drawn with care and every word of dialogue is written by hand, with intention. Nash explains the process of creating REX. Every panel is hand drawn, scanned, and filled in with Photoshop. A single panel is a full day's work from beginning to end. It's why he only posts once a week now—he couldn't keep up with it twice a week once AP classes became a thing.

"This is top secret stuff, Upstate."

A tear—*my* tear—splashes on REX #224.

I don't know when everything between Nash and me got so real.

Nash looks at me, eyes wide. "Whoa, hey. Why are you crying?"

"It's beautiful," I say. "*You're* beautiful."

Then I lean forward and kiss Nash because I want to remember this moment, this *feeling* while I still live in a world where Kels isn't real. It always starts off innocently, our kisses. Slow and sweet, until I'm tired of slow and sweet. Then I deepen the kiss and twist my fingers in his hair—did I ever mention how much I love his hair? His hands slide down to my hips and we rotate so I'm now straddling him and his lips are on my jaw, my neck, and oh my *God* I want.

I want, I want, I want.

Every week, I find that I'm the one initiating the next move, I'm the one pushing the boundaries closer and closer to the point of no return. I've kissed boys—I've even fooled around with some boys. Temporary flings with other temporary doc kids. We'd just make out and okay, *maybe* my bra would come off at some point—but that's as far as it'd go. I never let it go further, because I never *wanted* to.

With Nash, I want to. And it's so unfair, because I kiss him and touch him like I've known him for years because, well, I have. Sometimes when I'm like this, I forget that for him, it's only been six months, that we've only been officially *a thing* for thirty-four days.

Caught up in the moment, in Nash showing me, *Halle*, REX, I take his shirt off for the first time.

"I'm—I mean, I haven't . . ." Flustered Nash babbles, unable to find the word.

"Me either," I say.

I'm not exactly surprised, but I am relieved.

"Should we slow down?" I ask.

"Probably," Nash says.

We don't.

In between kisses, Nash slips my cardigan off my shoulders. Then he pulls my T-shirt off over my head.

It's cold, so I pull one of the fleece blankets over us. I'm still on his lap, kissing Nash, his skin hot against mine and oh my *God* this is so good. Nash's fingers graze my lower back and his hand slides slowly up, up, up to the clasp of my bra. I don't even feel self-conscious, not for one second.

But then his hands are gone and his lips are too far away from mine. I push forward to kiss him more but he pulls away.

"Oh my God." Nash pulls the blanket off and it's too bright. I blink to readjust to the florescent basement lights. When I do, Nash is putting his shirt back on. Inside out.

"Nash?" I ask.

He doesn't say *what?* or offer, like, any sort of explanation.

He just throws my shirt at me.

I'm not even joking. It lands on my head.

"My parents," he says. "They're, like—right upstairs. What if they—and we were . . . ?"

"Oh," I say. *Oh.*

I got so wrapped up in Nash, in *us*, I totally forgot about that. Andrea and David upstairs while we were . . . well, Nash is right. *Oh my God.* I pull over my T-shirt and button every single button on my cardigan. Brush out my tangled hair with my fingers. Sit up straight against a chair, like how we started, and let my breathing steady. I look at him, my cheeks flaming.

It's okay, though, because his are also on fire.

"That was the opposite of slow," I say.

"I wanted to."

"Me too."

"I just don't want our first time to be in my parents' basement while they're upstairs watching *Seinfeld* reruns."

Oh my God, you can legit hear Jerry's voice through the ceiling. I cover my hand with my mouth and laugh so hard.

"*So* romantic," I say.

Nash joins my laughing fit and we are okay. More than okay.

We restart the episode of *Stranger Things* and cuddle until I have to be home for curfew. I can't focus on the show because I can't stop thinking about Nash and me. How did we get so intense, so fast? I'm not sure.

But I am sure that I want to keep kissing Nash forever. Getting carried away with him forever.

I'm sure that I'm falling for him, and not only for a moment.

And I'm sure, I am *finally* sure that I can't keep this up. Nash shared REX sketches with me, Halle—and I said *I know* because I *do* know. Because I'm Kels. And as much as I'd like to continue to compartmentalize and pretend it doesn't matter now, it does. Of course it does. I can't keep doing things like this. I can't keep waiting for the right moment or finding reasons not to tell him.

I know I can't lose him; I don't know why I ever thought I could.

I know I might lose him, and if I do it's my own fault.

He was never going to wish Kels was someone else because she couldn't be. She's *real*. It's all been real.

He's not going to hurt Kels online or any of the other million excuses I've come up with.

If he hurts *me*, well—I probably deserve it.

March 1

BookCon @thebookcon 1hr
We are SO EXCITED to announce the fantastic lineup of our
very first Bloggers IRL panel:@BooksOnTape,@LilahClarkRead,
@OneTruePastry,@AnnalieseWritesYA, @MGPete,
@IambicPentara.
[101 comments] [584 ↻] [2k ♥]

Elle Carter @ellewriteswords 45min
WHAT. CC @AmysBookshelf @s_lee244 @Nash_Stevens27
PLEASE CONFIRM I AM NOT HALLUCINATING. HOW CAN
A GHOST BE ON A PANEL? I'M SHOOK.

Amy Chen @AmysBookshelf 40min
. . . you are definitely not?! this is WILD.

Samira Lee @s_lee244 37min
👀 👀 👀

Nash Stevens @Nash_Stevens27
I thought I'd never be more confused. I was wrong.

TWENTY

f Grams were still here, she'd be laughing so hard.

I'd tell her everything, the whole Nash situation, and she'd become the laughing tears emoji.

Not everything has to be this hard, she'd say.

I can still hear her voice, her laugh.

How has it been almost a year since we lost her?

It's a quiet ride to Stamford, to the Jewish cemetery where Grams is buried. Rabbi Goldman would say *laid to rest*, but I hate that phrase. Rest is a temporary action. Grams is stuck at the Stamford Jewish Cemetery forever.

Breathe.

I did not want to do this.

Cemeteries are the worst. The necklace that rests against my beating heart is more Grams than a plaque with her name on it and her decomposing body six feet under. I haven't been to a cemetery since my uncle's funeral, which triggered my first panic attack. So I can't understand how doing this is going to help anything. It's going to be horrible.

Ollie said we had to do this for Gramps. Gramps's voice broke when he asked us if we would come. And it's not just a trip to the cemetery—it's the unveiling ceremony, a Jewish custom. It's a small ceremony that occurs usually in the final months of the first year of mourning. Gramps says we'll say some prayers and the headstone with Grams's name on it will be unveiled.

How could we say no?

The minute I step out of the car, I wish I *had*. Tears start to fill my eyes and we haven't even left the parking lot. Spring emerges in a vision of cherry trees in bloom and freshly planted tulips. It'd be pretty if this weren't so terrible. Cemeteries shouldn't be beautiful.

We follow Gramps uphill toward the grounds where the rabbi will be conducting the ceremony. I fixate on the yellow and purple bouquet in his hand. He replaces her flowers every week, a Sunday morning ritual. Most grandpas read the newspaper. Mine goes to the cemetery. Today he leaves his fifty-second bouquet.

It scares me, loving someone that much.

When we arrive at Grams's covered placard I need to close my eyes and remind myself she's not here. Ollie holds my hand and I squeeze it so tight because I cannot cry. Today is not about me. I can do this for Gramps; I can be here for him. I can give him the biggest hug and say I still miss her too.

Gramps replaces the old flowers with the new before the rabbi starts the prayers.

"Still miss you, Mir," Gramps says. "Every day."

And . . . I burst into tears.

"I—I'm so sorry," I cough.

"Halle," Gramps says.

"I can't—"

I choke. Choke on my words, as always, and my tears. All I see is Grams in a box, Grams being lowered into the ground, strangers giving their condolences. Someday it'll be Gramps in the box. Then it'll be Mom and Dad. Eventually it'll be me, just gone, like I was never here. I'll be a *was* instead of an *is*. We all become past tense. Everyone. So what's the point of—

"Breathe," Ollie says, exerting pressure on my hand.

"It's okay, Hal," Gramps says.

"I can't be here," I say.

"Okay," he says.

He looks at Ollie, who nods, and we descend backward, just the two of us. Away from Grams, away from the plaques announcing the bodies buried underneath. Sometimes I squeeze my eyes shut and let Ollie lead me. He takes me down the hill and through the parking lot and into the back seat of the car. I reach for my cell phone in the cup holder, scroll through my apps without looking at anything, and I can breathe again.

I wipe running eyeliner from under my eyes.

"I'm the worst," I say.

Ollie shakes his head. "I am."

"No," I say. "You're so strong."

"I'm numb," Ollie says, pinching the bridge of his nose. "I miss her. But not like you do."

"Oh," I say, surprised by Ollie's confession. I always think my baby brother has everything together. Maybe he doesn't.

"I suck," Ollie says.

"No." I shake my head. "I'm pretty sure you're the best thing that happened to Gramps this year. Actually, no. I'm *positive*."

Ollie presses his back against the seat and closes his eyes. "If I let myself think about it, I get *so* angry. Grams ran *marathons* and she still got lung cancer. You can do everything right . . . and what? It doesn't even matter? She'll never get to see us do anything—graduate or go to college or fall in love or try and fail our way to success. It's bullshit."

I wrap my arms around Ollie. "Totally bullshit."

We stay like this for a breath.

When I let go, Ollie presses the heels of his hands against his eyes. "So much for numb."

We spot Gramps in the distance coming down the walkway, returning to us. I relocate to my spot in the front passenger seat, already wording and rewording all the variations of what to say next in my brain. Starting with *I'm so sorry* and ending with *I love you*. The words that fill the space between are still to be determined.

Gramps gets in the car and closes the driver-side door.

"Are you okay, Hal?" he says.

"I'm so sorry—"

"Stop," Gramps says. "Let me talk."

I swallow.

He twists the key in the ignition.

"You're allowed to say no to me," he says, surprising me. "Really, I promise. You kids never come, and I thought it was because of me, because I never thought to ask. You've been so strong for me since the start, so I didn't think it was because maybe you didn't want to, maybe you're not ready. That's okay."

"I hate cemeteries," I say.

"Me too," he says. "But someone's gotta keep the flowers fresh for her, you know?"

I take a deep breath, willing my heart not to shatter into a million pieces.

"I know."

Gramps backs out of the parking lot, because it's time to leave this sad place. I shift in my seat, reclining a few extra inches. Close my eyes because emotions are exhausting.

"I'm going to miss this," Gramps says in the quiet.

My eyes pop open.

"What?" Ollie asks.

"It's March," Gramps says. "This, our time together, it's almost over."

I blink.

Ollie blinks.

I'm pretty sure it's the first time this has occurred to either of us. He's right. School ends the beginning of June. Then, Ollie and I are supposed to spend the summer in Israel with our parents, until they wrap in August. Then it's college for me. For Ollie? It depends on Mad and Ari's next project.

"I'm shook," Ollie says.

Gramps frowns. "What?"

"Reality, Gramps," Ollie says.

"Reality," Gramps repeats. "Reality is I don't know what I'm going to do without you kids. Seriously. It was so hard being in that house alone."

It didn't hit me because my goodbyes have always been inevitable. Graduation, a stretch of summer, and then leaving for New York, fingers crossed. I am leaving Middleton regardless.

It's not simple for Ollie and Gramps—they've built a life here. Ollie looks like he's going to be sick.

"Can I stay?"

He asks so softly I'm not sure I heard him—and Gramps most definitely did not. Ollie clears his throat and repeats the question, louder, with more confidence.

"Can I stay?"

"Oh," Gramps says. "Um—"

"Please? I don't want to move again."

"That's not up to me, Oliver," Gramps says.

"But you'd let me? If Mom and Dad say yes?"

"Of course." Gramps doesn't hesitate in his reply. And judging by the stupid smile spreading across his face, he likes that idea too. I hope it works. I hope Mom isn't too stubborn to say yes. Ollie and Gramps are the most adorable duo, and staying in one place will be good for Ollie, I think. Middleton will be his home.

A Nash text buzzes in my lap.

See you at 6?

I text back, **Duh!** But my stomach twists.

We don't talk about the future of us, if there is a future of us. For Nash, it can't really be a conversation until the college emails fill our inboxes in two short weeks. For me, it can't be a conversation until Kels is a conversation. Dread flutters in my stomach, because Gramps has got me thinking about goodbyes, how they sneak up so quickly, and how it's the first time I've even had a home to say goodbye to.

I shake off the cemetery visit with a batch of buttercream frosting.

I dip my pinky finger in the bowl for a taste test.

It's too sweet.

Into the compost it goes.

Time for take two.

I ended up in the kitchen of Maple Street Sweets without quite meaning to. I knew I needed to bake, and I knew I couldn't bake at home. Not because Gramps won't let me. Because I *can't*. Not today. I asked Gramps if I could borrow the car and drove straight to the bakery on my Sunday off.

So here I am, baking trial cupcakes for the Ariel Goldberg event. It's three weeks away and I've been so caught up with Nash, I haven't even planned for it, like, *at all*. I scroll through One True Pastry's Instagram, back to when I did the epic cover reveal. The event cupcakes can't be identical to the cover reveal—there's no way, when I need to bake three hundred—but I *can* use it as inspiration.

How did I make the cupcakes look like a crime scene? I can't remember.

I spend too much time experimenting with food dye like I'm a scientist in a lab, until I achieve the exact swirl of red and gray frosting I need. I fill piping bags and practice swirling frosting until I'm convinced they're perfect. Because they have to be perfect. These aren't just cupcakes to post on Instagram, they are *Ariel Goldberg* cupcakes. They need to be the most epic, perfect cupcakes. A mix of flavors that will satisfy all cupcake lovers and frosting that is too pretty to eat. Almost.

Everyone knows me for my cupcake aesthetics.

Now, the taste has to match up.

I didn't think about that when I agreed to do this, but now it's all I can think about. What if everyone hates my cupcakes? What if the cake tastes like cardboard and the frosting is too sweet and I thought I could do this, but it's a disaster?

Also Alyssa Peterson wants *three hundred* cupcakes. I didn't even consider how I'd make three hundred cupcakes or how to transport them. I didn't think about getting it all done by myself or the risk of not living up to my brand—I just said *yes*.

I'm transferring my first batch of practice cupcakes to a plastic airtight container when the kitchen door swings open behind me. I don't even bother to turn my attention to the door—Diana and Max have been in and out all afternoon to refill the shelves with the overflow pastries on the cooling racks.

"You okay, Upstate?"

I spin to face Nash and the cupcake in my hand falls to the floor, frosting down.

"Sorry," Nash says. "I didn't mean to—um, sorry. You weren't answering your texts, so I called Sawyer. He said you've been here all afternoon—he sounded worried. And I know Miriam's unveiling was this morning and that was probably really hard. So I am here! Hi!"

He picks my cupcake off the floor and he is so close to me as Kels right now. He could recognize my cupcakes, recognize the specific frosting colors. He retweeted my *Read Between the Lies* cover reveal. If he took a step back and saw me, I mean *really* saw me and the cupcakes, he could put the pieces together.

For the first time that doesn't make me tense or panic. This time I want him to.

"What time is it?" I ask.

"After eight," Nash says.

I blink. "Wait, really?"

Time has no meaning in the kitchen, but I didn't realize how zoned out I was in the name of One True Pastry. I was supposed to meet Nash for dinner two hours ago.

"I'm so sorry," I say. "I don't know where time went."

"Are you okay?" he asks, waving off my apology.

"Fun fact: I stress bake," I say.

Admitting this truth feels like my two worlds are colliding.

"Clearly," Nash says.

I scoop the leftover frosting into Tupperware to bring home.

"Seriously, though, are you? Okay?"

"I bolted before the mourner's kaddish."

"So. Not great," Nash says.

I shake my head. "Not great. I didn't know what to do after

except come here. We used to bake together and just—I feel so much closer to her *here*."

"That makes sense."

"I really hate cemeteries."

"I'm not a big fan either."

Nash wraps his arms around me and for the first time all day, I can relax. It occurs to me that in a way, I wouldn't have Nash without Grams. Everything leads back to her. Without her, I never would've learned the art of the perfect cupcake. I wouldn't have a blog, it wouldn't be cupcake-themed, and Kels really, truly, would not be real.

I mean, Nash and I would've met eventually, here, and I'd only be Halle. But without Grams, I wouldn't have *known* Nash, I wouldn't have spent years in DMs and G-Chat becoming this boy's best friend.

Grams has guided me through every major moment in Kels's existence—from starting the blog, to making sure I had the best baking equipment, to editing my posts and reviews until the words and tweets felt as natural as breathing.

If she were here, I know what she'd say.

You know what to do, Hal. You don't need my notes anymore.

But even if she *were* here, it'd be up to me to fix this mess.

If I keep waiting for the right words, I'll never speak.

Nash wipes a tear off my cheek and I remember being right here months ago and thinking that I used to hate how he's always just *there*. I don't know why, because now it's one of the best things about Nash—his uncanny ability to show up when I need him.

"Cupcake?" I ask, offering the container to him.

"Sure," he says.

He plucks one of the cupcakes from the container, takes a bite, and chews it *so slowly* oh my God. Each bite is a millennium. I watch him on the edge of my seat, or I guess on my tiptoes, because his opinion matters. Like him showing REX to me. If I can't impress Nash, no way the cupcakes will measure up for my followers.

He swallows. Shrugs. "Kind of dry, tbh."

What. I gape, because One True Pastry cupcakes *are so not dry*.

He breaks into a huge smile. "Kidding! Wow, I got you."

I punch him in the arm. "I hate you."

"I solemnly swear that your cupcake is so moist. The *moistest*, dare I say."

Once again, I'm laughing and I can't stop because Nash loved my cupcake and *moist* is the grossest word on the planet and he knows it. Because Nash always knows just what to say to make me feel better without even trying. Because Old Halle *never* would've offered Nash a cupcake and I feel so good that I did. Because I shared part of Kels with Nash as Halle and the world didn't fall apart. In fact, it feels more whole than it has in a long time.

Because I have an idea.

I'm going to use three hundred cupcakes to tell Nash I'm me.

OTP cupcakes announcement

Ariel Goldberg @ArielGoldberg 1 hr
EXCITING NEWS! We will have @OneTruePastry cupcakes at
the READ BETWEEN THE LIES launch party at Central Square
Books!! Thank you SO much, Kels! Can't wait to taste! 😍

|

Kels @OneTruePastry 2min
SO EXCITED *runs away to bake*

[Nash Stevens and 252 others liked a post from Ariel Goldberg]

TWENTY-ONE

Today the College gods will decide my future.

I don't even have a chance to process if any .edu emails are in my Halle inbox before I am inundated with text messages from Le Crew.

Nash Kim
Halle
5:03 AM

Nash Kim
Wake up
5:04 AM

Nash Kim
It's college day
5:07am

Nash Kim
Hellooooooo
5:15 AM

Nash Kim
I'm dying.
5:30 AM

Molly Jacobson
WE'RE BOTH DYING
5:31 AM

Sawyer Davidson
You're not dying.
5:32 AM

Molly Jacobson
AUTUMN IS MIA TOO.
5:33 AM

Molly Jacobson
WHY IS EVERYONE ASLEEP ON THE MOST
IMPORTANT DAY OF THEIR LIVES
5:40 AM

This more or less continues until my alarm clock goes off at six-fifteen a.m. and I groggily text **STOPPP** in the group text.

Sorry, College gods, I'm not waking up early, not even for you. I hit snooze twice, like always, and roll out of bed at six-forty. This gives me exactly twenty-five minutes to choose an outfit and apply the bare minimum of makeup before Ollie and I run out the door to make it to school on time.

I choose high-waisted jeans and a beige off-the-shoulder sweater, then swipe mauve over my lips. The lipstick is a bit extra for a Wednesday at MHS, but it would be perfect for a Wednesday at NYU. *Dress for the life you want*, and all.

It's just another day, I remind myself.

Still, I can't help but check my email on the stairs, in the bathroom, at the kitchen table during breakfast. With every vibration in my palm that indicates a new text or email—my heart spikes. I definitely need to turn off notifications today. But then I double-check—even though I *knew* it wasn't going to be there yet. According to Google, NYU sends their emails out in waves throughout the day, because they *love* to induce anxiety.

As if my anxious brain isn't already in overdrive.

You're just an amateur blogger.

Your SAT scores are mediocre.

Rejected.

I toss my phone into my backpack, as if that will make a difference.

"Wait-listed."

Molly can't even look at us when she says it. She's too busy tearing her quesadilla into tiny, inedible pieces. Her eyes are wet but she doesn't blink, won't even shed a tear. Sawyer texted me in first period, but this is the first time I've seen Molly today, so it's the first time I can believe it's true.

"It's not a rejection," Nash says.

"It's not over," Autumn says.

Molly shrugs. "I don't know how to process this."

We don't know what to say to that—so we don't. Lunch passes in awkward silence, because what do you say to someone who's sort of maybe lost their dream? Molly took five AP classes this year. Molly is *valedictorian*. Student council treasurer. President of USY. If Molly Jacobson isn't enough for her dream—how am I possibly enough for mine?

"No word yet?" Sawyer asks Autumn, Nash, and me.

Sawyer's future is on lock. Last week, he signed his life away to UConn baseball.

"They're Division I *and* I can keep working at the bakery. It's kind of too perfect," Sawyer said to me during a shift last weekend. He had multiple offers from schools all over the country. He's absolutely Ollie's hero—if there was ever any doubt otherwise.

He's also a hero for handling our stress like a champ, tbh.

Molly blinks out of her trance. "I'm sorry. I'm so in my head right now! Please distract me. What is everyone else's situation?"

Autumn swallows a fry. "Well. I got into Loyola and Emerson. So . . . I'm going to film school! USC is still very much to be determined."

"I've heard from UConn and Wesleyan," Nash says.

I retie my ponytail. "I—"

Autumn's phone vibrates, loud, against the table.

Ten anxious eyeballs stare at Autumn's phone. It's the fifth time this has happened.

"I mean." Autumn swallows. "It's probably another false alarm."

"Autumn," Molly says, her voice level, "if you don't check your email right this second and give us some good news, I'm going to have an existential crisis. Right here."

Autumn inhales a deep breath and opens her email. My eyes dart around the table, from Nash to Molly to Sawyer to Autumn. We're all holding our breath. I'm positive. Autumn's eyes are glued to her phone and for a moment she's expressionless. Like a total statue. But then her eyes widen and her lips curve up and I almost burst into tears. Which, like, this isn't even *my* news. Pull yourself together, Halle!

"I got in," Autumn says.

Then she bursts into tears and it's *wild* because I've never seen Autumn cry.

"I'm sorry." Autumn wipes her nose with her shirt sleeve. "I don't know how to process *this*. I prepared myself for a *no*. I didn't think— like, I guess I never thought I'd actually—God, Molly, I'm so sorry."

Molly stands up from her seat, walks around the table to Autumn, and wraps her arms around her. "Why are you apologizing? You freaking got into USC! My existential crisis has to wait."

We're all freaking out and congratulating Autumn, who is absolutely glowing. The emotional whiplash is unreal.

Once Molly lets go, Autumn turns and wraps her arms around me. "I literally couldn't have done this without you. Thank you."

I shake my head. "Not true."

Autumn raises her eyebrows.

"Okay! Maybe just the dialogue part." I laugh.

"Director, Autumn Williams," Nash says. "Has a pretty sick ring to it."

"It really does," Molly says.

"Remember us when you're famous," Sawyer adds.

The bell rings, interrupting the celebration and reminding Le Crew that we are, in fact, at school and we do, in fact, still have AP tests to prepare for. Nash and I have calculus next and I don't even know how I'm going to process free-response questions. It's enough of a struggle on a normal day.

Le Crew splits off into every direction. Nash and I walk to calc and he asks—no, *insists*—that we check our email.

"Please. I need to know. Please. Please. *Please*," he begs.

He doesn't need to ask me twice.

Your NYU Admissions Decision appears in bold at the top of my inbox.

This is not a drill.

"It's here," I say.

"Mine too," Nash says.

We freeze in front of the English wing lockers. My heart is racing and my palms are sweating because in a matter of moments, I will *know*. And it'll either be the best day of my life or I will be commiserating with Molly for the rest of the year. That's probably what will happen, too, because of the SATs and I don't have any fancy leadership titles, only tiny film credits and a blog and a spot at a convention that hasn't even happened—

"Halle," Nash says. "On three."

One. Two. Three. I tap the email open, holding my breath.

On behalf of the admissions committee, it is my
honor and privilege to share with you that you have
been admitted to the College of Arts and Sciences
at New York University.

Nash and I look up from our phones and lock eyes.

He nods.

I nod.

Speechless, we both break into the stupidest smiles, I'm sure. In an instant, I forget that I am at school. I even forget about my strict no PDA rule and press my mouth against Nash's because—I, Halle Levitt, got into NYU. And so did he.

"Best day *ever*," Nash says.

"We're going to NYU?"

"We're going to NYU! I mean, hopefully after I tell my parents. Wow. I didn't think I'd *actually* have to tell my parents."

"It'll be okay," I say.

"I know. I mean, I don't *know*. But I think so. Maybe that's just the adrenaline talking." Nash laces his fingers through mine and exhales. "But first, to calculus?"

"What's calculus?"

At NYU, I'll *never* math again.

I float through the rest of the day, rereading the email between classes to assure myself that it's real, it's not a fluke, I'm going to NYU. Ollie has an art elective fifth period, so I text him to meet me by the water fountain next to my physics class and we silently scream together for thirty whole seconds before we need to get back to class. We'll celebrate tonight, Ollie promises.

"Gramps is going to *freak*," he says. "So will Mom and Dad."

NYU is reality. I'm going.

And that means Kels is going. Do I announce it on Twitter? How will Nash feel? Knowing he, Halle, and Kels will all potentially be on the same campus for four years?

Yeah, it's getting confusing for me too. But it won't be confusing for too much longer.

I have a plan.

"It sounds like congratulations are in order," Dad says.

"*Congratulations*, Halle!" Mom cries into the phone. "We're *so* proud of you!"

Gramps, Ollie, and I pass the phone around the kitchen table and wow, I wish my parents were here for this moment. I'd be suffocating, wrapped in one of Mom's tight hugs. Dad would ruffle my hair and I'd pretend to be annoyed he messed it up. Ollie would tell Mom to *please stop crying, for the love of everything*.

"Thank you," I say.

"Seriously, Hal," Dad says. "Grams would be blown away."

I pinch the bridge of my nose because I'm *so* done with tears today.

"I wish we were there," Mom says. There are thousands of

miles between us and still, she says exactly what I'm thinking. "I hate this. We missed too much. You're a BookCon panelist! You have a boyfriend! You got into NYU! Being here, making this doc—it's been amazing, don't get me wrong. But part of me *misses* Charlotte."

Ollie sits across from me at the table, protein smoothie in hand. "You hated Charlotte."

"Okay," Mom admits. "Maybe not *Charlotte*. But the *idea* of Charlotte. Us together in one place. Going to your baseball games. But now Halle's heading off to college and it's just going to be the three of us in L.A. through postproduction and—"

Ollie cuts Mom off. "Mom, I want to stay here."

"What?" Mom says.

"I want to stay with Gramps."

Gramps looks at Ollie with exclamation points of panic in his eyes. Ollie's eyes widen and he shrugs, like, *oops*. Sometimes, Ollie has literally zero tact. Actually, not even zero. Make that negative tact. But to his credit, he sounds a thousand times more confident than he looks.

It's so silent on the other side, I think they might have hung up.

"Hello?" I ask.

"We're here," Dad says. "Just—processing."

"No," Mom says. "No way, Oliver."

"I kind of love it here. Did you know I made varsity baseball? That I'm the only sophomore on the team?"

"Well, that's wonderful. But—"

"No," Ollie says. He's so worked up, face all red and blotchy like he's going to explode. "Middleton is home now. I have friends, I have a girlfriend. I have Gramps. Please let me stay. *Please*."

"A girlfriend?" Dad asks.

"Not the point," I say, though I can't help but be curious about when exactly Talia became Ollie's girlfriend and why I didn't know about this. I thought—well, I thought Ollie and I were back on track. Am I seriously still that checked out?

"It's okay, Mad," Gramps says. "Ollie and I have talked this through, and I'd love to have him stay. It's no trouble at all."

Silence.

"I think we need a beat," Dad says.

"Let us think on it, okay?" Mom says. "It's just . . . the idea of losing both of you? It's *a lot*."

"It's not *losing* me," Ollie says.

"We'll discuss it, okay? We love you," Dad says. "Congrats again, Hal."

"Love you too," Ollie and I say in unison.

The line disconnects.

"Well." I stare at the phone. "That went well."

Ollie covers his face with his hands. "I didn't mean to co-opt your college news. Ugh."

"You're an awkward Levitt at heart," I say.

"Not your best moment, Oliver," Gramps admits.

He'll get to stay, I think. I hope.

Ollie storms upstairs to his room, muttering *ughhhhhh* under his breath with every step.

• • •

I'm trying to start a new YA romcom, but I'm too distracted by the dreams-coming-true swoon.

So I drop the book on my night table and text Nash, because it's time to put the plan in motion. I almost want to blurt it out right now. But Nash is at a track meet in Hartford. And after everything, he *cannot* find out via text. This is one thing I have to do IRL.

> Hey
> 4:37 PM

Nash Kim
Hi.
4:39 PM

Why didn't I skip this meet?
4:40 PM

> Because you never skip track stuff
> 4:41 PM

Track season is well under way, and it takes up a lot of Nash's time after school. I hate how time-consuming it is as much as I hate running as a concept.

Ugh. We should be celebrating!
4:42 PM

> Totally!
> 4:45 PM

Maybe we can Saturday?
4:46 PM

Clearly, I am the queen of subtle segues.

Saturday is Ariel Goldberg. Saturday is Boston and cupcakes and the day I'm going to tell Nash the truth. We will have a cute day in the city and we will stumble upon Central Square Books. He'll recognize the cupcakes and look at me and a light bulb will go on and I won't even have to tell him because he'll just *know*. It'll be hard and confusing and, okay, maybe it will be terrible at first. He'll probably be mad. But I know what I'm going to say. I wrote it and rewrote it in my bullet journal.

I've even practiced on Scout.

No more going into this situation and hoping the right words will come out.

Finally, I *know* they will. He'll understand, because he's Nash. We'll be okay, because we're Halle and Nash. And Kels and Nash.

I can't Saturday. I have a family thing. I'll
probably miss bowling too, tbh
4:51 PM

Oh. I . . . did not anticipate Nash saying no.

Since we've been official, Nash and I have spent every single Saturday together. If I'm working, he hangs around Maple Street Sweets until I'm out. We'll grab food or catch a movie or even just walk around downtown until bowling. After bowling, we either hang at his house or mine. Usually his, because his house has a finished basement and mine has a living room and a dog who always seems to wedge herself in the space between us. Wouldn't he have told me sooner?

> Is everything okay?
> 4:52 PM

Yeah. It's a Nick thing, so like, I can't really get out of it.
4:53 PM

But Sunday is wide open!
4:53 PM

> Sunday works!
> 4:54 PM

I've had this *very specific reveal* planned for weeks, and not once did it cross my mind that he might not be able to go. I'm running out of time and ways to tell him the truth and I'm afraid that it's already too late, but I thought the Ariel Goldberg event would work if anything would.

Nothing can be too terrible when surrounded by books and cupcakes, I'm sure.

But now that won't happen.

BookCon is two months away. I need a Plan B—and fast.

April 1

Kels @OneTruePastry—April 1
See you soon @NYU!!! 😎 🤯 😭
[240 comments] [252 🔁] [2.7K ♥]

Direct Messages

Nash to Kels

Thursday, January 2, 2:13 PM

I hope everything's okay. I really wish you would've just talked
to me if it wasn't. It sounds so stupid now—but I thought we
had something real. I guess we don't.
Bye, Kels.

Wednesday, April 1, 5:04 PM

[Nash typing]

TWENTY-TWO

s it turns out, it takes minor deception and a lot of planning to bake three hundred bookish cupcakes.

I spent two days baking the cupcakes at Maple Street Sweets. It was the most difficult part, because I couldn't start until the Davidsons left. Sawyer thinks it's all for a chemistry project—which is only half a lie. Mr. Portman *did* assign a creative project where we are supposed to present chemistry in everyday life. Baking is kind of a perfect example of that. But Gramps is okay with baking again, so theoretically I could have done that at home. For the event, though, I need all the industrial equipment—I couldn't bake this many cupcakes in Gramps's kitchen even if I *wanted* to. Between Wednesday and Thursday night, all three hundred vanilla bean and double dark chocolate cupcakes have been baked and sealed unfrosted in airtight containers to keep them fresh.

Since frosted cupcakes don't last as long, frosting must happen at the last possible second. Which is why I'm spending Friday night not going to Shabbat, but in Gramps's kitchen, music blasting, meticulously frosting each cupcake with different colors of buttercream. I have three designs—black and white swirled with red sparkle sprinkles, red and gray swirled with edible pearls, and chocolate ganache with a white stripe, to have the whiteout effect of the title.

I don't know what's more of a miracle—Gramps letting me use the kitchen, or Gramps letting me *skip Shabbat* to frost cupcakes. Gramps does okay when I bake the occasional batch, but he keeps himself busy today. He goes to Ollie's baseball practice; they go out for dinner before Shabbat. All so I have plenty of time to frost and clean up before he gets home.

My phone buzzes. It's Nash. But not for me.

He liked Kels's most recent NYU tweet.

Kels @OneTruePastry 1hr
Apparently NYU has a Milk & Cookies club and WOW I didn't know how badly I needed that in my life?!?!

I switch my phone to silent. It's jarring, Nash suddenly engaging with Kels again. I have no clue what he's thinking—and it's not like I can *ask*. I wish I didn't tweet about NYU. Because it's like Nash suddenly remembered that Kels *is* real.

Kels ghosted Nash, but for whatever reason, he wants her to know that he's still here. The more Nash likes and engages with Kels's content online, the weirder Nash seems IRL. Maybe I'm overthinking. But yesterday, I asked him if he wanted to study for our impending AP exams before I had to work, and he said he had, you know, *so much* English homework and bolted. It didn't even occur to me until I got inside that *we're in the same English class*. And no, we did not have *so much* homework.

It's probably REX related. Or the Nick thing. Whatever that means.

I transfer two finished tubs of cupcakes to the basement storage refrigerator. Each container has two tiers, holding twenty-four cupcakes. Two containers down—eleven more to go. *God.* How did I think I'd be able to do this myself? These cupcakes are *endless*.

I fumble with my phone on my way back to the kitchen.

I'm going to text Nash and check in.

Hey
6:50 PM

Nash Kim
Hi.
6:51 PM

Hi? Period? It's so distant.

What's up?
6:53 PM

Just at temple, you know, getting ready for services.
6:54 PM

> Are you okay?
> 6:54 PM

>> Stomachache.
>> 6:55 PM

> It's not even a lie, honestly.

> Oh no! I hope you feel better for Sunday.
> 6:56 PM

>> Me too.
>> 6:57 PM

The service is about to start, but still I hope for some last message, a flirty emoji, anything. It doesn't come. Disappointed, I return to my mission of frosting two hundred and fifty-two more cupcakes, alone. I work methodically, focusing on one pattern at a time until I am on autopilot.

Is it self-centered to think his weirdness is because of the renewed possibility of meeting Kels IRL, because of me? It doesn't even make sense. What happened to Kels isn't real? He hasn't brought up Kels to me, not once, since *Fireflies and You*.

Still, he thought he loved Kels—that can't just go away. Even if he's mad or hurt or whatever he's feeling. But I'm pretty sure he loves me, Halle, too.

To him, it's a triangle.

But I know it's just a line.

It's always been a line.

. . .

It's Cupcake Day, and Faneuil Hall is the definition of too much.

Quincy Market, the food hall of Boston's historic shopping center, stretches endlessly in front of us. Food vendors line both sides of the path. Seriously, any food you want? It's in Faneuil Hall. Sushi. Pizza. Lobster. Ice Cream. Every choice is at your fingertips.

"Gotta get me some chowdah," Ollie says.

I almost spit up my sip of water. "Never say that again."

Ollie smirks. "Chowdah."

"Okay," Gramps says. "We get it, Ollie. Hal, what do you want?"

We've already walked the entire food hall, so I should be able to choose. But I don't know. There are too many choices. Too many tourists pushing past me every time I pause to read a menu.

"How about we get a pizza?" Gramps asks. "Can't go wrong with that."

I nod. Pizza is good. I can do pizza.

Gramps says he'll handle the food, so Ollie and I go search for a place to sit. It's nice out, bright and sunny, and everything is crowded inside. Spring is here, so we snag a table outside, in view of the live performers scattered throughout the promenade.

In the open air, away from the claustrophobia that is Quincy Market, I can *breathe* and enjoy this.

Three hundred One True Pastry cupcakes have already been successfully delivered to Central Square Books. In a few hours, people will be at the event, eating those cupcakes, tweeting those cupcakes. I'll meet Ariel Goldberg. Maybe, if I'm brave, I'll tell her they're mine, *I'm Kels.* I'll finally say it out loud, own it. She'll sign my collection of her books and the weight of carrying them around in my backpack all day will be worth it. Everything about this day will be a success.

You will be a success.

"Ready for tonight?" I ask Ollie.

He looks up from his phone, mid-Snapchat selfie. "I can't wait. You'll never be able to top this present. You peaked too soon. I'm sorry."

I laugh. "Challenge accepted."

"Are *you* ready?" Ollie asks.

"I think so. I just hope my cupcakes don't suck."

Ollie sticks his tongue out at his camera. "We both know your cupcakes don't suck."

"What if Nash hates me?" I ask.

Since I can't tell him here, today, like I wanted to, I'm going to tell him when we hang out tomorrow. I'll show him pictures from the event, pictures of the cupcakes, and have a leftover cupcake for him. It's not a perfect plan, but I've accepted that there will never be a perfect plan or the right moment to tell Nash the truth. I can't force things to stay the same. Honestly, I don't want them to.

I want him to know. I want him to know me.

Ollie lowers his phone, placing it on the table. "I'm not going to tell you what you want to hear."

"Great table, kiddos."

Gramps appears with the food and I'm grateful for the distraction because I almost definitely don't want to hear what Ollie was going to say. We dig in and I burn my tongue, biting into the gooey cheese pizza too fast. Ollie is obsessed with his *chowdah*, and I swear he's going to say *chowdah* every day for the rest of our lives, just so he can see me cringe when he does. Sometimes, Ollie says the smartest things and I forget he's fifteen. Then he says *chowdah, chowdahhhhh,* and I remember.

"Did Mir ever tell you about our first date?" Gramps asks.

We shake our heads and I lean forward, my elbows on the table, anxious for another Grams story. The best part of today, besides *not* dropping three hundred cupcakes during the delivery process, has been story time with Gramps.

Most of the stories begin with, "In college . . ."

It's jarring at first, imagining a Gramps who is in college, a Gramps not too much older than me, exploring these same streets more than fifty years ago. He and Grams met when he was a senior at Boston University. She was an editorial intern at a small press.

"I surprised her at her first improv show—"

Excuse me? This is brand-new information.

"Improv?" Ollie asks.

"Grams?" I ask.

Gramps laughs.

"I didn't know Grams was funny," Ollie says.

"She's not." Gramps shakes his head. "By *first improv show*, I meant *only* improv show."

Ollie snorts. "Aw, Grams."

I wonder what else I don't know about her.

So I ask Gramps questions I thought I never could.

Why did you ever think premed was a good idea?

When did you know Grams was the one*?*

How on earth did you both end up in Middleton?

Gramps answers every question and it feels so good being able to talk about the past—about *her*. Some days, I can tell it's still so hard for Gramps, but it's kind of amazing how far he's come, compared to how broken he was when we got here. Maybe it's being out of Middleton, but today, he laughs through stories, like the revelation that "Islands in the Stream" started as a dare at a frat party.

I hope this Gramps, *my* Gramps, continues existing when the magic of Boston fades.

I fall in love with Central Square Books.

This store is particularly adorable—each wall is a different bright and inviting color, the floor is a deep blue carpet, and the shelves are a rainbow of categories and genres and beautiful words. I could spend hours browsing just the young adult section. I could spend an entire Maple Street Sweets paycheck here, I'm certain.

"Enjoy Book Nerd Heaven," Ollie says at the door.

Gramps hugs me. "Eat an extra cupcake for me."

"Go Red Sox," I say.

Ollie and Gramps leave me to my books and my cupcakes and head for hot dogs at Fenway Park. Booksellers are in the process of setting up chairs in the event space that takes up the back corner of the store. I peer from behind one of the middle-grade shelves, watching them as they line up row after row. They come in and out of the EMPLOYEES ONLY door and I wonder if my cupcakes are hiding somewhere behind that door.

Twenty minutes ago, Alyssa Peterson tweeted a behind-the-scenes photo of *Read Between the Lies* with one of my cupcakes and Twitter *freaked out*. My mentions are insane. I've avoided Twitter since—the hype is way too much pressure, honestly.

I'm not the only teen aware of the chairs; as soon as setup is complete everyone appears out of nowhere, claiming chairs with tote bags and backpacks. I drop my tote on an end seat in the third row. With a decent seat successfully claimed, I weave my way through the crowded space and back to the YA section. I squeeze past people in tight aisles and wow, when did it get so crowded? Seriously, it's like I turned around and the small crowd became an Ariel Goldberg mob.

My heart spikes every time my skin accidently brushes against a stranger's. I weave through the aisles of books, past the long line of teens purchasing *Read Between the Lies,* and push through the doors of Central Square Books. The cool air feels good against my flushed skin. I collapse onto a bench in front of the store, cover my face with my hands, and *breathe*.

It's too many people and the space is too small and oh my God, *my cupcakes*—what if everyone thinks they taste terrible and I am here to *witness* the embarrassment firsthand?

I imagine the hate tweets.

OTP cupcakes are pretty . . . pretty AWFUL!
should've stuck to the aesthetics, Kels . . .

The email from Alyssa Peterson was one of the most excit-ing things that has happened to my blog, besides BookCon, but I'm overconfident when it comes to my cupcakes. My whole life, everyone has told me how great my baking is. By "everyone," I mean my parents, Ollie, Gramps, and Nash—AKA the people who would never in a million years tell me that it sucks. For all I know, my cupcakes could be the worst.

If they are, the whole Twitterverse will know in an hour.

One True Pastry will never recover. Maybe NYU will change its mind.

Breathe.

I stay on the bench until the speed of my heart slows down and the panic subsides. Until I find the confidence that brought me from Middleton to Boston with three hundred cupcakes. Until I remember that at every one of my parents' wrap parties, One True Pastry cupcakes were the dessert of choice for entire film crews.

My cupcakes are the *moistest*, according to Nash.

They got noticed by Ariel Goldberg. By BookCon.

I am good at what I do. No, I am *great* at what I do.

The event starts in fifteen minutes, so I find the courage to venture back inside the store. I weave my way through the crowd. A semicircle of bodies has formed behind the last row of chairs—and that semicircle is five people thick, with a small gap so that people can walk down the center aisle.

At the end of the aisle, I see the chair that Ariel Goldberg is going to sit in. Two rectangular tables are set up—one for books and wow, yeah, one for my cupcakes.

They look amazing, on display like that next to the book. I got the frosting colors *just* right. It's a perfect Bookstagram.

Shoulders back, eyes forward, I march down the aisle and toward my bag—which is miraculously still saving my third-row seat. Book nerds might be passionate AF, but we respect seat saving rules.

It's a good sign. Tonight is going to be good.

Settled in my seat, I finally feel able to scroll through Twitter to check the pre-event buzz.

I search all the appropriate hashtags—#ReadBetweenTheLies, #OTPCucpakes, #ArielGoldberg, #KelsCupcakes—and retweet my favorite posts.

Retweets will have to do. I'm not unveiling that I'm here today.

It's five minutes till six and my pulse quickens—this time from anticipation.

It's surreal, honestly. Being here and living this moment where online and IRL blurs and it's okay because I am—

"Halle?"

My eyes snap up and my stomach plummets to the floor. It's not. I mean, it can't be. What? He's in Connecticut. He has a *Nick* thing.

"N-Nash?" I sputter.

"What are you—?" he asks, eyes wide in alarm.

Then they flicker forward, to the cupcakes.

Back to me.

Cupcakes.

Me.

"Kels?"

April 6

Ariel Goldberg @ArielGoldberg 1 hr
Look at these beauties thanks to @OneTruePastry!!
#ReadBetweenTheLies 😍😍😍
|

Sophie @unicornbooks 37min
SOUND THE ALARM, I AM 99% SURE KELS IS HERE
|

Elle Carter @ellewriteswords 5min
. . . and I'm 99% sure that's @Nash_Stevens27 with her?! cc
@AmysBookshelf @s_lee244
|

Amy Chen @AmysBookshelf 3min
WHAT.
|

Samira Lee @s_lee244 1min
👻 👻 👻 ???
|

Elle Carter @ellewriteswords 25s
lol that hand holding is the opposite of romantic
|

Samira Lee @s_lee244 now
brb blowing up nash's phone as we speak

TWENTY-THREE

'm wrong," Nash says. "Tell me I'm wrong. *Please*."

And that's how I know I'm the reason he's here.

Not me, Halle.

Me, Kels.

There never was a Nick thing—it was always a Kels thing. With this realization, my cheeks flush pink and I clench my fists so tight I make fingernail marks in my palms. Focus on the pain of nails attempting to break flesh.

I knew Nash probably still had some feelings and questions. But this is more than that. Nash came all the way to *Boston* to maybe meet another girl, and that *hurts*. Even if that girl wound up also being me—he didn't know that.

"I can't," I whisper.

Nash blinks, still *so* confused. "Kels?"

The second time he says my name, it is twenty levels too loud and suddenly it is chaos. Random pairs of eyes flash to us, to *me*. A blonde girl behind Nash asks if it's true, if I'm Kels. She may as well have screamed because it sets off a ripple effect of questioning for confirmation, of professing their fandom, of gushing over my cupcakes. People pull out their phones and start taking photos and in an instant, my face is going to be plastered all over Book Twitter. My anonymity is officially gone. And not in the *Hey, you made these awesome cupcakes and have amazing book taste* type of way I'd always imagined.

Nash stands. He takes my hand and pulls me through the crowd, through the noise, to the quiet outside. Away from the cupcakes and Ariel Goldberg fans asking if I am Kels, *excited that I'm Kels*, with absolutely zero awareness that my whole life is blowing up right in front of my face. The moment we're away from the crowd, Nash drops my hand like it is on fire and continues straight out the door.

I push through the double doors after him and even though he's stopped out front I don't stop walking. I put as much space between Kels and Central Square Books as I can. I focus on speed walking in wedges that pinch my toes with every step. Cross the street and turn the corner, *don't stop*. I don't know what to feel first, who to feel it for.

Halle is freaked because she is caught red-handed in her lie.

Kels is overwhelmed by her whole online world exploding.

Halle is crushed because Nash lied too.

Three blocks later, I am sitting on an empty bench, my arms wrapped around my knees. Nash arrives and paces back and forth the length of the bench. He runs a hand through his hair and I know he's waiting for me to speak, but I've never been so lost for words.

I don't know who I'm angrier with—Nash or me.

"I'm still, um, processing," Nash says. "This doesn't make sense? You're Kels."

He needs to believe it, so I flip my phone screen to show him One True Pastry's Twitter account. To show him my blown-up notifications, the pictures, the excitement surrounding the fact that *I*, *Kels*, showed up to the Ariel Goldberg event. Even bigger news to Book Twitter? Nash and Kels being spotted there. *Together*. IRL.

"Kels," Nash repeats.

I swallow my scream. "A Nick thing?"

His mouth drops open. "Well—"

"There never was a Nick thing. It was a Kels thing."

"Holy shit, Halle. Does it even matter? You're the same person!"

"You didn't know that!" I say.

"Yeah but you *did*. Rewind. Let's talk about *that*. You're Kels."

He still says it like it's another language.

I nod. "I'm Kels."

"Kels," he repeats. His voice cracks and I want to bury my face in my knees. He sits next to me on the bench and closes his eyes and I know he's pressed rewind. Back to every moment I sort of slipped, every chance he had to put the pieces together. Every time he mentioned Kels and I nodded along. Every time he told me the stories of his life that I already knew. Every time he texted me, Halle, and me, Kels, simultaneously.

The sunrise.

Molly's party.

It's all clicking, just way too late.

His eyes pop open. "This is so messed up."

"I know."

"You're so messed up," Nash says.

His words stab me in the stomach.

"Nash," I say.

"No," Nash says. "This is such bullshit. I told you about BookCon. I showed you REX. *I told you how I felt about Kels.* God. You knew that and you ghosted me and I had no idea why. Do you even know what that was like? But you've been right here the whole time. How could you not tell me?"

"I was scared." It's the answer behind all the excuses and justifications. Really, that's all it ever was. It was never about Nash or protecting OTP. I was just too scared.

Nash laughs, like, *That's the best you could come up with?* "Of what?"

I pick the threads on my ripped jeans so I don't have to look at him. "Honestly? Kels is way cooler than me, right? At first I thought you'd be disappointed if you knew."

Nash blinks.

"At first? Halle. It's *April.* It's been *seven months.* We're in a *relationship.*"

"I know."

"All year, you lied to me. Pretended not to know me. You lied to all of us." He clenches his fists at his side.

I cringe because I hate that word. That's who I am to him now. A liar.

"I liked that you liked me," I blurt out.

His fists unclench. "What?"

"Online? As Kels? I don't stumble over my words. People *care* about what I say. *You* cared. She's me without the anxiety that comes with *being* me. When we met, I didn't even know how to *friendship* IRL. But you still liked me. I don't know. I liked that. And like you said: Kels isn't real. This is. We are."

"Were," Nash corrects. "We *were*."

There it is.

"Nash," I say.

"Were you ever going to tell me?" he asks. "You're doing the panel, right? How did you think this would go down? Did you think I'd see your picture when they announce the schedule in a few weeks and go, *Huh, Kels is actually Halle. Cool.*"

I shake my head. "I asked if you had plans today. *This* was supposed to be the plan. I wanted to bring you here. I wanted to geek out together over meeting Ariel Goldberg and eat cupcakes and *I wanted to tell you here.* I wanted to show you."

Nash laughs. "*Right.* That would have made it way less of a betrayal."

I knew there wouldn't be a perfect plan. That I just had to do it. But now I am Halle the Liar. Nothing I say will matter.

"I loved you," Nash says, and my stomach falls another ten stories.

New tears fall fresh because it's already in past tense and he's never even said it in present.

Nash bites his lower lip. "I need to go—I need to . . . God, I don't know."

"I'm so—"

"Stop." Nash stands so fast he trips over a crack in the sidewalk. He doesn't fall, just stumbles forward a few steps in his
whirlwind to rush out of my life.

I reach for his hand to steady him.

He freezes and I sigh because his hand is warm and it's in
mine.

It's selfish, stupid to think he'll stay, talk it out more, try to
forgive me, but for half a second I do.

When I open my mouth again, he pulls away.

"Later, *Kels*."

Before I can react, he's gone, stomping on the pavement like
he's crushing the pages from our history underfoot as he runs
down the street.

April 6

Samira Lee
KELS. WHAT IS GOING ON?
8:42 PM

Elle Carter
WE ARE SO CONFUSED. YOU MET NASH?
AFTER YOU GHOSTED HIM?
8:43 PM

Amy Chen
I know we're not supposed to be talking to
you since you decided you're over being
friends with us, or whatever, but seriously?!?!
8:44 PM

Elle Carter
The photos are pretty awkward, tbh. Did you
not know he was going to be there?
8:46 PM

TWENTY-FOUR

Grams is probably second-guessing my publicity career right about now. Honestly, so am I.

Publicists are supposed to *fix* problems, not *cause* them.

Photos spread through the YA Twitterverse like wildfire, and not of the cupcake variety.

Kels and Nash have gone viral. Online, our friendship is no secret. We comment on each other's content, retweet posts, and chat in public Twitter threads. So the entire YA online community and REX fandom are kind of losing their minds reposting the photographic evidence of *us*—Kels and Nash—*together*. One follower proclaimed in a REX subreddit that Nash and I are an OTP.

The photo is hideous, it is everywhere, and we're both caught in the hype.

Curled up on the couch with Scout, I open Twitter on my laptop. I know it's a bad idea. I'll spiral down the rabbit hole, into this alternate universe where Kels and Nash are together and the book world is just *happy*. This is the last place I should be right now. But I have to—

Nash Stevens @Nash_Stevens27 23min
Blindsided

I click on Nash's page. The gray FOLLOWS YOU banner is not next to his handle anymore. He's hurt. He's making a statement. Calling out the lie in the photo. Everything is about to get so much worse. Nothing is private anymore. Not who I am. Not who I love. Nothing.

I click on the tweet.

Sophie @unicornbooks 21min
wait. so you're NOT with @OneTruePastry? what did she do?!

Olivia Brooke @livlaughlove333 15 min
are we cancelling Kels? cupcakes are overrated!!

Lilah Montgomery @lilahrose424 12 min
Why are we assuming this is KELS'S fault?

Deja Louis @dejavuwho 8min
#cancelonetruepastry

That's only the beginning. People are taking sides. Over a one-word tweet.

Sometimes, I really hate Twitter.

"Stop." Ollie sits next to me, closes my laptop, and swipes it from my grasp.

"Give it," I say.

"Nope. Not happening."

I reach for my phone on the side table and *surprise*, it's not there.

"Oliver."

He shakes his head. *Nope.* Gramps passes through the living room on his way to the kitchen and Ollie throws my phone to him, almost like the intervention was choreographed. Gramps catches my phone and slips it into his back pocket. He doesn't say anything, doesn't even stop walking.

Gramps knows the Nash situation and it's the most embarrassing part of our relationship. When Nash left me on the park bench around the corner from Central Square Books, I don't even remember how I got back to the hotel. I *do* remember Ollie and Gramps returning from their baseball game, high on the Red Sox's victory, only to find me curled up in bed, hysterical. It really freaked Gramps out, I think. He tried to talk to me, but I went mute. I didn't speak, not one word, the entire ride home to Middleton.

Ollie told him everything—in unnecessary detail.

"Ollie, *please*."

Scout's head pops up, alert.

Ollie holds my hand and I don't even realize that it's shaking—that *I'm* shaking—until he steadies me. My vision blurs. The feeds were moving faster than I could read them and being cut off sends a shock of panic through my system. I need to know what the world is saying, even if I don't speak back. Is Nash going to tweet more information? Will everyone hate me? I don't know how to respond. I just know I need to, well, *know*.

I close my eyes and count the beats of my erratic heart until it steadies.

I wipe my nose with my shirtsleeve. "I need to see it."

"Not productive. Is now a bad time to say I told you so?" Ollie asks.

I don't even have the energy to flip him off. He's right.

"Twitter will die down. I give it twenty-four hours at most. Let's face it. You're not *that* interesting."

Insert Angry Sister Glare here.

"He's pissed. *Obviously*," Ollie says. "Collecting the receipts isn't going to help."

"He unfollowed me," I say.

"I'd unfollow you too," Ollie says.

"Please. Give me. My laptop."

"No," Ollie says. "Take another hiatus, Hal. You seriously need it."

Ollie takes my laptop upstairs and we are not okay.

Nothing is okay.

"I can't do this."

"Halle," Gramps says, his tone even. "You're going to school."

We're parked in the MHS student drop-off area, Gramps and me. Ollie's long gone, off to lock up his baseball stuff before first period. We were supposed to walk in together, Ollie and me. But I'm frozen in my seat. I *can't*. The idea of walking into school? Of seeing Nash? Facing Le Crew? I can't do it. I *won't* do it. Nope. I need more time. One pajama day with Scout was not enough. I need infinite pajamas days.

Kels is back on hiatus. Can't Halle be too?

"I'm going to fail my calc test," I say.

"That's probably true," Gramps says. "Who cares, though? You got into NYU."

"Gramps."

"Hal," Gramps says, "you can't hiatus from life. When people mess up, there are consequences. So I'm sorry, I love you, but you're going to school. You can't avoid him forever."

"Not forever. Just until I figure out what to say."

Gramps starts the car. "Isn't that the problem? You waiting to figure out what to say?"

My eyes widen. Gramps is right. He's also *savage*.

"Either you go to school today, or you come to the Jacobsons' seder on Wednesday."

Passover starts Wednesday night and under no circumstances will I be attending *anything*, never mind a seder, at Molly's house. It's a tragedy, because honestly, I was *totally* looking forward to my first proper seder. A few weeks ago, Nash explained to me how it goes down at Molly's—less party than Rosh Hashanah, more prayer and reflection. And great food.

Defeated by Gramps's ultimatum, I reach for the door handle. "Okay. *Fine.*"

The passenger door swings open and I pick my backpack up off the floor, my movements stiff. I slam the door shut and leave Gramps without saying goodbye, angry because he's *right*, this is what I do. I bite my tongue. I wait for moments to present themselves, for the right words to appear out of thin air, and they never do.

Nash hurt me too, but it never would have happened if I had just told the truth. He needs to know how sorry I am. Even if it comes out all wrong, I have to at least *try*.

I tie my purple cardigan around my waist and push through the double doors. I have five minutes until first period. If we were still us, we'd be hanging out by Nash's locker, sipping on iced coffees and discussing *King Lear* before we head off to debate act one, Socratic seminar style. I bolt toward the English wing, taking the stairs two at a time and ignoring the stares from students who are heading to first period in every direction. Because if Nash is still at his locker, I need to catch him.

A five-minute chat won't fix us. But I won't make it through the day if I can't talk to him first.

I turn the corner to the English wing and exhale because it's mostly empty, but I see Nash—he is still *here*; I'm not too late. He's at his locker, rummaging through his backpack as if he can't find what he's looking for. He's chewing on his lower lip and his hair falls into his eyes.

He looks *awful* and it rips my heart in half because it's my fault. I did this.

I approach him. "Nash?"

Nash does not react to the sound of my voice. His bloodshot

eyes do not snap up to meet mine. He doesn't flinch. Nothing. I'm standing two feet away from him, but it's like I'm not even here. He digs through his backpack and I'm, like, if he hasn't found what he's looking for already it probably isn't there.

"Nash."

He pulls *King Lear* out. Zips his backpack and tosses it over his shoulder. He turns away and starts walking down the hall toward Mr. Walker's class. I get that he's angry. I deserve it. But *talk to me. Yell at me.* I know I messed up bad—but I want to fix it. He won't even look at me. He'd rather pretend he doesn't hear the sound of my voice. It's like I'm nothing.

"Nash." I wipe away the tears that roll down my cheek.

I hate how desperate I sound, how desperate I *am.*

He doesn't turn around.

And it hits me.

I'm being ghosted.

At lunch, I hide in the library, in the comfort of drafting OTP posts.

Really, what choice do I have? Nash and I have not made eye contact *once* today. It's kind of an impressive feat, considering we have almost every class together. Like, I was banking on accidental awkward eye contact to happen at least *once*—for Nash to see that my eyes are bloodshot too. He doesn't. All morning, we move from class to class, very much *not together.*

Of course, Le Crew is Team Nash.

They're by his side in all our overlapping classes, as silent as he is.

Yesterday, Molly and Autumn texted me.

Molly Jacobson
Nash is wrecked. Please tell me there is a
logical explanation because this is too messed
up.
3:31 PM

Autumn Williams
I always told him not to trust Kels. I never
thought we couldn't trust YOU
3:33 PM

I didn't see the messages until Gramps handed my phone back to me this morning. I wanted to answer them, wanted to explain myself. I get it. Nash isn't the only one I hurt. I lied to them too. But today they're as icy as Nash and I know it's not worth wasting my words.

Le Crew are Nash's people.

I need *my* people.

But I probably lost Amy, Elle, and Samira too. Still, they *deserve* an explanation—Kels just *ghosted* them along with Nash. I became too involved in my Halle/Kels drama to see I was literally giving them up just to maintain an unsustainable lie.

After finishing my lunch, I open my DMs, type a message, and send it before I change my mind.

hi. i miss you guys so much. everything is such a
mess and i'm a mess and i'm so sorry i ghosted
you. it wasn't about you it was about the nash
stuff and i have a lot to explain. too much for
one text but i needed to start somewhere so
hello. hi. i'm halle.
12:21 PM

I stare at my screen, waiting for a response, terrified of more
silence.

But like always, they start typing immediately.

Elle Carter
It is very Not Okay, Halle/Kels.
12:24 PM

i want to talk, for real. i'll explain everything.
12:25 PM

Amy Chen
nash told us the gist. you've known him since
september???? you've been DATING???
12:27 PM

Samira Lee
You've seriously been in Connecticut this
whole time? What else have you lied to us
about?
12:27 PM

> please just let me explain
> 12:30 PM

Elle Carter
We video chat on Fridays. I'm inviting you
because there is no logical way you can
explain this via text.
12:31 PM

Amy Chen
it's going to be a tough enough sell via
hangouts tbh!!!
12:31 PM

Samira Lee
If you ghost us again, I'm done.
12:32 PM

> i'll be there
> 12:33 PM

"So *this* is how we meet."

Elle's enunciation is exactly like how she texts, I swear. If we were texting right now, this would be capitalized. Her arms are crossed, her dark brown eyes looking directly into the camera, straight into mine. There's no more filter between us. Her braids are tied in a topknot and she's wearing a NaNoWriMo winner T-shirt from a few years ago.

"Hey," I say, delivering an awkward wave. It's the most social interaction I've had all week.

Amy pushes her thick black glasses up on the bridge of her nose. "This is so weird."

Samira says, "What do we even call you? Kels? Halle?"

Her voice has a Southern accent I'm not expecting. It's all so jarring—my friends, with faces. Not that I'm not looking at their faces every day. But those are pictures. Posed. Not faces with expressions with emotions. Not faces that scream, *You owe us an explanation, so get talking*.

"Kels is a pseudonym. My real name is Halle Levitt. I'm not an army brat and I didn't move to Georgia in September. I moved to Middleton to live with my grandfather. My parents are actually kind of famous? Well, in the documentary world. So I guess they're not that famous . . ." Shit, I am definitely rambling. "But you probably knew my grandma. Miriam Levitt? Anyways, I didn't even know Nash lived here, not until I bumped into him at the library my first day here. And I was so freaked, I didn't tell him . . . and then it eventually got to the point where I couldn't tell him—and I really messed up."

"You've been friends with Nash for years. You didn't know where he lived?" Samira asks.

I shrug. "People from Connecticut usually say, 'I'm from Connecticut.' Like, there is literally nothing distinguishing about Connecticut. Trust me."

Amy snorts. "Fair, I guess. But you were just . . . friends with him all year? While you were still texting him as Kels?"

"That's really messed up," Elle says.

"It didn't feel that way at the time. Not at first. At first, it felt like I needed to protect Kels and Nash's friendship, you know? I always move and leave, so I didn't want anything to change for this one impermanent stay. I didn't mean to fall for him."

I feel my cheeks heat with the admission.

"What?" Elle asks.

"Kels," Amy says.

"Halle," Samira says.

I tell them everything. The fake love triangle. Winter formal. The movie. REX.

"But you knew he was in love with Kels, right?" Elle asks.

I shake my head. How many times have I shook my head at my phone when we talked? For the first time, my gestures are visible. "Not until he told me."

"I'd say no one is that oblivious . . . but maybe you are?" Samira says.

"Nash has literally always loved you," Amy says.

I cover my hands with my face and shake my head. "He was my best friend. I didn't love him. Not like that. Not until I knew him."

Amy dips a carrot in hummus. "I wish you'd talked to us."

"We could've shut this shit down so fast," Elle says.

"I think that's why I didn't tell you. Seriously, I'm so sorry. For being distant. You've always been there for me—I hate that I made you feel like I didn't care about our friendship. I just got in so deep . . . I didn't know how to get out and even when I wanted to, I was sure you'd never forgive me. And I know you still might not. But I love you guys."

"We feel like we don't even know you," Samira says.

"It's kind of a lot of lying to process," Elle says.

"Process," I say. "I'll be here after you do. If you can."

"I want to," Amy says quietly.

For the first time in what feels like an eternity, I exhale.

"It's just . . . a lot," Samira repeats.

Elle looks past the computer screen and removes her earbuds. Nods and puts her earbuds back in. "I have to run," she says. "My brain has exploded, but I'm glad we talked."

"Me too," I say.

"Well. It was weird to meet you, Halle/Kels," Amy says.

"Good weird?" I ask.

"I haven't decided yet," Amy says.

The line disconnects and it feels like we have a long way to go. But if something good came out of this whole mess, it's the smallest possibility of weekly video chats with Amy, Elle, and Samira. It felt good, being myself with them.

I'm not sorry the truth is out, I'm only sorry *how* it came out.

I'm not sorry I'm Kels.

So I know what I have to do.

April 11

Halle (aka Kels) @OneTruePastry 19min
HELLO, TWITTERVERSE. this is me (and scout!) #shelfiepic.
Twitter.com/we3dkfl8 (1/4)

Halle (aka Kels) @OneTruePastry 17min
my name is halle levitt. my grandmother was miriam levitt, former editor-in-chief of empire children's, & I'm a book blogger/
cupcake enthusiast. I thought the pseudonym would let me
grow OTP independent from that legacy—instead, it made a
mess of my IRL relationships. (2/4)

Halle (aka Kels) @OneTruePastry 13min
I get that this is weird. I'll be on hiatus until June to focus on
studying for AP tests & finals. Scheduled posts will still go up!
school is A LOT right now . . . but my DMs are open for Qs.
And I'll see you at BookCon! (3/4)

Halle (aka Kels) @OneTruePastry 11min
If Halle is too weird, you can still call me Kels! That's cool!
(4/4)

TWENTY-FIVE

I haven't baked a single cupcake in a month, not one batch.

Every time I try to bake, I can't. At work, I stay behind the register and out of the kitchen. At home, I screw up vanilla bean batter and throw it in the trash, bowl and all.

Yesterday, Nash tweeted he's going to NYU.

Nash Stevens @Nash_Stevens27 18hr
So thrilled to announce that I will be studying studio art @ NYU!! Can't wait to learn from the best and up my content game for everyone!
[147 comments] [87↨] [2.2k ♥]

Nash is going to NYU. He told his parents and they're letting him go. I'm *so* happy for him. But I hate that I don't know what happened and that I wasn't there for him. I know how hard that conversation must've been. I hate that I want to reach out to him so bad but I can't.

We're nothing. I have no right to ask.

Online life is otherwise surprisingly fine. It seemed like *such a big deal*—deciding not to split myself anymore, to tell the internet I'm Halle. To take ownership of my identity—and my mistakes—before BookCon.

In the end, no one really cared.

Kels, my persona, is something I built up in my head the whole time. The content is the same, and besides a few trolls, everyone has just accepted it. As Ollie predicted. They're over the Nash-Kels drama now that we're both back to posting regularly and haven't said anything else.

The online world keeps turning, though, and buzz builds on Twitter re: all things BookCon. There are pre-con giveaways, raffles for tickets to exclusive events, and all the swag promotions. I tweet cupcake promises I might not be able to keep. With each new tag, my heart flutters with a combination of excitement and anxiety.

But the panel is called Bloggers IRL, right? I want to be honest, to be *myself*, at BookCon.

Plus, last night the BookCon gods released the full schedule for panels, ARC drops, signings, everything—and wow, planning the weekend is more of a process than I ever imagined. I spend most of my study period mulling over the schedule, writing the priority events in a notebook, and fitting the puzzle pieces of this weekend together. I'm planning to live tweet the weekend as much as possible from the One True Pastry account while I'm there and write recap posts when it's over, so I have to think about what will be most exciting for my followers, too.

Nash sits two rows in front of me, and I watch him doing the same thing.

It's the first time hope flutters in my stomach in *weeks*, but as soon as I see a panel called Are Pictures Literature? On the Modern Consumption of Graphic Novels, moderated by best-selling graphic novelist Michael Yoon—I know why Nash is going to BookCon.

It isn't for me.

Part of me can't stop hoping he checks out my panel.

Even if he doesn't love me anymore, I want him to see the full picture of *me* just once.

I'm trying to salvage too-liquid frosting with more powdered sugar when Ollie enters the kitchen and asks if we can talk.

"Not about Nash," I say.

He opens his laptop and scowls at me. "Um, no. About me? And my life?"

Seriously, how long am I going to be the worst sister on the planet? I can't remember the last time I asked how he is, how he's doing. I've been so in my Nash feelings that I never even asked him how baseball season is going or when he and Talia became a thing.

I leave the frosting bowl on the counter and sit next to Ollie at the table.

"I'm sorry. Really sorry. What's up?" I ask.

"I kind of did a thing."

He turns his laptop to face me and it's opened to an email.

Subject: *Re: Junior Counselor Candidacy at Camp L'Tovah*
Eyebrows raised, I read.

Hi Oliver,

We are pleased to inform you that you have been accepted to the junior counselor program at Camp L'Tovah. We were impressed by your application, and after we spoke last week it is evident that you are a perfect fit. Attached is all the necessary start paperwork, important dates, and camp handbook to read at your convenience. Please confirm that you are accepting the position by May 30th. Orientation begins June 15th.

Welcome to Camp L'Tovah!

Sincerely,
Abraham Ben-Yehuda

I reread the email three times before reality hits. Ollie Levitt. My brother, who can't keep a *kippah* on his head if his life depended on it, is going to Jewish summer camp? Ollie barely knows the *shema* and he . . . is going to *junior counselor* a group of tiny Jewish kiddos? This is *incredible*.

"How did you even—?"

"Molly," Ollie says.

I nod. "Of course."

"I just . . . needed *something* to keep me here. The camp runs for six weeks and it's right outside New Haven, so it's kind of perfect. We'll visit Mom and Dad in Israel for a few weeks like we promised, then I'll bestow my wisdom on third through sixth graders for the rest of the summer while living with Gramps. It'll be great, and I'll get to stay. Do you think it will work?"

"I don't know. But it could help Mom see how serious you are," I say.

"Every time I bring it up, she shuts me down. I know she misses us. I miss them too. It's not about that. It's about staying in one place so I can take baseball seriously. I want to play in college, like Sawyer, you know?"

"That makes sense. Mom and Dad will get it, I think. They let us stay here when I explained my blog stuff to them. They're all about chasing dreams, you know?"

Ollie nods. "I hope so."

"I'll talk to Mom," I say. "If you need backup."

Ollie closes his laptop. "I think you mean *when* I need backup. Thanks."

"Of course. How did you bamboozle Abraham Ben-Yehuda into hiring you?"

"I, um, pretended to be a Yankees fan."

I gasp. *"Ollie."*

"I know. Don't tell Gramps."

"We both know I'm going to tell Gramps."

I forgot how good it feels, laughing with my brother—laughing in general.

"Whatever. I got assigned to sports and rec. So basically, I'm getting paid to teach kids how to throw a baseball. I'd do that for *free*, dude."

"Did you tell Talia?"

"We broke up weeks ago."

What? Did I seriously not notice that my brother was also going through a breakup? Now that I think about it, I haven't seen Talia around the house in . . . a few weeks.

"You didn't—"

"With all the Kels stuff, I don't know. It didn't seem important."

I shake my head. "It's *so* important."

"It's no big deal, honestly. We're better as friends."

"You're okay?"

He stands. "I'm awesome. I am a camp counselor. Well, assuming the parents let me. Still, I . . . need to ask Gramps if he has an extra *kippah*. Or five."

"I'll be here with the bobby pins and backup support."

Ollie pauses at the bottom of the stairs. "Thanks, Hal."

"I'm sorry I've been a mess. I'm sorry I *made* the mess. You were right. You told me so."

He pulls out his phone and opens an Instagram story. Presses record.

"Let Halle Levitt state for the record that I, Ollie Levitt, am always right."

I return to my cupcake batter. Because it's definitely true, but there's still no way I'm letting Ollie get that sound bite on the record.

. . .

Gramps comes home from class a few hours later and I have to accept that cupcakes are hopeless.

Attempt number one ends in half a bag of powdered sugar spilled on the countertops. Attempt number two, I use special dark chocolate cocoa for the batter and it is bitter times a million, so I dump the batter in the trash. Attempt number three, I forget how to fill a piping bag and lose half my batch of semi-decent frosting to the kitchen sink.

This is not working.

My phone buzzes on the powdered sugar counters with a new Nash tweet.

Yes, I still have notifications turned on for him.

It's just an #amreading tweet but I like it anyway. I know I shouldn't. I know it's desperate. But Twitter gives me the ability to interact with Nash in a way that I can't IRL. It's like reverting back to before all this started. With Twitter, I can say, *I still see you.* With Twitter, I can say, *I'm still here,* even if he doesn't respond.

Nash knows this move. He did it himself, after all, when Kels tweeted about NYU.

So I like his tweets, I read every review he posts on Outside the Lines, and my graphic novel TBR has become as long as my YA TBR.

Forget the kissing and the falling and getting caught up in the fact that my life somehow became novel-perfect—I will never even think about kissing Nash again, about being anything more than his friend, if he'll let me apologize. If it's possible he'll forgive me.

Every wrong choice was supposed to be in the name of not losing our friendship.

But that was never up to me.

And now, because of me, it's all up to him.

My brain is a constant loop of cupcakes. BookCon. Nash. Cupcakes. BookCon. Nash. Cupcakes. BookCon. Nash. Cupcakes. BookCon—

"Hal?"

Hands wrap around my shoulders.

I drop the battered spatula in the sink.

"Halle."

I turn around and, well, Gramps looks legit *freaked*—kind of like the first time he caught me using Grams's stuff to bake. But it's been okay for a while, more than okay, so I don't understand what is with the spooked face. I—

"Sorry, I'm—"

Gramps guides me to the table. "Sit."

I sit.

"I want to talk to you—"

"How was class?" I blurt out, because *I want to talk* is the scariest combination of words.

"Um, that's what I want to talk about."

I frown, because I wasn't expecting this. "Okay."

"There is no class," Gramps says.

My eyebrows scrunch together because I am so confused.

"I don't have any classes this semester." He scratches the back of his neck. "After Rosh Hashanah—well, I started going to a bereavement group in New Haven. I wasn't doing well, I know you know that, and Mrs. Jacobson suggested it." Gramps coughs. "I wanted to be okay—or at least, uh, functional. For you kids."

"Oh." This is a lot to process.

"I had decided you should have her books, but building the bookshelves? It was an exercise, well, from my therapist."

I chew on the inside of my cheek. "I wish I knew that."

Gramps sighs. "I didn't know how to tell you. It felt weak. But it's the best thing I've ever done. I can talk about her. I can build bookshelves and eat cupcakes and read her favorite books— the memories aren't so suffocating anymore. I needed help."

"That's not weak."

He dips his finger into the frosting bowl on the table. "I know that. I guess what I'm wondering is—do you?"

"Um, I've never thought about it."

It's the truth—the thought of therapy has never crossed my mind, not once. I know crowded spaces and too-loud voices trigger panic attacks. I know that if death even crosses my mind in the dark when I'm trying to fall asleep, I'll be tossing and turning for hours.

I know my anxiety. I know Ollie can always calm me down.

Except Ollie won't always be there. I mean, it's not like I can take him to NYU with me.

I know my triggers, but do I really know how to deal with them on my own?

I don't know.

"Well, you're always welcome to come to a group session with me. Open invitation. If you want to. Whenever you're ready—and if you're not, that's okay too. I know you're going through a lot, and I don't know how to help. I hate that. But this might. Help, I mean."

I close my eyes. *Breathe.* "I'll think about it."

Gramps nods. "Okay."

I stand up, certain that this too-real conversation is over for now.

"One more thing, Hal," Gramps says, and my butt reglues itself to the kitchen chair. "It's about BookCon. I've thought about this, um, a lot. And as much as I want to be at your panel, I can't do it. I just . . . I'm not ready yet, I'm afraid."

I swallow. "Okay."

"I'm sorry, Hal. I'll accompany you to New York, of course. But I don't want you to think—"

I shake my head. "I promise I don't."

"I'm proud of you. Mir would be too, you know."

"Gramps. Stop it. I'm blushing."

"I only speak truth."

I stand up, transferring the dirty bowls from the table to the sink. "I screwed up. Bad."

"Everyone screws up. Let me be proud."

I point to my flaming cheeks. "Nope. Stop it."

He sighs. "Fine. You're the worst. Please tell me there are cup-cakes on the counter."

Of course the cupcake container is freshly stocked with Maple Street Sweets cupcakes. Sawyer baked this batch himself, and they're almost as good as mine. "Red velvet or vanilla and chocolate?"

Gramps narrows his eyes at me. "What do you think?"

"Cream cheese frosting?"

He nods. "Cream cheese frosting."

May 28

Mom
Just submitted the waiver for Ollie. I can't
take him to LA with us just because I miss him.
You're right. Thanks for making me listen last
night. ♥
4:39 PM

Mom! I'm SO glad.
4:47 PM

it'll also selfishly be nice that ollie will only be
a train ride away. i wish you were only a train
ride away . . .
4:48 PM

Mom
I know, babe. But you'll be thanking me in
December when you're visiting us during
winter break!!!
4:49pm

Dad

4:50pm

that's definitely true
4:52pm

Mom

we'll celebrate when we see you! two more
weeks until graduation. i cannot wait to give
you a hug! warning: i might never let go.
4:53pm

Dad

🐗 ❤ 🐗 ❤ 🐗 ❤

4:55pm

???
4:57pm

TWENTY-SIX

So." Elle taps absentmindedly on her desk. "What are we going to do about Nash?"

It's the fifth time I've talked to my friends—and each time we feel closer to okay. I wish I had joined the video chats *years* ago. I hate how much I've missed. Amy's had to cut back on the booktubing, because as it turns out, biochemistry is a ridiculous major. She spends most of her time in the library studying, and can't remember the last time she's read a book for fun. Elle's currently working on an R&R, a revise and resubmit, for an editor at a major publishing house—which is taking up all her free time. Samira has won some local photography awards for the pictures she's taken for her school newspaper.

It's so nice, this new normal: sitting back and listening to my friends talk about their own lives and their own drama. Until it inevitably circles back to me.

"I don't know," I admit. "He's so mad."

"He's mad because he's heartbroken!" Amy says.

"It's been almost six weeks, Amy," I say. "I miss him so much. But he still won't even *look* at me. I might have to accept that it's over."

"I refuse to believe that," Samira says.

"Not that we'd know," Elle says.

Besides updating REX, Nash has otherwise been pretty off the grid.

"You need an apology strategy," Amy says. "I'm thinking big and grand gesture-y, just so we're clear."

"*Super* grand gesture-y." Samira nods.

"I—" I'm cut off by a knock on my door. "One sec."

Gramps pokes his head in as I press mute on my mic.

"Hey, Hal. You've got some visitors downstairs."

I frown, confused. "Really?"

"I told them you'd be right down."

Gramps is gone before I can even ask who's here.

I unmute my mic. "Sorry, guys. I need to run. But re: grand gesture . . . I am open to anything."

"Don't give us that much power," Elle says.

"We'll think of something," Samira says.

"Later, Halle/Kels," Amy says.

I shut my laptop and head downstairs feeling the weirdest mix of nausea and hopefulness.

"Hey."

Molly and Autumn are at the bottom of the stairs, waiting for me. Here. At Gramps's. We haven't spoken words to one another since before I broke their best friend's heart.

"Can we sit?" Autumn asks.

"We're going to sit," Molly says.

I nod. But I'm so confused.

They hate me.

They're Team Nash. I accepted it weeks ago. I lied to them, too.

I swallow. "Hi."

Silence.

Molly and Autumn look at each other.

Then at me.

Then back at each other.

"Hi?" Autumn asks. "Seriously, Hal?"

"Where is our explanation? We've been waiting"—Molly looks down at her smartwatch—"*six weeks.*"

I blink. "What?"

"You didn't answer our texts," Autumn says.

"You didn't defend Cordelia during yesterday's Socratic seminar," Molly says.

"You pick the *real sport* option in gym just to avoid us," Autumn says.

"We can continue," Molly assures me.

"You iced me at school," I say. "I thought—"

"Us?" Autumn frowns. "We reached out. *You're* the one who disappeared."

They're right. I don't speak at all during the *King Lear* unit even though *King Lear* is epic. I *do* choose all the terrible gym activities—basketball, ring hockey, soccer—even though I can't sport. I have bruises all over my body to prove it.

And they *did* reach out first. I never answered their texts. But when they didn't talk to me in class I just assumed it wouldn't change anything. I thought I was making it easier by avoiding them. I thought that's what they wanted.

"Hal," Autumn says, "talk to us. Please? What's going on?"

I want them to yell at me. I want to be chewed out.

They just wait to listen and I don't deserve that.

"Didn't he already tell you everything?"

I can't even say his name.

"Nash is hardly saying anything," Molly says.

"He's *miserable*," Autumn says. "Kind of, well, like you."

I chew on my lower lip. "I figured you'd hate me."

"Well, you don't get to just mess up and disappear!" Molly yells.

Autumn nods. "We tried to give you some space, because we saw a lot of the Twitter stuff. But yeah, that's not how this works."

"I've tried texting him and—"

Molly rolls her eyes. "I'm not talking about *Nash*. I'm talking about us—your two most awesome lady friends? Hello? I mean, we *are* friends, right? Because we have tried so freaking hard to be your friend, Halle."

I drum my fingers against my thigh. "Right."

Autumn laughs. "Convincing."

"You're supposed to be Team Nash," I say.

Molly's nose scrunches, confused. "Team—? Halle, this isn't *The Hunger Games*. Nash is my best friend, so of course I'd be lying if I said I'm not pissed for him."

"Honestly? I'm pissed for *me,* too," Autumn says. "I can't believe you've just been lying to all of us like that. We knew about Kels. We knew how Nash felt about Kels. We *told you.* And you just—acted like it didn't matter."

"It always *mattered,*" I say. "That's why this happened. It mattered too much."

"So talk to us!" Molly says. "We want to hear you out. At least, I do. I want to know why you did it."

"He misses you, even if he's too stubborn right now to admit it," Autumn says.

"We miss you too," Molly says.

I bite my lower lip. Hard. "Me too."

Over Sawyer's cupcakes, I summarize One True Pastry's origin story.

It was to separate myself from my Book Famous grandmother.

I didn't know I'd get so popular. I didn't know he'd become so important to me.

I was ready to tell him myself, I swear.

I was just scared.

I'm sorry.

It feels good, talking to Molly and Autumn. It probably would have felt even better if I had trusted them before it all fell apart.

"Is there a chance of, like—will he ever forgive me?" I ask.

Autumn shrugs. "Maybe. But he's hurt and stubborn and the best grudge holder in the universe—even better than *Molly.*"

"It's true. When I was eight, Nash had one of those, like,

motorized kid cars and he legit *ran over* my Barbie dream house. He felt so bad, he burst into tears. I didn't speak to him for three months. That Chanukah, Nash got one of those fancy glass Star Wars chess sets, right? Well, the first time we played it, I dropped a few of the pieces and Luke Skywalker's head fell right off. Nash didn't speak to me for *four* months."

"He's over it now," Autumn assures me as she crumples her cupcake wrapper into a ball.

Molly swallows a sip of water. "Barely. Nash wallows. It's a character flaw, but he usually comes around."

"I didn't break his rook, Mol," I say.

Autumn covers her mouth full of water with her hand—like she wants to burst into uncontrollable laughter. Water dribbles down her chin, but she manages to swallow most of it. Her hand doesn't move from her mouth and she is silent cackling like crazy.

Molly and I stare at her, expressions blank.

"Am I the only one who thought that sounded dirty?" Autumn asks.

"Clearly," Molly says.

"A hundred fifty percent yes," I say.

Our trio of laughter is loud and I know I'm still a work in progress, but I'm learning. Friendship—*real* friendship—isn't easy. It's destroying Barbie dream houses and screaming in movie theater parking lots and screwing up, sometimes badly. It's a mess of lines drawn in the sand and questioning loyalties and answering difficult DMs. It's making comparisons and exposing insecurities.

But it's also bowling by our own rules. Laughing until our

stomachs cramp and tears stream down our cheeks. It's knowing that I have people, real people, from all over the country in my pocket, always a text or tweet or lunch table away when I need them. It's knowing the world might be a trash fire, but it's less trash when there are people to help navigate the darkness.

Friendship is messy. Hard. Infuriating. Awesome. Fragile. Durable. Impossible. Worth it.

Always worth it.

BookCon, Morning

Elle Carter
BOOKCON DAY. Totally wish I could be there.
Kill the panel! Network! Steal all the ARCs!
8:59 AM

Amy Chen
ESPECIALLY THE NEXT QUEEN OF STONE
BOOK FOR YOUR BEST FRIEND WHOSE
FORGIVENESS YOU'RE STILL EARNING
9:01 AM

Samira Lee
Subtle, Amy. Also, pretty sure you can't steal
an arc!!
9:02 AM

Samira Lee
If you don't find Nash at the Michael Yoon
panel, I stg Halle/Kels
9:03 AM

Elle Carter

He's been thinking about texting you.

9:07 AM

Elle Carter

But you did NOT hear that from me!!

9:08 AM

Molly Jacobson

HAPPY BOOKCON DAY! REMEMBER TO
TELL US EVERYTHING PLEASE

9:07 AM

Autumn Williams

spare no details, obviously

9:09 AM

Sawyer Davidson

NASH WANTED TO TEXT YOU THIS AM. HAS
HE?

9:11 AM

Molly Jacobson

SAWYER.

9:11 AM

Autumn Williams
SAWYER.
9:12 AM

Sawyer Davidson
#sorrynotsorry
9:13 AM

TWENTY-SEVEN

Teens and their moms flood into the Javits Center by the hundreds.

We're a block away, walking west on 34th Street toward 11th Avenue. Every doubt, every anxious thought I have wraps its tendrils around me in these final moments where I am cocooned by family. With Gramps on my left and Ollie on my right, I feel safe amid the rushing crowds. But I'm going to have to step away from that, from them, and enter the gigantic glass box that is Javits. I love books; I really hate crowds.

My pulse quickens with each step that brings me closer to the chaos.

"Can I do this?" I mumble to myself. "No, not a question. I can do this."

Ollie hands the cupcake container to me. Inside are two dozen BookCon-themed cupcakes. I whipped them up at two a.m. because while no one asked me to bake—it wouldn't be One True Pastry without cupcakes. Maybe I'll offer them to volunteers and the other members of my panel, or maybe we can raffle them off to attendees afterward. Either way, they're the first successful batch of cupcakes I've baked since I started therapy two weeks ago, and I will take that small victory.

"You *can*," Ollie assures me. "If you can't, well, you have me on speed dial."

I frown. "No I don't."

Ollie rolls his eyes. "*Metaphorically speaking*. You know what I mean!"

Now, Gramps frowns. "But don't I have you kids on speed dial?"

Ollie shakes his head. "Sadly, the speed dial has been reduced to metaphor status, Gramps."

My phone buzzes with texts from Le Crew—*my* Crew.

I show Ollie the texts and for the first time, hope flutters in my stomach.

Inside, I am going to find Nash because he can avoid me in Middleton all he wants, but he can't avoid me at BookCon. I'll remind him that once upon a time, he wanted to be at BookCon with Kels and, well, here I am! Here, amid the books, I will apologize for my lie—but I will also prove to Nash that I am *me*.

I don't know if he'll forgive me, but I do know this is the best shot I've got.

These texts are proof. I've never been more thankful that Elle and Sawyer can't keep secrets, not if their lives depended on it. Nash knows this. So, like—if he told *both* of them that he was thinking about texting me, it probably means that he wanted me to know. Right? Even if he didn't follow through.

"You got this, Hal," Ollie says.

"Totally." Gramps gives me a thumb-up.

I laugh, because grandpas are not supposed to say "totally."

Ollie and Gramps hug me goodbye, leaving me alone before I have a chance to change my mind. They're off on another bro adventure, their first of many now that Ollie gets to stay. The condition was that we'll spend all school holidays together in L.A. Which isn't even a condition—I was planning on doing that *regardless*.

In mere moments, Gramps and Ollie blend in on the crowded sidewalks and I am alone.

I reread the texts one more time for an adrenaline boost before pivoting to face the Javits entrance.

Breathe.

I go in.

Perks of being Halle/Kels: I skip the queue.

The show floor is basically what heaven looks like. A maze of booths filled with books and swag. The smell of paper and ink, fresh off the presses. And tote bags. So many tote bags. I'm free to wander the floor and be an attendee until thirty minutes before the panel, when I will have to go pick up my cupcakes stored in the speakers' lounge, meet the other panelists, and prep. Yesterday, the moderator emailed us a short list of questions—so I am prepared-*ish*. Notecards are tucked in my back pocket, the beginnings of answers jotted down in longhand.

I spend the morning pretending I'm at BookCon with Grams. I peruse the stands for all the major publishers and my favorite independent presses, attend ARC drops every hour, buy the newest titles released by Grams's imprint, and keep my eyes peeled for Nash.

I don't know which are longer, the signing lines or the free tote bag lines, no joke.

I catch a glimpse of Lola Daniels signing ARCs and I just about pass out because *whoa*. Authors are everywhere. Industry people too. Like, as I'm scanning the crowds for Nash, I look the other way and make eye contact with Kristen Ellis, an agent I follow on Twitter.

"I think I know you from Twitter," I say.

Kristen raises her eyebrows. "Oh?"

"Yeah. I'm Halle," I hold out my hand. "From One True Pastry. Better known as Kels."

Recognition flashes in her eyes—*thank goodness*—and she takes my hand. "Oh! You did Grace Tran's cover reveal last year. Your cupcake cakes are *amazing*. It's so nice to meet you!"

"Thank you," I say. "Seriously."

"Can I get a selfie for Instagram?" Kristen asks.

I blink, processing the fact that a *literary agent* wants to take a photo *with me*. "Of course."

Now that Kels has a face, there's really no point in hiding it. We pose for the photo and Kristen tags me in her Insta story before we part ways. Wow. That was *so* cool.

I was so cool.

The Javits Center is overflowing with book lovers on a mission to attend their top panels, to meet their favorite authors. Everyone is so hyperfocused on their carefully curated schedules.

I continue to explore the show floor as just a teen who loves YA, like everyone else.

But Nash, the boy who is always everywhere, isn't *anywhere*.

At noon, I attend the Superheroes in YA panel because I'm certain he'll attend. The conference room is packed with more than two hundred people—but as far as I can tell, not Nash. I slip out of the room before the panel starts.

I text Sawyer.

He is here, right? This isn't a joke?
12:05pm

Sawyer Davidson
No but that's a good idea for next time!
12:07pm

I double back to the Empire Publications booth, since it's in the center of everything. On one side of me, a large group of hopeful teens and aggressive parents are battling for a box of ARCs. On the other side, people are receiving exclusive tote bags.

It's chaos.

I am surrounded by chaos.

Breathe.

". . . I can't believe he drew a panel for you!"

". . . you better save that for when he's famous . . ."

I turn toward a group of tweens squealing at a piece of folded-up notebook paper. The girl holding the paper has long red hair and is in a NIMONA T-shirt. The other two are taller, both in graphic tees featuring their favorite comic book characters.

Red holds the piece of paper to her chest and sighs. "He's so cool."

"Chill, Lana. He's just a blogger."

Lana's face turns as red as her hair. "Shut up and be jealous."

"Hey," I say, without quite thinking about it too hard. I *don't* insert myself into other people's conversations. But when I see the sketch, I see the swirl signature.

It's a Nash original.

"Can you tell me where you met him?"

The tweens eye me suspiciously.

"I'm his friend."

Lana crosses her arms. "Sure."

If he just did this—Nash could literally be *right here*.

I need these girls to talk.

"Wait." Lana's eyes narrow.

She nudges the blonde girl and they start whispering to each other. Blonde girl pulls out her phone and opens Twitter. She shows the screen to Lana and their eyes widen.

"Kels?"

I smile. *Yes.* "Hi."

"OTP totally got me through seventh grade," Lana says and I die because—well, that *matters*. Lana points in the general direction Nash went after they'd met. I thank her profusely, for reading, for helping, for all the things. She asks for a selfie and if I can sign one of her bookmarks.

I am somehow a star. It's so weird. But amazing.

Lana sends me to the back end of the Empire booth, where I see staffers lining people up for the next signing. The queue is long, wrapping around the corner and winding back toward the autographing area where Michael Yoon is. The graphic novelist that Nash came here to see.

Oh my God, Nash is totally in this line. My palms turn slick and all the papers fall out of my hands. Cursing under my breath, I bend over and collect my stuff, shoving all loose papers into one of one my five tote bags.

No, I do not *need* five tote bags—that's not the point.

I stand straight and wipe away the sweat that has accumulated on the back of my neck. Re-tuck my on-brand cupcake-patterned T-shirt into my high-waisted jeans. Smooth the bumps out of my ponytail. Check my lipstick.

Inhale.

Exhale.

I search the sprawling line, but it isn't simply one line. There are lines everywhere. It's kind of a mess and if he's here—I can't even begin to track him down. Maybe this shouldn't be a surprise. There are too many people, too much noise. I had no clue there'd be *so much*. Or that the Javits would be a giant maze filled with passive-aggressive—and straight-up aggressive—YA fandom. As I'm getting pushed out of the way by a ten-year-old, or being chastised for the cutting I didn't do by a mother, I think *Can't we all just get along? Isn't our mutual love of all bookish things civilizing?*

I check my phone and it's almost time for me to meet up

with my fellow Bloggers IRL panel members. I don't have the brainpower—or *time*—to keep looking for Nash.

Maybe I should just text him. Kels would.

Hey, Nash. I'm here.

Hey, Nash. Are you in the Michael Yoon line?

Hey, Nash. Meet me at x location at y time. Please.

I type and retype every variation of *I'm here* before settling on:

> well. we're both at BookCon. it's pretty much
> nothing like how I'd imagined it. but my panel is
> in E110 at 2. is it stupid to hope you'll show up?
> probably, but I'll save you a cupcake anyway.
> I really hope you will.
> 1:23pm

I press send before I can change my mind, and retreat downstairs to the designated panel meeting point—relishing these final moments where I am just an invisible teen who loves YA, just me.

I am so not qualified to be on this panel—what were the Book-Con gods *thinking*?

I'm seated between Celeste Pham and Lilah Clark and I have forgotten how to speak. I mean, my logic brain has known since BookCon announced panelists that they'd be here. But somehow the fact that I would be here, with them, *sitting next to them*, did not compute.

Celeste hosts Books on Tape—the number one bookish

podcast on the internet. Lilah is a booktuber with over a quarter of a million subscribers. The other four panelists are equally daunting—Annaliese is fifteen, agented, and a total star on Book Twitter. Pete advocates for diversity in middle grade. Sarah runs the best monthly #bookstagram challenges. And Tara rose to Book Twitter fame with poetry—every book review she writes is in iambic pentameter.

Each panelist that I am sitting alongside makes One True Pastry look meager. I am totally starstruck.

Stella McQueen, an editor at *Bustle*, is moderating. In the moments before the attendees enter the conference room, she introduces herself, and reminds us that of course we'll have a rapid-fire round and Q&A at the end.

Energy radiates from Celeste and Lilah.

"Is it Halle or Kels?" Celeste asks.

"Halle," I say. "I'm Halle."

"One of those cupcakes better be for me," Lilah says.

Pete reaches across Lilah and takes one off my plate. I bite my tongue and let him do it, even though the platter I've designed is now asymmetrical—a perfect twenty-four become twenty-three. Prime numbers make me twitchy.

Annaliese leans across Celeste. "Red velvet?"

And that is how the Blogger IRL panelists come to savor a One True Pastry cupcake in the moments before we begin. I pass them out, tongue-tied, but it's okay because I realize I don't have to speak or explain or draw any more attention to myself. My cupcakes speak for me.

Pete licks chocolate frosting off his fingers. "These are great, Cupcake Queen. Color me impressed."

"Thanks."

I still can barely process that they know who I am.

Sitting between two bookish icons? I, Halle Levitt, have peaked.

I will not squeal, though—that cannot happen. Today, I am a professional. A mutual. Not a fangirl. I can be a fangirl tonight, on Twitter, when I retweet the professional panel photos and post selfies of my own.

I glance at my phone and it is ten minutes until start time. Right on cue, the doors to the conference room open and attendees flood in. I count them by twos as they come in and my heart spikes to new heights every ten people.

Two. Four. Six. Eight. SO MANY PEOPLE.

Twelve. Fourteen. Sixteen. Eighteen. AHHH.

None. Of these. People. Are. Nash.

Focusing on the door is driving me mad, so I shift my eyes down to the notecards in my sweaty palms—so sweaty that ink has smudged and transferred onto my skin. *Shit*. I try to decipher the more illegible notes, try to remember what I wanted to say. I can't remember and oh my God, I am going to blank out. Right here. Onstage. Okay, it's not a stage. It's like an elevated platform. But still. What is my name? What does OTP even stand for? I don't know anything. I don't—

Celeste swipes the cards out of my hand, crumples them in a ball, and drops them on the floor.

"I get it," she whispers. "I almost passed out before my first panel from the nerves. But you'll sound rehearsed. Notecards mess with your brand authenticity."

I dig my fingernails into my palms. "Um. Okay."

"You be you," she says. "Trust me, *that's* why everyone is here."

"Not the cupcakes?" I ask.

She smiles, surprised. "Okay, mostly the cupcakes."

Microphone feedback echoes through the speakers. Stella stands and everyone claps and I've been to enough panels in my life to know that this is how it begins. It is happening, the moment that defined my senior year, the hour I've been counting down to since an email landed in my inbox six months ago. This day has been so hyped in my brain—I don't know how to process the fact that it is happening, *actually*.

"Welcome to the first Bloggers IRL panel! This year, Book-Con invited six of the most innovative book bloggers to—"

My phone lights up on my thigh. A notification. From *Nash*.

It takes everything in me to flip my phone so it's facedown. He's not here. So I can't be distracted by him. Not now.

It's panel time.

Each blogger introduces themselves, starting with Tara because she's seated next to Stella. I'm fourth to go, and I stumble through my introduction, in which I try to sound goofy and whimsical. I think I succeed, but blank out immediately after, so it's impossible to tell.

Stella asks her questions and I answer when it's my turn. I

cannot wipe the stupid smile off my face as I am thrown questions about blogging and cupcakes and being a teen voice in YA and even *Fireflies and You* and handling controversy on social media. Stella smiles at my answers, people laugh at my jokes, and I am *killing it*.

The first few questions, I ask myself, *What would Kels say?*

But honestly? I don't have to try so hard.

I am the Kels that everyone expects me to be, and she doesn't feel like a persona anymore. I hope Nash is here to see that. I hope he sees *me*. The girl who will forever avoid *The Lord of the Rings* fandom, who will talk books with him anytime, who will bake the most extra cupcakes because they may be for eating, but they're also for stress relief and brand building. The girl who is good at bowling but bad at finding the right words.

The girl who loves him.

I wasted an entire school year justifying the differences between my digital friendship with Nash and my IRL friendship—but were they ever that different? *Really?*

I don't think so.

I hope Nash doesn't think so either.

#BookCon

BookCon @BookCon 2hr
AFTERNOON REMINDER! Follow #BookCon all day to stay
up-to-date on all events and win swag!

Lana @Lana_and_Lola 15min
HI EVERYONE @OneTruePastry IS THE ACTUAL SWEETEST,
JUST FYI #BookCon

Lana @Lana_and_Lola 13min
ALSO, @Nash_Stevens27 WILL DRAW FOR YOU #BookCon

Lana @Lana_and_Lola 10min
And . . . I think @Nash_Stevens27 & @OneTruePastry are
okay? I MEAN, HE'S AT HER PANEL RN SO?!?! #BookCon
[47 comments] [125 ♺] [532 ♥]

Elle Carter @ellewriteswords 42s
WHAT #BookCon

Samira Lee @s_lee244 37s
#OTP #BookCon

Amy Chen @AmysBookshelf 25s
PLZ LET THIS BE TRUE 🙏🙏🙏 #BookCon

TWENTY-EIGHT

have one final question for Kels before we start taking audience questions."

Stella bats her eyelashes at me—which means whatever comes next will slay me.

"In this community, there's a lot of discussion of maintaining a brand identity and authenticity in these online communications. We all know you *and love you* as Kels—so I think a lot of people are wondering, who is Halle Levitt, and why share your identity now?"

Silence reverberates throughout the conference room.

Before the panel, Stella assured me that she'd avoid any questions regarding the Halle/Kels situation. I should've known she was full of shit. I guess in a way I kind of did, as I had an answer prepared on my crumpled-up notecards just in case. But Celeste was right: I don't need them.

"The way I look at it, Kels is my pen name. I don't regret that—I never have. Lots of people create under pen names. Blogging as Kels gave me a platform and a community that never would've existed, I don't think, if I'd created my blog as Halle Levitt, because it would've tied me to my grandmother. Nobody in the universe was a bigger Miriam Levitt fan than me. I *worshipped* my Grams. But I needed to know if people thought my content was good. I'd never know, not for sure, if I started my blog as Halle. Also, while the internet has given me so much, it can be a cruel place. I wanted to shield myself from that."

I swear the entire audience hears my heart beating through the microphone.

I look up at them and pause because leaning against the back wall, his arms crossed, is Nash. *Nash is here.*

Breathe.

"For the record, I love being Kels from One True Pastry. I will still post all the cupcake aesthetics on Instagram and write all the YA reviews. The only thing I regret, if I'm being totally honest, is letting One True Pastry overtake my life. Nash, I am so sorry."

Stella McQueen's jaw drops to the floor.

My fellow panelists' jaws follow suit.

If I'm speaking in clichés, it's because I just became one.

Nash stares at me, his eyes wide.

Then he bolts toward the back door. The exit.

Stella blinks. "On that note, I believe it's time for audience questions!"

Microphones are set up in both aisles, and those who want to ask questions stand and move toward the microphone closest to them. I look at the clock—in the fifteen minutes between now and the panel's official conclusion, Nash could be anywhere. He will be gone—the magic of BookCon will fade, and he will without a doubt never forgive me. Especially after the tweets that are sure to surface re: my very public apology.

I should go.

"I have a question for Kels and Annaliese."

My eyes shift away from the exit, back to the Q&A. A girl stands at the microphone, wearing an #AMWRITING T-shirt. "Hi. My name is Mel and I'm a teen writer. Both of your brands rely heavily on being teen voices. So I'm curious—what's the plan when you're, you know, not teenagers anymore?"

I laugh. "I ask myself that question every day."

"You should," Annaliese says. "It's your problem before it's mine."

The audience laughs and I'm grateful for a question that pivots away from Nash. "I guess the plan is to stay on the path to becoming a publicist and being sure to advocate for teen voices in-house when I do. I'll always read and love YA. But it won't always be *for* me, you know? So then I have to make sure to advocate for the teens it *is* for, like my grandmother always did."

The heads in the audience nod and I relax into my seat.

I can't make Nash forgive me.

I *can* finish this panel strong.

After the panel concludes, I bolt. Down the hallway of conference rooms to the food court. I'm starving and somehow it's the only place I can think he might be.

I spot his neon blue sneakers first.

He's sitting at one of the food court tables, furiously texting—so focused on his phone he doesn't even hear me say his name, doesn't even notice me sit down.

"*Nash,*" I say.

He jumps and looks up. "What was *that*?"

"Um—an apology?"

He shakes his head. "It's a PR move."

I blink. "What?"

"To Book Twitter, I'm now the asshole who walked out on your extra public apology."

I blink, shook by Nash's anger. "No. That's not—how could you even think that? I said I'm sorry because *I am sorry*. I know you don't believe me, and I promise it's the last time I'll say it. But I need you to know that I am so, *so* sorry. I never should've lied to you, especially when things got real between us. There were so many moments where I almost said it—but then you said something or I got scared and . . . I couldn't find the words. So I kept waiting for the right time, but I'd already missed it. The second I met you? I should've told you. The second I knew I loved you, I wanted to. But I didn't."

My words hang in the air, the weight of the rambling mess crashing on my shoulders.

"I can't believe I said that out loud."

"I can't believe you said that out loud," Nash says, his expression softening.

The scent of freshly made French fries wafts through the food court and my stomach moans, reminding me that I haven't eaten today. I want fries, and wow, I want them *now*.

Shut up, stomach. So not the time.

I cover my face with my hands, wondering why I am the way that I am.

When I open my eyes, Nash has silently disappeared and I can't believe it. I know he's pissed, but to just run away? I clutch my stomach, which is still making the god-awful *give me fries* noises, the panic of the empty table doubling the rate of my heart. But then I look over my shoulder and exhale because Nash is in the fries line.

He comes back to the table with two large fries, a packet of ketchup for him, and honey mustard for me. Because honey mustard is the superior dipping sauce of choice, obviously.

But I've never dipped fries in honey mustard in front of Nash.

My heart swells with this realization.

It's a Kels thing. A running argument. We got into a stupid Twitter war over it. Polls and all.

But Nash got it for me, Halle. It's a me thing.

Nash's nose crinkles when the first fry makes contact with the honey mustard.

I dip another fry in the honey mustard and hold it out to him.

He shakes his head.

I shrug because it's his loss, really. We eat the rest of our fries in silence and Nash sticks with his ketchup. It sucks because I already said so much, and there's so much I still want to say. But I don't want to overload him and Nash is giving me *nothing*.

This sucks.

"This sucks," Nash says.

I want to laugh or burst into tears or both.

"Yeah," I say. "It really does."

"I just . . ." Nash pauses. Breathes. "These last two months have been really hard, Halle."

His voice breaks when he says my name and I can't.

"I know," I say.

"But, like, you don't. At all."

I look down. "You're right," I say, softer.

"I'm sorry I pretended going to OTP's event was a Nick thing. That was not my best move. But other than that, I've never lied to you. Not about my feelings for Kels. Not about my feelings for you. And it's still really hard for me to wrap my brain around all the lying. I've been trying to put myself in your place, asking myself what I would've done if the roles were reversed. I'm trying to understand. But I don't, like, at all. The moment I knew you were you? I *would've* told you."

I fidget with a crumpled-up napkin.

"I didn't mean for it to go as far as it did," I say. "First, it was because I was scared to—but then it was because I didn't know how to."

Nash leans back in his chair. "But why were you scared? I would've been happy, you know. I would've been so happy."

"I guess I thought maybe if you got to know me, you wouldn't be. Happy."

"That's dumb," Nash says.

"The most dumb," I concur.

We stand and wander aimlessly down the hall, both way too fidgety after we inhaled our fries to sit still. We wander back toward E110, the room that hosted my first-ever panel appearance. I *did* it. I spoke words on a panel in front of an audience and I didn't puke or pass out. Which means I can do it again. Someday. If I want to. This is the world I want to be in. I'm here.

But I want Nash to be here with me too.

I open the cupcake container. There is one red velvet left, so I pick it up and place it in his palm before he can say no. It's now or never, I decide.

Cupcakes make me brave. Books make me brave.

Grams makes me brave.

"I mean it, you know. I really love you, Nash Kim. But it doesn't matter. None of the other stuff matters if we're not talking or reading or laughing—if we're not friends."

He freezes. "Friends?"

I nod. "We were good as friends, right? Before I messed up. But I won't do that anymore—mess up, I mean."

"I've been so mad at you," he says.

My shoulders slump forward. "I know."

"But I'm mad at me too. I should've known—or, like, seen it coming at least. Obviously, I wasn't paying enough attention. Because I should've seen it. I should've seen *you*."

People swarm around us in every direction as the panels let out, moving on to their next destination. So many people in one space, yet somehow, I'm able to block out the noise. Somehow, it's only Nash.

I chew on my lower lip. "I'm different online."

"But, like, you're not. Not really. Not in the ways that matter. I kinda fell in love with you twice, Halle Levitt. I don't think that's a coincidence."

My face is on fire, I'm sure of it.

I'm also sure there's officially a stupid smile on my face.

"You don't have to say that," I say.

"Halle?"

"Yeah?"

"Stop."

Nash's mouth smashes against mine and I kiss him back and oh my God, we're kissing again. At BookCon. In New York City. His hands are around my waist and mine are in his hair and wow, I missed him.

I can't help but hope this is the first step back to okay.

Because I'm not thinking about whether I'm Halle or Kels.

Because I am Halle.

I am Kels.

I am *me*.

ACKNOWLEDGMENTS

Publishing *What I Like About You* has been an absolute dream come true. Writing is a solitary act, but I would not be holding my debut novel in my hands without the guidance, support, and love from my friends, family, and publishing team. So now it's my chance to gush about what I like about all of you! (Sorry, I had to!)

To my agent, Taylor Haggerty, thank you so much for believing in this book from the beginning, for finding its perfect home at S&S, and for your positivity and enthusiasm every step of the way! Every day, I'm so grateful that I have you in my corner and that I'm a part of the Root Literary family.

To my editor, Alexa Pastor, working with you to bring this book to life has been the most incredible experience. Thank you for loving Halle and Nash as much as I do! I feel so lucky to have an editor who not only believes in my books, but believes in me. You push me to be a better storyteller and this book is a culmination of our vision. I'm so proud of what we created together!

To the entire team at S&SBFYR, thank you for all you do behind the scenes. Justin Chanda, Anne Zafian, Chrissy Noh, Karen Masnica, Lili Feinberg, Lisa Moraleda, Katrina Groover, Chava Wolin, Michelle Leo, and Julia McCarthy, thank you all for your part in getting this book out to the world! And thank you to the art and design folks who made this book so beautiful—Krista Vossen, for the adorable cover design, Sinem Erkas, for illustrating Halle & Nash so perfectly, and Hilary Zarycky, for the above and beyond interior design.

Being selected for Pitch Wars 2017 changed everything for me, so a huge thank-you to this incredible organization and community! To my mentor/writing mom, Rachel Lynn Solomon, thank you for literally everything. You were the first person to believe in this book and working with you was one of the best experiences of my writing life. I'm forever honored that you chose me and I'm so grateful for our continued friendship. I would not survive publishing without you!

Thank you to everyone who has read *What I Like About You* at various stages of the writing process. Kelsey Rodkey, Carlyn Greenwald, Sierra Elmore, Maggie Soares, Auriane Desombre, Haley Neil, and Jenny Howe, thank you for reading my trash drafts and always being a sounding board during the creative process. You're all such talented writers and amazing friends—this book is so much stronger for your feedback.

What I Like About You would not exist without my friendship with Rosiee Thor and Al Graziadei. We met as teenagers on inkpop who dreamed of being published authors. Ten years later, look at us! We're doing the thing! My friendship with the two of you inspired me to write this book and it would not exist without all the writing sprints, brainstorming sessions, and an entire decade of inside jokes. I love you both and I cannot wait to hug you someday, IRL.

Thank you to the friends who remind me that there is a world outside of publishing. To Allie Bassett, for being the one person IRL who loved talking about books as much as I did, for reading (and hopefully burning) my earliest work, and for being the longest and best friendship I've ever had. To Kyle Richard, for listening to the highs and lows over a bottle of pinot grigio and always making me laugh. And to Jamie Servidio, for being there for me through all the debut emotions at the day job. There is no one I'd rather sit next to forty hours a week.

Sam Cheung, thank you for making me laugh every day, for always wanting to celebrate even the smallest milestones, and for making sure I ate proper meals when I was on deadline. You are a real-life romcom hero, truly.

Vanessa, thank you for the inside jokes, dramatic readings, and endless laughs. We've been through all the sister angst and came out as best friends. Thank you for giving me space to write for a reasonable amount of time before banging on my door when we were kids. If I knew how much I'd miss seeing you every day, I'd probably have put the laptop down sooner.

And finally, to my parents, Margery and Arnold, thank you for always taking my dreams seriously. Dad, thank you for reading to newborn me in hospital halls, ensuring I'd love books from the moment I was born. Mom, thank you for always seeking out my words. Teen me hated that you tracked down my online profiles, but it truly meant the world that you were so engaged and encouraging. Thank you both for always saying *not if, when.* I love you.

Turn the page for a special sneak peek
at Marisa Kanter's next book,
As if On Cue!

t is six a.m. and I am debating the opposite of "frozen" with Reid Callahan.

"It's 'melted,'" I mumble into my pillow, salty, because how dare he wake me up before the sun on a Monday? In my current state of bleary-eyed rage, I throw a pillow vaguely in the direction of my doorframe, where Reid is standing.

"No way. The opposite of frozen is definitely boiled. I'm serious. 'Boiled' is the only valid title if you're going for parody. 'Melted' is fundamentally flawed."

"*You're* fundamentally flawed."

He snorts, and I hear the clink of metal against ceramic. A spoon swirling in cereal. By now, I'm used to Reid in my house in the early hours of the morning, mastering complex arpeggios on the clarinet under the instruction of my father. Reid is pretty much the only person in the entire universe who matches Dad's intensity for a musical instrument. Which means he's *always* here.

It's kind of unbearable.

"Why are you here?" I ask.

"It's Monday," Reid says slowly, as if I don't know the days of the week. Monday morning lessons have been a thing since school started two weeks ago—and will continue to be a thing that makes Monday even *more* Monday for the duration of my junior year.

"I mean *here*, Reid. Why are you in my bedroom?"

"To pay up," he says.

He nods toward my desk, where a large iced chai from Kiskadee sits on top of an elephant coaster. Of course, he decides six a.m. is the perfect time to deliver my *Wow, you actually wrote a play* chai. Winning a bet against Reid Callahan is still always losing, in a way.

"Your timing is impeccable."

I fall back onto my mattress and roll over, facing the wall and closing my eyes in an attempt to return to my dreamscape. Before Reid woke me up with three staccato knocks, I was sitting at a table read for my big-budget Broadway play featuring the Chrises. We were staging a fight scene between Pine and Evans. Hemsworth leaned over to whisper in my ear, *You're bloody incredible, Jacobson*. And I didn't brush off his praise or downplay my talent—I owned it. Thor called *me*, Natalie Jacobson, incredible. I *felt* incredible. In my dream, playwriting became more than a high school hobby. It's possible.

Reid flips the switch next to my door and my eyelids twitch as synthetic light tries to push through them. "Don't want you to oversleep!"

"Thanks," I deadpan, sitting up because I am now officially awake and Reid has Won. I reach for my glasses while my eyes adjust, already plotting my revenge for his ruining of the epic Pine-Evans fight scene.

"You're welcome." Reid's hazel eyes meet mine. They seem to change color depending on what he's wearing. This morning, they pick up his blue button-down. "The least you can do is be on time, considering you're wasting Mrs. Mulaney's."

It's so elementary, I almost laugh as I move from my bed to the adjacent desk and start weaving my disaster curls into two disaster braids. Any other day, I'd fire back a snarky retort. Not today. Because today is the culmination of an entire summer writing with my best friend, Henry Chao. Before homeroom, we'll enter scene and deliver a dialogue to Principal Mulaney about why *Melted* deserves to be our fall play—a performance that has the potential to shift the entire fate of Lincoln High School's drama department.

I can't afford to be distracted.

"Bye," I say.

I shut the door on Reid and reach for the chai on my desk. Straw between my lips, I take a long sip. It doesn't quite taste like victory, but it's still a Kiskadee chai. Therefore, delicious. I enjoy it, unfazed by Reid's basic insult because with *Melted* I have a chance—a *real* chance—at convincing Mrs. Mulaney that keeping LHS's drama department intact is just as valuable as new band uniforms.

Seriously, Reid's biggest problem is being an outfit repeater. When the school committee announced that "significant budget cuts" were coming for extracurricular activities at the end of sophomore year, the drama club had an emergency meeting. It was initiated by me and our former advisor, Miss Bryant, who quickly jumped our sinking ship of a drama program for a full-time faculty position teaching theater at Boston Arts Academy. But when Reid heard about the cuts, he didn't flinch. It's *that* obvious the band is relatively immune from total destruction, thanks to a passionate band director who, over the course of a decade, revitalized the band program from the ground up.

That teacher? It's none other than Aaron Jacobson. Reid's teacher. My dad.

It's complicated.

I pick up the pillow I launched at Reid and toss it on my bed on the way to my closet. Today's aesthetic is comfy and confident, like how Mom would style herself for meetings with her publisher. This is that important. I pull a new floral T-shirt dress off its velvet hanger, rip off the tag, and pair it with a denim jacket and white sneakers. To complete the look, I swipe a clear pink gloss over my lips.

Satisfied, I stuff my laptop into my backpack and I'm on the move. Downstairs, the kitchen smells like raspberry hazelnut coffee and burnt toast, the scent of creative anxiety.

I pause at the bottom of the stairs when I catch sight of the kitchen table scene.

Mom sits at the head of the espresso wood table, staring intently at her laptop screen. Reid's next to my mom, his button-down now unbuttoned to reveal a white graphic T-shirt that says MUSIC IS MY FORTE, with a spoon in one hand and *The Fundamentals of Musical Composition* in the other. Dad sits across from Reid, sipping on coffee and sorting through papers that spill out of his Band Bible—a three-inch blue binder with his certified non-sensical organization system. Last year, I created the most beautiful color-coded filing system for his monster binder. He was *not* pleased. How Dad transformed Lincoln High School's concert band and orchestra into a nationally recognized, award-winning program—yet cannot accept the convenience of alphanumeric order, page numbers, and *labels*—is beyond me. But no matter what, he's always in band mode, his back-to-school haircut still slightly too short, his salt-and-pepper beard slightly too long.

My stomach clenches, witnessing the comfortable quiet that is the three of them together.

"How's the solo coming?" Mom asks Reid.

Reid's eyes flicker up from his reading. "More work ahead. How's the book coming?"

Mom closes her laptop and smirks. "More work ahead."

He nods and raises his coffee mug. "Solidarity, Aunt Shell."

Reid is the only person who can get away with calling my mom any variation of "Shell." Aunt Michelle was simply one syllable too many for toddler Reid. I wish he dropped the "Aunt." It makes me feel like we're related—which, no, we absolutely are *not*.

Being the children of dads who were childhood best friends does not a family make.

"You're too hard on yourself," Dad says, looking up from his "organized" chaos. Is it the new music for the homecoming game? Is it a set for his jazz band, Lincoln Street Blues? Who knows! "Both of you."

Reid brushes off Dad's words with a shrug and looks up, his

eyes meeting mine from across the kitchen. "Hey, Nat."

Enter me, the girl who always seems to arrive before her cue.

"Morning," I say, reaching for the box of blueberry Pop-Tarts above the stove. I take the entire box and slide into the chair across from my mom.

"You're up early," Mom says. Her hair is a messy bun of curls, now two shades darker than my own from the dye job masking her gray roots. Beside her laptop is a half-eaten apple and an elephant mug filled with what I'm sure is lukewarm coffee. Plastic purple reading glasses are perched on the tip of her nose as her eyes remain trained on her screen. "Nervous?"

My eyes focus on the apple, its exposed flesh already brown. Better than yesterday, when there was nothing left but seeds and core. On Mom's best writing days, the apple stays untouched, her fingers dancing on the keys, no chance of breaking their rhythm for a bite. On those days, Mom is Michelle Jacobson, *New York Times* best-selling author of *The Lola Diaries*.

I can't remember the last time Mom forgot to eat her apple.

"I'm ready."

"So, can I read it *now*?" Mom asks.

I perform the shrugging girl emoji for Mom.

If she reads it, she'll encourage me. She'll critique. She'll call me a playwright.

"You can read it when it's real," I say for the thousandth time. "That's what you'd say."

Mom's lips press into a thin smile. "I know, Lee."

Her voice begs me not to press further, so I don't. Before the pressure to follow up *Lola*, Mom was a force in publishing and proof that writing could be more than a hobby.

Now, I see my mom stare at a blank Word doc for hours. I hear the defeat in her voice when she says, *I know, Lee*.

And even though my stomach dips, everything inside of me is relieved to not love it like that, to not be following in her footsteps. I love theater, but writing and directing is a hobby, and that's all it will ever be. I'm not sure what Adulting looks like for me—I don't even know what I want to go to college for—but I do know it won't be my parents' life. Dad's symphony orchestra dreams landed him as an overworked and underpaid high school band director. Mom's burnout is so intense there are days she doesn't get out of bed.

I've seen firsthand what art can do to a person who loves it too much.

The mental toll of tying your financial security and self-worth to a creative pursuit.

"Well I read it," Reid interjects. "The title needs work."

Mom's eyebrows shoot up. "*Reid* read it? Wow. That hurts."

I swallow a piece of my Pop-Tart. "It's not like I had a choice."

"You bet that I couldn't name every *Survivor* winner," he says, closing his book. "You basically handed it to me."

He even named them in order. It was bizarre.

I mean, who still even watches that show? It started before we were *born*.

I roll my eyes, but honestly? It wasn't the worst bet to lose. Last week, when he was reading my script at breakfast, he didn't even hear me come down the stairs, he was so absorbed in *Melted*. Before I made it across the kitchen, he laughed. Genuinely laughed. Like he got it.

It honestly did not compute. Because we do not get each other, Reid and me.

It's actually funny, Reid had said, his mouth full of Froot Loops. *You're funny.* Then he smiled at me and I almost forgot how much I hate him.

When I reached for the box of Froot Loops and it was empty, I remembered.

Mom stands. "I guess I'll have to take Reid's word for it."

"Off to do some productivity sprints?" Dad asks.

"More like prep," Mom says. "Now that my syllabus is approved, there is *so* much prep."

Dad waves at his chaos binder, like *exhibit A*. "Relatable."

It's going to be Mom's second year teaching creative writing at Emerson College, a side hustle that pays the bills while she impatiently waits for inspiration to strike. And bills we do have. Mom spent most of June in Ft. Lauderdale looking for a caregiver for my bubbe, after she fell down the stairs and broke her hip. In July, our air conditioner busted in the middle of the hottest Massachusetts summer in, like, two hundred years. And a few weeks ago my dad learned that his budget for new supplies got cut in half—forcing him to purchase new music for the fall Harvest Festival out of pocket. All summer, it has been one unexpected expense after another.

Mom always says bad things happen in threes.

I say don't pick a career that relies on creative whims to pay the bills in the first place.

"All romance writers this semester?" I ask.

Mom nods. Romance is her brand, the literary space where she has made her career. Readers have been waiting nearly four years to see how she follows up *The Lola Diaries*.

"Maybe it'll be inspiring," Reid says.

Mom's smile turns terse. "That's the hope."

"*Nirvana* always gets me through a long prep session," Dad suggests. "Just don't forget Delia has lessons with Rabbi Sarna at three." My twelve-year-old sister is in full bat mitzvah prep mode, eating, sleeping, and breathing Vayishlach 36:40.

Mom waves away his reminder. "We have a tasting with the caterer after."

Dad nods. "Four-thirty."

"Good luck today, Lee."

Mom squeezes my shoulder then tucks her laptop under her arm and retreats to her office in the name of class prep, leaving me alone with Reid and my dad. Pretty much the worst combination. Before I have a chance to form words, they're in their own musical world.

"Six weeks until the Harvest Festival," Dad says.

Every fall, the concert band performs at the Lincoln Harvest Festival in Pine Hill Park. The Harvest Festival is a community event filled with hayrides, farm stands with local produce, and so many cider donuts—pretty much peak fall in New England energy. A few years ago, Dad proposed that it also be a performance opportunity for the band, where the marquee event is a classic film score. Past performances have included *Casablanca, E.T.,* and *Gone with the Wind.* It's an event that the town has come to anticipate and is excellent—both in terms of the local media attention it receives and the boost it gives to small businesses that participate.

Star Wars: Episode IV—A New Hope is this year's Harvest Festival score and the hype is already building, thanks to Aaron Jacobson's local news debut in a piece highlighting how the band's participation in the Harvest Festival has increased turnout.

The screen time has absolutely gone to his head.

It's a cool story, objectively.

But, like, the school committee does *not* need another reason to obsess over the band.

Neither does the town, for that matter.

Because as a town, Lincoln is as average as it gets. Our sports teams are mediocre. We don't have a marching band. Our drama club is small. Our entertainment options are a movie theater, a bowling alley, and a mall with every store that's in every town.

But Lincoln's concert band and orchestra program?

They are exceptional.

Reid shifts the conversation to his current role: recruitment for the jazz ensemble.

"We need more percussion," Reid says.

"Makayla's—" I start.

"Rosalind Levy is sick on the snare." Reid says, cutting me off. "Which will make up for losing Tricia, I think."

Dad nods. "Cool. Good to know."

I wait for Dad to ask me about Makayla's sister, who is an incredible drummer. He doesn't. He continues talking to Reid like I didn't try to speak, like I couldn't possibly contribute something valuable to this conversation.

Like I wasn't once a musician myself.

"We won't know for sure until we hear how everyone meshes."

I am invisible.

Finally, after another Pop-Tart and what feels like endless band chat, Dad closes his binder and heads to his studio in the basement to set up for Reid's lesson. Reid stands and brings his cereal bowl to the sink, so I reach into my backpack for my laptop, ready for thirty sweet minutes of alone time, just *Melted* and me.

I open the file.

"It's not too late for *Boiled*."

I jump, my fingers jamming into my keyboard. "Why are you so fixated on this?"

"Imagine if Adina could instantly *boil* anything she touches. She'd be unstoppable!" Reid says. "Think about it. Artists need to be open to criticism, Natalie. Collaborative."

"Right. Except we're not collaborators."

Reid's jaw tenses. "I know."

"So why are you still standing here? Don't you have a clarinet to blow?"

Reid nods and takes a step backward. "As a matter of fact, I do."

He descends the stairs, not missing a beat. His cheeks don't flush, not even when I emphasize "blow." Reid woke me up before the sun and co-opted my parents . . . and I couldn't even make him blush? Literally everything makes Reid blush. I'm seriously off my game.

What a waste of a line, honestly.